WHITE FLAG DOWN

ALSO BY JOEL N. ROSS

Double Cross Blind

DOUBLEDAY

NEW YORK LONDON TORONTO

SYDNEY AUCKLAND

WHITE
FLAG
DOWN

JOEL N. ROSS

PUBLISHED BY DOUBLEDAY

Copyright © 2007 by Joel N. Ross

All Rights Reserved

Published in the United States by Doubleday,
an imprint of The Doubleday Broadway Publishing Group,
a division of Random House, Inc., New York.
www.doubleday.com

DOUBLEDAY and the portrayal of an anchor with a dolphin are
registered trademarks of Random House, Inc.

Book design by Gretchen Achilles

Library of Congress Cataloging-in-Publication Data
Ross, Joel N., 1968–
White flag down / Joel N. Ross. — 1st ed.
p. cm.
1. World War, 1939–1945—Europe—Fiction. I. Title.
PS3618.O8455W47 2007
813'6—dc22
2006026773

ISBN 978-0-385-51389-0

PRINTED IN THE UNITED STATES OF AMERICA

1   3   5   7   9   10   8   6   4   2

First Edition

WHITE FLAG DOWN

In June of 1941, two years after signing a non-aggression pact, Nazi Germany invaded the Soviet Union. Within six months, the Russians lost a thousand miles and three million men—and in 1942, the relentless German Wehrmacht swept into Stalin's namesake city, Stalingrad. Combat seethed in the city streets, ten thousand Soviet soldiers died in a single day fighting for a single hill.

Then, in mid-September 1942, Hitler ordered a "final offensive" to capture Stalingrad. Yet on October 7, the German army paused. As General von Richthofen, commander of the Luftwaffe, wrote in his diary: "Absolute quiet at Stalingrad."

After months of combat, a sudden silence rose on the eastern front.

But why?

CHAPTER 1

Despite the chill of the brisk English morning, heat prickled Lieutenant Grant's neck and a trickle of sweat ran down his spine. He shrugged off the discomfort: in thirty minutes, flying photo recon over Nazi-occupied France, he'd be grateful for the warmth of his Irvin flight jacket and trousers.

He stepped from the mission briefing with his navigator, Sergeant "Racket" McNeil, who whistled in disbelief. "This one's a doozy, Lieut."

"Easy enough," Grant said, heading across the airfield.

"I dunno—any closer to Germany, we'd smell the sauerkraut."

"They want recon, we'll give 'em recon."

Racket was a rangy kid with an easy grin, but this smile looked forced. "And be back by dinner."

At the dispersal pen, Grant pulled himself through the nose hatch into the cockpit of the Mosquito, settled into the pilot's seat, and saw the camera in Racket's hand. "Bringing your handheld?"

"For souvenirs," Racket said. "Something to show my grandkids."

"At the rate you're going, you already have some."

"The English girls like me, what can I say?" They were stationed near an Oxfordshire village—half-timber houses and a high street pub that sold warm bitter beer—and Racket had wasted no time meeting the local fauna. "But if what I hear about Frenchwomen is true . . . brother, you can drop me over Paris."

Grant laughed and completed his preflight checks, then twirled a finger at the RAF flight sergeant, who gave the thumbs-up. Grant hit the starter button and the propeller revolved lazily before catching with a puff of smoke and a bark from the exhausts. As the port engine settled into the rough idle of a cold Merlin, he started the starboard motor, watching the temps rise to ground levels. He ran through his after-start check, turned from the dispersal pen, and rolled to the eastern end of the runway.

"Clear blue skies," Racket said.

Grant examined the heavy gray clouds. "Should've requested a navigator with eyes."

"Who needs eyes? You've got Pinpoint McNeil."

"The met officer says it's clear over France." Grant swung the Mossie into line and trimmed the rudder. "Hope he's not as drunk as you."

He flicked the magneto switches, advanced the throttles, and the Mossie rolled down the runway, heavy with fuel. The western hedge rushed toward them, and a light tug on the stick pulled the undercarriage from the ground and into the sky.

Racket told Grant about his new girl and her mother, like some radio drama, then there was nothing but engine noise and clouds, and heat seeping into the cabin from the radiators. When Grant had arrived in England, sent by the Eighth U.S. Air Force to fly photo-reconnaissance flights with the RAF, he'd laughed at the British. The photo-reconnaissance unit flew PR.I and PR.IV versions of the Mosquito—wooden aircraft, plywood and balsa and glue. Then he'd flown one, and stopped laughing: wood or not, Mossies could fly.

Racket broke the silence. "You know why they sent us spitting distance from Germany, Lieut?"

"For photo recon?"

"On account of General Eaker's new intruder force—using bad weather as a cloak for blind-bombing operations. I figure we're prepping for them."

"Where do you hear this shit?"

Racket fiddled with the nav system. "I also heard you saw combat in China, flying with some civilian outfit."

"Yeah. CNAC."

"What's that?"

"Chinese National Aviation Corporation."

"You flew into war zones—why didn't you join a fighter group?"

Because he'd lost his edge in Nanking, in 1937. "I fly what they tell me."

"Speak fluent German, too, don't you?"

"What's that got to do with anything? Check we're on course to find the IP, Racket."

Because they were beyond GEE range, pinpointing the initial point for the photo-recon run took all of Racket's attention. He managed, though, then edged into the glazed nose of the Mosquito to trigger the cameras and said, "Looks like the met officer was drunk after all."

The world below was a featureless white, cloudy as a cataract. "We'll take another run," Grant said. "Under the clouds."

They took two more—then a Focke Wulf 190 dropped from nowhere, running at them from the front.

Racket swore. "The hell did he come from?"

Grant flew into the attack, turned the nose down, and opened the throttle.

"Another Focker," Racket said tightly. "Behind and—"

"I see."

"Watch the—" Machine-gun fire pocked the side of the Mossie, the noise drowned by the explosion of 20-millimeter cannon shells. "*Damnit!*"

Grant screamed downhill, into a bank of clouds. "Racket?"

"Starboard side's smoking."

"Where are they?"

"Can't see beans—" A short intake of breath. "We're leaking glycol, Lieut."

Grant checked his instrument panel. "Starboard's in the red. Temp's rising, and we're losing fuel. We're not getting back to England, find us a—"

One of the Fockers broke cover a hundred yards away. "Shit."

Grant cut the starboard engine and boosted the port, torquing the Mossie into a thick gray mass, holding his breath and staying inside the cloud. "Gimme a hint, Racket, we're almost outta time."

"Head southeast."

"Germany's east."

"*South*east. Switzerland."

The fuel gauge edged lower and the starboard temp rose—they wouldn't be back by dinner. The cloud cover finally thinned, the needle touched red, and Grant said, "I want you ready to bail, Racket."

"I'm not going anywhere."

Because after the navigator bailed and the pilot released the stick to follow, the damaged Mossie could spin and trap him inside. "That's an order, Sergeant."

"Climb back here then, and we'll arm wrestle for—" Racket's voice turned tight. "There! Another Focker, at ten thirty."

"Where? I don't—" Grant saw the bogie and felt his heart catch. "That's not a Focker, too damn fast."

"That's a—" Racket raised his handheld camera. "What *is* that?"

"I never saw anything like it. Nobody has."

"Look at her go—" A constant *click-whir*, Racket snapping photo after photo. "There's nothing keeping her in the air."

"There's nothing keeping *us* in the air, Racket."

"She's got no propellers, how the hell is she flying?" *Click-whir, click-whir*. "She saw us, she's veering off."

"And radioing for help."

"Swastika on the fuselage, she's German and too fast to—damn. Gone already."

"You got pictures?"

"Sure, but what *was* that?"

"Some kind of prototype." Grant swung them into the clouds. "With a fighter patrol for cover. Are we in Switzerland?"

"A prototype? That thing is *Flash Gordon*, we gotta tell 'em back home, show 'em the pictures."

"First we have to *get* home. We in Switzerland yet?"

"Maybe. Yeah. Almost."

"Check your maps, find a—" Grant cocked his head. "Do you hear that?"

"What?"

"The engine." A high hollow whine, a bad omen. Too low to bail out, and he couldn't get any altitude. "We're gonna land soon and we're gonna land rough."

And the next time they broke the clouds, they were flying into a mountain.

Grant corkscrewed blindly, and instead of exploding against rock, they were trapped in a craggy snow-dusted valley, the mountainsides blurring past. No way out, rats in a maze, and the only direction they were headed was down, the port engine roaring and starboard coughing—

"Lieut!" Racket shouted. "There! There!"

The alpine meadow shimmered into sight like an oasis in the desert, but this was no mirage. His face slick with sweat, Grant relaxed his shoulders and exhaled, his hand gentle on the stick. The valley walls squeezed the Mossie, the meadow grew larger, and a stillness rose inside the speed and the noise. He felt nothing but the slow beat of his heart, heard nothing but his own breathing—yet saw every outcropping of rock, every windswept tree, every pretty shrub that could send them cartwheeling.

Speed steady at 210 knots, lower, steady, lower—

And the starboard engine seized in a deafening clatter.

Grant fought to keep the nose up, slamming the throttles shut as the port propeller shattered on impact and the Plexiglas nose broke and turned the Mossie into a giant shovel, scooping rocky earth into the cockpit.

Black smoke coiled under the gray sky.

Grant's ears rang and his mouth was full of blood; he sat stunned and staring. Then he heard the sizzle of fuel dripping onto hot exhausts, saw the smoke rising from the shattered engine cowlings—and snapped back. One spark and they were dead. He reached for the escape hatch in the roof, but it was already gone, demolished in the crash.

He fumbled at his harness, dragged himself to his feet and saw Racket slumped in his seat, belts tight across his chest, his face a clotted mask of blood—but alive. He called his name then shook him, with no response. Got himself through the roof hatch and leaned back inside, hooking Racket under the shoulders and using his own body weight sliding down the fuselage to pull his navigator out. They fell hard, then Grant dragged him across the meadow and crouched to check his wounds. The mountain tilted—Grant staggered and collapsed and lay there, deafened by the cold wind.

After a time, he stood and sprinkled sulfa powder on Racket's cuts and dressed them with a compress bandage. Didn't know what else was wrong, didn't know what else to do. Except Racket still held the strap of his handheld camera in his fist.

Were they even in Switzerland? If this was Germany, and that prototype aircraft radioed in a sighting, he could expect company.

And Racket needed a hospital. Grant turned in a slow circle, almost losing his footing on the uneven ground, and picked out the largest fir tree at the edge of the meadow. He fell to his knees and buried the camera, wrapped in oilskin, among the roots.

Back in the meadow, Racket's face was as white as the mountaintops, his breath fast and shallow. Nothing Grant could do but go for help, and pray he was in Switzerland. He chose a direction and started walking.

Through the trees, a hundred yards below him, two army trucks and an ambulance drove along a snaking dirt road. By the time Grant stumbled from the woods they were gone, headed up-mountain. He lifted his head and saw black plumes of smoke from the Mosquito waving like a banner in the sky.

An ambulance, already on the way to Racket. So now what? Depended on the country—if this was Germany, he'd get the camera and hightail south, across the border. If Switzerland, he was on velvet: talk to the American consulate, tell 'em where to find the camera, and sleep easy.

He walked downhill through the woods, paralleling the dirt road—roots catching at his boots and branches slapping his face—until the sun dipped behind a mountain peak. The ringing in his ears grew steadily louder, but he didn't realize until he saw the fenced pasture that he was hearing the rush of a nearby river running through a mountain town.

He crossed the pasture toward a barn. Halfway there, a farmer stepped from a shadowed pen, wearing heavy boots and a home-grown hat, and called to him. He didn't understand a word, and the relief almost knocked him over: the farmer was speaking Swiss-German, he was safe in neutral territory.

Grant went toward the barn. "American. *Ich bin Amerikaner.*"

"The airplane," the farmer said, in regular German. "You crashed."

"*Ja*. My navigator's hurt, I need to talk to—"

"Come, come." The farmer led Grant around the barn to a stone-walled house overlooking a green valley. "You stay, you wait. I send my son."

Grant sat on a weathered bench. The farmer asked him something, but he didn't answer. Cowbells sounded in the distance, and the scent of pine and manure rose on a chill breeze. The view was unreal, too vivid, too panoramic, like a dream—like part of him was still in the cockpit watching that meadow loom larger and closer.

He looked at the clouds until tires crunched on the drive, and a tall soldier stood before him, with a coal-scuttle helmet and a rifle.

"You are the pilot?" the soldier said, in unaccented German.

Grant checked the man's uniform, saw buttons with the Swiss cross. He nodded, and answered in German. "You found my navigator?"

"He's in the hospital already. They are looking after him, yes?"

"I need to talk to the American consulate."

"First you talk to us," the soldier said.

A medic came and checked his eyes and pulse, then he was strapped on a gurney, sluggish and shocky. The clouds slid away, and he was looking at the riveted metal roof of the ambulance. He faded out, shaken by the hard rattle of the mountain road.

CHAPTER 2

The first morning in the quarantine hotel, Grant lay on his bed, watching light filter through frilly curtains. Floral wallpaper, polished pine furniture, and a muddy painting of the Alps. And his new clothes were folded on the dresser: a shirt and jersey, trousers and a greatcoat and gloves and a beret. Only one thing he still needed—to get Racket's handheld camera to the U.S. consulate and pin a name on that German bogie.

Had he really seen an aircraft flying without propellers? Sure, it probably didn't have a cockpit, either. Or wings.

He shook his head; he knew what he'd seen. He got into his clothes and looked out the window at the main street of a rustic alpine village hemmed in by mountains—a small tourist town, lined with shops. He didn't know who to ask about contacting the consulate, or—

A knock sounded at his door, and Grant called, "*Ja?*"

A heavyset man with graying temples entered. "Lieutenant Grant," he said in slightly accented English. "You are feeling better?"

Grant glanced toward the window. "I'm feeling like I crashed into a Shirley Temple movie. What is this place?"

"A resort hotel." The man smiled softly. "You see how generously we treat our guests?"

"The bunch last night aren't gonna win any prizes."

"You were debriefed last night?"

"After the doctor gave me a clean bill. They had a questionnaire, a Red Cross form."

"Ah, yes. You did not answer?"

"No—I fell asleep. You're here to ask me again? You're an officer?"

"Me? Oh, no, I'm a reservist, that is all. My commander knows I have English, from visiting family in America, he sent me to talk with you. I will now proceed to ferret out all your secrets." His brow furrowed. " 'Ferret out'? That is correct, no?"

"That's fine."

"Because I've heard both ways, 'ferret out' and 'flush out.' "

"Either one." Grant looked at the man. "You wanna hear my name, rank, and serial number?"

"You gave those the same day you crashed."

"I did? That's still a bit blurry."

"You must be hungry, yes?"

"No, I'm—" Grant stopped. "Half starved, actually."

"Then come, the dining room is serving."

"What about the ferreting?"

"Believe me," the reservist said, opening the door, "there is no rush."

"And Racket?" Grant asked. "My navigator, Sergeant McNeil?"

"Stable. He has several broken ribs, as well as the blow to his head. He is getting exceptional good care—if one must crash, Switzerland is not the worst place for it."

"Better'n Germany," Grant said.

They went down a corridor to a dining room with big square

windows full of sunlight. Tables dotted the floor, half of them clustered around the stone hearth, the other half overlooking a picturesque farm and a distant waterfall. Swiss soldiers murmured at two of the tables, and an old woman in an apron stood behind a long trestle table laden with food.

"Do you have any coffee?" Grant asked her, in German.

"Yes, of course." She eyed him speculatively. "Your German is very good."

"Good enough to ask for food is all."

"No—you speak as well as I."

"I can't cook, though," he said. "So your job is safe."

She tutted and poured a cup of coffee. He piled a plate with rolls and cheese and cooked greens, then crossed the room to sit with the reservist. "What now?" he asked.

"You spend two weeks in quarantine. Here, in the hotel."

"Get a little rest." Grant spread marmalade on dense grainy roll. "Then back to England?"

"England? No, you're an internee now, Lieutenant, and—"

"An internee?"

"Well, General Guisan uses the term 'POW,' but—"

"Guisan? Never heard of him."

The reservist sighed. "We Swiss have no general in peacetime, we only elect one at times of war or national emergency—Guisan was elected three years ago."

"He says I'm a POW?"

"The Hague convention dictates that belligerents on neutral soil be kept from the fighting. By force, if necessary." The man smiled, a little wistfully. "You'll spend two weeks inside the hotel, in quarantine, then you'll have the run of the village."

"For how long?"

"Until hostilities cease."

"The end of the war?" Grant snorted. "The air force spends twenty-five thousand dollars training a pilot, that's what I heard."

"So you are valuable equipment?"

"Yeah, and I shouldn't be rusting away in some postcard town in Switzerland."

For the first time, the reservist seemed taken aback. "You don't like the village?"

Grant asked the only question that he cared about: "Have you notified the U.S. consulate that I'm here?"

"Of course—last night, after you were transferred from medical observation."

"When do I meet them?"

"The military attaché is already on the way. Brigadier General Leeger. He'll arrive at any moment."

Grant smiled over his coffee mug. "Guess I'll stick around, then."

"Only one road leads down the mountain—this is a pretty prison, but a prison nonetheless."

"One road's all it takes."

"There is no reason to run that risk." The reservist leaned closer, and the humor left his face. "Listen closely, Lieutenant, I am not proud, but here is the truth. There are those in my government whose allegiance is . . . unfortunate. If a German flier lands here, he refuels and returns to Germany. There is a five-kilometer zone, *inside* the Swiss border, in which only Germans may fly."

"In Swiss airspace?"

"Precisely so. Most Swiss have a horror of the Nazis, but there is a saying: All week we work for Hitler, and on Sunday pray for Churchill."

Grant put his fork down. "What are you warning me against?"

"Against the notion that you landed in a production of *Heidi*. If you try to escape, they'll toss you in a punishment camp—and if you succeed, they'll shoot you at the border."

He didn't know how to read this guy, with his warnings and his rueful smile—but it didn't matter, not yet. As long as a brigadier general was coming, he was sitting pretty. He said, "I'm getting another plate."

"Please, enjoy the feast. Food is rationed, you know—I had to dig my roses over to grow potatoes."

"Then why the spread?"

"Hoping a full belly will loosen your tongue." The man tapped an envelope on the tabletop. "The Red Cross form—again. Are you sure you won't answer?"

"Pretty sure."

"Ah, well," the reservist said, clearly unconcerned. "I've done my duty, I'll try again this evening. You play chess?"

"No."

"Perhaps I'll teach you." The man stood. "Until tonight, Lieutenant."

Grant told him goodbye, and watched him leave. Hadn't even gotten his name. Still, plenty of time for that—for chess and potatoes and figuring a route to the French border—once he told the attaché about the prototype aircraft and the camera hidden at the crash site.

After another plate of cheese and bread, he left the room, feeling the Swiss soldiers watching him. He passed his room, prowling the corridors until he found the front door: unguarded, with a single clerk at the desk. He climbed to the third floor and followed a carpeted corridor around the perimeter of the hotel, checking doors. No roof access, but he wouldn't get any real altitude anyway. He opened a window instead, the wind loud after the calm of the corridor. The mountains formed an impassable prison wall, with farmhouses on the meadow slopes standing as sentry boxes. One lonely road snaked through the village and around a distant hill: the only way out. He committed the details to memory, shut the window. Not planning on leaving yet, anyway—not until he briefed Brigadier General Leeger on the handheld camera.

On the second floor, he paused at a bookshelf. Ran his finger over the spines of the books. An encyclopedia, a few dozen novels, some guides to birds and mushrooms. A few books in French, a calculus textbook . . . and a pictorial guide to Switzerland, twenty years out of date but with plenty of maps.

He grabbed that one, plus a few novels for cover, and went downstairs. When he turned the corner to his hallway, three men stood at the open door of his room.

"You're Lieutenant Grant." The nearest man spoke perfect English, his face jowly and his necktie tight as a fist under his dress uniform—U.S. Army brass. "Where were you? You were told to wait here."

Grant saluted. "I didn't get that message, sir."

The man smacked a swagger stick against his polished cavalry boots. "In the future, see that you do."

There was nothing to say to that, so Grant looked from him to the other men, one a Swiss officer, the other an aide with a clipboard.

"I am Brigadier General Leeger," the jowly man continued. "I trust you got *that* message, at least?"

"Yes, I—"

"Perhaps you heard I retired from the service, Lieutenant? Is that the problem?"

"I'm not sure there is one, sir."

"I've lived six years in Switzerland as a civilian, this is true—but duty is not something one forgets. I know this country and I know my duty, and you will be guided by me, is that clear?"

"Yessir. Any word of my navigator?"

The aide said, "He's still in the quarantine hospital, and recovering as well as can be expected."

"Excellent medicine, the Swiss." Leeger inspected Grant through narrowed eyes. "You seem to have walked away unscratched."

"Yeah, I aimed for a soft patch of mountain."

"Do you find humor in an injured crew member, Lieutenant?"

16

The man was a prick on a pony, but Grant had nobody else to tell about the camera. "No, sir. Can we talk privately, sir?"

"I came for three reasons, Lieutenant. First, to see that you are being treated accordingly." Leeger looked at Grant, then at the quiet corridor, and nodded. "Which you clearly are. Second, to offer to send a telegram in advance of the official notification."

"Notification?"

"That you failed to return to base. Your family will get an alarming telegram if you don't inform them first that you are safe. What is your home address?"

Grant looked at the Swiss officer. "Can we talk privately, sir?"

"There is nothing you cannot tell me in front of our Swiss friends."

Not a fight worth having about a telegram—but he couldn't mention the camera in front of the Swiss. He said, "Okay," and gave the aide his mother's address.

"My third reason, Lieutenant," Leeger said, "is to issue orders. You are not to attempt to escape from Swiss custody, is that understood?"

"U.S. Code of Conduct," Grant said. Captured airmen must try to rejoin their units.

"I'm aware of the Code of Conduct. This is a direct order, Lieutenant. You are not to entertain any notion of escape. Further, there will be no delinquency of any sort, is that understood?"

"I understand perfectly."

"Then we're finished. Unless you have a question?"

"I'd still like that private word, sir."

"I already told you there is nothing you cannot say here. Now—are we finished?"

"Yes, sir." Because a prick like Leeger, strutting around in cavalry boots, would dig his heels in at any hint of defiance. Better to call the consulate and talk to someone else. "Except—is there a number for the embassy, if I need to contact you?"

"I sincerely hope you won't."

"No, but if—"

"In that unlikely case, speak to the corporal here."

"I'd rather have the number," Grant said.

The brigadier general tapped his boot with his swagger stick. "I believe I've made myself clear."

Grant looked from the man's fleshy chin to his eyes—shifted forward and let him see how small and soft he was. "Still," he said. "Sir."

After a silent moment, Leeger cleared his throat. "Give him the number," he told the aide.

Back in his room, Grant flipped through the pictorial guidebook to Switzerland. If you knew the lakes you couldn't go too far wrong— except for the mountains. Still, no reason to play this rough, trekking cross-country. Easier to catch a train to Geneva, where France was a stone's throw away. Only question was, when should he move? Well, the first stop was a pay phone in the village to ring the consulate about Racket's camera: that had to happen today. Yeah. Make the call, then lay low around the hotel for a few days, taking stock. Right now all he needed were coins for the phone and a fix on the crash site, to tell the consulate where to find the camera.

He flipped to the map of Bern canton—that's what they called them, cantons instead of states—and saw he was a long way from the German border. They'd crashed north, maybe in Jura or Basel or Aargau or . . . where?

He bent over the book, trying to pinpoint the crash site. Flipped back and forth, then shook his head. "Shit."

No idea. That mountain could be anywhere, he'd been too busy trying to land wheels-down to get a fix. Racket could find the crash site blindfolded, but Grant didn't know where to start. He closed the book. The consulate would find the site when he gave them reason, told them about the camera.

He stepped into the hallway, where two soldiers leaned against the wall.

One of them offered a pack of smokes. "*Wollen Sie eine Zigarette?*"

"*Danke.*" Grant took one. "*Haben Sie Feuer?* I left my lighter in my other flight jacket."

The soldier chuckled and gave him a book of matches. "You know you aren't to leave the hotel, yes?"

"Yeah." Grant set fire to the cigarette. "Where's the laundry?"

"The housemaid will take your clothes."

"I thought I might introduce myself." He showed them one of Racket's grins. "Never met a Swiss girl before."

The soldier laughed, said something in Swiss-German to his buddy, and told Grant to try the basement.

He said *Danke* and headed downstairs—no better place to find loose change for a pay phone than a laundry—but when he stepped inside, the "girl" was his mother's age, and she shooed him away before he could talk her out of a nickel, or whatever they called a nickel here. Back in the hallway, he checked the book. "Rappen" or "centimes," that's what the Swiss coins were called. He needed rappen, needed a restaurant or a bar, to sweep a tip from a tabletop.

Back in the lobby, the black-haired clerk fiddled with a ledger. What next, break into a room? Too conspicuous—he'd head into the village and steal change from a car, or rifle through someone's house. Bad options, but better than nothing.

He eyed the clerk: oughta try the easy way first. He tapped the bell on the counter and the man raised his head. "Yes?"

"Do you have any playing cards?"

"Of course, please." The clerk opened a drawer and gave Grant a pack. "Enjoy."

"Thanks." Grant turned away, then back. "Oh—and how about a few francs?"

"Pardon?"

"We're playing poker, I don't have a stake. Five or ten francs, put it on my tab."

The clerk bit his lip. "I'm not sure I ought to do that."

"I'll pay you back in chocolate and cigarettes. C'mon, five francs."

"I really don't think . . ."

"How about poker chips, you have any poker chips?"

"I'm sorry, no."

"Loose change? All I need's enough for an ante or two."

The clerk drummed his fingers on the ledger, chewing his lip.

"Go on," Grant said. "I'll give you half my winnings."

"And if you lose?"

"Then you get the whole thing."

The clerk shook his head, but reached into a pigeonhole for a change purse and poured a few coins into Grant's palm. Mostly bronze, with a few zinc or nickel—one of 'em oughta fit a pay phone. Grant thanked him and headed toward his room, then turned onto a wooden deck with wrought-iron tables and chair. He spent a quiet hour skimming the guidebook, giving anyone watching time to get bored. Finished reading about Lake Geneva, flipped through the pictures of the Salève—a mountain range on the French border—then lay the book on the table and stepped close to the hotel wall, like he was returning inside. He'd hop the railing and follow the hedge into the village, there oughta be a pay phone at the post office or a corner store. He put a hand on the railing, then stopped at the sound of an engine approaching: a Swiss army van swinging into the hotel driveway.

When the big soldier stepped onto the deck five minutes later, Grant was sprawled on a bench, staring blankly at the distant waterfall.

"Lieutenant Grant?" the soldier said, in a deep respectful rumble.

Grant turned. "That's some view."

"But I hear you don't find our conversation so enjoyable."

"What're you talking about?"

"You just say name and rank and serial number."

"Oh. Yeah, I'm funny that way."

The big soldier grunted. "The captain wishes to see you."

"Well, I'm not going anywhere."

"In the village."

"The village? What about quarantine?"

The soldier shrugged. "The captain says."

"Fair enough." Grant stood, suppressing a smile. Everything was falling into his lap. "What's your name?"

"Engleberg."

"Who's the captain? I thought the brigadier general said 'corporal.' "

"No, that's a different man." Engleberg led him into the hotel, down the corridor. "This is Captain Dubois." He stopped outside Grant's door. "I am instructed to pack your bags. You'll meet the captain at the Sterner Tavern, yes?"

"Pack my bags?"

"You're being transferred—sent to your embassy, perhaps."

Better and better. "The Sterner, right. Thanks."

The lobby echoed with emptiness, the black-haired clerk gone from the front desk, no soldiers or hotel staff. Outside, the breeze stiffened and Grant followed the sidewalk toward the center of town. Past a dozen private homes, a grocer, and a drugstore—but no post office, and no pay phone.

A block away from the tavern, a uniformed man stepped from a doorway. He pointed his pistol at Grant's chest and barked: "*Halt! Hände hoch!*"

"Wait!" Grant raised his hands. "I'm here with permission. I'm meeting Dubois."

"I'm Captain Dubois." The man's sharp brown eyes glinted behind his eyeglasses. "And you assaulted the desk clerk, attempting escape."

"What? No—"

"It's a good thing you're so closemouthed, Lieutenant." Dubois gestured with his pistol. "We can't have you talking to the wrong people."

The captain's gaze shifted and Grant half turned. He caught a flash of motion over his shoulder—Engleberg swinging a rifle butt at his head—and the world turned inside out.

CHAPTER 3

The freezing wind shook an eddy of fine black dust from the pocked wall against which Major Eduard Akimov sat, wrapping his bare feet in *portyanki*, strips of coarse cloth. Not easy, with his missing left arm. Still, at least he could see, despite the hour: a pillar of flame rose from a burning factory across the city, and the pall of smoke over Stalingrad reflected the glow, a charred orange light like dawn.

Akimov watched the black dust settle around the base of a stone chimney that towered over the ashes of a wooden home. He'd been cut off from the regiment he commanded for two days now, with only twenty-eight men. No radio, no support—fighting deaf and blind in the ruined city, and hugging the Hitlerites close enough to smell their breath. Keeping the enemy near so any Luftwaffe air strike would kill their own people.

Pyotr approached and squatted beside him. "We just got a message, sir. From command."

"They fixed the signal cables?" Cables snapped every day, destroyed by tank or mortar or grenade. "Or please, tell me the radio is working."

"A runner got through," Pyotr said.

"Lucky man."

"He's the third one they sent."

That was life on the front, the German Sixth Army driving the decimated Soviet Sixty-second back toward the great sluggish Volga river. Stalingrad had burned into ruins months ago—they lived in basements and sewers and caves, fought in the wreckage for every house, every hallway.

"What message?" Akimov asked.

Pyotr jerked his thumb westward. "Get to the square. Cross and create a 'breakwater.' "

Akimov gazed across the rubble. "Is that all?"

"They're expecting a panzer push. If Fritz reaches the Volga, he'll cut the army in half."

"A 'breakwater,' Comrade Major?" the boy Sasha asked.

"A bulwark of defensible houses," Akimov explained. "We'll slip forward with a small fighting patrol—"

"Ten or twelve men," Pyotr told the boy. "And tonight, you're the twelfth."

"Clear the houses," Akimov said, "and fight off the counter-attacks."

"But . . . for how long?" the boy asked. "Only twelve men?"

"Until the consolidation group comes," Akimov said. "With men and ammunition and food."

"They'll reinforce us soon?"

"Or we might get resupplied by biplane," Akimov said, not quite answering.

"Might not," Pyotr said. "They told—"

A field gun banged and the boy cried out and clutched his rifle. Another bang, the chatter of automatic fire, and the boy looked at his feet and said, "They told us that once we crossed the Volga, everything was different, we'd find courage. But I, I—"

"Courage is knowing what trembles on the scales," Akimov told him, quoting the poet Akhmatova: " 'The bravest hour strikes on our clocks, let bullets—' "

"You recite one more poem, Comrade Major," Pyotr said, "I'll shoot you myself."

Akimov chuckled. "You'll get used to it, Sasha, soon enough."

"No," the boy said. "I'll die. I'll die here."

"One or the other," Akimov told him, not unkindly. "Those are your only two choices."

Akimov finished wrapping his feet and headed to the cellar, the boy dogging his heels.

"I'll be the twelfth man?" Sasha said. "In the fighting patrol?"

"Just do as the sergeant says," Akimov said. "You'll be fine."

"Will you be with us, Comrade Major?"

"Fetch an arm from Fritz," Pyotr told the boy, "and sew it on the major's shoulder. Then he'll come along . . . despite his rank."

"Anything else in the message?" Akimov asked.

"Something about 'Not a single step back.' "

Akimov ducked through a ragged brick doorway. "Good of them to remind us." He nodded to the guards on the ground and glanced toward the riflemen sprawled invisible on the rooftops. "We'll cross the square and make a breakwater, then."

He stepped beneath the skeleton of a building, careful of his footing on the rubble-strewn floor, and into a trench camouflaged by piles of bricks and charred beams. Then ducked into the basement of a half-destroyed toy store—their garrison, their sanctuary and head-quarters. The lamp glowed low, not quite reaching the corners of the wide room with its fire-blackened walls and skittering rats.

At a makeshift table of heaped plaster, the skinny sniper Rabinovich licked his spoon clean and tucked it into the top of his boot. "Fish stew," he told them.

"You've been to the river?" Pyotr asked.

"The Hitlerites catch the fish." Rabinovich shrugged. "Eating them is the least we can do."

"They catch the fish?" Sasha asked. "The Germans do?"

"Bombs stun them and they drift to the surface," Pyotr told him. "Watch your fingers around Rabinovich, he never stops eating. That's how the major lost his arm—he fell asleep and Rabinovich started chewing."

Rabinovich cheerily told Pyotr to fuck his mother, and across the cellar the Pole stood at attention. He'd worshipped Akimov ever since a *politruk*, a political officer, tried to arrest him for keeping a diary on the front. Illegal, but Akimov wasn't going to lose a man for bullshit like that. At least, he thought the Pole worshipped him: Who knew? The man only spoke Polish. Still, he could toss a grenade through a window blindfolded and around three corners—that was enough.

Akimov threw him a halfhearted salute and sat beside Bobrikov.

"Numbers 47 and 49," Bobrikov told him, looking up from a city map.

"For the breakwater?"

"*Da*. Those are best, Comrade Major."

"You trust your map?" The walls of Stalingrad crumbled too quickly to map, streets crushed into dead ends and buildings into craters.

"And my memory."

Grishuk raised his head from the corner where he'd been dozing, using his boots for a pillow. "Still happy to be here?" he asked Bobrikov.

"There are worse places."

As the son of an "enemy of the people," Bobrikov had been assigned first to a labor battalion, doing forced construction with convicts and conscripts, eating frozen potatoes, living in trenches where men died of exposure and exhaustion. Only Akimov understood how he could think Stalingrad was an improvement.

Akimov nodded. "Numbers 47 and 49, then. How are we for grenades?"

Bobrikov told him, and Pyotr said, "The question is, how are the Germans?"

"They've probably got one or two."

Grishuk said, "At least Oallah will have a good reason to hit the dirt."

"Oallah" was what they called Husami—a Tajik who spent half the day on the ground, praying "O, Allah," and the other half absolutely motionless, turning himself into a chunk of fallen plaster. The best scout you never saw, and not bad with a flamethrower, either.

Those six were all that remained—uninjured—of Akimov's "men of Rostov," the battalion that fought rearguard with him at Rostov. The rest of these men, though . . . farm boys who'd never seen an electric light before the army, telephone operators and tobacconists, college students driven back to the Volga over the corpses of their countrymen. Two million dead in a year? Three million? The Red Army was commanded by ideologues who believed the propaganda they spewed, lapdogs chosen for loyalty instead of competence: with perfect faith in the inevitable victory of Communism, they'd never planned for defense, only offense. Why bother defending, when victory was assured?

Akimov kicked Grishuk's foot. "Get your boots on."

"Me? I'm this close to a good night's sleep."

None of them slept, not in this hell of ear-shattering clamor, with the stink of piss and sweat and gunpowder everywhere. "Maybe the breakwater has a feather bed," Akimov said. "You can sleep there."

Pyotr laughed and told Sasha, "You too, boy. Let's go."

Sasha said, "What? Where?"

27

"Across the square."

"Now? Already? Now?"

"In three days," Akimov told him, "you'll be an old hand, hard as cast iron."

"Three days," the boy whispered, looking at Akimov with pleading eyes. "Will you come with us—"

"Grab your grenades," Pyotr growled at him. "Ten of them. And a spade. You know how to clear a house?"

Akimov rubbed the stump of his arm and listened to the clatter of ammunition belts and PPSh submachine guns, the clink of grenades. He watched Rabinovich stroking his rifle, sleepy-eyed Grishuk yawning himself into readiness, the Pole checking his saber: the others used bayonets, but not the Pole. He'd been a horseman, once. Two of the new men, the redhead and the Ukrainian, each took six kilograms of dynamite, and the other four, mortarmen cut off from their company, prepared the 55-millimeter light mortars. In the corner, invisible unless you knew he was there, Oallah crouched over his flamethrower.

Not a traditional assault team, but Akimov was satisfied as he surveyed them. Then his gaze settled on a white-faced Sasha adjusting his forage cap, and he shrugged. Well, what the hell—if a leader didn't lead, what was he?

He patted his jacket and took a grenade, and Pyotr stepped beside him and murmured, "Tell me you're not coming."

"That wouldn't be my first lie, Pyotr."

"Don't be an idiot, Edik—" Edik was his nickname, for Eduard. "You'll just be in the way."

"They'll fight harder with me there."

"We all will." Pyotr glanced at Sasha. "But that's not why you want to come. You're a major, a field-grade officer. Whatever else your father did, at least he—"

"The ranks flatten as the front shrinks, you know that. With a hundred meters between the Nazis and the Volga, even the generals are affixing bayonets."

"Not the one-armed generals. Put the grenade back, you can't even pull the pin."

"You remember the day we met?" Akimov asked, with a soft smile. "At Kharkov?"

Pyotr snorted and turned away, knowing not to argue.

Akimov led them from the cellar, the boy at his elbow. He eyed the ruined street, heaps of wreckage cupped inside the husks of buildings, shallow shell craters edged with dirt. Oallah hissed from behind the remains of a garden shed, and they slipped around the corner, over the rubble, and into the water pipes.

Akimov crawled slowly, pools of stagnant water seeping through to his elbow and shoulder. Even Oallah with his flamethrower moved faster than a one-armed man—Akimov's stump burned and his breath turned ragged, following Pyotr's boots in the darkness. They finally turned, at Bobrikov's muttered instruction, into a concrete chamber, past a pile of bodies charred from fire and bloated from water: civilians.

At a pair of metal doors long-exploded by a mine, Akimov nodded at the Pole, who touched his saber with a hungry smile and led them upward, under the roiling sky.

At the edge of the square, the air stank of blistered iron. They inched forward, the bold advance measured in centimeters, past a smoldering mattress and an upended perambulator, over the muscle and guts of the city: concrete and stone flayed into view like a pig carcass hanging in a butcher shop. Halfway across the square they took cover behind a blackened tank and a toppled statue.

Akimov looked at his wristwatch. Not yet.

He couldn't see the boy Sasha, but he heard his whisper. "How did the major really lose his arm?"

"Quiet," Pyotr told him.

Akimov glanced at the rooftops. Cut off from army headquarters, ordered to take a breakwater—and Pyotr was right, he couldn't fight anymore, couldn't even use a grenade. On his watch face, the second hand swept in a slow circle.

"We were fighting rearguard," Pyotr murmured, to Sasha. "This is in Rostov, trying to slow Fritz before he overran us from behind, a massacre. The major's battalion . . ." Pyotr's words faded under the rumble of Stalingrad, then returned. "Then a German soldier breaches the house with a grenade in his hand. We're all standing there holding our dicks, until the major jumps him from the landing, in a bear hug, and traps the grenade underneath the German. The grenade blows. The major's arm is wrapped around. Poof."

The boy said something Akimov didn't hear.

"A year out of prison," Pyotr said. "And he loses an arm."

"Prison?"

"Akimov was in the gulag for three years. They paroled thousands of officers after our losses in Finland. Turns out you need officers to win a war." Pyotr laughed softly. "Who knew?"

"The gulag? Why was he in the gulag?"

"Denounced for anti-Party activity."

"But—"

"Ask him yourself, his nose is an inch from your ankle."

The minute hand on Akimov's watch ticked over. He clucked his tongue, stood into a crouch and ran across the rubbled square with his men. The Germans caught sight of them—too soon—and squeezed off bursts from a machine gun. One of the men grunted, and the German fire was answered with the woof of the 55-millimeter light mortars, perfectly timed, and the unhurried crack of Rabinovich's rifle from the rooftop.

Akimov rushed the house, his Nagan revolver useless in his hand, and a dozen explosions sounded as one long deafening crash, the Pole and Pyotr throwing grenade after grenade through the windows and gaping doorways of the first floor, the house belching smoke and debris. Bobrikov raced fearless through the dust into the house and sprayed the first room with his submachine gun—the two

Germans at the window already dead—and the redhead tossed a grenade down the hallway, Grishuk taking the other two doors and Pyotr the chasm in the wall, explosions surrounding them, two and three grenades followed by the spray of submachine-gun fire. Akimov felt the cruelty rising in himself, the calm carelessness of battle, and shouted at his men, "Next room, go! More grenades! Now, now! Rip through the wall!"

They took half the floor, then a German stepped from the pantry, firing around the corner, and stitched Bobrikov in half, and he fell against the wall and dragged himself ten feet and stumbled inside the pantry, and the blast of his grenades blew his leg in half at the knee, his boot hit the ceiling and left a red-brown stain. Deafened, shouting, and half blind, Grishuk cleared the parlor, stumbling on Bobrikov's torso, and Akimov caught a glimpse of something and screamed—the ceiling! a hole in the ceiling! the fuckers shooting down!—and a stream of fire from Oallah's flamethrower singed his hair and burst upward, and Akimov emptied his Nagan, screaming for the Pole, for Jesus, for Grishuk.

The Germans fought for the living room, tooth and nail. Akimov had the Ukrainian blow a hole in the floor, and Oallah went beneath to burn them out. Pyotr finished them with his PPSh, and the Pole hunched behind a bullet-pocked icebox and fired bursts at the stairwell.

Then a sudden pause, the city holding its breath, and Akimov turned to Pyotr. "Where's the boy? Sasha?"

"In the square."

Dead already. "Shit. I need a cigarette."

"In Moscow, they charge two rubles a puff."

"See how lucky we are?"

"Yeah, Bobrikov is right."

"Was right," Akimov told him.

Pyotr shook his head. "Not Bobrikov?"

"Yes." They didn't speak for a moment, then Akimov eyed the stairwell. "Two more floors and we've secured the building."

"Do it the easy way, or the hard way?"

Akimov laughed, his ears still ringing. "There's an easy way?"

"You're the commander, you tell me."

There wasn't an easy way.

They cleared the upper floors.

Six weeks ago, a German panzer division smashed through the lines and attacked antiaircraft batteries operated by volunteer girls, half of them Stalingrad high-school students. Never trained to repel ground attack, they brought the antiaircraft guns low and fought the Sixteenth Panzer Division to a standstill. After a brutal exchange of fire, the antiaircraft batteries fell silent, the panzers advanced—and the girls rose from the ashes and beat them back.

Again. And again. And again. They battled the Germans through one entire night until dawn, and all the next day to sunset. They refused to retreat, they fought the panzers until the moon rose and the last girl died, still firing.

And so? What did slowing the Sixteenth Panzers matter? Did they save the street, save the city? Win the war? Akimov shook his head, kneeling beside the ruined bodies of Grishuk and Oallah and Bobrikov and the redhead whose name he'd already forgotten. You never knew, never knew if one bullet, one moment, one inch would tip the balance. You never knew what trembled on the scales.

His head bowed, he told Pyotr, "Smash through the walls. Make firing places for the machine guns—we need more antitank rifles. Put the men in the cellar and the rooftop, the panzers can't elevate that high. Did the mortarmen bring mines? We need a field outside. Where's Rabinovich?"

"Here," Rabinovich said, from the doorway, his face smeared with dust, the boy Sasha slung over his shoulder.

Akimov straightened. "He's alive?"

"I didn't carry him all this way to bury him," Rabinovich said.

The attic was exposed to the sky, the roof blown away. A lattice of beams like ribs arched over them, and through the blackened rubble Akimov saw a glazed red flowerpot, hatboxes spilling from a smashed wardrobe.

He checked the skyline, then nodded to a half-fallen wall and told Rabinovich, "Dig in over there."

"There?" the boy Sasha said. He'd woken shaken, with a nasty gash on his forehead, but strong. "They'll see him."

"When the sun rises, he'll be in shadow."

"Fritz likes to fight from eight to five," Rabinovich dug his spoon into a tin of meat. "Office hours."

"And we just wait?" the boy said. "After all that?"

"That was the simple part," Rabinovich said, around a mouthful. "Now the fighting begins."

"How are you with that rifle?" Akimov asked the boy.

"I—I'm good." The boy nodded. "I'm good."

Three days later, troops broke through lines and established supply routes. Now Akimov had artillery spotters, snipers, machine gunners, signal troops, medics. Antitank gunners, barbed wire, a minefield, a communications trench from the basement. They'd repelled seven attacks: corpses rotted in the crossroads, white smoke curled from a smoldering tank, and the angry howl of machine guns never stopped, day or night. So much for office hours.

Nobody slept. Sleep was as remote and fantastic as silence. Life before numbers 47 and 49 faded into a distant blur—he'd been born here, stinking and hungry and cold, ears burning and throat hoarse from shouting orders.

"It's true you were in the gulag?" Sasha asked, in the cellar.

Akimov nodded. "Kolyma."

"And from there . . . from prison they immediately made you an officer?"

"They gave him a bath first," Pyotr said.

"They didn't *make* me an officer," Akimov told Sasha. "I was a captain already."

"Well, but they gave you a command?"

"Straight from the gulag. They needed expertise."

"The comrade major knows men in high places," Pyotr explained. "His father, for one."

"Ah! Your father had you released?" Sasha asked.

"Perhaps," Akimov said. "If he felt my freedom was in his best interest."

Sasha smiled uneasily. "Surely no father would do less for an imprisoned son."

"He's the reason I was imprisoned."

"That can't be true."

"Akimov's father didn't approve of his marriage," Pyotr said. "Or his divorce."

"Even so, he—"

"He didn't approve of the comrade major joining the Bolsheviks. He approved even less of him joining the Bolsheviks so long before he himself did."

Sasha shook his head. "I don't understand."

"His first loyalty is to himself, that's all," Akimov said.

A shadow fell across them, and a *politruk* stood in the doorway. "Speaking of loyalty, Major Akimov, you're to come with me."

. . .

Akimov followed the *politruk* into the trenches, across the city to staff headquarters, a department-store basement with storm lanterns hanging from pipes in the vast damp darkness. Dim shapes crouched around a smashed display cabinet, eating dry sausage, drinking water from a helmet.

The divisional commander told Akimov, "You took the buildings."

"And held them, Comrade Colonel."

The colonel prodded a map with the point of his pencil. "Then we have a stronghold, here—our front line. And where's theirs?"

Akimov tapped the map in the same place. "We captured the sink, they have the toilet." An old joke, but in the darkness men laughed. Akimov continued, more quietly. "We've held the breakwater for three days. How much longer?"

"Until the end."

Before Akimov could answer, the *politruk* tugged him toward the far end of the basement. "Please, this is a matter of some urgency."

"Good. The faster we deal with it, the sooner I can return."

"That won't be possible, Major Akimov."

"To return to my men?"

"The dossier says you're a romantic, reading poetry and praying Mother Russia will tuck you in at night—but you aren't some sergeant commanding a single platoon."

Akimov massaged his stump. His missing arm ached before rain, ached in the morning, ached with a sudden premonition of trouble.

"You have new orders, straight from the top, you—" The *politruk* grimaced at Akimov's arm. "Need you fondle that?"

"You've seen worse."

The man's face sharpened. "I've done worse." He stopped at a table in a dark corner, with a bottle of vodka and dented tin cups. "I've seen prisoners scratch holes in concrete with nothing but fingernails—and motivation. There's nothing I won't do for the Party, because I understand what is at stake. Can you say the same?"

"Numbers 47 and 49 are at stake. What do you want from me?"

"Come." The *politruk* sat at the table. "Join me."

Akimov remained standing, watching the man. What kind of orders came from a political officer, a foot soldier of the NKVD? None that he was eager to hear, but still—a lieutenant in the NKVD effectively outranked a general in the Red Army.

"They had imported lobster in great mounds," the *politruk* told him when he finally sat. "Butter in silver boats, trout stuffed with cream bread and bacon."

"Where?"

"First pour us drinks."

Akimov gripped the bottle between his knees, removed the cap, and filled two cups.

The *politruk* eyed his empty sleeve. "You're clever with that—*without* that. I heard you lost an eye, too."

"It healed."

"There's still a scar, like a white spiderweb. They had fresh oranges and *gadazelili* and butter rum cake."

"We played this game too, in prison. 'The banquet of heaven'—imagining menus, remembering meals."

"This is no game. Six weeks ago, Churchill was in Moscow, eating trout stuffed with cream bread. He admitted there will be no second front, the British won't open a beachhead to draw the Nazis away from us."

"Am I supposed to be surprised?"

"You're supposed to say 'Yes, Comrade' and do what you're told. As are we all."

"Yes, Comrade." Akimov drained his cup. "If that's all, I should be heading back."

"You're not returning to the breakwater."

"To where, then? The tractor factory?"

The *politruk* lifted Akimov's duffel from beside his chair. "You're leaving Stalingrad to save Stalingrad."

"I don't understand."

"Orders from the top. First you fly to Ankara—"

"Turkey?"

"And then Switzerland. You lived there for years, didn't you, as a child? You speak French and German?"

"Switzerland? I left Switzerland, I came back, I fought in the October Revolution, in the Civil War, I—"

"Your wife stayed."

"I don't have a wife."

"Magdalena Akimova. She never came back."

"*Magdalena*?" Akimov's phantom arm throbbed. "She divorced me twenty years ago."

The *politruk* downed his vodka. "She has information we need, and no love of the Soviet Union. A tsarist, isn't she? Still, they say she knows something that might save Stalingrad—and maybe she'll listen to you."

"She never did when we were married. What is this about?"

"That's all I know," the man said. "You're flying to Switzerland to find your ex-wife."

CHAPTER 4

On Grant's sixth day in solitary confinement, the strut finally tore free from the roof. He dropped his arms to his side, shoulders burning and fingers numb, and breathed in the stench of the cell, leaning against the wall to stay upright. When the dizziness passed, he propped the strut, half as long as a baseball bat with the same heft, behind the doorpost. Now all he needed was the chance to use it.

Despite the rain lashing the roof— and the nickname of his cell, *Dunkelkammer*, the darkroom—a line of daylight smoldered at the base of the door. The room was a rectangular box the size of a closet, with four thick plank walls. The wall opposite the door backed onto the prison-camp stables, where horses stamped and shifted and bunched piss-damp straw into his cell through a half-inch gap over the concrete floor. Behind the side walls were a pigsty and the guards' toilet. Twice a day the door opened and Private Engleberg poured cabbage soup from a slop pail into a tin pan.

Grant paced the cell, working the pain from his shoulders. He could live with the stink and the darkness, but he was getting weaker—if he didn't move soon, he never would. He needed to find the crash site and get the camera. Oh, and convince the consulate to listen to an escaped prisoner accused of assaulting a civilian.

Easy enough.

After he'd been suckered from the quarantine hotel and pinned with assault and attempted escape, they'd shipped him to Wauwilermoos prison camp. Far cry from a resort hotel: prisoners slept in a freezing barracks on straw-covered boards crawling with lice, with an overflowing slit trench for a latrine. Watery soup with chunks of gristle, a weekly hose down by the guards—at least Grant thought that it was weekly, he hadn't been in a week before Captain Dubois summoned him for a "debriefing" then tossed him in solitary when he refused to answer.

More eager to throw Grant in a cell alone than to hear any answers. It didn't make sense. Except maybe there was one thing Dubois wanted more than hearing what Grant saw on the border: he wanted to keep him quiet. What had he said, back in that postcard village? *We can't have you talking to the wrong people.* This had to be about the prototype aircraft. And it was big—why else go to all the trouble? So the pilot of the German aircraft had spotted them, then the Germans alerted allies in Switzerland, like Dubois. And now here Grant was, locked in a punishment camp before he could tell anyone what he'd seen.

But who'd believe him? Nobody knew he had more than his memory, nobody knew he had film. Nobody knew the camera was still buried on that mountainside. Even Racket didn't know the camera was hidden or—

A shaft of pale light cut the darkness as the cell door opened, catching flecks of straw floating in the clammy air. Grant lifted a hand to shade his eyes, saw Engleberg in the doorway, armored in brightness.

"Hey, sweetheart," he said in German. "Dinnertime already?"

"Not for hours," the guard said, and he wasn't Engleberg.

"Burri? That you?" Private Burri was the best of the guards, a strapping farm boy with a lazy drawl. "I had Engleberg the whole time I'm in solitary, he won't even say hello. What'd I ever do to him?"

"Called him 'sweetheart'?"

"He likes that, it makes him blush."

Burri snorted. "Engleberg?"

"The big teddy bear. Ten to one he's Bernese."

"No more gossip, Lieutenant."

That was bad news. During Grant's days in the regular prison population, Burri let him grill him about Switzerland and current events; "no more gossip" killed Grant's only source of information. "What happened to 'we're on the same side'?"

"I have my duty."

"I'm still a downed pilot, still an American, still a—"

"Prisoner," Burri said. "If you'd stayed in the quarantine hotel, you'd have a clean bed and skiing lessons. Instead, you escaped and ended here."

"I told you about that."

"A dozen times. You were framed. Sure, you and every other prisoner in the camp. Now come, you're due at the Kommandantur for a discussion."

"With Dubois? Probably wants to talk about those skiing lessons."

But what would the commandant really want? To learn if Grant had seen the prototype aircraft on the border. If he hadn't, he could be safely released. If he had, he'd be kept in prison for the duration. That was the only way to keep him from talking. So how could Grant convince Dubois he hadn't seen a thing? No idea.

He stepped outside, onto the mud-splattered wooden boardwalk, leaving the roof strut behind. He couldn't take Burri without surprise, not as weak as he was, not when they were expecting him at the Kommandantur. At least he still had a feel for the bird's-eye view from flying photo recon. He could map Straflager Wauwilermoos in his mind: the camp surrounded by a double fence of barbed wire, patrolled by armed guards with attack dogs. Three gates—Schötz, Santenberg, and the pedestrian entrance—led outside, while the camp interior was divided by another barbed-wire fence, with two gates separating the smaller northern section from the larger southern. Grant's building, the stable and darkroom, was on the dividing line, with the infirmary and the prisoners' quarters to the north and the rest of the punishment camp in the forbidden south.

The rain wet his face and shoulders, and Burri said, "You smell like an ape."

Grant shrugged. "How's your girl?"

"She's well, *danke*."

"You take her to the cinema?"

"We saw *Kings Row*." Burri squinted toward the perimeter. "She said next time, we see the musical comedy with Marika Rökk."

Grant felt the bristle on his chin. "You got a razor?"

"When pigs fly." Burri produced a threadbare blanket from under his coat. "But I brought a towel."

"Zofingen is north, right?" he asked, taking the blanket. "With the Gothic church? And Brittnau had the girls' school in the old château?"

"Please, Lieutenant!" Burri glanced toward the distant guards. "Don't speak of that, I was wearing a cap when I told you."

"Wearing a cap?" Some Swiss-German expression. Grant scrubbed his wet hair with the blanket. "Talk German, Burri."

"I was drunk, I shouldn't have told you."

"And the war?"

"Am I your news service?"

"Last I heard, the Germans were at the gates of Stalingrad."

"They're inside the city now, fighting in the streets." Burri shook his head. "There was a newsreel at the movie, Hitler vowed he'd take Stalingrad by the end of the month."

41

"Which month?"

"This month. Now move."

Grant followed Burri past the infirmary, cold muck oozing between his toes. The air smelled of wood smoke and sulfur. At the interior gate—an X of heavy lumber, coiled with barbed wire—one of the guards flicked a cigarette butt at him, but the ember drowned in rain before hitting his thigh.

The other side of the gate, past a bare patch of earth, the Kommandantur dominated the camp. Burri brought Grant inside, to a room with a peaked ceiling and windows pearled with mist. A potbellied stove squatted in the corner and Commandant Dubois sat at a table with a pewter ashtray and a porcelain figurine broken in three.

"Take a seat, Lieutenant Grant," Dubois said. "You don't object if I speak German?"

"Depends what you say."

"You speak like a native." Dubois's dark hair stuck to his forehead, and his eyeglasses magnified sharp brown eyes. "Do I detect a hint of Bavaria in your accent?"

"Have you got any glue?"

"Pardon?"

Grant nodded at the broken figurine on the table. "I'm good with my hands."

"Private Burri, there's glue in the hutch, if you please." Dubois steepled his fingers. "Let me begin by asking, what exactly was your mission?"

Grant arranged the ceramic shards in a row: a girl with rosy cheeks, yellow hair, and a peevish mouth sitting on a glossy green hillock.

"Why, Lieutenant, does an American pilot conduct photo reconnaissance in a British Mosquito?"

"Good machines, Mossies."

"You'll answer eventually," Dubois said. "I am in no particular rush, and solitary confinement eats at a man. You were flying a mission over France, photographing Strasbourg?"

The porcelain shards didn't mesh, Grant couldn't make the jagged white seam disappear. "What's in Strasbourg?"

Dubois forced a chuckle. "You tell me. You were three hundred miles from the last Allied bombings."

"Looking for Paris. My navigator wanted to meet some French girls."

"You were two hundred miles from Paris."

"That explains why he didn't."

"Mosquitoes are British machines, and you are Eighth United States Air Force. Flying reconnaissance over France, you're discovered by a German air patrol and your airplane is punched full of holes, yes? Simple, so far. You couldn't return to England, so you emergency land in Switzerland. Ah, but you are caught! Quarantined at a hotel—soft treatment—this is all quite ordinary."

"You ever crash into a mountain? Not so ordinary. Neither is getting framed for assault."

"I tire of your fantasies of persecution." Dubois removed his glasses and pinched the bridge of his nose. "There is something you are not telling me."

"You want my serial number again?"

Dubois leaned across the table. "What are you not saying?"

"What are you not asking?" Grant raised his head from the figurine. "Who's behind you, giving the orders? What are you after?"

A brittle silence, as Dubois sat back in his chair.

"I'm an ordinary Allied pilot," Grant said, "shot down on an ordinary mission—and Wauwilermoos is a federal prison. Forget how I got here, I never even saw a military tribunal—you're violating the Geneva accords ten ways from Tuesday."

"Switzerland didn't sign the accords."

"The *Geneva* accords."

"Signed *in* this country, not *by* this country."

Grant glanced at Burri. "You didn't sign the accords?"

The guard shook his head. "*Nein.*"

"How about the Swiss Alps?" Grant asked him. "You got any Alps here?"

"We're neutral," Burri said. "There was no need to sign."

"Good theory, 'til you're on the wrong side of the barbed wire."

Dubois cleaned the lenses of his glasses with his necktie. "You were classified in the military manner until you escaped—that is a criminal offense. And don't tell me about the Code of Conduct, not when your military attaché personally instructed you not to escape."

"Leeger's a—" Grant switched to English. "Leeger's a prick on a pony. He's not my commanding officer."

If only Leeger had listened, given Grant five minutes in private. Didn't much matter that he was stuck in prison, but that prototype aircraft needed to be brought to light. Especially now, with Dubois going to this much trouble to keep him from talking, dragging him into prison to ensure he spoke to nobody at all. Must be following German orders. What else could be behind this?

"He what?" Dubois said. "I don't understand."

Back in German, he said, "Leeger's not my CO."

"I'm your commanding officer now, Lieutenant."

Grant swung at Dubois. Before he connected, Burri clamped his shoulder and shoved him back into his chair. Moving too slow, like he was under water.

"Look at you, Lieutenant." Dubois shook his head. "You can't fit two pieces of crockery together. Good with your hands? After six days in solitary, you couldn't swat a fly, shaking like an old man."

Grant lifted his hands. They were trembling.

"Six days," Dubois said, "and I have you in custody four more months. You stay in solitary *für d' Fuchs*. In vain. You punish yourself for no reason."

"We done here?"

"Almost. Tell me what you're not saying, and I'll release you from solitary. Remain stubborn, and the next time you see daylight will be 1943."

"I'm a pilot," Grant said. "I've seen plenty of daylight."

Dubois's eyes glinted. "And what else have you seen?"

"I once saw a monkey riding a bicycle."

The commandant stood. "Come along."

Grant followed him out the rear door, where the rain turned to a fine gray mist that veiled the sun. Dubois stopped on the wooden landing and said, "This is the War of the Races, Lieutenant, despite what you've been told. Last week, Reichsmarschall Göring spoke on this subject: the clash is not between governments, the only question is whether the Aryan German or the Bolshevik Jew rules the world."

Grant watched the fog drift past.

"Tell me what I want to know," Dubois said. "I'm a strict man, but fair—I can make your time here easy. Or hard indeed."

"You're not so bad, Dubois. Nothing wrong with you a bullet wouldn't fix."

"Return to quarters, Lieutenant Grant."

Grant went down the steps into the mud. *Was* this about the prototype? The camp had Swiss criminals—murderers, rapists— had Poles, Brits, Cypriots, Frenchmen. One German deserter, a broken kid who thought he was a traitor, but Grant was the only American . . . so far. Maybe that explained Dubois's interest. No, that wouldn't explain being framed at the quarantine hotel. And tossing Grant into solitary . . . Dubois had to know they'd seen the prototype. Or that they'd seen *something*. Maybe he'd just been ordered to keep Grant on ice, talking to nobody until further notice. The Germans wouldn't want news of that prototype known. Still, would they care this much? A couple of U.S. airmen with a tall tale, who'd listen?

Nobody knew about the camera, nobody knew they had proof.

And nobody would listen, even if he escaped—not without the camera. Especially now that he was officially a criminal. Problem was, he couldn't find his way to the crash site without Racket. Well, plus he was stuck in solitary confinement in a punishment camp, slogging barefoot through cold pebbled mud.

He walked halfway to the interior gate before he realized Burri wasn't beside him—glanced back and something solid and dark lunged past his elbow. Bunched muscles and glossy fur landed in the mud, haunches thickening, gathering for a spring.

Five years ago, Grant had overheard a drunken argument, maybe in Burma, maybe Hong Kong, about how to fight a dog. One man said, stuff your forearm into the dog's teeth and fall backward—put your other arm at the base of the neck, whip the dog above and behind, and snap its spine with its own weight.

So Grant moved his left arm, and was on his back in the mud. The dog stood on his chest, scouring his face with steam. Bright eyes burned under the furrow of the dog's brow and the mud leeched warmth from Grant's shoulders. Time slowed, and the camp receded: there was nothing in the world but the dog's bone-white teeth.

At a distant command, the dog backed away, hackles raised. Drizzle touched Grant's cheeks, and he lay there staring into the gray sky. Burri's face appeared, and strong hands pulled him into a seated position. Then a pair of boots drove divots into the mud: Dubois, cheeks blushed with excitement, eyeglasses fogged. "They are not good scent hounds, Lieutenant, but with a scent like yours . . ."

The guards laughed, and Burri lifted Grant to his feet. Good to feel human warmth again, a human touch. He stumbled for a few steps, then found his feet, and leaned on Burri through the interior gate, past the toilets to the darkroom.

He put a hand on the wall and said, "Gimme a second."

"She bit you?" Burri asked.

Grant shook his head, and when the ground stopped tilting went halfway inside the darkroom door. "You saw my hands?"

"I saw."

"Shaking like an old man. Tell me something, Burri. Are we on the same side?"

Rain trickled from the roof, and Burri shook his head and turned away, his voice soft. "I'm sorry."

Grant said, "Me too," and stepped from the doorway, swinging the roof strut.

CHAPTER 5

T he blow caught Burri behind his ear, the strut cracking against bone, and he sagged to his knees. Grant hit him again then stood trembling, breath ragged and palms stinging.

Beyond him, the camp drowsed—water dripped from gutters and pocked the boggy earth. He dragged the guard's limp body to the middle of the cell, plowing a path where filthy concrete showed through straw. Goddamn Burri, the best of the guards, a good kid loyal to a neutral country. But neutrality, shit—not with a five-kilometer boundary *inside* the Swiss border for German flyers only.

Grant leaned close. "Burri?"

No answer but a soft wheeze. Grant unlaced the guard's boots and pulled them onto his own muddy feet. Wrestled himself into Burri's overcoat and trousers, propped the cap on his head, and cracked the door.

Foggy halos pulsed around downturned electric lights. Grant took the sodden blanket he'd used as a towel past the infirmary to the double perimeter fence, checked he was alone, and tossed the blanket over the top line of barbed wire. He could climb the first fence without too much damage, maybe slip under the next in the mud. And then? Fifteen miles from Lucerne, to the southeast or southwest.

On foot. Over mountains, for all he knew. Unarmed. With dogs on his scent.

And there was nothing for him in Lucerne. He needed to bring the camera to the consulate, but first he needed Racket to find the crash site—and had no idea how to find him. Secreted in a hospital, somewhere in Switzerland.

He looked at the blanket draped over barbed wire. He couldn't do this, flying blind.

He returned to the darkroom, raising a hand to the fog-blurred shapes of two guards strolling toward Schütz gate, and nudged Burri, still curled on the floor. The shallow breathing didn't change, so Grant grabbed his wrist and dragged him halfway outside, face-down on the muddy boards, then stepped back into the cell and crouched in the thickest gloom. His legs trembled and the darkness shimmered like an oil slick. Something was wrong with his eyes. Something inside him had snapped like that ceramic figurine, and the bone-white edges wouldn't join.

He closed his eyes but the shimmering remained.

Shadows moved behind sheets of fire.

Nanking, 1937. Around the darkened street corner, a girl pled in Chinese. Grant glanced at Martin, a small neat man in wire spectacles who couldn't fight his way out of a lemonade social. Martin wasn't looking toward the girl's voice, though, he was eyeing a pile of rags in the gutter.

"Still alive?" he asked.

Grant crouched over the rags, an old Chinaman curled inside a threadbare smock, and shook his head. Dead—Grant knew from the smell alone, disemboweled by a bayonet.

"Beyond help, then," Martin said.

Grant looked toward the darkened street corner. "*She's* not beyond help."

"We can't interfere."

"Interfere now, or bury her later."

"If we miss this appointment, Mr. Grant, we'll bury thousands."

Around the corner, the girl's scream cut through the roar of flames before choking into silence. Surprised male laughter sounded, then quieted into the singsong chatter of Japanese.

Grant stood from the dead old man. "I can't walk away again."

"You'll do as you're told," Martin said.

He pulled his .45, hearing the soldiers coming closer.

"Put that away," Martin said. "There are five of them—"

"I got seven bullets."

"I spent two weeks on my knees pleading for the Japanese to respect the neutral zone, there are tens of thousands of refugees—attack these soldiers and you endanger them all. Lower your weapon. *Now.*"

Grant holstered the .45 a moment before the Japanese soldiers turned the corner, two of the older men teasing a younger one, who blushed and fiddled with his rifle strap. When Martin offered a polite greeting, they bowed and smiled and escorted Martin and Grant down empty echoing streets to their meeting with the commander.

Martin made his case, and the commander apologized: there were enemy combatants in the neutral zone, and he couldn't, for the safety of his own troops, keep the zone off-limits to his men.

Grant stood apart from the negotiations, his palm itching for the weight of his sidearm. But this was Martin's show, and maybe Grant didn't much like him but he respected him. He obeyed him. Martin was tougher than dirt, never passed the buck, never froze or fumbled: he fixed what he could, ignored the rest. And saved thousands.

Martin wore the commander down, extracted a promise about safe passage and troop restraint, and said he'd be back tomorrow to continue the conversation. On the way out the door, he murmured to Grant, "And *that* is how one saves lives, Mr. Grant."

"Talk 'em to death. Would've been quicker with a bullet." Grant looked at the tidy Swiss man. "We're coming back tomorrow?"

"And every day, until he reins in his men."

Three hours later, just after sundown, Martin sent Grant for medical supplies. Drawn by the light, he'd circled around a fire raging at the ruined granaries. The Japanese culled a dozen girls and women—some as young as nine—from huddled families, and doused the rest with gasoline. They tossed grenades into the fire and after each blast the screams grew fainter.

An old woman in a peasant shirt fell to her knees, pleading with Grant in Chinese. He nodded, yes, his face stung by the fire, and led the woman and a boy with a bloody bandage for a face past the Yangtze river, clotted with bodies and makeshift rafts. Down an alley in a wealthy neighborhood, a shout of laughter echoed from an open doorway, and the girl with the long neck stepped outside with immaculate care, like the road was paved with broken glass. She was from a good family, the daughter of the house, couldn't be older than sixteen, with bite marks on her bare shoulders over the white shirt hanging limp and dirty like a swan's broken wings.

Grant knew the story, he'd seen it a hundred times: she'd watched her father and brothers bayoneted, watched the soldiers rape her mother and sisters and kill them, keeping her for last. A hundred times in two weeks.

From some impossibly deep well of strength the girl with the long neck gathered her dignity, raised her chin, and took another step, then spun slowly and sat, and he saw they'd cut off one of her breasts. She was naked except for the shirt, and one hand automatically attempted modesty. Grant had covered her with his jacket, face averted, nothing he hadn't seen before—and something shattered inside him. He'd lost the clear snap of automatic response, the hair trigger of instinct—he'd been rendered useless.

. . .

A shout jerked Grant awake.

Shadows broke the rectangle of light at the open cell door, and guards dragged Burri fully outside, his feet jostling through the doorway. Then the door swung shut, the darkness deepened, and Grant steadied himself—if they remembered the lock he was finished, but why lock an empty cell?

Boots squelched in the mud, a guard yelled, "He went over the fence, I found a blanket—" Metal jingled in the stables, soldiers falling into formation and dogs straining at leashes. At least they couldn't smell him, not in here. The sounds faded, the chill of the rain-damp overcoat soaked into his shoulders and, finally, the line of gray light at the concrete floor dimmed and died. He brushed straw from his trousers, stepped through the door, and hunched against the drizzle. There was only one guard at the interior gatehouse, but one was enough—they knew him at the interior gate.

He went into the guards' toilets and splashed water on his face. Now what?

Stormy air blew through gaps where exposed rafters ran to the eaves outside—and inside, to the peak of the roof, the gaps forming narrow crawl spaces untouched by the light of the bulb swaying on a metal chain.

He eyed the rafters. Could he squeeze through to the other side of the wall? Get to the southern half of the camp without passing the gatehouse? He hauled himself onto the sink, grabbed a water pipe, slick with condensation, and pulled himself upward. Wedged a boot on the sink housing, swung his other leg up, and levered himself into a crawl space, one hand pinned to his side, the other in front like the antenna of a blind insect. The shaft narrowed under the peak of the roof, then fell away into dark space, and he inched forward, four feet, five feet . . . and got wedged inside.

He hadn't panicked when the Focke Wulf 190 dropped from the clouds, firing bursts at his Mosquito, or during the crash—but now he couldn't breathe, arms wedged and legs trapped, impossible to turn his head. His heart seized and his skin itched and he couldn't scratch.

An arrhythmic tapping startled him and he started sweating, imagining guards entering the toilets behind him and seeing his legs—but the tapping was only his arm trembling against the wall. Shit. He took a breath and edged forward until dirty light filtered from the downslope of the crawl space. He shifted an inch at a time through the bottleneck until he suddenly lost purchase and slid down the other side of the crawl space.

He fell onto the hard-packed floor of the stables. He could see the corps buildings through the open stable door, and to his left the Kommandantur and the quartermaster's barracks, the depot and warehouse. He rubbed his shoulder and limped into an empty stall, breathing deep to keep from shaking. There'd been a time when he would've set the camp on fire and strolled away by the light of the blaze. Well, he was older now.

The stables were empty except for one swaybacked nag with rheumy eyes and concertino ribs. She scoffed at Grant and someone entered the stables behind him and said, in German, "Fucking mud."

Grant grunted his agreement.

There were two thumps, the man kicking dirt from his boots, then silence. Grant fed the horse a handful of hay, glanced over his shoulder, and the man was gone. Maybe. He adjusted his cap and headed across the clearing toward the Kommandantur, twenty yards that felt like a mile. Through the back door, down a narrow corridor to Dubois's office . . . where the door was locked, and flush with the jamb.

Goddamn Swiss engineering. He headed outside, counting his paces, and around the side of the building, held Burri's doubled cap against the pane and rabbit-punched. Glass tinkled. He unlatched the window and climbed through, groping until he found a desk lamp. He pulled the cord and there was a writing desk and file cabinets, a wooden swivel chair and a map pinned to the wall.

He went through the drawers, found half a dozen scented handkerchiefs, a penknife, and—in the cabinet—dozens of files. Personnel reports and inmate dossiers, a handful of letters signed "Heil Hitler" with a heavy grease pencil over Dubois's home address. Requisition forms, army manuals, a yellowing scrapbook . . . but no mention of Racket or the hospital.

Grant spun in the chair and eyed the map on the wall. There was another way to find Racket. After he escaped.

CHAPTER 6

The prison camp smothered in gray-green aquarium light, the search for an escaped prisoner leaving the grounds quiet. Grant adjusted his grip on the stack of desk drawers in his arms. He'd dumped the contents in Dubois's office, so the drawers were lighter than they looked, and obscured his face. Just a man in a uniform, running an errand in the middle of the night. He walked toward the exit and checked the guardhouse: three soldiers huddled drowsily in their jackets for warmth.

He angled toward the open gate, carefully not looking at the cars and vans parked outside. As far as the guards knew, the only loose prisoner was long gone, why stop a fellow soldier?

He was ten feet from the gate when a bearded soldier in the gatehouse shot him an incurious glance and reached for a pen. Shit—he wasn't gonna pass unchallenged.

He kicked the door frame. "Wake up, you lazy fucks."

The bearded guard said, "What? I'm awake."

"And the other two? Sleeping on duty? You wearing a cap?"

"What?"

"Sleep it off when you're not on duty," Grant growled. "If I'm running around this time of night, you can stay fucking awake."

"Calm down," the guard said.

"That's the problem, too much calm. Give me the key. The key to the van."

"The van?"

"The van, the goddamn van." From behind the stack of drawers, Grant nodded toward the military vans parked beyond the gate. "You think I want to carry these all the way to Zurich?"

"Zurich?"

"What are you, a fucking echo? The keys. You want Dubois riding your ass?"

The man raised his hands in aggrieved surrender. "Fine, take them."

Grant's fingers trembled, fitting the key into the ignition, but he drove away steady enough.

An ancient wall bordered Lucerne on the north, with a moon-touched lake to the east, and a river bisected the town, spanned by a crooked footbridge. The map from Dubois's office lay crumpled on the passenger seat beside Grant, and the fuel gauge edged lower as the wheels hushed over rain-soaked streets, raising plumes of spray.

A man with an umbrella stood under a sign for the National Quay, lawn tennis and lake baths. Grant ran down the window. "I'm looking for Brüggligasse."

The man pointed with his umbrella. "In Musegg."

Back the way he came, through Schwanenplatz, past a big church where sluggish fat raindrops freckled the windshield. He turned at the Kornmarkt, found Museggstrasse in the shadow of the ancient wall. Followed the street the wrong direction, and ended in the museum district, but back the other way, the gas needle below empty, he found Brüggligasse.

The house had wrought-iron gates and a stone chimney. He parked down the street and checked the front doors. Locked. Side doors, too. The old coal-chute cover shifted easily, though, and he crawled into pungent blackness, missed a handhold and sprawled onto uneven ground. He fumbled through cobwebs into a white-washed stone hallway and a cool earthy breeze brushed his face— the root cellar.

Another door, and he was in Berlin: swastika flags flanked a podium stacked with pamphlets, and an enlarged photo of Hitler hung in the place of honor. It was Dubois's house all right. There was a gun cabinet with bolt-action rifles, an old Gewehr 98 and the shorter standard issue Karabiner 98k. Pistols, too, an 8-millimeter French Lebel, a Mauser, a couple of Walthers. There was a death's-head SS dagger in a sheath and in a glass drawer, half hidden by a riot of red stamps, was a Great War Stielhandgranate, a stick grenade with a wooden handle like a hammer.

Grant loaded the Lebel and drew a bead on the photo of Hitler across the room. His hands shook, the gun barrel jittering like a drop of water in a hot skillet. He replaced the pistol, grabbed the death's-head dagger. The blade slid from the sheath and trembled.

He wasn't good with his hands anymore, but this wouldn't need a soft touch.

Upstairs, he found the front parlor, sat on the davenport, and slipped Burri's boots off. Maybe Dubois hadn't returned home, maybe he was hunting Grant outside Wauwilermoos. Maybe Grant could curl onto the cushions and sleep for a week.

The stairs were gritty under his bare feet. On the second floor, he found a snoring lump in a four-poster bed crowned by half a dozen pillows. He switched on the lamp, the hilt of the dagger cold in his palm. A grunt sounded from the bed, the whisper of cloth under the counterpane, and Dubois lifted bleary eyes toward the light.

"This time," Grant said, "I ask the questions."

There was a catch in Dubois's breathing. "Wha—" His voice cracked. "Grant?" He pulled himself against the headboard, wearing striped pajamas and a floppy nightcap. "You can't—you can't be here."

The room smelled of camphor and cologne. Outside, a dog barked and another answered.

"You assaulted a guard," Dubois said. "You escaped the camp. You're in deep water now, my boy. When they find you, you'll regret it."

"*You* found me."

"You don't frighten me, Lieutenant."

"No?"

Dubois worried the counterpane with his fingers. "What do you want?"

Grant turned the death's-head dagger in his hands. He wanted a shower and a shave, a hot dinner and a good night's sleep.

"Tell me what you want," Dubois said.

The dogs stopped barking. The silence was as suffocating as the cockpit of a Mosquito, the radiators oozing heat.

"Say something, goddamn you."

"My navigator, Racket McNeil. Oliver McNeil."

"Sergeant McNeil, yes." A pause. "He's being looked after, his injuries treated. We help internees, I can help *you*. Turn yourself in, Lieutenant—there's nothing to prevent you. Burri is not seriously injured. You'll appear before a military tribunal, how does that strike you, how does that sound?"

"Where is he?"

"McNeil? In the hospital, I imagine."

"Where?"

"Surely, Lieutenant, you don't think—"

Grant leaned closer. "What town?"

"In Neuchâtel!" Dubois said. "In Neuchâtel!"

"Where's that?"

"To the northwest, on the lake—" Color flooded into Dubois's face. "You're going back for him."

"You think?"

"I know."

"Not smart, Dubois."

"Smarter than you." His brown eyes shone. "He's an injured man, only a fool would—" He stopped suddenly at Grant's expression. "What?"

"You know where I'm headed."

"To Neuchâtel, of course—" Awareness dawned, and Dubois stilled. "I won't—I won't tell anyone." The whites of his eyes seemed to brighten as Grant showed him the dagger and stood. "Oh, God, no, please, I'm a—I'm a neutral, I'm an officer."

"You're a dead man." Grant pressed the man against his mattress, lifting the knife in his hand. "You set me up."

"Please, in the name of God, this is murder."

"What do you want with me? Why all the questions?"

"I don't, I'm not—"

"I'll only ask once more," Grant said, then didn't.

Dubois breathed hard into the silence. "I heard—I was told that you—before you crashed, you may have seen something. A sensitive location, or a—an industrial area, I don't know."

"You don't know."

"They told me to learn what you saw. To learn if you saw anything. They told me it was most important to keep you from speaking to anyone, I must move quickly, prevent you from reporting in. Keep you quiet. They said—I couldn't control you in quarantine, so . . ."

"So you ordered me to leave the hotel." Grant tapped the blade against the pillow. "Engleberg took care of the clerk, and together you captured an escaped felon."

"I'm a loyal soldier. I do what is necessary."

"Who told you this? Who told you I saw something?"

"A contact."

"In Germany?"

Dubois didn't answer, breathing hard.

"The patrol who shot me down reported my location? Sure, then the Nazis called you to keep me from talking."

"Yes."

"They think I stumbled onto something. What do they think I saw?"

More breathing. Grant pricked Dubois's cheek with the dagger and he blurted, "Yes! Yes, I don't know. You were seen by an aircraft. I received a call, the evening you crashed. I was told to keep you quiet. I discovered where you were being taken and—the rest was easy. That's all I know. That's all I know."

"You're a Nazi."

Dubois flushed. "I am a member of the National Socialist Party."

"Get up."

"A—a proud member."

"Fucking idiot." Grant dragged Dubois from bed. "I didn't see anything before we crashed, I was too busy trying to stay in the air." He shoved the man down the corridor to the linen closet. "Open the door."

Dubois opened the door with a shaky hand. "Don't—"

Grant pushed him inside. "If I hear a single noise, I'll take you in the bathroom."

"Into the—?"

Grant showed him the dagger. "For the drain."

He blocked the door with a sea captain's chest, then started a bath and soaked in the scalding water. The stink of solitary confinement had seeped into his skin, into the muscle and bone. He lathered a shaving brush and shaved, then drained the bath and started another.

A hospital in Neuchâtel. Easy enough.

He clipped his nails then rifled through Dubois's closet until he found a suit that almost fit, a pair of socks and too-wide shoes. He put on a tie and a watch, and downstairs grabbed a briefcase and hat. Found money and papers in the rolltop desk—found a map, too. Neuchâtel didn't look far: shove Racket into the van and head to the crash site for the camera. Then the consulate would listen, Brigadier General Leeger be damned.

In the kitchen, he drank a jug of milk, found dense grainy bread and smooth white cheese. When he finished, he put apples and the rest of the bread in the briefcase. He was forgetting something: map, money, food, clothes. He sat at the table, missing something big, like flying a plane without landing gear.

He rested his head on his outstretched arm. Get Racket, find the crash site, bring the camera to the consulate . . . all he needed was the keys and a tank of gas.

Drive to Neuchâtel, park behind the hospital, down a dank stifling alley where the stink of burned flesh curdled the air, where the sound of laughter meant the opposite of pleasure and the girl with the long neck stepped into the road, crescent bruises on her pale skin, blood staining her stomach and legs, her shoulders wrapped in Grant's jacket.

Boots marched past the alley, a slow hollow thumping, with brittle edges and the smell of sauerkraut, and Grant opened his eyes to the uneven thud—

Where was he? The barracks, the darkroom . . .

Dubois's kitchen, listening to an insistent banging. A slatted rectangle of light draped across the table in front of him: morning in Lucerne, shining through the window. Like an idiot, he'd slept— wasted the night and killed his lead.

He grabbed his hat and briefcase and stood, and his legs buckled. He fell into the chair and breathed until the smoke cleared from his eyes. Gathered himself to stand, but his legs didn't work. The steady knocking grew louder, construction on the street or a gate banging against—

No. Dubois, upstairs, beating his way out of the closet.

Grant put his palms on the kitchen table and pushed up from the chair. When his legs stayed under him, he went into the hall to the stairway. Ought to climb up for a quiet conversation with Dubois, but that was a lot of stairs. He stepped through the front door and the damp street reflected the sun, brighter along the curb where the light caught a ribbon of water.

Down the street, the van was gone.

Grant stared at the curb, his mind blank. Dubois would be free in ten minutes, and knew he was headed to Neuchâtel. Steal a car? Not with this much traffic on the streets, not when he couldn't trust his legs—not when the one thing missing was his nerve.

Two blocks over, peeling whitewash flaked from the ancient town wall like sunburned skin, and Grant walked until he hit the river, then went along a quay lined with flat-topped trees. He crossed a covered bridge with a roof painted like an illustrated Bible, and was hit by a wave of fatigue. He was out of the prison camp, he'd found Racket, he oughta be popping champagne—instead he was breathless as a broken old man.

At the *bahnhof*, he bought an express ticket for eleven francs and sixty centimes. He couldn't do this alone, and he only knew one person in Switzerland: Martin's wife, Anna Fay.

CHAPTER 7

The front doors of the Variété Theatre swung open and three couples emerged, the women chattering in empire-waist gowns and fur stoles, the men a dark silent backdrop. Anna Fay watched them for a moment, then stepped from the taxi, smoothing her brocade evening dress. She smiled brightly at the women, pretending her dress pumps weren't pinching her toes—she'd bought them ten years ago, expecting to soon shed her childbearing weight.

She laughed to herself: instead, she'd shed her expectations.

Up the stairs, she slipped from the nighttime chill into the theater lobby, where perfume and cigars thickened the air. Although the play had ended half an hour ago, the crowd remained, laughing and smoking and drinking from a bar only slightly depleted by the war. She slipped around the edge of the room, holding the package—an empty stationery box, prettily gift wrapped—by her side.

At the staircase, a woman behind her said, "Anna, darling. Is that a present for me?"

She turned and found Rosine, all angles and dark sleepy eyes. "I didn't expect to see you here."

"The Undersecretary of Customs and Finance came for the play."

"Why aren't you flirting with him, then?"

Rosine made a noise in her throat. "I am—he's watching from the balcony."

"Where?"

"Don't look! He's with his wife." Rosine tapped the gift-wrapped package with a varnished fingernail. "Tell me it's a rope of pearls. I haven't any pearls."

"Go away, I'm meeting someone."

"A bashful lover? It's about time, darling."

"Rosine, shoo!"

The girl drifted away, and Anna felt the attention of the room shift, felt herself forgotten. Good. She trusted Rosine, but she wore a mask in the social whirl that Anna hardly recognized. Not that she blamed her, of course.

Anna lingered at the edge of a conversation, waiting for the approach. The source she hoped to meet tonight was more than ordinarily cautious, and for good reason: the stakes were more than ordinarily high. With her reputation for fervent anti-Fascism and disregard of the censors—based on articles written for the newsstand papers and a few privately circulated journals—Anna was periodically contacted by people hoping to shine a bright light on the darkness of Swiss-German cooperation. The woman who'd arranged this meeting had alluded to the document Anna most wished to discover, a Nazi memorandum on the status of German-Swiss economic negotiations. Months ago, she'd unearthed a smudged mimeograph of an early draft, written by Reichsminister Karl Clodius, which had made German reliance on Switzerland painfully clear:

- Switzerland represents our only means of obtaining freely disposable foreign exchange. We cannot, even for two months, forgo foreign exchange transactions in Switzerland.

- Even limited Swiss deliveries of finished goods are indispensable.

- Among Swiss arms contracts are consignments of specialized technical equipment whose delay would seriously affect the German tank and remote-control programs.

- Only half of the 470,000 tons of coal currently being dispatched to Italy via Switzerland could be conveyed there by other routes.

The Clodius memo proved there were men in the Swiss government, in banking and industry, whose hands gripped tight the financial reins of Hitler's Thousand-Year Reich. Anna needed to find them—and force them to act against the Nazis.

If only this woman would show herself. She tapped the gift-wrapped package against her hip, increasingly anxious as the crowd thinned. Yet this wasn't another dead end. The telephone call had come yesterday, and something in the woman's tone convinced Anna that she was genuine.

"May I speak with Madame Fay?" the woman had asked, in accented French.

"This is she."

"I have read some of your articles."

"Yes? May I help you?"

"I think you can be trusted. I possess certain information, newsworthy information."

Anna reached for her notepad. "Please go on."

"About Swiss-German financial dealings."

"To whom am I speaking?"

"We'll meet soon enough. I worked for a man who arranged a sham deal between Swiss and German industries. I saw the paperwork. I *have* the paperwork."

"A sham deal?" If Anna investigated every unethical financial transaction, she wouldn't have time to sleep. "The commissions are too high, or—"

"They launder money between Switzerland and Germany. This isn't greed—isn't *merely* greed, but politics . . . at the highest level. This violates the laws of neutrality."

"You worked as this man's secretary?"

"Don't press me. There are others who want this information, who'd pay me or . . . or worse." The woman's voice wavered for a moment before she regained her assurance. "This man, my ex-employer, he is not to be trifled with."

"And his name?"

"Not on the telephone. He's dipping his fingers into something new. I investigate him still."

"Tell me his name—tell me *something* I can confirm."

"I'll give you confirmation when we meet."

"You have evidence?"

"*Oui*. A memorandum."

Anna felt her breath catch. The Clodius memorandum? "About Swiss economic support of Germany?"

"And the Federal Swiss Police, and our security apparatus, and a group of investors who—" The woman stopped, her voice suddenly brittle. "Enough. You are in Bern. The night after tomorrow . . ." A newspaper had rustled over the wire. "Here, after the evening show at the Variété Theatre. Bring a—some way I can recognize you."

"How do I know this isn't a goose chase?"

"You know."

True enough. Anna had believed her already. "I'll be there."

"Bring a gift-wrapped package," the woman had continued. "That's how I'll find you. A present—though you'll be getting the gift."

The woman's mixture of fear and assurance had convinced Anna of her sincerity—and even now, watching the last of the theatergoers leave the lobby, an hour after midnight, she didn't truly doubt her.

Finally alone, she stepped into the cold night and the empty streets. The Old Town of Bern rose on a sandstone ridge above the Aare river, with medieval fountains and arcades jostling under the bristling Münster tower. Broad lanes extended from the single span of the Nydeck bridge, branching through the city toward Buben-bergplatz. Not even two miles home, but a long walk after an exhausting night—she'd missed the last tram, of course, and the taxi rank was abandoned.

Only one car passed before Anna turned down Münzrain toward her shortcut. She leaned against a wall under the vast stone belly of the Bundespalast and ran a finger along the heel of her shoe. Had the woman been frightened away? Had she truly intended to come? Hardly mattered—Anna was obliged to explore every dead end, she owed that to herself, to her husband. To Switzerland.

Farther along the street, she slipped through the unfastened gate of a railcar, climbed the maintenance stairs, and stepped onto Taubenstrasse, where her house at the edge of town backed onto acres of vineyard that allowed for hidden approaches. She went inside, kicked her pumps from her feet, and massaged her arches until a ghostly shape drifted to the stairway landing: Christoph, pale hands gripping the railing, black eyes heavy with sleep. Only ten, and solemn as a priest—he was his father's son, a mixed blessing.

"Go back to bed," she told him.

"You said you'd be home for dinner."

"We can talk about dinner tomorrow," she said, "and how it arrives on the table."

"I'd rather have you than dinner."

"This is a busy time."

A somber pause. "You always say that."

"It's always true, dumpling."

"Don't call me that."

"Go to bed, Christoph—you've school tomorrow."

He drifted away like a wraith, and she peeled the gloves from her arms, removed her velvet tam, and unpinned her hair. Upstairs, she opened Christoph's door. His white face turned toward her from the bed, a beautiful brooding boy, pale and dark as a Romantic poet.

"Sleep well," she said.

"You too, Maman."

But after wrestling her duvet for an hour, she didn't sleep at all. She slipped into her bathrobe and went downstairs to the laundry where she put the kettle on the gas ring. Sprinkled a layer of starch in the saucepan, added water, and kneaded the lumps with her fingers. She swirled the boiling water into the saucer, wrung the clothes in the mangler, and took the hot iron from the pad.

The heat and whisper and rhythm of the work soothed her, the fabric smooth in the wake of the iron. Poor Christoph, so bright and so finely tuned. Steam rose to bathe her face, yet when the phone rang she felt a chill: good news never came at this hour.

She stepped into the corridor to answer. "Hello?"

"It's me." Lorenz, a manager at the Palace Hotel. "I have information."

"You're at the switchboard?" she asked.

"At the hotel, yes."

Which meant he couldn't speak completely candidly. "What's wrong? You need me there now?"

"No, Anna, I'm sorry, I—this can wait until morning."

She twisted the telephone cord. "I'll come now."

"Don't bother, I shouldn't have called. A woman spoke with me this evening. She wanted to apologize for missing you at the theater, she was afraid to go inside, she thinks she's being followed and—"

"Lorenz, did she give you anything? A document?"

"No."

"Her name?"

"She was afraid to—"

"You arranged a meeting for me?"

"I got her name, Anna. She took a room using an alias, paid cash. But I searched her luggage for labels and—"

"She checked in? Is she still there?"

"She stayed for an hour, and left. And no, I didn't arrange a meeting, and I don't know where she went—not out the front door, I can tell you that much. Her name is Magdalena Loeffert."

"Spell the last name."

"L-O-E-F-F-E-R-T. Magda. Magdalena."

"You checked the directories?"

"Of course," Lorenz said, "and spent an hour on the phone. Her most recent address is an apartment in Geneva. According to the superintendent, she's moved."

"That's all you found, her old address?"

"It's late—tomorrow I'll learn more. She's important?"

Anna unwound the telephone cord. "She worked for a man who arranged a Swiss-German financial deal, to launder money."

"She's in government, then?"

"Or near enough. I'll ask Pierre-Luc."

"Which one is he? Your editor in Bern?"

"*Oui*. Pierre-Luc Soyer. He knows the personnel of the federal government like you know fancy automobiles."

"And he'll tell you?"

"No." She'd need some ruse; Pierre-Luc was not a man who involved himself in controversy. "Let me handle that. You search the room again."

"She was only there an hour, perhaps two."

"Then why bother to book a room at all?"

"Perhaps she wanted a nap."

"At your rates? Maybe she *was* being followed, and the person found her. Search the room, Lorenz, then find me at the newspaper tomorrow morning. I'll arrange an early appointment with Pierre-Luc."

She said goodbye and nibbled the brass cap of a pencil from the telephone table. Why would the woman check into the Palace Hotel? The hotel was the scheming heart of political Bern, the conference rooms and bedchambers hummed with seduction and intrigue. Why would Magda Loeffert, afraid of discovery, book a room there?

Anna returned to the laundry and ran the iron along the shirt collars and cuffs. Pierre-Luc could track down Magda Loeffert for her, if he chose. She couldn't rely on his principles, though; she must rely upon his pity instead. She'd written two articles, far too controversial for him—she'd offer them, and after he refused perhaps he'd place a few phone calls on her behalf.

She pressed the shirt pockets and the front panels, and ironed the handkerchiefs. There. Now she'd accomplished something; now she could sleep. Upstairs, she lay the laundry on her bed and crawled under the covers, curling into the weight of the clean clothing, the scent and the warmth.

CHAPTER 8

A kimov stepped from the airplane in Belpmoos, a small town five miles south of Bern, struck by the silence. He blinked at the gentle smokeless sky and stared in disbelief to the picturesque horizon. Once, he'd known the names of the alpine peaks, but now other landmarks loomed larger: a twisted iron gate in a Stalingrad square, the basement of a dry-goods store, the kitchen of number 47 and the back parlor of 49.

Two men stepped beside him, one on each side like a prison guard. "I'm Vladimir," one said. "This is Vladislav. They call us Little Vlad and Big Vlad."

The smaller of them was big as a draft horse. "Am I supposed to guess which is which?" Akimov asked.

They eyed him with a bleak respectful suspicion, stamped from the same mold as his escort from Ankara . . . but these two might actually know something. They ushered him into a stuffy airport office with paneled walls, where Akimov stretched his arms—his arm and his stump—and caught a flash of disgust on Little Vlad's face.

He looked at the man. "Where are we headed?"

"The hotel."

"Which hotel?"

"The Palace."

"In downtown Bern? What're we, hiding in plain sight?"

The man shrugged. "We have half the floor, Comrade Major. You adjoin the deputy commissar."

"Who's he?"

A disbelieving smile rose on Little Vlad's face. "You don't know?"

"Nobody told me anything—nobody knew anything."

"Ah, of course not. This news cannot be allowed to reach the front."

"Bad for morale," Big Vlad said, in a deep rumble.

"What news?" Akimov asked.

"What *did* they tell you, Comrade Major?"

"I'm instructed to find my ex-wife. She has something of value to aid the war effort."

"This will be a regular family reunion, then. The deputy commissar's name is Akimov."

"My father?" Akimov felt himself grow still. "He's here?"

"He returns to the hotel tonight."

Akimov hadn't seen his father in five years, not since the betrayal and the trial that sent him to the gulag. Even in his nightmares, his father's face—watching unblinkingly from the courtroom bench—was a featureless blank. A perfect reflection of the road his father had chosen. Such a long distance from Akimov's first memory, of his father's open laughing face, surrounded by a halo of sky. So far from a childhood trip in the Russian countryside in an open carriage, seeking the sanctuary of his father's arms at the rumble of a sudden thunderstorm. And even in Switzerland, he remembered a quiet afternoon drifting in a shabby dinghy his father had rented on a sudden whim, taking him from classes to fish. Talking for hours of nothing, casting hooks into the glassy water.

And now. A deputy commissar, in Switzerland, his father's hidden hand still moving him like a pawn on a chessboard.

He exhaled slowly. "My father."

"Yes, Comrade Major."

"Then he's still alive." And Akimov would be forced to face him. "A pity."

The Vlads exchanged a glance and remained silent.

"Any news on Magdalena?" he asked.

"No."

"She's still missing?"

"Her address is a Geneva apartment—we've watched and entered, searched every corner, but haven't yet found her. So they bring in the ex-husband, maybe he'll have better luck."

"She's gone from her apartment? You checked her friends, her work?"

"Yes and yes."

"What does she have that will aid the war effort?"

"Ask your father, Comrade Major."

"It's true, then? She does know something?"

"What she has could stop the bloodshed at Stalingrad."

He snorted in disbelief. "Does she know what she has, then? And how important it is?"

"No, she thinks it's just proof of a Swiss-German money-laundering scheme. Talk to the deputy commissar," Little Vlad said. "He'll tell you what he wants you to know."

"Deputy commissar of what?"

"You don't know your own father's rank?"

"He's moved up in the world. Easier to rise when you climb over corpses."

The Vlads shifted uncomfortably.

"And until he arrives?" Akimov asked.

"Rest."

"And waste a day?"

"You're part of a trade delegation, liaising with the Swiss." Little Vlad tossed Akimov an overstuffed envelope, wrapped tight with a rubber band. "Documents and information. Some Swiss francs."

Akimov caught the envelope between his hand and chest. "You're certain Magdalena is gone from Geneva?"

"From her apartment, at least."

He asked how long they'd been in Switzerland, if they'd searched Geneva themselves, if they had recent photos of Magda.

"Ask your father," Little Vlad said. "Briefing you isn't our job."

Akimov put the envelope in his satchel and watched an airplane trundling down the runway. "The soil in Stalingrad is so hard you can't break through with a shovel, did you know that? You need an ax or a pick. The ground gives nothing in Stalingrad, try digging a grave. You think my job is grave digging? No, our jobs are whatever—"

"Pardon, Comrade Major," Big Vlad said, as a car pulled outside the office. "But it's time to go."

Akimov looked from one man to the other. "Where's the bathroom?"

"We'll be at the hotel in fifteen minutes."

"I'm not asking permission."

In the bathroom down the hall, Akimov measured himself in the mirror over the sink. He looked old and lean, like rawhide, with scars around one eye and a downturned mouth that expected all news was bad. Bad news: the reason he was in Switzerland, the reason his father was here, the reason they were so eager to find Magdalena that they'd shipped him from the front. Should he wait at the hotel for his father, as instructed? No—there was no man to whom he owed less obedience, no man he wanted less to see. They needed him to find Magda, he believed that much, even if he didn't know why. So he'd find her and be back to the front in another two days.

Playing games in Switzerland was worse than stupid, and he refused to be his father's pawn. Still, he had no choice but to help. If they lost Stalingrad, they lost the war . . . and they were on the verge of losing Stalingrad. He couldn't refuse any chance to aid the war effort; his duty to Russia trumped his distrust of his father.

He returned to the hall and told Little Vlad, "I'm going to Geneva. Where do I hire a car?"

"What? No. You must wait for the deputy commissar."

"I wasted years waiting for him," Akimov said, stepping past.

"We'll escort you," Little Vlad said. "Please."

"You think Magda will let you close? She'll see you and start running."

"She won't see us. She's not even there. And if she is, she won't see us."

"Why risk it? I can't have you two scaring her away. I'll return tomorrow morning at the latest."

"This is—you do this only to anger your father."

"No," Akimov said, "that's simply an added benefit."

"But what will I tell him?"

"The truth—you couldn't stop me."

At the front of the airport, Akimov hired a taxi at the queue, and they pulled slowly away. Into Switzerland. Smooth paved roads snaking under cold mountains, around hills, and over ravines: even the clouds looked Swiss, plump and knowing. At Lausanne, he told the driver to wait outside Gare Centrale, a railway station perched on a narrow terrace. Twenty years gone, yet everything looked the same—the choppy lake and tobacco factories, the castle and cathedral, the viaducts and bridges and breakneck staircases.

Inside Gare Centrale, the switchboard operator told him Magda's telephone was disconnected. He memorized the address, dismissed his driver, and boarded the next train to Geneva.

Closer to Magda than he'd been in decades, yet he felt nothing. The emptiness surprised him—he'd loved her blindly, achingly, the sway of her hips and the sheen of her hair. The bite of her wit, her curiosity and restlessness. But that had been a different life, before the army, the betrayal, the gulag. What remained of the boy he'd been, consumed by love? A distant fondness, nothing more.

Both born in Russia, he and Magda had met in Switzerland, at the embassy where his father had been posted—an ambassador before the Revolution, erudite and cultured, a lion among jackals. Magdalena's parents were diplomatic servants, and Akimov's father, in those days before he'd remade himself, frowned on his son's "infatuation" with the servant girl. Magda was acceptable for dalliance, but nothing more.

So Akimov married her, drunk on class equality and Magda's warm white skin. He'd been a committed Communist, his eyes on the bright and inevitable future: a society without class or exploitation, without greed or violence, armies or police. He quoted Marx to his then-horrified father: "I can do one thing today and another tomorrow—hunt in the morning, fish in the afternoon, rear cattle in the evening, criticize after dinner . . . without ever becoming a hunter, fisherman, herdsman, or critic."

And he'd returned to Russia to join the Red Guard, to fight for a society in which there'd *be* no fighting—but Magdalena hadn't followed, as she'd promised. She'd divorced him instead.

Two decades since he saw her, and now he stood outside the apartment in which she lived—or had lived, until last month. In Les Eaux Vives, around the corner from the park, one of eight quaint buildings with small courtyards and modest charm. Strange to walk on uncratered streets past unscarred walls—to see children in school yards and hear unhurried traffic winding through narrow unguarded streets. He eyed the building, measuring the windows for grenades and the roof for snipers, then shook his head. *Geneva*. If Magda had "something of value to aid the war effort," he'd find her, simple as that. For the millions dead and the millions yet to die—for the wounded hope and pride of Mother Russia.

He rang the bell twice, then took his knife from his satchel and forced the front door. On the second floor, sunlight pooled in the corridor under a window near Magda's door, and Akimov gripped his knife—and stopped. A padlock hung from a new bolt, secured across the jamb.

Back outside, he checked nameplates until he found M. COUIL-LARD, MANAGER.

A pink-faced man opened the door to his knocking. "Yes?"

"Good morning," Akimov said. "Monsieur Couillard?"

"It's afternoon. You're looking for Madame Loeffert?"

"Well—yes. I am."

"She's gone, these three weeks and more, and you lot can stop bothering me." Couillard stepped back into his apartment. "Good day."

"Wait! Wait—I'm her ex-husband."

The door stopped, half closed. "Monsieur Loeffert is dead."

"I'm her first husband, from—we were nineteen. I'm only in Switzerland for a week, I heard she's missing. I—I'm concerned."

"You're Russian, then?"

"Here with a trade commission." The door wavered, so Akimov pressed onward. "All day long I'm in meetings about quality control for ball bearings and range finders. You don't know what tedium is until you start dreaming in millimeters."

The man almost smiled. "Her ex-husband?"

"She divorced me when I returned to Russia."

"No children?"

"*We* were children. But no."

"Can't say I blame her, choosing Switzerland over Russia."

"Neither can I," Akimov lied.

"Well, there's not much I can tell you. She moved last month, and I haven't seen her since. She's paid until the end of the year."

"You must have something, some paperwork of hers?"

Couillard nodded. "Credit and bank information. All confidential. Even if you *are* her ex-husband, you have no rights."

"There's no forwarding address? All I'm asking for is a number to call, someone who might know where she is."

"Her post is being held at the central office. Show me your papers, maybe I'll let you look at the empty walls in—"

A shot echoed in the narrow street. Akimov dropped behind the stone steps, scrambling for the Nagan revolver he'd left in Stalingrad, trying to locate the sniper. Unarmed and alone in a strange city, without men or cover, naked in the sights of an enemy he couldn't see . . .

Couillard blocked his view of the rooftops, his face hard. "A car backfired."

Huh. Akimov stood slowly, and brushed dirt from his pants.

"Some trade negotiator," Couillard said. "You lot broke into her apartment once already, I had to buy a damned padlock. Get yourself gone, or I'm calling the police."

"I'm her husband, her ex-husband—"

The door cracked closed, sharp as a gunshot. At least this time Akimov stayed on his feet.

CHAPTER 9

Anna Fay shifted on the visitor's chair in the cluttered newspaper office. "Certainly, Pierre-Luc, if that's your final decision—"

"You know I can't print this article," the editor said. "Don't be angry. Let's speak of something else. Your son is well?"

"I'm not angry." She tapped the typewritten pages on the desk between them. "I'm disappointed."

"You know perfectly well this article cannot be printed."

"I know *you* won't print it." But that wasn't her goal, her goal was to shame Pierre-Luc into getting her access to Magda Loeffert's records.

"What would you have me do?" he asked. "I'm answerable to the military penal code. If your article goes beyond the bounds of objective journalism, I'll be held accountable."

"Do you dispute my facts?"

"No, but—"

"You find them subjective."

"I don't argue with your facts, but your presentation. You report only on the negative."

She listened for a moment to the clacking of typewriters from the secretarial pool, the ding and swoosh of the carriage return. "Christoph is well, thank you. Do you remember the first of my articles you refused?"

"About the 'J' stamp."

Anna nodded. In 1938, the Swiss Federal Police asked the Germans to mark the passports of Jews by stamping the passports with a "J"—and she hoped to prey on Pierre-Luc's guilt for refusing her article on the subject. "And two months ago, when I located the police circular . . . do you recall?"

"Of course."

" 'The borders are closed to those fleeing for reason of their race,' a naked attempt to exclude Jews. Then Dr. Rothmund"—the head of the Police Section of the Justice Department—"started mass expulsions of refugees."

"Three years ago," Pierre-Luc said, "when a thousand Jews fled Hamburg on a steamship, the United States sent them back to Europe—and the Third Reich. We're not alone in this."

"We're Swiss," she said. "We know better."

"This is my concern: you report only the damaging stories, your facts are true but unfair."

"I wrote last month about Grüninger." A police superintendent who'd allowed three thousand refugees into the country illegally. "He's a hero."

"And how did the story end?"

"With the facts. He was fired for his heroism, lost his pension and his career."

"It's not so simple, Anna." Pierre-Luc's voice was tired. "You want to give the Nazis an excuse to invade?"

She tapped her article on his desk. "This isn't about refugees, it's about the Swiss Nazi Bund, the League of Swiss in Greater Germany, the SVV. The goals and high-level members of the Swiss Nazi frontist groups."

"There's nothing illegal in joining the Schweizerischer Vaterländischer Verband."

"Nothing illegal in printing its membership lists, either."

"Unless the list includes military officers. Bircher"—the founder of the SVV—"is president of the Swiss Officer's Society."

"He's organizing Swiss medical teams to treat Nazis on the battlefield."

"Who told you this?"

She lifted an eyebrow. "Sources. Who also tell me Bircher has dinner with the interior and finance ministers, he's supported by Pilet-Golaz and General Guisan, who—"

"Watch your mouth, Anna."

"Guisan cannot be criticized?"

"He's a good man."

She scoffed. "He means well."

On September 1, 1939, a week after the Nazis and Soviets signed the non-aggression pact, Germany invaded Poland and the Swiss spent the next ten months watching the neutral states of Western Europe buried beneath the avalanche of the Wehrmacht—Denmark and Norway, Belgium, Luxembourg, and the Netherlands. At home, rumors spread of German troops in the Black Forest: Swiss civilians fled from the border towns in convoys of cars, mattresses strapped to roofs. Britain abandoned the Continent, the United States passed the Neutrality Act, Italy declared war, and Nazi columns marched through the Arc d'Triumph.

With the capitulation of France, Switzerland was a shallow island in a mutinous sea. The collaborationist French president spoke of the "crushing superiority" of the German armed forces; Churchill said Britain faced an imminent threat of invasion. And Marcel Pilet-Golaz, the president of Switzerland, gave a radio address declaring Switzerland's intention to adapt to the "new order in Europe," urging the Swiss to prepare for a "German future" and to trust the government like a "führer."

Dozens of Swiss frontist groups—Nazi sympathizers and agitators—merged into the National Movement of Switzerland, the Swiss built factories in "Greater Germany" and allowed German quality control inspections on Swiss soil. To placate the Fascists—and to secure German coal for heat and industry—two-thirds of the Swiss army was demobilized. The Swiss gave Germany the French financial reserves and all orders for military equipment placed by Norway, Britain, and France. The Third Reich ruled Europe, and Switzerland accommodated the new reality.

But Swiss general Henri Guisan was not so easily cowed. He withdrew the army from the borders and began constructing a national stronghold—the Réduit—in the heart of the Alps. He abandoned the lowlands and most of the population, leaving the major cities defenseless in the face of a Nazi onslaught. Instead, he built an alpine fortress extending from Sargans to Saint-Maurice to the Gotthard, in cliffsides and hidden caves, invisible to the Luftwaffe and inaccessible to the Wehrmacht. If an attack came, the Swiss troops would dig in . . . and destroy the alpine railway tunnels.

Mountain fighting, even against Switzerland, would not deter Hitler, but the threat of exploding the tunnels might. For years, almost two hundred German trains a day rolled through the Saint Gotthard tunnel, through the heart of the Réduit, carrying thousands of tons of steel and iron. Though Switzerland was surrounded by the Third Reich and the federal government sought to placate Germany, General Guisan gave his country a bargaining chip: the alpine railway passes. If the Nazis invaded, Guisan would sacrifice the valleys and farmland, the cities and the seat of government—everything but the alpine heights. The Nazis would prevail, yes, but they would pay dearly.

Yet with this partial victory Guisan was apparently content. He raised the cost of an invasion beyond all proportion to the benefits . . . then allowed the frontists to flourish in the army and the press.

"Even if I were inclined to print this," Pierre-Luc said, "the Department of Political Affairs has issued arêtes and the newspaper's doors would be barred before the ink was dry. This idealism of yours . . . you learned that from your husband. Martin did good work with the Red Cross and in China, but you can't bear the weight of the world alone."

"You may be right."

"Have I ever been wrong?"

"Not that you've admitted."

He laughed, but there was a tinge of self-disgust. Good. She opened the tabbed folder on the desk, and slid a second article to him. "Perhaps this piece, then? At the rate Christoph outgrows his clothes, I could use the money."

Pierre-Luc balanced his spectacles on his nose. "Summarize, as I read."

"The Swiss franc is the most useful currency for the Nazi munitions industry, yes? Only with Swiss francs can Germany buy Spanish manganese for gun barrels, Portuguese wolfram for aircraft construction, Turkish chromium for ball bearings."

"A précis, Anna, not an international tour."

"You can't listen and read at the same time."

He glanced over the page. "Continue."

"The Germans can't buy enough raw materials without Swiss francs, this is their Achilles' heel—the goods they need are only obtainable on the world market with foreign currency and gold. They can't buy what they need with reichsmarks. The Nazi war machine is a bonfire, and having consumed all available fuel there's nothing left to burn."

"Less poetry, Anna."

"In 1940, our government fed the Nazi fire, granting 'clearing credit' loans to the Reich—200 million Swiss francs in 1940, 850 million in 1941, and more this year, with—"

"How much more, this year?"

"I haven't a number."

"How do you know it's higher, then?"

"Sources. These interest-free 'clearing credit' loans not only—"

"Interest free? That can't be."

"It is. The clearing credits break the law of neutrality, Pierre-Luc. We cannot—"

"Wait." He dropped the article into the open folder. "You have proof?"

"Almost." Once she found the Clodius memorandum. "Not yet."

"You want to accuse the government based on what?"

"Sources and reportage. Run the article, Pierre-Luc. At least give me a column."

Pierre-Luc removed his eyeglasses. "You know I can't."

"I remember a time when your greatest editorial concern wasn't the military penal code."

"I'm sorry, Anna. If there's anything else I can do for you . . ."

Finally! "Well . . . perhaps you could help me locate a source? A woman named Magda Loeffert." She spelled the last name. "She works in the government—or did, fairly recently."

"Federal or cantonal?"

"That's what I want to know. Where did she work, in what office, for whom?"

"Ring the disbursement offices, check the employee rolls—you're a journalist, you don't need my help."

"Yes, but if you call directly I'll know in ten minutes."

"Why?"

"I'm working on a story."

"I've seen the sort of stories you work on." He swiveled in his chair and stared out the window. "I can't help you."

"Call Herr Leuenberger; you're old friends."

"Leuenberger wouldn't know."

"At least tell me who you'd ask."

Pierre-Luc sighed. "I'd ring Johannes Perret, at the Kantonale Dienststelle für Verkehrsfragen."

"The Transport Bureau?"

"We were at school together—but you, he won't help." He raised a hand as she began to speak. "And no, I won't call him. Now please, Anna, I'm a busy man."

She wasted ten minutes trying to change his mind, then told him Martin would be ashamed and left. Down the hall, she pressed the elevator call button and listened to the distant rattle. She'd learned nothing of Magda Loeffert. Maybe the whole thing was a goose chase, but knowing the Clodius memorandum existed, knowing there were documents that might alter the course of the war . . .

She turned away before the elevator arrived, went down the hall to an empty office, and sat at the desk. The switchboard connected her to Johannes Perret's secretary at Kantonale Dienststelle für Verkehrsfragen, and she said, "Good morning! This is Mademoiselle Boulanger, from Pierre-Luc Soyer's office. Monsieur Soyer has a quick question about one Magda Loeffert. L-O-E-F-F-E-R-T. You have access to her payment records?"

"Her payment records?"

Anna said, "*Oui.*"

After a pause, the secretary said, "For Monsieur Soyer?"

"He said I should call Monsieur Perret's office."

"One moment."

There was a click, and Anna waited. Times like these, she wished she smoked. A man half entered the office, paused in the doorway, and looked at Anna, his brow creased.

"Five minutes," she mouthed, pretending she was taking notes.

"But, um—"

"Five minutes," she said, more sharply, and he left.

The secretary returned to the phone. "Madame Loeffert, yes, we have her records. Executive secretary at the Federal Wood Syndicate."

"The wood syndicate? That's a government body?"

"Joint private-public enterprise. She left for a position at a financial services firm, apparently."

Anna nodded to herself. A financial firm was more promising than a wood syndicate. "She departed on good terms?"

"There's nothing in her file but praise."

"Which firm? I mean, her new job?"

Paper rustled. "That's not listed."

"But you have Madame Loeffert's current address?"

"Certainly. In Geneva." She gave the old address. "Do you need me to repeat the—" The secretary spoke to someone on her side of the line. "Hm? Yes, of course."

A man's voice came on the phone: "This is Herr Perret."

"I'm calling for Pierre-Luc Soyer," Anna said. "He wanted—"

"I just spoke with Pierre-Luc, Mrs. Fay."

Merde. "Ah. Well, we're almost through here."

"Not 'almost,' " he said, and rang off.

Outside the newspaper office, Anna stepped onto the sidewalk and a chill wind tugged the brim of her hat. At least she'd confirmed Loeffert's background: the woman wasn't a crackpot, wasn't a dead end. She bowed her head against the cold and passed the tram stop to the Gurten railway, where she and Martin had dined years ago, at the garden restaurant atop the long green hill.

A horn beeped, and a stately maroon cab of the Palace Hotel glided to the curb. Behind the wheel, Lorenz touched his black chauffeur's cap in greeting, a burly man with a close-cropped beard that narrowed to a devilish point. Despite the hat, he looked more like hotel management—which he was, one of the managers—than a driver.

Anna slid into the cab beside him. "My poor feet."

"Soak them in Epsom salts." Lorenz turned off the avenue toward Helvetiaplatz. "I've told you and told you."

"Any news on Magda Loeffert?"

"Well, first, I'm sorry I called so late last night, I—"

"Never mind that—you searched her room?"

"The bed was made, the closets empty. No signs of a struggle, the people in adjoining rooms hadn't heard anything."

"You asked them?"

"I told them a story about a housemaid and a broken picture. The woman hadn't used the phone." He slowed at the Telegraph monument. "Even the wastebin was clean but for a sheet of crumpled paper."

"A sheet of paper?"

"Blank."

"*Merde.*"

He turned onto the bridge, the tires rumbling. "Back where we started."

"No good to anyone." Anna watched the buildings glide past. "We need to find something that can be *used*, Lorenz."

That was her solitary goal; she no longer cared for stories, only leverage. She was no longer a journalist but a party to the fight—in this war nobody was neutral, and the Allies were losing the covert battle against the Germans. The Americans lacked any real network in Switzerland, the hub of European espionage—even the French were more established, and they hadn't a country any longer. At the moment, despite British efforts, Allied intelligence was an orphan child. Increasingly, Anna's fellow Swiss were joining the fray, and curiously many of the key players were women. Countess Wally Castelbarco, daughter of the composer Toscanini; Mary Bancroft, studying for her doctorate in Zurich under Dr. Jung; Elizabeth

Wiskemann at the British embassy; and Anna herself—amateurs, all of them. The best Swiss agency was the Bureau Ha, privately funded, privately staffed, and privately run by an army captain. One man's hobby, more reliable than the official channels rife with German sympathizers.

Then there was Aktion, the Swiss National Resistance Campaign, mostly civilian, fighting the frontists, fighting appeasement—fighting the federal president and his cronies. They printed a weekly sheet, *Information of the Week*, for which Anna sometimes wrote . . . but were more a political club than an intelligence service.

And who were the professionals? The Germans, who ran a training camp for saboteurs at Panoramaheim, had dozens of frontist groups, tens of thousands of supporters, and infiltration into the highest reaches of government.

Still, she and Lorenz and Rosine did what little they could, for Switzerland—the first democracy and the finest—and for Martin, whose standards she'd never meet. They drove in silence past Bundesgasse: They needed something they could use. They needed Magda Loeffert.

CHAPTER 10

A shroud of steam rose between Nadya Loeffert and the two policemen on the railway platform outside her second-class compartment. She bowed her head in prayer—*Most Holy Mother of God, deliver me from misfortune*—but when the steam faded the policemen were still there.

She worried her silver necklace, wishing for the cool leather of a *lestovka*, a prayer ladder, in her hand. The men wore the uniforms of Swiss Alien Police, Fremdenpolizei, nothing to do with her—yet *his* connections were everywhere, this Swiss industrialist who so frightened her mother. Were they searching for her? *He* couldn't know what she'd done, at least not yet.

The ticket collector passed her compartment, chanting the name of the next station—"Walenstadt, Walenstadt"—and through the half-open window came the gasp of an arriving train, the cry of iron brakes. On the platform, the younger policeman stood under the brass placard of the station, talking with his middle-aged comrade: then he looked up and met her gaze.

Nadya lowered her head and felt herself flush. *Most Holy Mother of God, strengthen my soul and banish my despair.* She'd do anything for her mama, who'd sent her on this errand, yet she couldn't ignore the shiver of fright and regret.

She risked a glance outside and saw the policemen boarding her train. Her breath caught, but there was nothing to fear. This was not Germany where the SS rampaged in the streets, or the Soviet Union where believers were purged—this was Switzerland. In any case, the Fremdenpolizei wouldn't enter her compartment. If *he* knew what she'd done, he'd have stopped her already, before she'd delivered the document.

The train lurched forward, and Nadya's eyes watered against a rush of air carrying the scent of leafless trees. The white-walled houses and parish church of the village slid away, and telegraph poles blurred past as the train curved into an alpine valley. Then the frosted glass door of her compartment swung open and the Fremdenpolizei entered.

Nadya steadied herself against the seat, her gaze fixed on the window.

There were haystacks in a meadow beyond the oily black telegraph wires dipping and rising, merging and breaking like the wake of a steamer. The policemen murmured together, and she watched silver railroad tracks disappear toward Lichtenstein and Lake Constance, parallel lines stitching through the mountains.

The young policeman cleared his throat, and addressed her in German: "A beautiful afternoon, Fräulein."

"*Oui*," she said, still facing away from him. Her German was accented with Russian, but she spoke French like a native.

"And the evening will be lovely," he said, this time in stilted French.

She turned and smiled uneasily, afraid to offend him, afraid of the older policeman reading a newspaper across the compartment.

"Did you read of last week's rally?" the young policeman asked. "At Oerlikon Stadium, with fifteen thousand Nazis pretending they were celebrating the harvest? Mostly German. Some Swiss, too, but with them we have no—how do you say in French?—*Jurisdiktion*."

"*Juridiction*," she said, pretending to look inside her purse.

He laughed. "*Juridiction*. The Swiss citizens don't come under our *juridiction*."

There was a shriek and the electric lights flickered into darkness as the train dove into a tunnel. Through the window, the stone walls glinted with condensation.

"What brought you to Graubünden?" the policeman asked.

"Visiting relatives," she lied.

"Ah! I wonder if—"

The train emerged into abrupt brightness and the policeman was too close, his smile too wide. Nadya drew back and almost fumbled her purse to the floor. Why so afraid? She'd already delivered the document, the danger was past. But she'd never seen Mama so troubled, moving from one boardinghouse to another, asking Nadya to carry this document to a mountain retreat.

"I wonder if I know them?" the policeman said. "Your relatives."

She shook her head and turned again to the window, through which a mountain lake shone pale green in the fading light. "What a pretty sight."

"The Walensee, mademoiselle."

Beyond the sheer cliffside banks of the lake, a ruined castle crumbled above a village ringed by orchards. She wanted nothing more fiercely than to be left alone. Could the policemen be working for *him*? She needed to pray for guidance, but if she crossed herself with two fingers, the right shoulder before the left—following the old rite of the Russian Orthodox Church—they might think her a foreigner. She prayed inwardly instead: *Most Holy Mother of God, preserve me from every evil and cover me with your protecting mantle.*

She was granted courage, a warm confident glow, and spoke politely, without fear or awkwardness, until the ticket collector called "Zurich" and the train rumbled through the Käferberg tunnel. She stood when the train stopped, and the older policeman lowered his newspaper and told his comrade, "Check the luggage voucher."

"Do we have a voucher?"

"Run along, Romeo."

The young policeman colored and left the compartment, and the older man looked at her and said, "Russian, hah?"

She nodded, her head suddenly hammering.

"Bolshevik?"

She shook her head.

"Outside your canton?" He folded the newspaper. "Take care where you travel, Fräulein. Now quickly, before you miss your connection."

Pale with relief, she took her portmanteau into the corridor. The porter helped her down the steps and directed her to the connecting train, downstairs and across the platform where the sound of her heels was small and lonely, and the ferrous tang of trains mixed with the damp of the two rivers that straddled the station.

She set her portmanteau on a bench and a gentleman in a fawn-colored jacket said, "Miss Nadya Loeffert?"

"Yes?"

"Please come with me."

"I—I have a pass." She hurried after him, her strap slipping from her shoulder. "But excuse me, are you from—"

"Montreux-Oberland Railway," he said. "You purchased a combined railway and motor-post ticket?"

"I'm sorry, I don't understand."

Around the corner, he grabbed her wrist and spun her. She opened her mouth to cry for help, and a hand clamped across her face.

"Come quiet." The man pricked her neck with a knife. "Or come cut."

. . .

An ugly man with a sack of babies stuffed a chubby infant into his gaping mouth; a strange statue anywhere, but in the heart of Switzerland? Akimov scanned his guidebook, swaying in the seat as his motor coach rumbled past the fountain. The statue was the Kindlifresserbrunnen, the Child-Eater Fountain, which marked the ancient city limits of Bern—built to frighten children from venturing too far from home.

Wasn't only children who ventured too far. Akimov could almost hear the old *zek*, a fellow prisoner in the gulag, reciting one of Akhmatova's poems:

> *A soothing voice said to me:*
> *"Flee your lost and sinful land, leave Russia forever. I'll wash the*
> *   blood from your hands, and draw the shame from your heart . . ."*
> *But I stopped my ears, to keep these unworthy words from staining*
> *   my grieving soul.*

The motor coach swayed onto Marktgasse and heaved to a stop, and a towheaded boy and his mother boarded. They sat in front of Akimov and the boy kneeled backward on his seat to regard him with an unblinking stare.

"*Guten Abend,*" Akimov said.

The boy's stare widened.

"*Bonsoir?*"

"*Buona sera,*" the boy said, leaning closer.

Blond as that, and he spoke Italian? Akimov ruffled the boy's hair, soft like corn silk. "*Buona sera, figlio.*"

"How do you tie your shoe?" the boy asked, in Italian.

"Hush!" his mother said. "Keep still."

"But his sleeve is empty as a sack!"

93

His mother tugged her son around and didn't quite look at Akimov: "*Scusilo, signore.*"

Akimov smiled his lack of offense, and at the next stop stepped into the bright busy street. Odd to be called *signore* instead of *maggiore*, wearing civilian clothing like a disguise.

Down the block, a doorman bowed him into the Palace Hotel, and he stood in the lobby under a lofty ceiling painted like a French cathedral. Leafy plants shone with hothouse health, couches and chairs gathered in quiet conclaves on the arched balcony, and even the elevator operators were impressive in uniforms with braided epaulettes.

Akimov checked the number on his key and rode to the fifth floor. He'd stayed in Geneva last night, spoken to Magdalena's neighbors, the shopkeeper on the corner, the local pharmacist. He'd learned nothing, except that she quit her job weeks ago, her parents were long dead, and he was tilling dry ground: everyone with whom he spoke was suspicious and reserved. They'd already been asked . . . and he still didn't know why his father—and his father's masters—wanted Magda found.

Down the corridor, he let himself into his room, slipped his satchel onto the chair, and shook his head at the cream curtains and eiderdown blankets. Impossible that such things existed, while two thousand kilometers away a hundred soldiers died for a single intersection in a—

"It's good to see you, Edik," a man said, from the sofa in the corner.

Akimov stopped, his chest suddenly tight.

"Close your mouth, you look like something on a fishmonger's slab." His father's warm eyes creased with humor. "You must have heard I'm leading the negotiating team."

The years had been kind: his father's thick mane of hair now a striking white, his voice still commanding, his eyes still incisive, and his shoulders still broad and strong. But despite all the years, Akimov still found himself momentarily speechless.

"Please, Edik," his father said, growing serious. "We need you to find Magdalena, yes. But I also . . . I need to explain."

"There's nothing to say."

"There is. Why I denounced you, why I stood at your trial and—"

"Tell me about Magdalena."

"At least listen, Edik. I'm your father. You owe me that much."

"I owe you years of hunger and years of pain. The scars on my face, the friends I saw killed. Do you want me to pay you what I owe you?" Akimov exhaled, trying to control his shaking voice. "Tell me why I'm here. Nothing more."

After a moment, his father looked away. "You had no luck in Geneva?"

"You're a deputy commissar now? NKVD?"

His father gave a grave, leonine nod.

"One of Beria's men, and so highly placed." Akimov didn't try to keep the scorn from his voice. "Your loyalty was rewarded, then. I congratulate you."

"You should. Without that show of loyalty—"

"Betraying me to the gulag. Quite a show."

"Without that, I'd never have achieved my rank. And listen, Edik—*listen!* I've spent three years whispering in Beria's ear, telling him we must prepare for the Nazi invasion. You know who remained after the purges: lapdogs. Lapdogs who couldn't admit the necessity of planning for an invasion. Do you want the fate of Russia to rest in *their* hands?"

"You sent me to the gulag for whispers and a dacha. A fair trade."

"How much good did I do? I don't know. I'll never know. Without my whispers, might we have lost Moscow?" His father shrugged. "We're balanced on a knife's edge, the distance between victory and defeat is measured in inches. I betrayed you, yes. For Russia. Would you not have done the same?"

"Where is your bodyguard?"

"In the adjoining room. Little Vlad is unhappy with the stunt you pulled at the airport, leaving so precipitously."

"You were always incapable of doubt," Akimov said, lifting a glass vase from the sideboard. "Are you so confident I won't kill you?"

"I am, yes."

He stepped closer. "Do you doubt I have good reason?"

"I know you, Edik, as well as you know me."

"Prison changes a man."

"You'd no more kill your father than—"

"Than you'd kill your son?"

His father fell silent. The vase was cool and smooth in his hand, and his phantom arm tensed with the urge for violence. He wanted to crush his father's arrogant face and resonant voice, erase the man from his present and his past. But he wouldn't. He couldn't.

"No luck in Geneva, then?" his father finally said. "No sign of your wife?"

"She left me twenty years ago."

"Ex-wife, then."

"No, no luck."

"Precisely as you were told. Our contacts in the Rote Kapelle"—the Red Orchestra spy network—"tell me that while they don't know where Magda is, they certainly know she's not at home. A day wasted, Edik."

"You can call me 'Comrade Major,' " Akimov said. "I needed to check for myself. When I start trusting men like you, I'll be completely useless. The sooner this is done, the sooner I return to the front."

"You serve a higher purpose here than in Stalingrad. There you fought a battle, here you fight the war."

Akimov eyed the room. "And such a comfortable war, too. What do you want with Magda?"

His father patted the sofa, inviting Akimov to sit. "These are hard days, Edik—Comrade Major. The Germans are winning the war, and if Stalingrad falls we may not recover." He poured two glasses of kirsch. "If there was ever a time to seek an understanding with the Nazis, that time is now."

"An understanding?" Akimov said, still standing.

"A cease-fire."

"We've gone that route before, signed a non-aggression pact and they betrayed us." Akimov looked into his father's untroubled eyes. "Nobody trusts a traitor twice."

"Almost immediately after the Nazi invasion, the West feared we'd treat with Hitler again—the U.S. assistant secretary of state, a man named Berle, suspected us of making a separate peace with the Nazis as early as July 1941."

"One month after they invaded?"

"Diplomacy can happen in a flash." The deputy commissar swirled his glass. "On August 14, 1939, Hitler's foreign minister, von Ribbentrop—"

"I know who von Ribbentrop is."

"On August 14, he contacted Stalin. Five days later, the economic agreement was signed, and four days after that the non-aggression pact. In nine days, the world changed. We already signed one pact with Hitler, and the West is concerned we'll sign another." He leaned forward, his white hair sweeping across his brow. "They're right to be concerned."

"According to whom, this American politician?"

"He's not alone. The British expected we'd sue for peace two months later. In early 1942, Lord Halifax warned Washington we'd—"

"Americans and British," Akimov said, dismissively.

"And a few months ago, the German Communist Party in Moscow urged an 'indestructible bond' between Germany and Russia."

"You can't be serious."

"Beria believes a truce with Germany is to our advantage, especially while Stalingrad teeters on a knife-edge."

"Beria, your master."

"Careful what you say."

"What will you do, send me to the front?"

A low rumbling laugh. "A truce at this moment would serve the Soviet Union better than a dozen fresh divisions, and now the West admitted they won't open a second front—"

Akimov finally sat. "You're serious."

"I'm in deadly earnest, Edik."

"You said you're 'leading the negotiating team'? Not a trade deal—you're negotiating a peace with Germany?"

"A cease-fire, at least. Now that—"

"Do you know of the 588th Night Bomber Squadron?"

"I'm not a—"

"They fly a dozen missions a night, every night, in rusty decommissioned biplanes, not even a third as fast as Messerschmitts. Bombing behind German lines, you can't imagine the iron that takes, the ninth mission of the night, the eleventh, the twelfth. They cut their engines and glide to the target, no sound but wind through the bracing wires . . . then the bomb blast. And they're girls, twenty years old—the Nazis call them the *Nachthexen*, the night witches. Young girls are flying a dozen flights every night behind enemy lines. And you're making eyes at the Nazis behind their backs?"

"Think what you're saying, Edik. You—"

"In August we lost 40,000 civilians—civilians—in one day. And you're making peace."

"I didn't raise an idiot—think before you speak. This means an end to the battle, an end to the battle of Stalingrad. Is that not what you want?"

Akimov shook his head, fogged by his father's presence.

"No bomb runs, no dead civilians, no bullets and bodies. No night witches, no young girls dying. Tell me, is that not worth fighting for?"

Yes. Fighting to stop the fighting. But hearing the truth spoken in his father's lying voice . . . he couldn't respond, couldn't believe.

"Quiet in Stalingrad," his father continued. "The rubble cleared, order on the streets—and time. Time to rally, to fortify, to rebuild. To bury the dead."

Akimov nodded slowly. An end to the battle of Stalingrad—with a signature on a scrap of paper, instead of a mountain of corpses. He let the possibility seep into him, warming him better than the liquor. "This is why I'm here?"

"The West won't help us. Churchill refused to open a second front, Roosevelt broke his vow to invade Europe before '43. This is the only path to victory—buy time now and spend it wisely."

"And the Germans?" Akimov asked. "The Sixth Army is fifty yards from the Volga—why would they sign a pact now?"

"The first pact was a jewel in von Ribbentrop's crown and he wants another."

"He's one man."

"Goebbels supports a settlement, as do many of the lesser military men, the realists. Stalin himself gave a speech reassuring them that we don't aim to destroy the German military: 'Hitlers come and go, but the German state remains.' We hope the officers understand."

"And Hitler?" Akimov asked.

"Dreaming his dreams, loath to negotiate in earnest. That's why you're here."

"Ah. Finally we come to Magda."

His father set his glass on the table. "She contacted the Red Orchestra and told—"

"She contacted them? She hates the Party."

"Perhaps, but she loves Russia. She has a document, proof of a money-laundering scheme, which can be used as blackmail against an influential Swiss."

"Then we can force the Swiss to make peace?"

"Don't play the fool, Edik. Your wife claims this Swiss financier can starve the Reichsbank of francs and foreign exchange. She says he's the key to their coffers. They can't fight a war without money."

"So we use Magda's document to blackmail this Swiss banker to do what? Force the Germans to sue for peace?"

"This will merely serve to . . . tip the scales. Financial leverage may convince Hitler to listen to reason."

"Not one of his strengths."

"They've already agreed to unofficial, exploratory meetings, Edik—that's why we're here. But we must have that document, at any cost."

"Switzerland can't be so influential as all that."

"Without Swiss help, the Reichsbank will fail by next March. The Swiss are the key to the Germans, and your wife the key to the Swiss."

"You say she contacted you. Why do you need me?"

"She arranged a rendezvous, and didn't appear. I think she decided to approach the Americans or British instead. My men are watching their embassies."

"To catch her?"

"If possible."

Akimov nodded. "Or at least to keep her away from the West, yes?"

"Indeed. They'll fight any cease-fire talks, tooth and claw. We need you, Edik. My men might scare Magda off, but you won't. You, she'll meet."

"If I can find her."

"Or if she hears you're looking—then she'll find you." His father leaned forward, eyes grave. "You'll do this?"

"Be your pawn? After you betrayed me once?"

"Not *my* pawn—Russia's."

Akimov's phantom arm itched, and he couldn't scratch it. Did the man truly expect him to track the only woman he'd ever loved across Switzerland, on the orders of the NKVD? But his father would never betray his country—Akimov knew that like he knew the beat of his own heart. Whether ruled by the tsars or the Party, his father served only one master: Russia. And the lessons of Akimov's childhood were rooted deep—he was exactly the same. No price was too high for a cease-fire in Stalingrad.

"Of course," he said. "Where do I start?"

The deputy commissar tossed him an envelope. "Here."

Inside, he found a matchbox printed with silver script, a Zurich address scrolled below the words MUSCOVITE CLUB. And two photographs: one showing Magda at the lakeside, her black hair shot with gray, the other cut from their wedding photo. Akimov and Magda standing together, happy children.

"Preliminary talks begin in three days," his father said. "If you fail, hundreds of thousands of your countrymen die."

CHAPTER 11

When the mail slot clattered downstairs, Anna returned the phone to the cradle and worked the crick from her neck. Hours of calling contacts, and she still hadn't found anything of note about Magda Loeffert.

She wandered into Christoph's room and folded his pajamas. He left the house in such a rush these days, dreading school but refusing to tell her what was wrong; poor boy, so bright and so deep, like his father. She opened the window and an upwelling of air from the terraced vines brushed her face. Over the vineyard, a range of mountains formed the horizon, and her gaze moved beyond the peak of the Niesen to the Wilde Frau, the wild woman, her far-flung inspiration. Or aspiration, at least. She closed the window—she was the Zahme Frau herself, the tame woman. Perhaps she should leave the heavy work to those more able, to Aktion and Bureau Ha. They were good people, Martin's people, better than she—but crippled by Swiss notions of neutrality and morality.

She plumped Christoph's pillows—and laughed, in sudden surprised understanding. The answer was so obvious. She trotted downstairs, called Lorenz, and said, "Why throw away a perfectly good sheet of blank paper?"

"What?" he said. "Hello? Anna?"

"The woman, Magda Loeffert—you found a sheet of paper crumpled in her trash."

"Yes, a blank sheet."

"And why throw away *blank* paper?"

A momentary silence, then Lorenz said, "Good Lord. The housemaid—the incinerator. I'll call you back."

She ate a bowl of cauliflower soup in the kitchen, not allowing herself hope, then went to the front door for the mail—two circulars and another letter from her mother-in-law informing her that she was a bad parent to Christoph.

She was composing a reply when the phone rang. "Yes?"

"Lazy housemaid," Lorenz said. "I got the page."

"And?"

"Blank—but there are impressions on it, from the previous page. I ran a pencil over them. A series of . . . words, I suppose. Are you—"

"No! Truly?"

He laughed. "Yes, truly. Are you ready?"

She got her notepad. "Go on."

"There are nine lines. I'll spell them as well as I can. The handwriting is odd, old-fashioned, and these are second-page impressions, so don't hold me to any of this. Line one: capital *O*, space, capital *M*, small *n*, *p*, *a*, capital *A*, small *o*, small *p*. Line two . . ."

When he finished, she eyed her notepad:

```
O MnpaAop

Yepy

6pyHCBNK MoHameHT

PeageHCy KadpN
```

AxeTN AeN NaKN

NpoMeHenA Aa NaK

Ae NopT

AxopAxe & KN

MaKa6N YaNen

"Then a date and time," Lorenz continued. "Six thirty p.m., October 11."

"The eleventh?"

"Could be the twelfth. Or the seventeenth. I think it's the eleventh."

"Any ideas what this means?"

"None."

"Magda Loeffert knows *something*," she said. "If this is code, we must break it. Keep looking for her."

She hung up and stared at the nonsense words on her notepad. She couldn't solve a cipher—she could barely finish a jigsaw puzzle. She wrote the names as a single series of letters, and squinted at the result. Perhaps this was a replacement cipher, with each letter—

A chill touched the back of her neck, and she raised her head from the notepad. Someone was in her house.

The wind scrambled uphill and banged a loose shutter against the work shed, and Anna started toward the front door, where Martin's rifle was in the coat cabinet, in a rack above the hats. Every Swiss man kept his government-issued carbine in his house, and while she hadn't fired the rifle more than a dozen times, she knew how to load it and she knew how to aim and she knew how to pull the trigger.

She took three steps toward the foyer and the bathroom door opened and Christoph stepped into the hallway, facing away from her.

"Christoph!" she said. "You frightened me half to death."

He stopped, but didn't turn. "Sorry, Maman."

"What are you doing home?"

"I forgot something." He headed for the stairs. "In my room."

"Christoph?"

"Down in a moment."

"Christoph, turn around."

He turned, and his lip was swollen and split, with dried blood spattered on his shirt and tie.

"Oh, dumpling." She took his face in her hands. "Only the lower lip?"

He pulled away. "It doesn't hurt."

"I'm going to speak with your headmaster this time, I won't—"

"Please don't, promise you won't."

She sighed. "Let's take you upstairs. Was it the same boy?"

He didn't answer.

"You told the school nurse?" She rubbed his back as they walked to the stairs. "She sent you home?"

"I needed a new shirt," he said.

She pretended that was an answer. "A new tie, too." She tried humor: "It's meant to be striped, not spotted."

He stopped on the landing and studied himself in the glass covering a photograph of Martin. She stood behind him, hoping he knew she'd always stand behind him.

"What would he say?" he asked.

"Your father? He'd say, 'Whoever slaps your cheek, turn to him the other.' "

" 'Whoever takes your shirt, give him also your coat,' " Christoph said. " 'Blessed be the peacemakers.' " He caught her eye in the reflection. "You argued with him about that."

"You can't remember."

"You said making peace is not always a job for the meek."

"You were four years old!"

"I was five."

She took his hand. "Come, Mr. Memory, and wash your face." They went to the bathroom and she inspected his puffy lip, cut raw against his teeth. "Give me your shirt and tie, and your jacket."

She brought his soiled clothing downstairs and into a bath of cold water. The stains were fresh enough that meat tenderizer mixed with cold water would dissolve them. She made the paste in the kitchen and heard him on the stairs.

"Christoph?" she called. "Your shirts are in the closet, where they always are!" He remembered an argument from years ago, but couldn't find his own closet. "Have you eaten lunch?" She stepped into the parlor and straightened a pillow; this time, she'd sit him down and ask about his trouble at school before letting him out of the house. "If you're hungry, I can—"

There was a footfall behind her, Christoph in the doorway, still bare-chested, his lips berry-red against his white face. In a small voice he said, "Maman . . ."

There was a hand on his naked shoulder, big and rough and crossed with veins. A man stood behind him, with flat pale eyes and a face in which all softness had been chiseled away. The man said, "Anna Fay."

She didn't answer. He had his hand on her boy.

"I'm Grant," he said. "There's a man in the vineyard, watching your house, he's got a pistol under his arm."

The name meant nothing to her, she needed to stay calm, needed to get Christoph away. Then she realized: *Grant.* From China. But Grant was American, and half a world away—this nightmare was in her foyer, speaking German like a native, his hand on her son.

She'd read Grant's letters for a year; she knew him. Not his face, but his heart. This man wasn't Grant.

• • •

He'd almost lost his nerve when the bare-chested boy tumbled downstairs to investigate the front door opening. Could've been a kid back home looking for a swimming hole, wearing a fat lip like a badge, except for the pressed trousers—and Martin's grave eyes.

Then Martin's wife stepped into the parlor, and he told her about the man outside. With hardly a glance, she moved to the cupboard by the door and reached for the rifle rack, standing on her toes. She was shorter than he'd expected, with wavy hair curling to the collar of her housedress, and lusher—a figure built for painting on the nose cone of a bomber. She opened a drawer and turned toward him, the rifle pointed at the floor. A good weapon, the Swiss K31 carbine, she pulled the bolt back, took a stripper clip from the drawer, and on her second attempt synched the clip with the grooves in the receiver. She pushed rounds into the magazine with the thumb of her small competent hands and slapped the bolt home. She still wore her wedding band.

He stepped forward and she raised the rifle to her shoulder, sighting at his head.

"Stop, don't move," she said, her voice tight. "Step back."

"Anna—"

"Back!" A touch of hysteria. "Get away from my boy."

"I'm Grant, from China. I—you know me."

"Christoph, run and get Joris. Quickly now!"

The boy's smooth shoulder slipped from under Grant's hand, his bare feet slapped the floor as he ran. Was this Anna Fay? Maybe she wasn't shorter and lusher—maybe this wasn't her. Could they have known he was coming? He couldn't think, a wave of malarial weakness rose from his knees. At the back of the house, a door crashed open as the boy shoved outside.

"Don't move," she said. "Don't move."

"A rifle at this range, you only have one shot."

"I'll fire, I swear—"

"Don't aim for the head." He tapped his sternum. "Center of mass."

"Raise your hands—don't move."

He went into the parlor, where everything was deep yellow and sky blue over Oriental carpets. There was a column of oval paintings on the wall, and three framed pictures on the mantel among porcelain knickknacks. A lamp with a stained-glass hood stood beside the sofa and a scrolled iron newspaper rack rested on the floor.

Grant sat on the sofa next to the newspaper rack. "You still studying English?"

She stood in the doorway, the rifle at her shoulder. "You say you're Sergeant Grant?"

Smart woman. "Lieutenant."

"Why are you here?"

"I don't have anywhere else to go."

"Why Switzerland?"

"I crashed into a mountain. Put the rifle down, Anna."

She drew a bead on his chest and stepped into the room. "Tell me something only Grant would know."

"See that ring, at the rear of the bolt body?" He looked at the rifle. "If it's turned horizontal, the firing pin is locked, you can't fire or reload."

She glanced to the rifle—the ring was vertical—then back at him.

"You're armed," he said. "I'm Grant."

"I swear I'll shoot."

"That's what I'm afraid of."

"Don't push me. Tell me something only you'd know."

He showed her his empty hands and tried to smile.

She sat in the brocade chair and rested the rifle across her lap, one hand on the butt, the other wrapped loosely around the barrel.

He said, "I saw Martin killed."

Her throat clenched. She shouldn't have lowered the rifle, but the way the man looked, threatening with his bare hands. If she lifted the rifle again, she'd shoot and still be afraid—what if she missed, what if she only wounded him?

"How did he die?" she asked.

"You never saw a picture of me, but Martin kept your picture by his bed."

"My husband didn't indulge in that sort of easy sentimentality."

"You and your son, in a double frame."

"Nonsense."

"You're wearing"—he squinted toward the window—"a light dress with a square neck, and your head's tilted, your eyes half closed like you stepped out of the bedroom. Your hair's wavy and longer—and I thought brown, not—" His flat eyes flicked toward her. "Red? Auburn?"

"Brown."

"Your hair was down to your waist, Martin said."

"How did he die?"

The man rubbed the back of his neck. "He died in China."

"That's not what I asked."

"The end of '37," he said. "The Chinese army abandoned Nanking. They knew they couldn't win . . ."

"And then?" she prompted, to keep him talking, give Joris time to arrive.

"The shelling stopped. The Japanese came through the gates. A month earlier, some Westerners—businessmen, scholars, relief workers—they'd established a safe zone, a neutral zone in the city for refugees."

"My husband knew about neutrality," she said.

"That was November. Yeah, Martin was on the committee, the International Committee of the Nanking Neutral Zone, but by the time the Japs advanced, the population of the city tripled, hundreds of thousands of refugees came, old men, women, girls . . ."

"You were with Martin?"

"They took the city."

"How did he die?"

The man listened to wind rattle against the bow window.

"Will you tell me?" she asked.

"No."

"I know the worst already."

He shook his head.

"I know Martin chose to die," she said, "instead of coming home."

"I never told you that."

"You never wrote the words," she said.

"He didn't suffer."

"I have the right to know."

"There's nothing to tell."

She fingered the rifle. "So you *are* Grant."

She and Grant had exchanged dozens of letters in the four years since he'd sent a carefully penned note following the official notification of Martin's death. He'd offered polite commonplaces, and she'd replied with a letter of uncharacteristic bitterness—from grief, or shock, or anger. She'd been surprised to receive an answer from the unknown Mr. Grant, sketching the outlines of Martin's life in China, surprised and grateful, but he'd never told her the details of her husband's death. His letters were understated and observant—though his spelling was atrocious—not traits she'd associate with the lean hard man sprawled on her divan like a wild dog.

He shrugged, almost apologetically. "Yeah."

"What're you doing here?" she asked.

"Running," he said. "I need—"

"Running from whom?"

"Who've you got? The police, the army, guard dogs. I was flying a photo-recon mission for—"

Joris burst into the room, his rumpled waistcoat flapping, his rough baggy trousers damp at the knees. He roared threats in Italian and the barrel of his old pistol swung across the room and found Grant.

110

CHAPTER 12

Grant froze, his right hand draped over the couch.

The man came closer, onto the rug, in front of the couch—too close—and Grant pivoted, knocking the Luger with his left forearm and heaving the iron newspaper rack around the sofa arm with his right. The gun swept past his ear and didn't fire, and the rack smacked the Italian on the chest, newspapers parachuting to the floor.

Grant grabbed his shirt and yanked—took the gun and shoved the man to the floor, putting the Luger to the back of his sunburned neck.

"No!" Anna said. "Grant, no! He's a friend."

She spoke machine-gun Italian, and the man turned his head; he had to be sixty years old, his face bronzed from the sun, skin tough and wrinkled as a peasant in a woodcut. Grant had almost stepped on a guy old enough to be his father.

"This is Signore Joris." Anna shot a dark look at Grant. "He looks after the garden—he keeps an eye on me and Christoph."

"More than an eye."

"He's seventy-one years old," she said.

"Doesn't look a day over sixty."

Anna glanced toward the door where her son stood, his face pale around Martin's dark somber eyes. "Put a shirt on, sweetie," she told him.

The boy disappeared, his footsteps padding upstairs, and Joris grabbed his cap and said a couple mouthfuls, some of which must've been goodbye. Grant said the same to him, then was alone with Mrs. Fay. Anna Fay. His eyes were level with her waist, and her dress wrapped her hips tight before falling in folds around her calves.

She turned to him. "What have you brought into my home?"

"I was flying photo recon over France. My navigator, Racket McNeil, and me, we needed an extra run due to cloud cover and a Focker—"

"Is this a long story?"

"Not really."

"I don't like you in the front parlor," she said. "We'll go upstairs."

"I can't stand."

"What?"

"My legs . . ." He shook his head.

"You walked into my house well enough, you took Joris's gun away. What's wrong with your legs?"

"Not sure."

She looked at him with an expression he couldn't read, then offered her arm. He stood unsteadily, leaning into her small rounded strength, and his legs stayed under him. They shuffled into the hallway, the woman his crutch. She paused a moment, looking toward the mail slot where a single letter sat in the tray, her eyes sharpening then turning away.

"You're stronger than you look," he said.

"Don't get too comfortable."

He tried a smile. "That's not a problem I have."

She gave him that same unreadable look, and they climbed the stairs one at a time, his right hand gliding up the smooth banister and his left arm curled around her waist.

He said, "I won't stay long. I don't know when they'll be moving Racket."

She led him down a cool hallway toward a bedroom washed by peach light through gauzy curtains. "Racket is your navigator?"

"Yeah. I need to find him." He sat on the bed. "I need your help."

"What you need is rest. Then we'll talk."

Anna slipped into the hall and closed the door quietly on the exhausted American. She needed him out of her house: if she were caught harboring a fugitive, she'd be of no use against the Germans. When he woke, she'd send him away. Maybe Joris had a place he could stay while he recovered. Anywhere but here.

She went downstairs to the mail slot—to the letter that hadn't arrived with the day's delivery. A plain white envelope, with a feminine scrawl across the flap: "Missed you at the theater, and your house isn't as private as I'd hoped." Magda Loeffert. She must've seen Grant enter, and been frightened away. "I'll contact you soon. I have documents about the barracks deal which prove what the enclosed suggests—"

Anna opened the envelope and flipped through the contents. A purchase order of wooden barracks in Switzerland—the wood syndicate?—for shipment to Germany, some town called Dachau. A waste of time, simply one more deal with the Reich. But reading the next page, her pulse quickened: the Germans shipped the wood to Switzerland, then purchased the finished goods for thirteen million francs.

They'd supplied the raw material then bought the finished products at an inflated price. This wasn't just another deal—this was money laundering. Anna scanned an acknowledgment of payment and read a marginal note in Magda Loeffert's hand: "Barracks deal initiated on direction of Waffen-SS and the SS Economic-Administrative Main Office, to legally transfer funds to Switzerland. First shipment, April 1942."

The SS was arranging deals in Switzerland? The Waffen-SS was a combat cadre, she thought—and the Economic-Administrative Main Office? She didn't know.

She went through the pages twice more, tamping down her excitement. This deal was traceable, thirteen million francs must've left a trail. To where? Implicating whom? If the connection to the SS was traceable, even Pierre-Luc would print her article: and the weight of Swiss opinion, already opposed to the Nazis, would crush the backroom deals and collegial economic collaboration.

She slipped into her wool jacket and opened the door. Grant could stay overnight: she hadn't time for anything but finding this woman.

CHAPTER 13

The white-and-gold telephone squatted sullenly beside the calf-leather desk blotter, and Ernst Villancourt turned away from the infernal machine. Here he was, on the cusp of the greatest triumph of his career, reduced to this—pacing the carpet, waiting for the ring, his hopes rising and falling like a child's rubber ball.

The first call, at dawn, had sparked a sudden warmth after days of chill: Herr Pongratz had finally found the girl Nadya. Thank the heavens! He'd use the girl to force her mother, the cursed Magda Loeffert, to return the stolen documents. He'd finally be free of this blackmail. But thirty minutes later, the second call brought bleak desolation: the girl had disappeared in a crush of traffic at the railway station. And finally the third call: though he hadn't found the girl, Pongratz would await her return trip through the Zurich station.

And so Villancourt waited, through the morning and all afternoon, gnawed by dread as evening approached. He took himself in hand—couldn't allow his anxiety to undermine his productivity—and pressed the button to buzz Hugo, his blighted nephew and temporary secretary.

Hugo entered, the pimpled scarecrow, and blurted, "Herr Rothenbuehler's still in the anteroom, Uncle. Waiting. In the anteroom. Sir."

"Hugo, you spotted stork, did I ask about Herr Rothenbuehler?"

"No, Uncle. Sir."

"Regarding that telegram, might I trouble you to take a few notes?"

"He's here about confirmation of the freight forwarding. Herr Rothenbuehler is, I mean. I'm sorry."

Villancourt arched an eyebrow. "And does Rothenbuehler expect me to go tramping about the Basel rail yard like a junior clerk?"

Hugo shifted uneasily. "No, sir?"

"Then we have nothing further to discuss. Now, regarding that telegram. If you please."

Hugo folded his gangly length in the upholstered chair, his notebook ready and his bony knees jittering. Villancourt cursed his sister, inflicting this plague upon him. At least the boy was trustworthy, more than could be said for that criminal, Frau Magda Loeffert.

"Have a list prepared of our daughter companies in German territory," Villancourt said. "Württemberg, Baden, and et cetera. They are the fastest-growing sector of the firm, we must know by precisely what margin. Industry thrives on belligerence, Hugo. There is nothing like the adjustment of a border to inspire the stock exchanges. Now—what percentage of our firm's output is delivered to the Reich?"

"I don't know, Uncle Ernst."

"Eighty-six point two percent, precisely the Swiss average." Due entirely to his own unceasing effort to achieve conformity. "And with eighty-six percent to the Reich, our chief customer is hardly in doubt."

That was how he'd present the matter to Chairman Ochsner and the board, to secure an additional 800 million francs of clearing credits to Germany. Given the Nazis' enormous appetite for precision-engineered Swiss goods...well, there was no arguing with commerce. Besides, what was the alternative? Creeping Bolshevism, that's what.

"We must expand into the newly acquired German territory. That is the long view, Hugo, you slab of cheese. Whether the Germans win or lose, the establishment of neutral business flourishes. Chairman Ochsner will be more than pleased. That is all, have that list prepared—now back to your desk."

At the door, Hugo said, "Um, Herr Rothenbuehler waits in—"

"The anteroom, yes. Carry on."

Villancourt adjusted the knot of his tie, paced the room a dozen times, and still the telephone did not ring. He decided against kicking the writing table, concerned he'd scuff his shoe. His latest triumph was Eclipse French Dressing and Satin Polish, a new brand of blacking; difficult to locate in the wartime economy, but worth the effort and no reason to scuff the excellent shine. He finally set himself to cleaning the nib of his favorite pen when the phone sounded.

He snatched at the receiver. "Yes? This is Villancourt."

Pongratz said, "It's done."

"You found her? She returned?"

"The package arrived at the station, and is now secure in the vault."

So the girl was locked in her cell, and the danger had passed. Villancourt's stomach unclenched. "Excellent! Bless you twice, Herr Pongratz! Now inform Magda Loeffert that she must return the documents she stole, or suffer the consequences."

"Loeffert is gone."

"Gone? What do you mean, gone?"

"Not at home," Pongratz said. "She's not in Geneva."

"She's gone?"

"And her apartment is closed. The neighbors haven't seen her in weeks. I was lucky to find the girl."

"Ask *her* where her mother is, then. Find this blackmailer, Pongratz, I don't care how. Find her, and tell her the girl's life is in her hands—either she returns those documents, or her daughter suffers. This is ridiculous, we secured the girl to control her mother and now we can't *find* her?"

"This shouldn't be a problem. Except Herr Kübler requested my return to the embassy."

"Your return?" Pongratz was on unofficial loan from Herr Kübler, the Foreign Office representative at the German embassy. "I'll straighten him, you find the woman."

"I'll ask the girl tonight."

They hung up and Villancourt rang the embassy. Waited three minutes to be connected to Kübler, then said, "I still need Pongratz."

"Haven't you anyone of your own? I mean, a Swiss who—"

"Men like him are rare. Rabid dogs don't often heed their master's commands. I know who I need, Kübler."

"When will this *end*, Herr Villancourt?"

"If this blackmail is circulated, I'm not the only man who'll suffer."

"But the barracks deal—" Kübler paused. "Surely thirteen million francs isn't so consequential. We'll fund the intelligence network though another route."

"The money doesn't matter, Kübler, but Magda Loeffert uses the blackmail to demand access to my records." Villancourt tapped his pen against the desk blotter. "If I agree to her demands, she'll be in a position to stop the clearing credits, and if I don't—and she airs the blackmail—the clearing credits will end. Because I'll be under investigation. Do you follow?"

"Well, of course, Herr Villancourt, I'm not suggesting—"

"I care about this blackmail because it can ruin me. You care because if I'm ruined, say goodbye to 800 million Swiss francs, and hello to worthless reischsmarks. What will your masters say to that?"

"But this is nothing, this threat of exposure," Kübler said, heat rising in his voice. "You know the June 13 Doctrine." In June 1941, the Swiss Federal Council had instructed the press that all Swiss commentary hostile to German behavior should be prohibited. "If a newspaper exceeds Article 102, we'll simply have them prohibited. Nobody will publish anything untoward."

" 'Publication' is not the same as 'investigation.' This could ruin me without appearing in any newspaper. Shall I tell your superiors you care nothing for the clearing credits? Hundreds of millions of francs, perhaps even a billion."

"Of course you can use Pongratz," Kübler said, suddenly soothing. "And what else might I do to help? Only tell me."

"Don't fumble the negotiations with the Bolsheviks, that's all I ask. Remember the terms I requested." Villancourt turned his pen over in his hands. "And assemble a team of men, put aside for my use."

"Of men?"

"Five or six well-trained beasts, to be placed under Pongratz's command."

"I haven't men to spare, I—"

"Bring them from the Reich if you must. Remember, with great risk comes great return. Think of your promotion, of the public honors."

"Well, I suppose—"

"Success will be rewarded." Villancourt gazed out the window. "And failure, Kübler?"

"Well, failure is impossible, Herr Villancourt! Quite unthinkable."

Villancourt pressed him: "If success will be rewarded, what about failure?"

"With the combined influence of a leading Swiss firm, with your position on the government board and mine in the German embassy—"

"Answer the question, Kübler. If success is rewarded, then failure is . . . what?"

Across the wire, Kübler hesitated. "Punished."

Villancourt allowed a moment of silence on the phone, then answered: "My old friend, so melodramatic! Failure is merely an opportunity to reevaluate tactics. Now then, did you receive the package? My new secretary is not as efficient as I'd like."

After a moment, Kübler murmured, "Eclipse French Dressing."

"I swear by the stuff. Tell your man, he must wax the stitching first . . ."

Through the window, far below, the surface of the Rhine was calm in the dense, cloudy afternoon, and workers scurried at a distant cargo barge. The firm and the Reich expanded as one, and Villancourt must ensure that the growth continued unabated. Easily done—once he found Magda Loeffert, he'd control the upcoming negotiations. Well, Pongratz would ask her daughter for her location. He was quite a persuasive man.

CHAPTER 14

A floorboard creaked and Grant came alert, curled on rotting straw between dank cell walls—then the memory faded into the scent of orange peel and the warmth of flannel sheets. Another creak sounded and he rolled toward the door, saw Martin's kid standing at parade rest, wearing a school jacket and a fresh white shirt, his chin scraped and lip swollen.

"How long—" Grant started in English, then switched to German. "How long've you been there?"

"I speak a little English," the kid said, in German.

"Yeah?"

"Yes, sir. A little."

"Your father teach you?"

"I was six when my father died. Maman taught me."

"Well, your mother." Grant wrestled himself higher on the pillows. "She sent one of my letters back, marked with red. She didn't like my spelling."

"She used to be a teacher."

"Not anymore?"

"She's a newspaper writer now."

"She downstairs?"

"No, sir."

"At the office?"

"I think she's researching something."

"She left you alone with me?"

The kid shifted. "She said you're not so bad."

Grant took the water glass from the bedside table. "Sure, I'm irresistible."

"Plus," the kid said, "she thought you'd sleep through the night."

"I'm full of surprises. There any cigarettes in the house?"

"Maman doesn't like cigarettes."

"There's money in my pocket—" He tilted the glass toward the dresser. "Run and buy me a couple packs."

"I'm supposed to be in school, sir."

Grant grinned. "Then don't let 'em catch you."

The kid looked down, maybe hiding a smile—maybe just looking down—and moved to the dresser. Grant's clothes weren't there. "Maman must have taken them."

"My clothes?"

"To clean, to mend."

"Check the briefcase."

The kid popped the clasps and took out a bruised apple, a hunk of cheese, and the death's-head dagger. He looked at Grant, put the dagger back into the case, and found the change purse. He gave Grant a slow shy look, then headed for the door.

"Hey," Grant said.

The kid turned.

"And a lighter."

. . .

The next time Grant woke, the curtains were drawn and the only light was a glimmering from the hall. Two packs of cigarettes and a book of matches were on the bedside table beside a cutting board with slices of brown apple and chunks of cheese.

He ate the apple and cheese. His legs felt okay, and stayed under him as he walked to the bathroom. When he stepped back into the hall, the kid was standing at the banister in green pajamas with little sailboats, rubbing one foot against the back of the other calf.

"Still awake?" Grant asked, like maybe the kid was sleep-walking.

"Yes, sir." He stopped fidgeting. "I bought your cigarettes."

"You get caught?"

"No, sir."

Grant cracked his neck. "Oughta be in bed."

"I'm not tired, sir."

"I'm not talking about you," he said. The kid followed him into the bedroom and watched him sit on the mattress. "Where are my clothes?"

"Downstairs, I think. Um . . . what's wrong with your legs?"

"Your mother says I'm tired."

Actually, she'd said he was suffering from a combination of idiocy and exhaustion, and should've known a plane crash and a prison cell would whip a man.

"That's what she told me," the kid said, dubious.

"But you think I'm just lazy."

"Oh, no sir!"

Grant grinned. "You're okay, kid."

The kid took the cutting board from the bedside table. "The lighter cost too much, so I got matches instead."

Grant leaned against the headboard and closed his eyes. A little more rest, then he'd sneak Racket from the hospital in Neuchâtel, find the crash site and the camera. He needed to move soon, though, or they'd ship Racket to an internment camp—and he couldn't find the crash site alone.

"Is that okay?" the kid asked.

Grant opened his eyes. "Mm?"

"The matches."

"Sure, that's fine."

The kid waited a second, then started for the door, the sailboats on his pajamas moving like ghost ships through the darkness.

"Hey." Grant looked at the boy's split lip. "Who won?"

"He did, I guess."

"That happens."

"He called me a name." The kid toed the floor. "Then he pushed me and I pushed him and he hit me."

Maybe Martin would know what to say, but Martin was dead. "Most fights aren't worth winning."

The boy stood there.

"When you lose," Grant said, "you don't lose much."

"He'll do it again."

"They always do."

The boy picked at the cutting board.

"There's two kinds of tough," Grant said. "The kind that knows how to hit, and the kind that knows how to take it. This kid—what's his name?"

"Horst."

"Sounds like he's the first kind, but your father was the second—maybe you take after him. The second's even tougher, the second never knuckles under. Your father was rock hard. The man was a mountain."

"He lied to me."

"Yeah?"

"He promised he'd come back."

• • •

"We're closed, Frau Fay." The clerk at the federal office tapped the tabletop with his knuckles. "The lights are off, the curtains drawn, we wait only for you."

"Just one more minute," Anna said.

"You've had fifteen. Please, I must insist."

Anna sighed and stood from the table, rubbing the back of her neck. No luck finding anything useful about Magda Loeffert. The only child of elderly parents, both of whom were dead. Married twice, one daughter with the second husband. A long history of employment, attendance at various cantonal schools, the regular payment of taxes. Nothing to help Anna find her *now*. She pulled on her hat and gloves, buttoned her coat, and headed outside.

She hesitated on the sidewalk, then decided: the evening was still young.

At the side door of the newspaper, the night watchman recognized her. He asked after her health and ushered her downstairs to the archives, where she sat beside a bank of file cabinets as big and grim as an ancient mausoleum. Hours passed before she slipped her shoes back onto her feet and stood. No luck. She'd have to decipher Magda Loeffert's code, then: a task entirely beyond her abilities.

She stepped into the cool evening and caught a late tram. That sheet of paper Lorenz found in the wastebasket was her best bet. She needed the original.

Across the city, she found Lorenz sprawled on the velvet couch in his living room, a glass of liquor in his hand, watching the fire, his tie gaping and his eyes bloodshot: drunk. She sat beside him and tugged at her gloves, guessing why he was drunk—and felt a flicker of hope.

"Any news?" Lorenz asked.

"Magda Loeffert worked for the Swiss, Federal Wood Syndicate as a confidential secretary, and—"

"Who was her supervisor? Find that, and you've found your man."

"Her direct employer was a typing bureau that supplies cantonal and federal departments. She's worked for dozens of men, in offices with hundreds more."

"Oh. And her new job?"

"As far as I can tell, she doesn't have one. Perhaps that was an excuse to leave."

"She needed an excuse?"

Anna laid her gloves on the armrest. "Apparently."

"I don't know what you expect of this information." Lorenz scratched his beard, his face sickly in the firelight. "Secret codes in a wastebasket . . ."

"If we find proof of financial misconduct, we can end it. We can publicize it. We can show the men involved that there are consequences. That's the reason."

"The Clodius memorandum again, Anna?"

"Rosine's trying to learn more about that from the Undersecretary of Customs, but no—this is something else, the Nazis washing millions of francs into Switzerland."

"Why?"

"I don't know, not yet."

He stared into the fire. "Damn that girl. Damn this war."

"You had no luck?"

"No. Rosine still won't marry me."

"I mean with—"

"I know what you mean, finding Loeffert or deciphering her list. Of course I had no luck, we need a cryptographer."

"I'll speak with the colonel tomorrow." The colonel was Anna's most trusted contact in Aktion. "He'll recommend someone."

"Then we can wash our hands of this?"

"What's wrong, Lorenz? You're drunk because Rosine's speaking with the undersecretary?"

"I pray she's only speaking."

"I pray she's doing whatever's necessary. How did they meet?"

"I arranged it," he said. "As her procurer, I arranged the meeting."

A log cracked in the fire. "You aren't the only one suffering, Lorenz."

"If only she weren't so damn convincing. The undersecretary has a table at the Daetwyler. I made a reservation for two at the next table and told Rosine to prepare to be jilted by an imaginary suitor. She'll pull on some inappropriate frock and arrive in a cloud of . . . *Rosine*. She'll weep over her solitary wineglass and he'll comfort her. Perhaps tomorrow morning she'll know more."

"I hope she exhausts him, Lorenz. This isn't a love affair, it's a battlefield."

"I know, Anna—ignore me."

"And Rosine?"

"She'll do as she pleases."

"You could stop her with a word."

"She'd never forgive me." He swirled his empty glass. "She'd look at me and see the faces of all the people she could've saved. Be thankful you never loved Martin."

She closed her teeth around an angry reply—better to have Lorenz hurtful than hurt. "Where's the paper from Loeffert's room?"

"On the side table."

She crossed the room. "This is another copy."

"The original's in the safe."

"The hotel safe? Lorenz, I have my own copy, I don't need another."

"You wrote yours over the phone—on that, I copied her handwriting."

She looked at the blocky, off-kilter letters. "I'll go to the hotel tomorrow for the original."

"I didn't realize—"

"No matter. Do you have fondants? Oh, and I need to borrow some shirts, I have a visitor."

"A gentleman caller? Anna!"

"Hardly a gentleman," she said, forcing a laugh.

They spoke about Grant, agreed Rosine would know how best to smuggle him to England, and finished half a box of Lorenz's hoarded chocolates before Anna returned home. She found Christoph in the front parlor, curled on the sofa. Prickles of guilt rose on her neck: she hadn't prepared his dinner in a week, hadn't taken him to church in a month, there was nothing in the refrigerator, and the kitchen floor needed mopping.

She woke him with a kiss on his forehead. "Dumpling."

"Maman." He blurred a smile. "Don't worry. I made myself biscuits and cheese for dinner, and saw that Joris had some, too."

She brushed hair from his forehead. "And your homework?"

"Finished my mathematics, it was easy. I only left the house to buy Mr. Grant cigarettes."

She went cold. What right had Grant to send her boy on errands? What right had he to *talk* to him? Yet there was a glint in Christoph's sleepy eyes, a hint of boyishness she hadn't seen in too long. So she tucked him into bed and stood outside his door for a time, her mind quiet and dark, before going downstairs to the laundry room.

An hour later, she worked thread clippers around yet another seam, her hair plastered to her face, the lights overheating the cramped space. She straightened the hems, sponged the creases with a solution of vinegar and water, and pressed the lines from the trousers. This was the third pair she'd lengthened tonight, Grant was taller and broader than Martin, but thin from his ordeal in the punishment camp.

Downed Allied fliers in POW camps in Switzerland—another article that would never see print. She'd heard that interned combatants were housed in alpine villages and ski resorts, not sent to punishment camps if they attempted escape. Of course, most wouldn't make the attempt, but something else was driving Grant, something he hadn't told her.

She measured and chalked the cuffs, pressed and sewed the new creases. Folded the shirts into a basket and switched off the lamp. Upstairs, Grant's door was open a crack. She nudged the door with her bottom, light from the hall fanning into the room, and lay the folded clothing in a pile on the dresser.

"Anna," Grant said from the bed, voice thick.

"Go back to sleep," she said.

"Anna Fay."

"Yes?"

No answer.

CHAPTER 15

The doors of the train were locked, the windows boarded with planks. Two rows of electric lights in frosted-glass domes lined the long arched ceiling, and Nadya paced beneath them, casting a fan of shadows on the carpet and the wood-paneled walls. Her prison was a fancy passenger car, with three doors in the corridor: to the ladies' washroom, the shoe-shine room, and the gentlemen's smoking room that she'd claimed as her bedchamber. She stretched her arms beside her as she walked, running her fingers along both walls at once, tapping the fluted glass doorknobs.

After his first hissed threat, the man at the station hadn't spoken a word. He'd dragged Nadya through a cold open rail yard, and touched her where he shouldn't have. She'd jerked away, and he'd shoved her up a short set of stairs into a train, and locked the door. She'd begged for an explanation, for help, but there was no answer except the clatter of metal and the grind of far-off machines.

Even now, remembering, she caught the scent of rising panic. She touched the baptismal cross on her silver necklace. *O spotless Virgin, undefiled, unstained, ever-chaste and Pure Lady, Bride of God. O gracious Mother who art the hope of the hopeless . . .*

The corridor ended and she stepped into the passenger lounge, where the aisle was lined with blue silk love seats and cane tables. Thick curtains fell from bronze rods along wide windows all revealing the same view: the wood grain of the boards imprisoning her. She sat in one of the armchairs. She must stay calm, pray for understanding, and eat for strength. A meal had appeared in a dumbwaiter at the end of the lounge—on a tray with a spray of flowers in a cut-glass vase. How long would they keep her, how long before she heard another human voice?

Her eyes warmed with tears and she shook her head. *Most Holy Mother of God, banish my despair.* She kneeled in the aisle and crossed herself. "Strengthen my soul, most Holy Mother of God, banish my despondency."

Fifteen minutes later, she stood and straightened her dress. One did not *wait* for salvation, one *worked* for salvation—in "fear and trembling," as Saint Paul wrote to the Philippians—so she would escape.

She searched her prison, standing uneasily on a slippery cushion to inspect the ceiling, checking the smoking room, running her fingers along the humidor, worrying the edges of the carpet. And finally, in the shoe-shine room, she opened the cupboard and found a ribbed oaken grate bolted to the outside wall. She crawled into the cabinet. Four bolts secured the grate, and the wooden ribs were too thick to snap. She needed a way to cut the bolts, or perhaps gouge the wood from—

A key scraped in the lock of her prison door.

She scrambled from the cupboard, barking her shin against the shoe-shine booth hard enough to bring tears to her eyes. She smoothed her dress, standing in the middle of the room, and heard footsteps approaching.

The cold-eyed man from the station stepped through the doorway and crowded her backward until she was flat against the wall. He pressed himself against her and spoke into her ear. "Where is she?"

Too frightened to pretend she didn't know who he meant. "I don't know, back home, in Geneva." She even gave the address, God help her. "That's where we'll meet, where I'm meant to meet her. There. At the apartment."

"I've been there." The man took her earlobe between his teeth. "Where is she *now*?"

She started crying. "I don't know, I don't know, she didn't tell me. She was afraid, she—"

"How do you contact her?"

"I don't! I'm to meet her in Geneva, to wait until she arrives. Please, please."

"She has the document." He worried her ear with his teeth. "Why is she so afraid?"

"She—" Nadya couldn't invent a lie fast enough. "I don't know."

"Don't think, just speak. Who's she running from?"

"The Russians—the Soviets."

"The Russians know what she has?"

"No, but—"

His teeth closed hard around her ear. "I have all night."

"No! She told the, the Russians, she told them she has *something*, but didn't say what. She hates Stalin and the Party and—and she never met them, the Soviets. She told them she would then she didn't. She wants to give the—the document to the Allies, but—"

"But what?"

"The Soviets were following, they scared her away from the American and British embassies."

"And now? What is she doing now?"

"I don't know, I don't know—"

He pushed himself closer, his hands crawling over her breasts. "You *do* know."

"No, please, I—she didn't tell me."

He grabbed her hair in his fist, his nails scraping her scalp. "She did."

"She wanted to keep me safe, to—"

He punched her in the stomach with his other hand. She sobbed and her knees buckled, and he held her upright against the wall by her hair.

"Do you know what revolts me?" he asked.

She couldn't answer, couldn't breathe, and he threw her to the floor and stepped on her hair.

"The sexual act," he said. "Do you hear me? Nod your head."

Her scalp burned, but she moved her head an inch.

"It's revolting—the sweat and the smells, the barnyard noises. I'll ask you again, and if you lie this will be a long and tedious night." He ground his boot into her hair. "Do you understand?"

This time she nodded without being told.

"What is your mother doing now?" he asked.

"She—she's trying to find a reporter."

"To publish the document?"

"No—I don't know. She said—she only said, there was someone she'd try instead of the embassies, a writer, a reporter."

He asked her again and again, but that's all she could say, because it was all she knew. Then he asked her another question, the question she'd been dreading, because she had to lie.

He said, "Where were you coming from, on the train?"

"She sent me away. She was—she was afraid for my safety, afraid something would ha-ha-happen to me."

She allowed herself to break down completely, sobbing on the floor, praying for protection in incoherence. At length, her prayers were answered: the man left and she lay there trembling, breath catching in her chest. Then she stood, washed her face and hands, and knelt to pray properly—for guidance, for calm and strength. And for help: once the man discovered her lie, he'd return.

She wasn't granted calm, but resolve. She must escape. To save herself, to warn her mother. She ate a yeasty roll from the tray, gathering her strength, and returned to the grate in the shoe-shine room.

CHAPTER 16

The blackout shades were open, and a square of light shone on the hardwood floor. Morning. Pigeons scratched and cooed on the roof and Grant, warm under the bedcovers, eyed the silver light. No straw, no fleas, no dust—Anna probably swept twice a day.

China rattled behind him, the kid with a cup and saucer, his hair combed and tie knotted, his lip a dull red.

"Tea?" Grant asked.

Christoph handed him the saucer. "Maman said you liked coffee."

He took a long slow sip. A little cream, no sugar. "Wise woman."

"What about the other fights?" the kid asked.

"What other fights?"

"You said *most* fights aren't worth winning. What about the others?"

"You think this kid is worth fighting?"

The boy's narrow shoulders slumped. "I suppose not."

"You wanna know how to fight?" Grant sipped again. "Whoever hits first, wins."

"That's all?"

"Pretty much." Grant lifted the cup and the coffee stayed level. His hands were steady. His hands were steady, he was ready to move—find Racket and get to the crash site for the camera. "Would you look at that?" he said.

"Um," the kid said. "You've fought a lot, I guess."

"I've lost fights on three continents." He swirled the cup, darkening the coffee with the grounds at the bottom. "Four, if Australia's a continent."

The kid looked surprised. "Of course Australia's a continent."

"Then four."

"What if I don't want to be the second kind of tough?"

"Which kind was second?"

"At school, I mean. What if I don't want to lose?"

"He's not worth busting your knuckles."

"I'm not asking that, sir."

Jesus, the kid was too much like his father, grave and demanding. "Then hit him first and hit him hard and keep hitting. Don't check if you're winning or losing, just—"

"Mr. Grant!" Anna's voice cut into the room and she entered with a tray. "Christoph, you're due at school."

"It's ten minutes before—"

"Christoph!"

The kid left and they listened to his footsteps. There was a sudden atmosphere in the room, and Grant put the cup and saucer on the bedside table. He didn't know much about women, but he knew plenty about storms.

She set the tray on the dresser. "How's your coffee?"

"Light on the cream, no sugar."

"I remembered from your letter."

"Guess I'm—"

"Mr. Grant, you don't tell one child to hit another."

"Yeah, I—"

"You don't tell him to hit first and hit hard."

He could see her point. "I don't know much about kids."

"Consider that your first lesson."

"Yeah." There was a long pause. "I need to get to Neuchâtel, for my navigator. Do you have a car?"

"Are you sure he's still there?"

"Only one way to find out."

"I can think of two," she said. "The first one being the telephone. I have a friend, Lorenz, he'll check if your navigator is at the hospital."

"Does *he* have a car?"

"There's something you need more than a car: a plan. You intend to head back to England?"

"Yeah." After he got the handheld camera to the embassy. "Figured I'd head west 'til I hit water."

She arched an eyebrow, unimpressed.

"After I get Racket I'll talk to the American attaché," he said. "Brigadier General Leeger. The man's a prick on a pony, but he'll help us get back to England."

"A prick on a pony? Is that like 'a burr under my saddle'?"

"Kinda." Grant caught a flash of her watch when she turned toward the foot of the bed. "Shit, half the morning's gone." He threw the covers off and stood, then remembered his manners, saying *shit*: "Excuse me."

"Try these trousers, they may—" She turned back and made a choking noise, eyes narrowing.

Anna put a hand to her mouth.

Even under the dainty coverlet, Grant had looked severe, his body coiled and his eyes bleak. Breaking into her house, attacking Joris, talking about solitary confinement and escape. Sending her son for cigarettes, telling him how to beat another student. *Hit first and hit hard and keep hitting*. Then standing from the bed, his body all planes and angles, a foot taller than she, hacked from some coarse wood like a totem pole. There were dark curls on his chest with a bare slash from a scar, and the muscles of his arms etched like he'd been digging trenches. There was nothing soft about him; not his shoulders, not his body, not his eyes or mouth.

Except his briefs were yellow, embroidered with red roses.

He said, "What's wrong?"

"Nothing, nothing I—"

"Once I find Racket I'll be gone, and—" He stopped. "What?"

She shook her head, eyes watering. "You don't, that's not . . ."

"I thought you were crying. You're laughing."

"I—I'm sorry."

Grant said, "You're laughing at me."

She glanced at his briefs and the laughter bubbled over.

CHAPTER 17

The Russian coffeehouse was tucked behind a delivery office on a sooty block in northeast Zurich, with a view of the railway tracks. Akimov pushed through the door. A bell jingled overhead, and the scent of rye bread steamed the air. Empty tables crowded an off-white counter, and jars of pickled tomatoes and carrots and herring lined the wall.

Behind the counter, a hard-looking man with a drooping mustache stacked honey cookies in a chipped bowl.

"I smell *pelmeni*," Akimov said. Dumplings stuffed with beef and pork.

"No meat," the man said. "Only *vareniki* today."

Akimov bought two honey cookies instead. "I'm looking for the club, the Muscovite Club."

"If you have to ask . . ." the man said, in Russian.

Akimov answered in the same language. "You know what I have a taste for? *Kvashennaya kapusta*." Salted cabbage. "or a plate of *yazyk*. Is your horseradish any good?"

"Not too bad." The man looked at Akimov's empty sleeve. "You lose that recently?"

"Last year."

"Outside Moscow?"

"Rostov." Akimov said, taking a bite of cookie. "You tell fortunes, too?"

"Only misfortunes." The man grinned behind his mustache. "You're looking for the club?"

"I'm looking for my ex-wife." He showed the man her picture. "Magdalena Loeffert."

"Never saw her."

"I went to the club's old address, they sent me here."

The man jerked his head toward a swinging door behind the counter. "You're on the wrong side of the building. We share a kitchen."

"I get to the club through there?"

"Be my guest." The man swung the door open with one hand. "Comrade."

The kitchen smelled of sour cream and mushrooms, buttered chicken, and kasha cooking in an earthenware pot. There was the sizzle of potatoes sautéing with egg and salt, the splash of water boiling in a massive pot. A waitress pushed with her hip through swinging doors at the other end of the kitchen and Akimov followed her into a small dining room. Whitewashed brick walls and harvest tables, about half full of diners with the babble of Russian warming Akimov better than the sheets at the Palace Hotel.

The waitress told him the manager was in his office and he found the stairs and followed them to the second floor, where they left him between two doors and a hallway. Through one door, a gramophone played American jazz to an empty room, and through the other, four simultaneous arguments raged among a dozen Russians.

"—he flew to Moscow in an American Liberator," a bald man said, in a chair by the door. "With the United States Ferry Command at the wheel."

"It's not a wheel, you ape," another man said.

"In the cockpit, then, at the stick. *Pashol na kher*. He flew with a U.S. pilot, this is what I heard, escorted by Red Air Force fighters to Moscow—"

A tide of argument spilled from across the room, a sleek young woman insisting: "—because the Nazi filth, the panzer armies captured Krasnodar and Maikop, that's why!"

"And we destroyed the oil refineries before we retreated."

"*We*? Who is we? *You* didn't swing an ax." The woman's voice was pure scorn. "You can barely swing your little pencil."

Two observers roared with laughter, and Akimov stepped into the room and put his hand on the bald man's shoulder. "You were talking about Churchill?"

"Um—" The man eyed him with a quizzical smile. "You're Dmitri's friend?"

"Flying to Moscow, you said—" Akimov was interrupted by a shout of laughter across the room. "That was Churchill?"

"Yes, Churchill," the bald man said. "For a four-day summit with Stalin and Molotov."

The laughter stopped, and the arguments faded to a rumble as the club members noticed a stranger among them.

"On what date?" Akimov asked.

"Mid-August? I don't know."

So that much of what his father said was true—Churchill had met Stalin at least, and probably admitted that no help would be coming from the West. Akimov thanked the man and stepped toward the door, and a beefy man called from one of the couches, "Hey, Jackpot! Take off your coat, grab a chair. Who're you, then?"

Akimov looked at the man, at the middle-aged woman curled into an overstuffed chair, the redheaded youth sitting on an ottoman at the sleek woman's feet. "Just another homesick Russian."

"You stink of the military," the beefy man said.

Akimov adjusted the strap of his satchel. Wasn't sure if he

should respond—if the club manager didn't know where to find Magdalena, he'd have to ask these people.

"You hear what I say, Jackpot?" the beefy man said. "Or are you deaf, too? A one-armed bandit—you stink of the army."

"This is what loyalty smells like. You wouldn't know."

"Loyalty? You mean brutality."

"You can tell them apart? There are three kinds of Russian: those who fight for Russia, those who fight with Russia, and those who cower in Switzerland pissing themselves."

The beefy man charged Akimov. His friends held him back, and he snorted and pawed like a bull at the end of an iron chain. The sleek woman slammed a book onto a table, rattling coffee cups. "Idiots! Behave yourself!"

The beefy man muttered mutinously, but stopped struggling.

"I heard it differently," the woman said, approaching Akimov, her glossy black hair cut bluntly over Asiatic eyes. "There are three kinds of Russian: those who are in prison, those who were in prison, and those not yet in prison."

So she knew the look of a man who'd been to the gulag. "There's a fourth kind," he said. "I'm looking for the manager of the club."

She brushed a crumb of honey cookie from his lapel, her skin pocked with acne scars beneath face powder, and told him to come along. Dagger-thin in a violet dress, her hips sharp instead of round, she led him into the hall. Halfway down the corridor she stopped. "May I ask you two names?"

"Of course."

"Konstantin Nicolaevich Egorov and Timofei Nicolaevich Egorov."

He shook his head, not recognizing them from the camps. "I'm sorry."

"My brothers." Her face was a mask of indifference. "They released you from prison?"

"I was paroled to fight."

"So you're an officer?"

He gestured with the stump of his arm. "I'm a junior member of the commercial delegation, trading with the Swiss."

" 'Capitalism is the diseased transition between dead feudalism and healthy Communism,' " she quoted.

"Even a diseased transition," he said, "can be useful."

She shook her head and led him into a cramped book-lined office, where two men played chess across a desk that was half buried under stacks of newsprint. The man facing them filled his glass with vodka, his nose twitching like a rabbit's, looked at the woman and tapped the chessboard. "Next time we play, Oksana Nicolaeva, I'll beat you soundly."

She said, "This gentleman has a question for you, Roman."

Akimov took the picture from his breast pocket. "I'm looking for this woman, Magdalena Loeffert."

The rabbit-faced man—Roman—rolled a captured pawn in his fingers, not bothering to look at the photograph. "And you are?"

"My name is Akimov. I'm a . . . friend."

"You think there's so much suspicion back home, there's none left for us in exile?"

"I think nothing of you in exile."

The man twitched a broken smile. "You're a patriot, then?"

"I'm a Russian."

"And I'm not?"

"I don't care what you are. Do you know where Magdalena is?"

Roman gazed at the photo while the other man drank his vodka, then said, "Why should I tell you? One of the old guard, you think the Soviet Union is the future, yes? It's the pyre upon which the future burns."

"One man's pyre is another's hearth."

"They passed a law confiscating all grain in the Ukraine, and executed anyone who withheld a handful." He showed Akimov his cupped hand. "This much. Two million starved to death."

"There was a drought."

"There was a grain-procurement quota."

"You think they turned the screws too far?" Akimov said. "Maybe they did. I know about screws turned too far, but what stands against Germany now? Switzerland? The capitalists? Only one thing stands between Hitler and his Thousand-Year Reich: Russia. They used us hard, like a dispatch rider who kills his horse delivering a message from high command. The horse dies but the battle's won—has the rider gone too far? He did what was necessary."

"Easy to say, for the rider."

"The rider?" Akimov was surprised into laughter. "My friend— I am the horse, I have *always* been the horse."

The second man offered a glass of vodka to Akimov and said, "We're all horses."

Akimov raised the glass. "The only question is, which end?"

They drank and Roman opened the bottom drawer of his desk for a leather-bound book. "Magdalena Loeffert. No patronymic— she's Russian?"

"She married a Swiss."

The man peered at him. "So ask him."

"He's dead."

"How inconsiderate. Do you know her, Oksana Nicolaeva?"

The woman lighted a slim cigarette. "She's no friend of mine."

"Loeffert." Roman flipped through the book. "I don't know the face, but she could be a member. You want her address?"

"I want anything you know."

The second man slid a bishop through a minefield of pawns. "Don't cheat," he said, and left the room.

Akimov offered the woman the chair. She blew a lopsided smoke ring instead of answering, and drifted into the hall. He didn't want his back to the door, so he leaned against the wall and leafed through a book on beekeeping, reading about the fate of drones when winter approached.

Roman closed his leather book. "One Magda Lobacheva, no Magda Loeffert. She hasn't even been a guest, according to this."

"And according to you?"

"Never heard the name."

"You mind if I ask around?"

"Suit yourself."

Two hours later, none of the club members admitted knowing Magda. A pity, but not a surprise; still, if she had friends here, they'd tell her about the man so eager to find her. As his father had said, that was his best chance: not tracking her down but drawing her out.

He headed downstairs, and stopped in the vestibule to struggle with his coat buttons. When he finished, he saw the sleek woman behind him, watching—he fished two makhorka cigarettes from his pouch and offered her one. She took both, rerolled them with thin fingers and a flicker of her pink tongue, stuck one in her mouth and the other in his. He coaxed a flame from his battered lighter and told her good night and stepped outside to the bracing air.

The woman followed and stood beside him, her arms wrapped around herself. "You gave Roman no reason to trust you."

"There is no reason to trust me."

"There must be."

He smiled—he liked her lips and the goose bumps on her arms.

"Are you honest?" she asked. "Decent? Loyal?"

"None of those are reasons for trust, Oksana Nicolaeva. Do you know where the woman is?"

She took the cigarette from her lips and looked at the ember. "She came to the club four, maybe five times."

"Recently?"

"Last week."

"Did she mention any plans, a new address?"

"If you give me a reason to trust you, I'll tell you what I know."

"Trust doesn't require a reason," he told her. "That's what 'trust' means."

The woman put her cigarette back in her mouth. From the other side of the building a train whistle sounded, and Akimov blew smoke from his nostrils and said:

"There was a time when only the dead smiled, glad to be released.

. . . .

And when, mad from suffering, the condemned regiments marched,
And the shrill sharp steam-whistles sang farewell.
Dead stars shone above, and innocent Russia writhed
Under bloodstained boots, under the wheels of black Marias."

"Poetry and moonlight, Comrade?" she said, arching an eyebrow. "So romantic."

"Anna Akhmatova. More than poetry."

The woman sighed. "Magda Loeffert is perhaps a tsarist. She came to the club, yes. Hoping to meet someone. She said—I was on the balcony, I overheard her mention a meeting, a rendezvous in Bern. At the Bear Pit."

"The Bear Pit. Who with?"

"I don't know. A meeting at the Bear Pit's kiosk. That's all I heard."

"Thank you."

"What is the fourth kind?" she asked. "In prison, out of prison, not yet imprisoned—and what?"

"Our children, who will never know prisons."

She flicked her cigarette into the street. "You're an optimist? Still hopeful, after what you've survived?"

"Without hope, Comrade, I wouldn't have survived it."

CHAPTER 18

A breeze blew silvery ripples through the vineyard and Anna tucked her hair into a makeshift bun, sitting beside Grant on the sun-warmed stoop behind her house. They'd not spoken about her laughter but the effects lingered, his face not so harsh nor his body so tense.

Yet apparently his impatience remained. "I need to get to Neuchâtel," he said.

"We'll catch the next bus to the hotel. Lorenz will see if your navigator is still in the hospital."

"You don't have a car?"

"Not of my own."

He sipped his coffee and ate a chunk of bread. "Tell me about Joris."

"He looks after Christoph when I'm away, potters in the garden. He's a friend of the family. He worked for my grandfather; he says he's my inheritance."

"With a Luger."

"He's protective."

A quicksilver smile. "Christoph said you quit teaching."

"After Martin died." She looked at the vineyard. "I needed a change, and an income. A difficult time, not having a grave to visit, not knowing how he died."

He didn't acknowledge the hint. "You work for a newspaper now?"

"I freelance."

"Society pages? Births and marriages?"

She couldn't tell if he was mocking her. "Whatever pays for bread and coffee."

"Uh-huh. And the reason Joris is armed?"

"He worries," she said. "He found you a farmhouse, outside Thun, twenty-five kilometers from here. Your navigator can stay there while he recovers. So can you."

"A farmhouse?"

"Not a farm but an *Alphütte*, for a *Senn*—a cheese maker. He won't be there, he's gone by September, before the snow." She watched a bird hanging in a thermal over Dählhölzli Park. "It's a good place for you, safe and remote. Lorenz will check that your . . . What's his proper name? I can't call him 'Racket.' "

"McNeil. Sergeant Oliver McNeil."

"He'll check Sergeant McNeil is still in the hospital. Lorenz is persuasive on the telephone, or at least he's an officious ass, which amounts to the same thing."

"You trust him?"

"More than I trust you."

"Me? Shit, I'm just a—" He stopped. "Sorry."

She turned to hide her smile. She liked that he apologized for swearing, she liked his offhand familiarity—but she needed to get him out of her house. She needed to get Magda Loeffert's note from the hotel safe, and convince someone to decipher it.

"So we find Racket," he said. "I break him out, get to the—"

"As easy as that, Lieutenant?"

"Would you call me 'Grant'?"

"You'll break him out, no trouble at all?"

"Trouble or not."

"I see," she said. "And then?"

"Me'n Racket find the—" He stopped. "We have a little job, me and Racket. Then we wait at your *Alphütte* until Brigadier General Leeger arranges a way across France."

"A little job?"

"Shouldn't take long."

Sounded like trouble. "Then cross France to England? My friend Rosine says the Maquis—French Resistance—are worried about tension on the Vichy border."

"We'll see what Leeger says. I'll call him from the hotel, get things moving."

"France isn't the only way, Mr.—Grant." She shivered as wind rose from the river. "You never use your given name?"

"Not if I can help it. What's the other way?"

"I know it begins with an 'H.' Harold? Herbert?"

"No."

"Henry?"

"Hans," he said.

She laughed. "For an American, that must be . . . rare."

"Yeah. My mother's first-generation, she insisted. My father calls me 'John.' "

"At least it's not 'Adolf.' "

"What's the other way back to England?"

"Hans," she said, enjoying his discomfiture. "Hans Grant."

He shook his head at her amusement. "What's the other way?"

"Cross into Italy, take a boat from Genoa to Spain or Portugal. Then you're back in neutral territory—getting to England is easy."

"We catch a boat, no trouble at all?"

"Trouble or not," she said. "Hans."

He smiled, and showed his face to the sky. The clouds were

high and bright, the sun warm through the cold air. "You're not what I expected," he said.

"Good." She stood and brushed the seat of her dress. "Time to catch the bus."

The salesman draped a black-and-gold watch on the velvet stand. "The Gubelin cocktail watch, Herr Villancourt, I'm sure your wife would approve."

"My wife is vulgar," Villancourt lied. "Her approval is a curse. No, I prefer the look of the Titus."

"Then allow me . . ." The man displayed another watch. "The Girard Perregaux, fourteen-carat gold with a silver dial."

The door to the warm little shop jingled and Herr Pongratz stepped inside, no hint of his true nature visible as he gazed blankly at one of the bright glass cases.

Villancourt frowned. "Not quite right. An antique, perhaps?"

The salesman's hand flickered and another watch appeared, with a rectangular engraved face. "Bulova, lovely in a hinge-back case with a winding crown."

Villancourt asked the price, then shook his head. "She's not worth that much. Perhaps a trinket? One of those watch pins?"

"I know the precise thing. A jump watch. Quite a curiosity, and modestly priced."

"My wife knows nothing of modesty." Villancourt headed for the door. "No, there's nothing here for me."

Pongratz fell into step with him on the walkway of the covered arcade. "You have a wife?"

"She lives in a sanitarium, the poor dear, touched with nerves." He'd been forced to commit her: one was better served by sympathy for a wife's plight than dismay at her outspokenness. "Still, shopping for her clears my head. You have Frau Loeffert's current location?"

"The girl doesn't know."

"You're certain?"

"As I can be, given your limits."

"Don't disfigure the girl—she's worth a billion francs to your Führer; she's the only way we'll stop the blackmail. You learned nothing, then?"

"I learned this: after failing to contact the Allied embassies, Magda Loeffert approached a reporter."

"A reporter? None of this is publishable."

"That's what the girl told me, that her mother wanted a reporter."

Villancourt stopped and watched the passing traffic. "Then the best way to find Loeffert is through that reporter. What would a reporter do, after she approached him? First, he'd verify her background."

"He'd investigate Loeffert?"

"Clumsily. Journalists are never careful—the secrets they protect aren't their own."

"So we find out if anyone's been asking questions about Loeffert?"

"Precisely." He led Pongratz back to the watch store and bought the Girard Perregaux. "And if I might use your telephone?" he asked the salesman.

"Oh, certainly, sir."

"Privately. If you would step into the back room?"

"I'm sorry, I can't—"

Villancourt tapped the man's tiepin. "As a personal favor?"

"Erm," the salesman said. "Well, I'm not entirely allowed—"

Pongratz cleared his throat, and the salesman wasn't such a fool as to object. He scurried into the back room and Villancourt sat behind the counter and called three cantonal offices before getting the answer he wanted.

"Why, yes," the secretary said. "A gentleman called only yesterday, asking after a Magdalena Loeffert."

"Did he? And you told him . . ."

"I'm not at liberty to say."

Villancourt chuckled. "You're not at liberty to say what you told him, or you told him that you're not at liberty to say?"

The woman's voice warmed. "Both, actually. The tax rolls are confidential."

"What time did he call?" Villancourt would have the call traced—tedious, but necessary. "Can you tell me that?"

"In the morning, before nine. I'll tell you what I told him—"

"You needn't bother," Villancourt said, moving to replace the phone. "I'll ask him myself."

"Ah," she said. "You already know Herr Lorenz."

"Wait! Hello? Herr Lorenz?"

"At the Palace Hotel."

Villancourt almost giggled. "He left his name?"

"So I might return his call, if I was allowed to give information."

Herr Lorenz at the Palace Hotel. Villancourt turned to Pongratz, and smiled.

CHAPTER 19

Two bears sprawled in the leaf litter at the bottom of the lichen-stained stone pit, one laying on her back, legs obscenely spread, the other hunched against the pebbled wall. A dead tree rose from the middle of the pit, stripped of bark, and a third bear crouched on the mossy stone steps and stared at Akimov with small reproachful eyes.

He leaned against the fence and pretended to read his guide-book. The woman at the Muscovite Club overheard Magdalena arranging to meet someone at the Bear Pit's kiosk, but who—when?—why? Should he directly approach the man in the slope cap who finally unlocked the kiosk and arranged bags of roast chestnuts on the counter? No reason not to simply ask if he knew Magda, but a twinge of caution held Akimov back.

He wasted ten minutes at the newsstand, then shook his head. He wasn't trying to catch Magda unawares; if the man at the kiosk could pass a message to her, he'd be one step closer to success. He started forward and saw movement across the street, a lanky man strolling toward Alter Aargauerstalden and the Rosengarten.

A familiar gait. Back at the kiosk, the slope cap still bobbed behind the counter, but the man crossing the street was the original wearer—he'd switched caps and slipped out the rear of the kiosk.

Huh. The man was hiding something, a promising sign. Akimov followed him into the morning shade of a hill, along the western promenade to a bus stop. Through the trees, the city spread, rows of roofs stepping downhill from a high bridge, but Akimov saw another city:

For no price would we abandon this splendid
Granite city of fame and disaster,
The wide rivers of shifting ice,
The dismal sunless gardens—
And, softly, the Muse's voice.

He retraced his steps to the previous bus stop. When the bus came, he sat in back, not far from the doors—and his luck was good. The lanky man boarded, and together they rode over the bridge, down Gerbergasse past the stone arches and javelin spires of the Münster. The man disembarked and headed east, and Akimov followed him past the view terrace of the city casino, into a narrow lane leading toward the cool heart of Old Town. He lost the man twice, and found him again immediately. Could this *not* be about Magdalena? Had Akimov followed her trail to that kiosk only to be distracted by a man playing children's games?

He shook his head—impossible—and ambled along a street at the foot of one of Bern's lesser bridges, where the man ducked into a storefront with a green-and-white awning. A bookshop. Akimov slipped into the chemist's across the way, bought a pot of cherry toothpaste, and spent ten minutes lurking among bottles of lavender water until the clerk cleared his throat.

Well, what was he waiting for? The lanky man to lead him back to the kiosk?

He crossed the street. Despite the sign reading ANTIQUARIAN BOOKSHOP, the store contained only a single display of books, in a case spotlighted by hooked brass lamps. A jumble of mirrors, every size and shape, covered the wall to Akimov's left and his reflection followed him toward the rear of the shop.

A woman sat sidelong on a couch, sucking the tip of a pen, wearing a black skirt and green jacket, not far from a beaded curtain swaying in an open doorway. Her eyes slid toward him, but she said nothing.

"May I ask if you're the owner, Fräulein?" he said.

"Close enough to make no difference."

"You buy and sell?"

She tapped the pen against her teeth. "As you say."

"And the appraisals?"

"I have a staff."

Akimov's phantom arm ached. In Russian, he asked, "But you are the one to speak with?"

"*Da.*"

Ah, so this *was* connected to Magda. "Tell me about your business."

"Ask me."

"Why the mirrors?"

"To look at myself."

He summoned his meager charm. "Nobody can blame you for that."

She sucked her pen, unimpressed.

"What else do you buy and sell?" he asked.

"Items of value. Antiquities."

"You're a broker, a middleman?" When she didn't answer, he continued. "My friend recommended you."

"How pleasant."

"Tell me how it works."

"*Nyet.*"

He attempted a rueful smile. "The truth is, he's not my friend, he's my competitor—I know he deals with you, but I don't know why. I would like to buy that knowledge." He took his wallet from his breast pocket. "Could you appraise that for me?"

"Not for sale." She made a note in her pad, then arched a brow at him. "Did you enjoy the Bear Pit?"

The rueful smile fell from his face—the lanky man from the kiosk had led him here on purpose. The beads rattled and a thick-set man in an undershirt shoved through. Akimov raised his arm and the man grabbed his jacket and flung him into the back room, the beaded curtain whipping his face. The lanky man stood from a ratty couch, and before Akimov could speak the other man punched him in the kidney from behind. He gasped and the lanky man drove a fist into his stomach.

"Now you caught me," the lanky man said.

The thickset man pinned Akimov's arm behind his back. "You only have one arm, don't make me break it."

The lanky man scattered the contents of Akimov's satchel on the card table. "I spotted you at the Bear Pit and led you here to talk in private—so nobody can hear you cry. You understand? Now, who are you? Why are you watching?"

He couldn't think of a single reason to lie. "My name's Aki-mov. I—"

"Akimov?"

"You were expecting someone else?"

The lanky man scanned his papers, and snorted. "This is Loef-fert's ex-husband," he told his comrade. "The old man's son. Fuck-ing everything up."

Grant grabbed his hat from the kitchen table. He'd wasted too much time already—he needed to find Racket before they moved him from the hospital. "Catch the bus?" he asked Anna. "Is that the fastest way?"

"Faster than walking."

"How about your man at the hotel—Lorenz? Does he have a car?"

"You should worry less about transportation and more about leaving the house. You're an escaped prisoner."

"There aren't a dozen people in the country who'd recognize me."

"It only takes one."

"Does Lorenz have a car?"

She sighed. "He can get one."

"How do I find the farmhouse?"

"Wait here, Grant." She touched his elbow. "Please. I'll look into smuggling you back to England."

"First I have to get Racket and—do this other thing."

"You want to tell me about that?"

He adjusted the hat. "Not really."

"That is unacceptable," Anna said.

"Well, I can't tell you without—"

"I mean the hat. Here." She gave him a felt fedora from the hall closet. "It's Martin's."

"Fits okay," he said.

"Because you both have big heads."

A memory flashed—Martin's head—and he clamped down. This wasn't the time. They went out the back door, where Joris waved from the work shed.

Grant looked at him. "I should take the Luger."

"The last thing you need is a gun."

"Yeah, especially if you don't have one."

She shook her head, but called to Joris in Italian, and the old man handed over the gun with a crooked smile and a stream of words.

"*Grazie*," Grant told him.

He jabbered some more, and Anna said, "Why are you thanking him? He's telling you the pin is broken."

"The firing pin?"

"Yes, the firing pin."

"He's carrying a dud gun?"

"To scare away crows, he says."

"Well, good." Grant stuck the Luger in his waistband: stupid to carry a dud gun, but sometimes stupid was the best you had. "At least now I can stop worrying about crows."

They caught the bus and he sat five rows behind Anna—in case she was right, and someone recognized him—and watched the sunlight strobe through the windows and play with her hair. She stepped off at Bundesgasse, but Grant stayed: they'd meet in the hotel, after he'd called Leeger. Sure, the officious prick ordered him to stay put, but that was history now, and a military attaché couldn't leave an escaped airman hanging on foreign ground.

Grant would get the camera himself, bring it to the embassy, and drag Racket back to England, with Leeger's help or not. He nodded to himself and watched Anna walk away, graceful and erect. He could still see her laughing, covering her mouth, cheeks flushed. Laughing at him, shit. The best thing he'd seen since Lou Gehrig blasted a second homer in game three of the World Series.

The bus turned north, away from the hotel, rumbled over cobblestones and pulled to the curb. Grant followed a pair of office girls to the street and fell immediately into step with half a dozen Swiss soldiers, with helmets and greatcoats and rifles.

"Why are clocks in Bern painted sloppily?" a skinny soldier was saying.

"Why?" another asked.

"The Bernese are so slow, the minute hand knocks the paintbrush away."

The other soldiers groaned, and the skinny soldier glanced at

Grant and his pulse quickened. He nodded politely, ducked into a side street, and waited. Nobody followed, so he headed for the post office. He placed the call and got the runaround for ten minutes before Leeger's secretary came on the line.

"I need to talk to Leeger," he said.

"I'm sorry," she said. "He's not in the office at the moment."

That stumped him. Should he tell another embassy staffer about the Nazi prototype aircraft? Not until he had the camera. Without proof he was just a fugitive with a wild story. No, they couldn't do anything until he brought them the camera—but Leeger could start making arrangements now to get him and Racket out of Switzerland.

"If you'll leave a number where he might return your call?" she asked.

"My name is Grant," he said. "Lieutenant Grant, from Straflager Wauwilermoos. Tell him that, if he's there. He'll come to the phone."

"I'm sorry," she said again. "The brigadier general isn't in the office. If you'll leave a—"

"When's he getting back?"

"The brigadier general is expected to return this afternoon."

"I'll try him at home."

"He's away from home," she said.

"Well, when he gets back, tell him to wait for my call."

She said she'd pass along that message, and hung up.

That didn't break how he expected—but things never did. He pushed through the post office doors and lighted a cigarette on the sidewalk. Maybe this was better anyway. *First* break Racket out of the hospital and get the camera to the embassy, *then* talk to Leeger. His stock would be higher with that film in his hands.

Around a few corners, the Palace Hotel rose into view: half bank and half cathedral, with an elegant dome above double-peaked roofs and solid gray walls. A flight of steps curved from the sidewalk to the front doors, and a man leaned against the railing, wearing a drab suit with a matching hat, his left sleeve empty. His weather-beaten face was a stranger's, but Grant knew him: he was a commander, an officer. Even without a uniform Grant could tell he was outranked. Well, he was outranked by Leeger too, but there was rank you *wore* and rank you *were*. This guy didn't need the insignia.

There weren't any marks, but as he got closer Grant could tell the one-armed man had been given the business—he wasn't just leaning there, he was marshaling his strength. Grant touched a finger to his hat, but instead of asking for help the officer showed him a ghost of a smile.

Inside the hotel, Grant passed the concierge and headed for the broad sweeping staircase. The floors were waxed, the brass polished, and there wasn't a stitch in the upholstery or a smudge on the wall. He went to the lounge, all dark wood and etched glass, smelling of pipe tobacco and warm ale. He sat at the bar, pulled an ashtray close, and shook his empty cigarette pack.

The one-armed officer slid onto the next stool. "Cigarette?" he said, opening his satchel.

Just what Grant needed, a Swiss officer. "*Danke.*"

The officer dug in a tobacco pouch. "I hope you're not in a rush."

"Not much."

"Good." The man started rolling a cigarette one-handed, his tobacco powdery as sawdust. "Me, I am putting off the inevitable."

"That ever work for you?"

The officer laughed, deep and rough. "Never. You?"

"Not yet."

"Maybe there's a first time."

"That'd be one for—" he was going to say *for Ripley*, but that didn't make sense in German—"for the books." The barkeep came, and Grant asked the officer, "Can I get you a coffee?"

"I wouldn't say no to whiskey."

"Then a pint of bitter for me," Grant said.

The officer handed the finished cigarette to Grant. "Makhorka."

"*Colonel* Makhorka?"

The man laughed again. "I mean the cigarette. Tobacco stems chopped fine, a Russian treat."

Grant lighted the cigarette. "You're Russian?"

"Soviet trade commission."

Grant inhaled, then looked at the cigarette in surprise. "That's disgusting."

"An acquired taste."

"The Red Army dumped you after you lost the arm?"

A quick grin. "You're not Swiss, asking that."

"I'm Australian."

The drinks came, and the officer lifted his glass to Grant and killed his whiskey. "Much better." He put his tobacco pouch in his satchel, then winced and pressed his hand to his ribs. "And you? No longer in the army?"

"I never was."

"No?" The Russian's gaze flicked at him. "Air force, then. Or are you a sailor?"

"Do you need a doctor for that . . . ache?"

"Not as much as I need a pair of spectacles. The stairs at the Münster-terrasse are steeper than they look." The officer stood and told the barkeep, "On my tab." Then he turned to Grant and said something in Russian, maybe *goodbye*, maybe *take care*. Maybe *you're no Australian.*

The wind flapped Anna's skirt as she stood at the railing of the Palace Hotel's third-floor balcony, watching the river's sluggish current vanish around a distant bend. She heard the veranda door open behind her and turned with a hopeful smile: a good omen, the colonel being so prompt. Despite being Martin's childhood friend and her most trusted contact in the anti-Fascist group Aktion—and possessed of a wealth of knowledge—he tended to dismiss anything not on his weekly schedule.

He stepped ponderously through the door, a tightly wrapped umbrella at his side. "Mrs. Fay, what a charming rendezvous."

"And private," she said. "I've never known guests to come here."

"More fools they. You have a request?"

"I need someone to make sense of this." She handed him the sheet of paper Lorenz had found in Magda Loeffert's trash. "It's beyond me."

"You're breaking codes, now?"

"I will be, after you introduce me to a cryptographer."

He scanned the paper. "Is this about those government loans you're always chasing?"

"The clearing credits? I don't know."

"If this concerns the banks, you know I can't involve Aktion."

She watched a stubby boat float under the Kirchenfeld bridge and didn't answer.

"I can't help unless you give me more background," he said.

"You'll have to," she said. "Martin would want you to."

"He'd hardly approve of all this."

"Don't tell *me* what my husband would approve."

His turn to watch the river. "You believe this is so important?"

"I have a feeling, Colonel." She didn't want to mention the thirteen million francs, not yet—Aktion wasn't secure, and word could get back to the men involved. "I spoke to the source and I have a . . . a feeling."

"Feminine intuition?"

"You'll find someone to untangle this?"

"I have a friend," he said. "A Frenchman who might help, given a week or two."

"You see the date? I need this today."

"That's impossible, Anna. That date—there's no telling what it means."

"It means we don't have a week."

The colonel tapped his umbrella on the floor. "There's another way, perhaps . . . I'm thinking of a different man now, no friend of mine. His name is Schürch, I know him by reputation only. An enthusiastic amateur cryptographer . . . and a frontist."

"A Nazi? I'm supposed to ask him for help?"

"If this is truly urgent, perhaps you should do more than ask."

Anna tugged at her wedding band. "What? Send Rosine to seduce some frontist cryptographer? Have Lorenz ferret out his secrets? There's no time."

"There is another way, Anna. A faster approach, and less gentle."

"Force him to help?"

"If you're certain this is urgent, then yes. Unless you don't know anyone sufficiently thuggish to convince him?"

She said: "I know someone."

CHAPTER 20

The Palace Hotel game room was shaped like a fat Swiss cross under a domed ceiling, with card tables and billiards and a stone hearth. Grant racked for a game of eight ball near French doors opening onto a garden terrace, to pass the time while waiting for Anna. Sunk the one and two, then chased the three around the table until a shadow fell across the side pocket. He tapped the cue ball and raised his head.

The girl was long and lean, with an angular face—even standing still she was like a wild horse, skittish and graceful, with wary eyes and a proud neck. Probably had a fine high rump, too. Her hair wasn't quite contained by her little veiled hat, her smile wasn't quite contained by her wide full lips. She wasn't beautiful, but it didn't matter.

Her voice was smoky and warm. "*Alors, vous jouez au chat avec cette petite souris.*"

"I don't speak French," he said in German, then tried to prove himself a liar: "*Je ne parle pas français.*"

"*Mais si.*" But you do.

"*Nein.*" In German, he said, "Only German or English."

"*Anglais? Êtes-vous Britannique?*"

"No," he said in English. "I'm Australian." He didn't try the accent, though, he knew his limitations. "*L'Austra—Autralie?*"

"*Le pays du kangourou?*" She curled her hands and mimed a rabbit hopping. "*Ou le pays de*"—she put her pinkie over her upper lip, like a mustache—"*Hitler?*"

"Kangaroo."

"Ah. *Cela me rappelle une plaisanterie—mais elle n'est pas très drôle.*"

He didn't understand what she said but he liked how she sounded. She was young, maybe twenty, with big curious eyes.

"*Vous ne parlez vraiment pas le français?*" she asked. You really don't speak French?

"Um, *vraiment.*" In German: "My accent doesn't convince you?"

A smoky laugh, and she purred more French in her husky voice, every word sounding like an offer.

"No idea what you just said." He walked around the table after the cue ball, to get some distance and clear his head.

She leaned low over the table and aimed an imaginary stick at the seven ball. "I say, you play like the cat toying with her mouse." Her German was accented, and her clothes off-kilter, a fringed frock and lavender gloves past her elbows. "You torture and chase."

"Do you play?"

"*Non.* I only hunt—" She cocked her head. "How do you say in English? Big game."

So she was a professional, working the hotel. "I'm glad to hear it."

"Why glad?"

He rolled the cue ball to her across the felt. " 'Cause I'm not game at all."

"Not game?" She stopped the ball with one finger. "That is a—a double entendre?"

Her tone was so earnest, he couldn't help smiling. "Yeah."

"Not very a good one, I think."

"I'm not much with words."

She tilted her head. "Anna waits outside, beyond the terrace."

"Anna?"

"You are Grant. I am Rosine, my pleasure to meet you. *Faites attention avec Anna; elle ressemble à un petit chaton, mais elle a le coeur d'une lionne, et les griffes aussi.*"

Grant stepped through the French doors to the patio and followed a crushed-gravel path to stone steps. The hillside was a cascade of yellowing leaves, dotted with the occasional tree where Anna waited on a lower terrace. She saw him and slipped behind an arbor, out of sight of the hotel windows.

He caught her in a hillside hollow. "That's Rosine? Betty Grable could take her night course."

Anna broke a twig from a scoured pine with low-hanging branches.

"I've seen bombers with less oomph," he said.

She brushed past him, eyes grave. He didn't know what the problem was; he was wearing the hat.

"Racket's still at the quarantine hotel?" he asked, following. "You spoke to your friend?"

"Lorenz called, yes. Sergeant McNeil's been transferred to a hospital in Solothurn."

"Another hospital? What's wrong?"

"Nothing, only the first was for quarantine. He's recovering perfectly well."

"You got directions?"

She nodded.

"How about a car?"

"Grant, I'm working on something else, something important. My own 'little job.' I'm not sure—" She looked at the twig in her hand. "I don't know if I can help you."

He gave that a second. "Okay. I'll get my own car."

But getting Racket out alone, with Dubois waiting, that would be tricky. He watched Anna turn toward the river, her face touched by reflected light. Maybe she didn't have Rosine's horsepower—she didn't smolder and burn—but her offhand beauty ran deeper, like a vein of gold.

"Woulda been easy," he said, "before I lost my edge."

"Lost your edge?" She flicked the twig to the leaf-littered ground. "You broke out of a prison camp."

"This time they know I'm coming."

"Who?"

"At Racket's hospital, they know my name, and my face."

"How?"

"I made a mistake," he said. "I didn't kill Dubois."

She took his arm and led him down a path toward Aarestrasse, where they stepped around an old sandstone fence to the sidewalk. "Is there anything else you want to tell me?"

"Yeah, there is." He turned to her, and didn't speak for a long moment, then he shook his head. "I need a car. I need your help."

"Do you know how little this matters, Grant? Two Americans stuck in Switzerland?"

"It matters."

"Why?"

"We saw something, Anna—on the flight, something we need to report."

She measured him with her eyes. "I'll give you three hours. But I need your help in return."

"For what?"

"I need . . . I need a man frightened into compliance. Maybe worse."

"Worse than frightened? Use Lorenz."

"I need a man like you."

"What am I like?"

She touched his elbow. "You're willing to dirty your hands."

"Yeah, I'm a prince," he said. "If I lean on this man, you'll help me get Racket?"

"We'll leave in five minutes."

He lifted his head at the sound of an engine, a Messerschmitt flying low to the southeast, and put a hand on the small of her back to protect her. Then the Swiss crosses on the wing came into view, and he turned away before she could see the look in his eyes.

She said, "I'll get a car."

CHAPTER 21

The little Peugeot ran easily over the smooth Swiss roads, though every time Anna shifted, the map jerked in Grant's hands. Still, he'd learned that Solothurn was a town of twelve thousand, with a cathedral and a fountain and a clock tower in the market-place—and bisected by the Aare.

He turned to Anna. "The same river runs to Bern?"

"Of course."

"How long a trip is that by motorboat? In case there's pursuit."

She slowed behind a turning truck. "If there's pursuit, Grant, we're ruined."

"Regretting our deal?"

Anna mangled the clutch again and the Peugeot jerked forward, clattering over train tracks toward the river. "Ask me again in an hour, and once more after we find Herr Schürch."

"He's the only man in Switzerland who can decipher your message?"

"How many cryptographers do *you* know?"

Good point.

They crossed the easternmost bridge of the city, where a flock of little brown birds ran along the riverbank. Far off, there was the sound of bells and the creaking of a boat on the water.

"How seriously was he injured?" she asked. "Sergeant Mc-Neil?"

"Racket's tough. He'll be fine."

She made a noise in her throat, but when he looked over her face was blank. After he got Racket, she'd drop them somewhere he could lift a car. Navigate to the crash site, make a quick run to the embassy with the camera. Then he'd put some weight on this Schürch and leave Switzerland, with or without Leeger's help.

The hospital was a squat medieval fort with stone walls and arrow-slit windows, rising from well-tended grounds surrounded by sparse woods. An army truck hunkered in the circular drive, courtesy of Straflager Wauwilermoos, and two guards lounged against the bonnet.

Grant slouched in his seat. "Two guards at the front door, maybe one at Racket's room. I'll meet you back where the signposts are." He opened the door a few inches after the car rounded a turn. "You know what to do?"

"I'm a housewife," she said. "A mother."

"What you are," he said, "is a surprise."

She almost smiled. "Just go."

He went out the door and through a weedy bank into the woods. The plan was simple. She'd speak to Racket, posing as a representative of the Swiss-American Neighborhood League, tell him to slip away and meet Grant at the southeast corner of the property. She had letterhead from the league and a box of cookies to prove her good intentions. Grant would help Racket to the car and they'd be off.

He slunk through the woods until he spotted the hospital roof, then edged behind a shrub with a view of the driveway. The Peugeot was parked near the entrance—Anna already inside the hospital—and the guards stood at the truck, monuments to boredom. Five minutes passed. Birds hopped through the undergrowth, a yellow fly hovered by his head. Ten minutes. Why hadn't Anna returned to the car? Hand over the cookies, say a few words in English, and be gone. Fifteen minutes, and Grant's palms started to itch.

Twenty minutes, and the front doors opened and Anna emerged, her hair copper where the lowest curls brushed the cool blue of her dress. She got into the car and ground the gears a few times, and Grant imagined she flushed. Then she drove away, and he watched the driver's side window: the prearranged sign. Wide open meant she hadn't spoken with Racket, closed meant he was on the way.

She cracked the window three inches.

What the hell did *that* mean? He crossed the grounds behind the hospital, nodding at an old man sitting with a pale girl on a bench, then stepped around a hedge back into the woods.

He found the Peugeot down a narrow road beside a deep gulch, Anna standing with her head bare and her hair ruffled by the breeze. He trotted to a halt beside her, breathing hard.

"And to think," she said, "yesterday you needed help climbing stairs."

"Was your window open or closed?"

"A little of both."

"They wouldn't let you talk to him? He can't walk?"

"We spoke. He's walking on crutches."

"And?"

She watched fallen leaves somersault across the road. "He liked the cookies?"

"What went wrong?"

She wound her hair into a thick hank. "Why do you call him 'Racket'?"

"You don't think he should travel? Did you even . . ." The thought froze him. "You didn't tell him I'm here."

"I told him," she said. "He thinks we're related on your mother's side, I'm your German cousin."

Grant put his hand on the car door beside Anna's shoulder, and couldn't tell if the breath of autumn was her or the mountain forest. "Anna, tell me."

She took the keys from her bag. "He doesn't want to leave."

"What?"

"He wants to stay. In the hospital, in Switzerland. He did his duty and he was shot down. He's injured and he's—he's finished. He's done."

"He thinks he's *done*?"

"Grant, don't—"

"Wait here."

He grabbed the keys and went back into the woods.

In the hospital garden, the old man and the pale girl were gone from the bench. Grant snapped a handful of flowers from an overgrown bed and headed for a recessed side door. Locked. Maybe Dubois had posted guards down every hallway, but Grant was running out of options. He pushed inside the back door and was alone in a vestibule with bright walls and the scent of citrus and steel. Around a few corners, he found the stairs; the second floor was shaped like an *E*, with Racket's room in the middle of the crossbar, a dead end.

The thin-faced nurse at the station said, "Excuse me?"

He showed her the flowers. "The American is in 216?"

"Yes, 216."

"I won't be interrupting? No visitors?"

"No, go right along."

The room was as small as a monk's cell. Racket sprawled on the bed, digging in the tin of cookies. He tossed Grant a grin. "Thought you'd wait 'til nighttime."

Grant jammed a chair under the doorknob. "Cookies any good?"

"The almond's okay."

He took one. "You made an impression on A—" She hadn't used her real name. "On the woman. What're you doing?"

"What everyone does in a hospital. C'mon, Lieut."

"You're hurt that bad?"

There was a small plaster on Racket's forehead, and his chest was wrapped with bandages under his hospital pajamas. Grant couldn't see his ankle, but there was a crutch against the wall.

"I won't be playing baseball," Racket said. "If the Dodgers call, tell 'em—"

"Can you walk?"

Racket raised his hands in surrender. "You want to talk to my doctor? My ankle's sprained, I can't walk far. The ribs are broken, three ribs."

Grant nodded toward the bandage peeking from Racket's unbuttoned pajama top. "Wrapped tight as a Christmas bow."

"You walked away okay, huh?"

"Not a scratch." Grant put his hat on the dresser. "I've had broken ribs, Racket, I've sprained my ankle."

"You know what they said, the Swiss, when I woke up? 'For you, the war is over.' The war is over. I got the gate, Lieut, I'm done. A rib almost popped my lung. And this—" He touched the bandage on his forehead. "Another two inches, you'd be digging me out of a hole to carry me home."

"That would've been hell on my back."

"You know what? When my life flashed in my eyes, it was too

damn short. Look at—" Racket stopped when footsteps sounded in the corridor, and didn't continue after they faded.

Grant ate the cookie. "These are good."

"Yeah, they're like shortbread."

"They speak English here?"

"A little." Racket ventured a grin. "I'm teaching one of the nurses a few words."

Grant laughed. "I bet. They put any guards on you?"

"A guy named Dubois, a captain."

"Not here now."

"He's back and forth. Fussy old maid."

Grant opened the door far enough to check the corridor. "I need to get to the crash site, Racket—for your handheld camera."

"It's still there?"

"Hidden. I didn't want anyone wandering off with it."

"So nobody knows what we saw?"

"Or that we have proof."

Racket whistled. "Damn right you need to get back there. What're you waiting for?"

"I can't find the place."

"You don't know where we crashed?"

"I was busy flying. I need you to show me."

Racket grinned. "Couldn't find your own ass without a navigator. Well, gimme that crutch. Let's get moving."

"We'll stop in Paris on the way back home," Grant promised, propping the crutch across the bed. Racket was a good kid. "Wait a second, I'll check the stairs."

He stepped into the hallway and heard boots on the tile floor, three men coming fast around the corner: Private Engleberg from the prison camp, unholstering his sidearm, with Dubois half a step behind, and a young blond guard, face eager and afraid, gun drawn.

Grant tugged the useless Luger from his waistband and drew on Dubois.

The commandant barked, "*Halten!* Don't fire!"

Nobody moved except the nurse at the station, backing slowly away.

"Nobody fire," Dubois said. "Stay calm. You've been watched since you entered the grounds, Lieutenant Grant. You're alone, save for an injured man. Is that not correct?"

"Shit. Yeah."

"Lower your weapon, we'll talk this over like civilized men. One against three, your situation is hopeless."

"I want a tribunal this time," Grant said, defensively. "The real thing."

"And you'll get one."

Grant offered the butt of his Luger to Dubois. "I'd better."

"A wise decision."

Dubois reached for the gun and Grant grabbed his shirt and slammed him in the face with his forehead—pain flashed, and Grant felt the *crack* of Dubois's nose snapping, and maybe his cheekbone. Dubois's knees buckled and Grant hugged him close, dragging him backward toward the doorway, his own eyes watering from the pain.

Engleberg swore but Dubois's bulk in Grant's arms blocked his shot, and the young guard fired wildly twice, then blurted, "*Sheisse!* Sorry, sorry."

"Racket," Grant said in English, through clenched teeth, "time to go."

No answer but Dubois's guttural moan, so Grant backpedaled into the room and glanced at Racket. Too scared to move, propped against the headboard, staring at the ceiling like—

No.

CHAPTER 22

The wind rose high and uneasy, chafing the branches of a drooping spruce. Anna opened the car door, grabbed the pack of cigarettes Grant had left on the seat, and nervously picked at the label. He'd been gone too long—if anything went wrong, they'd look for the car, but he'd taken the keys and she couldn't drive away. She should start walking, should've started walking fifteen minutes ago.

She couldn't do all this, couldn't uncover an SS-funded deal, *and* help Grant, *and* force Schürch to talk. Hell, she couldn't even make Christoph tell her what was wrong at school. She tossed the cigarette pack back onto the passenger seat. Lorenz was a good man, but fashioned to following, not leading. Rosine was better used in dim candlelight than solid darkness. Perhaps Anna shouldn't have—

Leaves crunched and underbrush rustled, and Grant loped from a blind of pines, alone.

"You couldn't change his mind?" she asked him.

"Racket's dead."

"What? No, he's fine."

His eyes were hard over the splattered blood on his shirt. "Let's go."

"He can't be, that's impossible."

"He's dead." He took the keys from his pocket and stared at them. "God help me."

"What happened?"

"They're coming after us. Let's go."

Anna held out her hand. "Give me the keys."

"I'll drive."

"You look like hell, Grant."

"You drive like hell."

She slid behind the wheel and closed the door. That poor boy, Sergeant McNeil, so bright and alive. This was more than a barracks deal and an encrypted list, more than money and politics; this was life and death, and she didn't know if she could keep fighting. Her breath caught, and she closed her eyes briefly—she could and she would—and Grant sat in the passenger seat and gave her the keys.

"Head north," he said.

She exhaled. "Toward Germany?"

"They'll search south."

Anna started the car and followed the road through steep forest windings toward Weissenstein. A cliff of serrated rock towered overhead, a gentle green valley lay below, and the air smelled of winter. Next month, freezing mist would fill the valley and hoarfrost would sheath the trees. She glanced at Grant, sitting with the heel of his hand pressed to his forehead, perfectly still, like a hunted animal.

"What happened?" she asked.

"I don't know. He's dead."

"They were waiting?"

"I don't know, I don't know. I got to Racket's room, and one of the guards . . . Yeah, they were waiting, Dubois and two guards.

One of them pulled the trigger—from nerves, just a kid. Like Racket."

"I'm sorry."

"He refused to bail out when we were hit, Racket did. Refused an order, he wouldn't leave me behind. Now look at him."

She drove east in silence, past the workshops of the Swiss Federal Railway outside Olten, then down the bank of the Zugersee to Andermatt, avoiding Lucerne per Grant's curt order. Back at the hospital, Sergeant McNeil had thanked her for the cookies with a crooked grin and an eye to her figure, which would've been insulting if he weren't so boyishly enthusiastic. So much spirit, so quickly snuffed . . . but she needed to think of the future. She needed Grant to force Herr Schürch to decipher the code—there *had* to be a link between that code and the barracks deal—and she no longer knew how to convince him. She'd kept her half of the bargain, but would he?

"We were flying on the German border," Grant said. "We were hit—couldn't get back to England. We saw something, I don't know, an aircraft—five times faster than anything I've ever seen. The thing was—unbelievable. No propellers. I don't know how she stayed in the air . . . some prototype nobody knows the Nazis have. Racket had his handheld, his portable camera, he took a few shots."

He fell silent, and Anna said, "Then you crashed."

"Yeah." He tapped the cigarette pack against his palm. "I didn't want anyone walking away with the film, so I ditched the camera. I got knocked around, I was seeing double—an ambulance took me to the hospital, and I don't know where the crash site is. Racket's my navigator, he can—could've led me right to the spot. Pinpoint McNeil."

"And now?"

"He's dead."

"And the camera?"

"Still there. I need to find the crash site and bring the film to my embassy."

"Surely if you tell them what you saw, they'll send someone."

"That was the plan—then I got framed for escape and assault. And now . . ." He shook his head. "They're not gonna listen. Without the film, this is just a tall tale."

"You can't find the crash site without Sergeant McNeil?"

"No—can you? Maybe in an article at your newspaper?"

"The military keeps that sort of thing under wraps." She considered. "But yes, I imagine I could, given enough time. Perhaps a week?"

"Too long. I'll ask the brigadier general, Leeger."

"The prick on the pony," she said. "Will he tell you?"

He shrugged and fell silent.

She drove south, following the Furka Railway to Gletsch, where she stopped to fill the tank and ask if the Grimsel Pass—twenty-five miles of tortured roadway linking the Upper Valais with the Bernese Oberland—was open. The man told her yes, for another few days. At the foot of the pass a sign pointed toward Totensee, "Lake of the Dead," and she glanced toward Grant, but he'd fallen asleep.

She turned the car into the long packed-earth drive of the farmhouse, down a quiet branch road halfway from Thun to Goldiwil. Views of the choppy lake and the Stockhorn mountains peeked through the forest, and Grant woke so quickly she wondered if he'd been feigning sleep.

"Where are we?"

"The farmhouse Joris found for you, outside Thun."

He surveyed the driveway and the pasture, but didn't seem to notice the *Alphütte* itself, a homey ramshackle place with a neglected kitchen garden and an unevenly shingled roof. "I need a telephone, to talk to Leeger."

"What will you tell him?"

"That Racket's dead. That I need a fix on the crash site."

"And if he won't tell you?"

"I'll think of something. First I need a phone."

She parked in the drive. "We'll leave when Lorenz comes; he's bringing another car. So you—you and Racket could've kept this one. Won't be long."

He nodded and left the car to prowl past the paddocks and around the grain loft, out of sight. She waited in the driver's seat until the chill settled through her jacket, then entered the farmhouse kitchen, where baskets of potatoes and apples sat on the trestle table, and heavy rafters hung with drying herbs. There was a loaf of bread and a wheel of cheese on the counter, and canned vegetables and tins of meat on the shelves. Joris had been here. A woodstove connected to the next room, the *Stube*—the dining and living room—where it worked as a warming oven.

She needed Grant to strong-arm the cryptographer, but what could she do to convince him? Nothing but wait: so she waited.

A hawk wheeled through plumed clouds, and the smell of mulch and snowfall mixed in the crisp air. Grant circled the property, built at the edge of a glacial moraine, with stone retaining walls and a winter barn behind stacks of cordwood. Two levels, one for the herders and one for the livestock, with acres of sloping pastureland.

Quiet until a bunch of yellow-billed crows rose screaming from the trees, disturbed by a strange sound.

Grant stepped into the shaded musky hayloft, and in the silence heard Racket's voice: *When my life flashed in front of my eyes, it was too damn short.* Forget Paris, forget the girls and the jokes. Forget returning home to his mother, who wrote an endless stream of letters, and his father, a lay preacher who always added the same P.S.: "Let nothing disturb you, let nothing affright you. All things are passing. God never changes."

All things are passing. Yeah. Rest in peace, Racket.

Grant breathed in the scent of damp hay, finally heard the sound that had startled the crows: an Audi Cabriolet rumbling toward the *Alphütte*. A reflection of the blue sky slid along the car windows then turned black in the shadow of the house, and Grant knew the girl in the passenger seat from the angle of her chin, which made the man with the bearded banker's face Lorenz. Pebbles crunched and the car stopped and Lorenz stepped out, husky in a respectable brown suit, and opened the door for Rosine. She put a slippered foot on the drive, wrapped her gloved fingers around his hand, and stood an inch from him, her face tilted.

The two stood motionless for too many heartbeats, then Lorenz dropped the girl's hand and didn't touch her again as they went inside. Grant watched the road. Nothing happened after ten minutes, so he followed them into the old farmhouse.

Rosine sliced a loaf of bread on the kitchen counter. She was dressed like a little girl's idea of a Gypsy, with a long gentle face and bony shoulders. Something was different about her, though, something missing. Took him a second to realize what was gone: her oomph.

He glanced toward the murmuring in the next room—Anna and Lorenz—and said, "You can turn it off, like a light switch?"

"*Pardon?*"

"The sex appeal."

She set the slice of bread aside. "It is a mask I wear."

"That's some trick," he said. "What are you doing here?"

"I came with Lorenz."

"Why?"

"Because I love him. Also to take Anna back to Bern and leave you with the car, you and—" She blew a puff of air in that way Frenchwomen did. "I am sorry about your navigator."

He took a hail-pocked apple from a wooden bowl, smooth and cool in his palm.

"And you?" she asked. "Now you leave the country?"

"Gotta call the military attaché first, tell him Racket's dead."

She put the wheel of cheese under her knife. "You will tell how he died?"

"Shot in the line of duty."

"Is that right?"

"The Code of Conduct is pretty clear."

"Ah," she said, noncommittal. "Would you like some cheese? Big slice or little?"

"Big."

"Your forehead is bruised."

"You should see the other guy."

She lopped off a chunk of cheese. "I cannot tell if you are joking—I think you don't know either. Put ice in a cloth and hold that to your forehead. Brush the hair forward to hide the redness."

Lorenz entered from the sitting room, tucking a fountain pen into his breast pocket. "Ah, Lieutenant Grant—but I should call you 'mister.'"

"Call me Grant."

They shook hands and Lorenz took his overcoat from the hook and didn't quite look at Rosine when he spoke to her. "You shouldn't have come along."

She raised her chin. "I missed you. I go too long without your company."

"And if we're seen together?"

"Nobody would look twice, seeing me with a man."

There was a silence like the pause between thunderclap and lightning. Grant said, "I need a telephone."

"Anna will take you to Bern," Lorenz told him, then turned to the girl. "Rosine, come along."

She wound her scarf around her neck, and Lorenz helped her

into her coat without touching her. Grant looked at the hail-pocked apple. Wanting what you couldn't have was easy; needing what you couldn't want, that was a trick.

After they drove away, Grant sat in the parlor, holding a rag of ice chips to his forehead, water dripping down his face. The ache had numbed—that ache, at least.

Anna entered and moved the rag aside to look at the bruise. "How do you feel?"

"Never better."

"You need a new jacket. There's one in the back room missing a few buttons, I'll sew them on."

"This jacket's fine."

"You'll be the only man on the train to Zurich wearing bloodstains. You think the police won't notice?"

"The train to Zurich?"

"Where Herr Schürch lives, the cryptographer." She sat across from him, knees together and back straight. "You're having second thoughts?"

He wiped his forehead with his sleeve, opened the rag and looked at the ice. "I'm having the urge to get that camera."

"The camera's not going anywhere."

"If the Germans put a squadron of those things in the air, we lose England." He put the rag back on his forehead. "I need to get a fix on the crash site."

"Let your brigadier general find the camera."

"I wouldn't trust him to fall downhill."

"Last spring, the Nazis funneled thirteen million francs into Switzerland," she said. "I don't know why, and my only lead is a coded message with today's date. I need a cryptographer, and I'm running out of time." She leaned forward. "The Reichsbank is teetering, Grant, on the verge of collapse. A group of Swiss bankers are supporting the German economy with clearing credits and—"

"You're losing me."

"Listen! How many Swiss are moving money for the Nazis? The same men are involved in this thirteen million franc deal and the clearing credits—they must be. Do you see? They're keeping the Reichsbank solvent. Without money, Grant, how will they build a squadron of these planes?"

"All I—"

"Are you the best man for getting this camera? A fugitive, an escaped prisoner? No. I'll send Lorenz, once we find your plane."

"In a week."

"Yes, there's no rush—unlike with this coded message."

"Send Lorenz to the cryptographer."

"He isn't like us."

He looked at her, surprised. "Are we alike? Martin and I were different as—"

"I'm not Martin," she said.

"No, you're not." A sudden fierce urge surprised him: he wanted to see her disheveled, her hair tangled and face flushed, her lips swollen. "Good thing, too."

She must've heard the hunger in his voice. She lowered her head and for a moment they listened to the wind. Then she said, "Have you heard of Roald Amundsen, the first man to reach the South Pole?"

He didn't answer, watching her, watching the play of light on her skin.

"He started with a hundred dogs," she said, "which he killed and ate on schedule. By the last push, only forty-two were left. This was his plan: at the final mountain—the Butcher Shop—they'd slaughter twenty-four dogs, and upon reaching the pole they'd shoot six of the remaining eighteen. An efficient plan, no?"

"Sounds like."

"He and his men reached the pole without loss of human life."

"What's the moral? 'Eat your sled dogs'?"

"Another man left for the pole, weeks before Amundsen—Captain Scott. But he was an animal lover; his men hauled sleds themselves and they arrived a month too late, found Amundsen's flag already planted. On the return trip, snow-blind and frostbitten, a storm caught them twelve miles from a cache of food."

"They died twelve miles short?"

"Not all of them. One died earlier, when he crawled into a blizzard. He was crippled with gangrene, he didn't want to slow the party. His last words were, 'I am just going outside and may be some time.' "

Grant's headache throbbed with his heart. "That takes guts."

"There's more. They were starving to death, they'd rationed every ounce of food, they had had scurvy and frostbite, but they still dragged thirty-five pounds of geological specimens 750 miles. Thirty-five pounds of rocks."

"Why?"

"A matter of principle," she said. "They promised they'd return with the rocks."

"Some principle—they didn't return at all."

"Which one is Lorenz, Grant? Captain Scott or Roald Amundsen?"

"There's only two choices?"

"For you and me, there's only one. Amundsen reached the pole first, his men survived. Can there be any question which man you'd emulate?"

"Nobody would choose Scott," he told her. " 'Eat your sled dogs.' "

"And that morning at the Butcher Shop, could Lorenz have checked the schedule and slaughtered twenty-four good and faithful dogs?"

Grant didn't answer. This was some kind of woman's conversation, with currents of meaning he didn't understand—but he still felt the water closing over his head. He went into the kitchen and tossed the damp rag at the sink, ate another apple, then returned to the parlor and leaned against the wall. Anna had unearthed a sewing basket and was putting buttons on a tweed jacket. He watched her work, intent and enclosed, lit by some internal glow.

"We'll leave when I finish this," she said, tugging at a thread. "First to Bern, and when you're satisfied I'll find the crash site, then to Zurich."

"Long as I can call Leeger."

"And then?"

"Then I'll meet your cryptographer."

"Good." She finished the button in silence, and started another. "You're staring."

"Yeah," he said. "What's with Lorenz and Rosine?"

"Lorenz won't touch her as a—" She tugged at a knot. "As husband and wife."

"I saw him not touch her; they're lucky the roof didn't catch fire."

"Still, he won't. You know why."

Because other men did. "Sure, but if she's—if your woman's a singer, let her sing for you. That's one of the benefits."

"I read your letters, Grant, I know you're not that unfeeling." Anna set the tweed jacket aside. "He won't touch her now so that next year, or the year after, they'll be different people, with different lives and different pasts. When they marry she will go to him as a—untouched."

"They're engaged?"

"Yes."

He shook his head. "Too European."

"They're in love," she said, "and at war."

"Okay." He couldn't see it. "I can see that."

She laughed. "Liar."

"Well, yeah." He smiled at her laughter, and raised his hands in defeat. "You have any cigarettes?"

"On the shelf."

"You want one?"

She shook her head and cut a thread with a pair of scissors. "Rosine was already raising money for refugees, Grant. The Swiss, you know, we accept refugees, except for Jews. If the Swiss Jews can't pay the price, they're turned back at the border. Rosine was a refugee herself, she had no money to contribute, so . . ."

"She's a Jewess? I thought she was a—*parisienne*."

"When I met her, she allowed herself to be kept by certain generous and influential men."

"To raise money for refugees. Then you recruited her?"

She nodded. "Now she raises information, too."

"For you."

"For a great deal more than me, if only I can make her sacrifice worthwhile."

"For the British? The Russians? Who are you—"

"The Russians." Her eyes narrowed. "Cyrillic."

"—trying to . . . What?"

"The note, the words." She crossed the room. "The letters are in Cyrillic, half of them, that's all."

"Russian? What note?"

She unclasped her bag for a sheet of paper. "The note I want to decrypt. Loeffert only used Cyrillic letters that look like French— none of the too-foreign ones. See here? That's why some of the *n*'s are blocky, the angular *b*'s and capital *A*'s. Do you speak Russian?"

"Not a word."

"I need a Russian dictionary, not a cryptographer."

"That's today," he said, looking over her shoulder at the date. "Tonight."

"If I'm right, we don't need Schürch." She moved to the door. "You drive."

CHAPTER 23

Grant overtook the rumbling lorry and looked at Anna. "Who exactly do you work for?"

"Nobody. Anybody. Watch the road."

He drifted into the right lane. "That's clear."

"We pass along what information we find, that's all, to whomever we can." Her coal-fire hair caught the sunlight through the car window. "Personnel of the German embassy, number of boxcars crossing the border, domestic secrets of frontists. Nothing but gossip and commonplaces. Until now."

"You think this woman, Magda Loeffert, she's the real McCoy."

"McCoy?"

"You think she's genuine."

"I know she is."

"And she left this note in a hotel room, half in Russian?" He tapped his cigarette in the ashtray. "She's playing a game."

"What game?"

"I don't know," he said. "And neither do you."

"She wrote the list for her own use, that's what I think. She threw away the second page because she's cautious—and afraid." She looked down the road. "Take a left where the sign says Kirchenfeld."

"When you fly into a cloud bank, you start seeing shapes."

"You think I'm seeing what I want to see?"

He shrugged. "I'm a pilot, not a spy. And you're a teacher, a mother, and a wife."

"A widow," she said.

He passed the Bernese History Museum, turned at Helvetiaplatz toward the bridge. Anna's silence thickened in the car, and he finally said, "Yeah."

"Tell me about Martin," she said. "How did they kill him?"

"Does it matter?"

"You think I can't bear knowing, but not knowing is worse. Imagining is worse."

"He didn't suffer."

"I know they didn't shoot him."

He looked at the traffic on the bridge. "Bayonet."

"And what happened to you?"

"In China?"

"Yes."

"Nothing, I'm still here."

She touched his cheek with gloved fingers.

"By the time I left China," he said, "I was Captain Scott. That's what happened. You think I'm the other guy, but I'm not. I lost my edge, I saw this girl, this highborn Chinese girl, I saw her die and— I'm like an empty gun, I've got nothing left."

"Tell me in plain German."

"There's nothing to tell. I lost my nerve."

"You saw too much blood," she said. "You lost your taste for violence."

"I had an edge and now it's blunted, that's all."

She took the cigarette from his mouth. "Maybe you didn't lose your nerve, maybe you found your heart." She killed the butt in the ashtray. "Are you a good soldier, Grant?"

"I'm nobody's idea of perfect."

"You're not so bad," she told him. "Park there. Call your brigadier general, and we'll meet at the hotel."

"You're chasing your tail with this woman," he said, pulling to the curb. "Because you think she's got what you need."

"We're all chasing something, Grant. We're all chasing what we think we need."

Anna entered the hotel through the service door, stepped into the stairwell, and found a note under the banister: "My office." Lorenz's handwriting. She went downstairs into a clean dim hallway, past the boiler rooms where her heels tapped bleakly along rows of locked doors. What if Grant were right, and this was a goose chase? What if her drive to honor Martin's memory resulted in nothing more than a neglected son? What if—

She stopped at an odd scuffle down the hall and called, "Hello?"

No answer but the whir of an exhaust fan. One of the janitors, most likely. She looked over her shoulder at the long empty corridor, broken by recessed doorways. Turned back, and a man was standing five feet from her—she gave a little shriek and pressed her palm to her chest.

"Pardon me, Fräulein." The man smiled in apology. "I'm a bit lost."

"Looking for your room?"

"Oh, I'm not a guest, I'm a commercial traveler, a salesman. Hoping to meet one of the assistant managers. A Herr Lorenz?"

"You might ask at the front desk," she told him. "Back upstairs, through there, and you'll be in the lobby."

He thanked her and left, and she went through the swinging

doors, climbed the half stairway to the offices. She found Lorenz at his desk, surrounded by open books, a cigar butt smoldering in the ashtray.

"I have news, Lorenz, about—"

"Wait." He offered her his cigar case. "Take one."

"You know I don't smoke."

"Then I'll have yours." He extracted a cigar and snipped the end. "We're celebrating. Turns out Loeffert is Russian-born, and—"

"The note's in Cyrillic, or at least some letters are—the rest is French, that's why I missed it. We don't need a cryptographer, just a Russian dictionary."

He tapped a book on his desk, sighing theatrically. "Always one step ahead of me."

"That's a dictionary? You already knew?"

"Her neighbor finally returned my call. He told me a bit more, too—but you probably already know."

"I don't know anything. What did you learn?"

"Her parents were servants at the Russian embassy. She married a businessman, Herr Loeffert, has a daughter, Nadya Loeffert, and a year after the wedding was widowed without two francs."

"Russian, so you looked for the Cyrillic?"

"Yes, it's not her handwriting that's odd, it's the letters themselves. In the note, she only uses Russian letters that look somewhat like French ones—phonetic spellings of words in three languages, her personal shorthand."

"That's all? Everything we've done—I asked Grant to strong-arm a frontist cryptographer just to read her personal shorthand?" Anna laughed in disbelief. "We're lucky it's not just a shopping list."

"Well, in fact, it reads 'milk, cheese, two loaves of bread . . .' "

"Liar! What does it really say?"

"I'm not sure yet. I've only figured out a few words."

"Must be important, or she wouldn't have used the shorthand."

"Not necessarily. She was an executive secretary, she must've taken many sensitive notes, she may have written this way out of habit. Accustomed to working in finance, I mean, and not wanting anyone to read her notes at a glance."

"But with more than a glance?"

He showed her a copy of the note, beside a Russian-French dictionary. "This one here is 'Mirador.' That's M-n-p-a-A-o-p, in Arabic letters, but Loeffert mixes them however she pleases. So Mirador, see?"

Anna nodded slowly. "Mirador is what?"

"I've no idea. Mirador Hotel? Mirador restaurant?"

"Each item is a place-name?"

"So far. Take this one, this one's clever." He tapped the page. "See 'Yepy'? That sounds out the English word 'church,' in Cyrillic letters."

"Church as in . . . *Kirche*?"

"Exactly. The English Church."

"Here in Bern?"

"Could be anywhere. As for the rest—I'm halfway through the list. This one is Promenade du Lac."

"In Geneva." She thought for a moment. "Or Lugano."

"Or Zurich or Lucerne . . ."

"And the date and time?"

Lorenz shrugged. "Far as I can tell, that's what it looks like. Today, this evening."

"Less than three hours," she said. "We need to cross-reference each of these places against all the towns in Switzerland. Find the one city that has every place mentioned—this is a list of rendezvous. What's next? This one with 'KadpN'?"

She ran her finger along the words "PeageHCy KadpN."

Lorenz consulted a chart of Cyrillic letters in one of the open books. "KadpN sounds like Kadpee, Kadpay, Kafay . . ."

"Café!"

"Ah, good. Then 'PeageHCy.' Starts with a sound like 'Py' or 'Ry,' maybe 'Peh' or 'Reh,' then the *g* is . . . there's no Cyrillic *g*. Then 'e-H-C-y' . . ."

She looked at the grid he'd made. "Pebensoo? Rygensch?"

"Regency. Régence Café."

In twenty minutes, they'd figured the rest: the Jetée des Pâquis, Rue du Port, George & Cie, and the Maccabee Chapel.

"Geneva." Lorenz rummaged in a desk drawer. "I've a map somewhere. Run to the travel bureau, get a guidebook. We can plot these like points on a graph."

She opened the door. "We have two hours, Lorenz."

A man stepped forward from the corridor—the salesman, the commercial traveler—and lifted his hand to her ear, like he was tidying her hair.

The underside of Lorenz's desk. Anna eyed the baseboard molding and the electrical socket from which two black cords sprouted. She didn't understand. She focused on a paper clip half buried in the carpet, ten inches from her face.

She heard the door close and a chair topple, and a half shout choke into a grunt. A reference book hit the floor and the pages unfurled. Brown shoes scuffed in the corner of her vision, and an electrical cord drew suddenly taut. A heavy thump, then a lightbulb shattered and shards of glass rained down, bounced, and caught in the carpet's nap.

"Get quiet," the salesman whispered, "or get cut."

She heard Lorenz struggle for breath. "Bastard. You bastard."

"Call for help and I kill your secretary." Something touched Anna's calf, and she felt the chill of air on her thighs, her skirt pushed to her waist. "I've no need of *her*, Herr Lorenz, the woman I want is Magda Loeffert."

"Never heard of—"

A blow, and a gasp. More scuffling, the whisper of cloth, then a faint clicking and a metallic hiss.

"No," Lorenz said. "No, please."

"Cigars," the salesman said. "Filthy habit. What's this, a snipper to cut the ends?"

"Don't."

"Fits nicely."

"Please." With rising panic. "Please don't, no!"

Shadows jerked from the floor to the wall. Anna couldn't remember how to stand, couldn't think of a reason she'd want to. Something rattled on the desktop, miles above, pages ripped from a book, over and over. A match flared.

"Oh Lord, stop, no, I'll tell you, I tell you everything."

"I know you will."

The sounds of struggle, then softly strained cries and muffled screams. A shoe scuffled desperately against the side of the desk.

"I'm removing the gag," the salesman finally said. "Don't scream." A choking noise, and a wad of crumpled pages landed on the carpet. "If you don't tell me what I want, Herr Lorenz, we start again at the beginning."

Anna heard jagged sobs and the desperate struggle for air.

"Start talking, or—"

"I will!" Lorenz said, panicked. "I will, just . . . please, no more. I'm looking for Loeffert, I work for a journalist, he pays me, he wants to find her—these are, this is a list, she stayed here, Loeffert took a room at the hotel. The journalist paid me to—she stayed here, she left this page. It's a list. In Russian and French. These are, they're places, in Geneva. Look. Look, they're all in Geneva."

"In Geneva. And this is today's date."

Anna curled her fingers, pressed her nails into her palm. Her head throbbed, the pain a cutting wire across her temples.

"Yes, today, in two hours. Please."

"The Regency Café," the salesman said, thoughtfully. "Who's the journalist?"

"Pierre-Luc, Pierre-Luc Soyer."

"I know your name," the salesman said. "I know where you work, I know where you live. Report this to the authorities, and we'll meet again."

A heavy weight slammed the desk three times. Anna lay on the floor. She couldn't hear Lorenz. She couldn't hear anything but her own heartbeat and a steady dripping *plop plop plop*.

The telephone hung on the cloakroom wall in the Viennese Café, where a row of big windows faced the street and white-linen tables gleamed with silverware. Grant dialed the number and waited for the connection, rolling his shoulders in the tweed jacket. He couldn't rely on Anna's nebulous "contacts," he needed to tell someone about the camera—but not Leeger, not unless there was no other choice. Well, he'd try to get the location of the crash site, then he'd see where he stood.

Leeger came on the phone, and Grant said, "Brigadier General, thanks for waiting."

"I didn't," Leeger said. "Where are you, Lieutenant?"

"The post office, sir. My navigator, Sergeant—"

"McNeil. He's dead, and you put two Swiss in the hospital, one of them a commandant."

Grant looked at the birdcage in the corner of the café, where silent yellow birds hopped from perch to perch. "He was shot trying to escape. I could use some help, sir."

"How about advice, Lieutenant?"

This was gonna be as easy as pulling teeth. "Yes, sir?"

"I offered you that already, in the form of an order: do not escape from Swiss authority."

"Yeah, I—"

"Disobeyed."

"The Code of Conduct—"

"You assaulted an officer of a neutral nation. You are solely re-sponsible for the death of your sergeant."

"What about the guy who shot him?"

"You find this funny, Lieutenant?"

"I'll answer charges back in England. Right now what I need is this: Racket left some personal items in the Mosquito, some letters I'd like to return to his—"

"You're at the post office in Bern?"

"What? No, Geneva."

"That's not what the switchboard tells me. Look outside, you should see the police approaching. They have your service photo-graph, they are aware you attacked a Swiss officer. Don't make this any worse than—"

Grant hung up and checked the street through the big windows. A few cars, a handful of businessmen, a scattering of housewives waiting for the tram. Maybe there were Swiss cops at the post office and maybe not, but this street looked clear: at least until the switch-board gave Leeger a better fix.

He slipped outside and headed down the block. The police had his picture—he wasn't just an escapee anymore, but a violent crim-inal who put an officer in the hospital. Only one thing to do: put himself in Anna's hands. He followed a streetcar down Schauplatz-gasse, to the edge of the plaza at the Bundespalast, the Federal Pal-ace. Soldiers stepped from side streets and rode past in army trucks, city workers wore martial uniforms, a traffic cop guarded the inter-section. Grant kept his eyes down, circled toward the Palace Hotel and pushed into the service entrance.

Found his way through a maze of corridors to Lorenz's office. The door swung open when he knocked, and he stepped inside and almost onto Anna's out-flung arm—sprawled on the carpet, skirt bunched at her waist, a trickle of blood across her temple.

"Anna." He knelt beside her, his throat suddenly tight. "Anna?"

Her unfocused gaze snapped to his face. "Lorenz."

"No, it's Grant." He ran his fingers over her scalp. "You took one to the head, you must've fallen—"

Then he saw Lorenz slumped facedown at his desk and he straightened, scanning the room. Nobody there, and no sound but the blood dripping from Lorenz's palm and soaking the carpet. No, not from his palm—from his severed pinkie.

"Something happened," Anna whispered, her voice vague. "Grant? Is that you? I think something happened."

He grabbed the phone and told the switchboard to send help. "Yeah, to Herr Lorenz's office. Any medical staff in the hotel—and an ambulance."

"Lorenz?" Anna said, her voice stronger. "Lorenz? Oh my Lord, is he—"

"He's okay." Grant tourniqueted Lorenz's pinkie with tape from the desk. "He's passed out, but—"

"I n-need to. Go now." She tried to push herself from the floor. "You have to. Take me. To Geneva now."

"You need a doctor, you're not going anywhere."

"This is the, the closest we've . . ." Her voice faded. "The man who did this, he's after Loeffert. In Geneva. The list—on the desk. Rendezvous. I have to meet her tonight." She crawled to her knees. "Before he does."

He took her in his arms. "Lorenz needs a hospital."

"You stay with him."

"The police have my photograph, I can't be here when they—" She saw Lorenz and paled. "Oh, sweet God."

She swayed, and he thought she'd faint. Instead, she snapped back into herself, standing with sudden strength and crossing to Lorenz, murmuring reassurances, her quick competent fingers moving over his burned and bleeding face, his broken elbow and severed pinkie. Lorenz groaned in protest then mumbled a few words, his voice little more than a gasp.

Anna leaned close, listening, a trickle of blood running from her temple to her chin, then turned to Grant. "Lorenz gave the man the list in the wrong order. You need to go to Geneva and meet Magda Loeffert. First stop, the *Au Mirador* teahouse."

"You're asking me to—"

"I'm not asking," she said.

CHAPTER 24

Akimov splashed English-rose bath salts into the steaming water and watched them drift to the bottom of the claw-foot tub. Smelled nothing like roses, nothing like salt. Maybe they smelled like England. He shifted uncomfortably, sloshing water over the edge, the beating at the bookseller having woken the pain of a hundred thrashings, a hundred boots. He washed the shiny pink of his stump, the bones grinding beneath stretched skin, and hummed the refrain from some half-remembered ditty: *Her son's been jailed and her husband's dead, say a prayer for her instead.*

He soaked until the ache faded, listening to the silent calm of Switzerland, then stood from the bath and brushed his teeth with the cherry-flavored paste from the chemist, watching his face disappear into the fog of the mirror. *This is Loeffert's ex-husband, fucking everything up.*

In the back room of the antiquarian bookstore, the heavyset man had roughly released him.

"You were told to find your wife," the lanky man had said, "or let her find you—not to interfere with us. You're tracking your wife in the wrong direction."

So they were Red Orchestra. Akimov had limped to the table, and started refilling his satchel. "You're the ones who sent her running."

"She's a wrecker, a kulak. Her country needs her and she's flirting with the West."

"You're so sure of—" He stopped at a sharp ache in his gut. "Of this document?"

"It ties a Swiss firm to the Nazis through a sham barracks deal. The Swiss get millions of francs, far in excess of what the barracks are worth. They use the money to start a corporation as a front for German intelligence in Switzerland."

"What has this to do with Russia?"

"Nothing . . . except your wife wanted to pry more records from her source, whoever he is, using this transaction as leverage. She's sure he's got his fingers in other pies. Like the Swiss support of the Reichsbank. And maybe these negotiations."

"You don't know even the name of her source?"

"Welcome to Switzerland, these firms wrap around each other like a ball of yarn. This document is one thread—we start tugging, the whole thing unravels. The Swiss loan billions to the Fascists, they—" The man sighed. "This blackmail could tip the scales, that's all. We must use the barracks deal to influence the negotiations. Your wife arranged to meet us, then vanished. She wants to go to the West instead."

"If she wants to," he'd said, "she will."

"She tried, and we were waiting. We spooked her, that's why we need you." The lanky man had shaken his head in disgust. "Now get the hell out, and tell your father the deputy commissar we need 15,000 francs. This shop is blown, thanks to you."

In the hotel bathroom, Akimov wiped the mirror clean with his palm and looked at his face. *Her son's been jailed and her husband's dead, say a prayer for her instead.* He shrugged, then dressed and knocked on the connecting door.

At the rumbling invitation, he stepped through.

The air smelled of velvet and scotch, and his father sat in an armchair, a book open in his lap. "Twenty years, Edik. How well do you remember Switzerland?"

"Another lifetime," Akimov said.

"Every month I'd leave the embassy on imaginary business, do you remember? I'd take you from school, we'd go sailing or hiking. Do you remember the mountaintop restaurant we found? You ate so much I threatened to roll you home."

They'd spent the day mushroom hunting, his father telling tales of "Ivan the Fool," magical stories of Russia, of spirits and heroes and home. "No," he said. "I remember none of that."

His father lowered his head. In a moment, he lifted the book from his lap, embossed with a gold cross with extra bars: a Bible of the Old Believers. "Then do you remember this?"

"Magda's Bible? You took it from my house?"

"After the arrest."

"I'm surprised you didn't burn it."

"A burnt offering? Well, sometimes a sacrifice is necessary, to propitiate the gods."

"I sacrificed 15,000 francs this morning." Akimov told the story. "And I'm no closer to finding Magdalena."

His father's eyes filled with disappointment. "How many men die at Stalingrad alone? Twenty-five thousand a week since July. There's quiet on the front, for two days now—two days without gunfire, imagine that. Yet three thousand of our countrymen die on the day we fail, and three thousand the day after that. Unless you find Magda, unless you—"

Akimov backhanded him in the face. "You think *you* can tell *me*?"

A heavy silence swallowed the sound of the slap. Akimov's father raised his fingers to his cheek, below his wounded eyes. "Of all men, you should understand. What would *you* not sacrifice for Russia?"

"My only son."

"Easy to say, until you must choose."

Akimov raised his hand again—in anger or surrender, he didn't know—and Big Vlad loomed from nowhere and rammed him against the wall. Little Vlad lifted a truncheon and—

"No!" his father barked, touching his bruised mouth. "Back in his room."

Little Vlad grunted and grabbed Akimov's collar. Dragged him across the room and shoved him through the adjoining door.

Akimov stumbled into his room, pressing the back of his hand to his cheek. That was all? One slap? All the rage, and he hit the man once and felt nothing but empty. The door slammed behind him and he went to the window. Cars crawled down the streets, people stood at fountains and shops. A city of ants, and he was no better.

After a time, a warbling chime rose behind him. He answered the phone and a woman's voice said, "Edik."

He sat on the bed. "Magdalena."

Silence on the line, yet he knew she was there. A silver thread connected them, from the mouthpiece of his phone down the wire to the switchboard, across the city to her room, into the receiver, warmed by her breath.

Finally she said, "Hearing your voice again, after so long."

"Yes." He closed his eyes. "You, too."

"We're old now, Edik. The world is old."

"You're forty, and still melodramatic as a child."

"Thirty-nine," she corrected. "Until next month."

"Remember your eighteenth birthday?"

"At that fleabag café in—" She stopped. "I don't even recall the town."

"I proposed."

"You were drunk."

"And impossibly young."

"We both were."

"I thought—" He laughed. "I thought I'd forgotten you."

"You thought you no longer cared, Edik. There must be a great deal you'd like to forget."

So she knew he'd been in the gulag. "Not a single day."

"Why? Because if you forget, you also forgive? Then you admit I was right, all those years ago?"

About the Revolution, the Soviet state. "You were half right."

"I heard you were looking for me, Edik. A friend at the Muscovite Club said you were staying at the Palace. I hardly believed it was you."

"They sent me here to find you. For the document you told them you have—and never delivered."

"You still obey them?"

"I still love Russia."

She was silent for a moment. "Can I trust you, Edik?"

"You can trust *me*." Meaning him alone, not the men with him, not the men behind him. "We need this document."

"The rot is too deep, I can't give this to anyone who—"

"Four days ago I was in Stalingrad, Magda. My men—I lost five men fighting for a kitchen. We're dying for empty rooms."

"What has this to do with Stalingrad?"

"Everything—what *else* is this about?"

"Ending Swiss support of the Nazis."

"Support? Your document can force the Swiss bankers to push the talks forward, to bring the Nazis to the table and—"

"What talks? What table?"

Didn't take a moment to decide he needed to tell her. "Cease-fire talks, Magda. They're negotiating for a truce, the precursor to another non-aggression pact."

"A Nazi-Soviet truce?" she said. "They told you this?"

"They shipped me from the front to find you, do you think they care so much about Swiss money laundering?"

"Another pact? That's—"

"The Germans are overextended, and we're one bad day from losing Stalingrad. There's an informal cease-fire in the city now, for the past few days—this can happen. This *must* happen. Talks start this week. Give me your document, and maybe the battle will stop."

"You care about ending the battle, Edik, I care about ending the war."

"Meet me, Magda. Let me see you. Let me convince you."

"You won't."

"Let me try. Where are you?"

Silence on the line. "Geneva."

"I'll be there in an hour."

"At seven o'clock, the Au Mirador tea room. Come alone, Edik—I'll be watching from afar. If I catch a whiff of the NKVD, I disappear."

She rang off, and he lowered the phone into the cradle, and the thought came from nowhere: Did she know he'd lost an arm? Still the nervous suitor after twenty years. He smiled. At least his breath smelled like cherries.

His father pushed into the room, flanked by the Vlads. "Well done, Edik!" He checked his watch. "A date at a tea shop, well done indeed."

The white-lettered sign of the Au Mirador tearoom shuddered as a lake breeze bustled along the Rue du Mont-Blanc. Grant stepped inside, and warmth wrapped him in the scent of chestnut puree and poppy cake. He removed his hat and the hostess said something in French.

He shook his head. "*Deutsch?*"

"A cold wind across the lake, tonight," she said, in German.

"I'm looking for a woman," he told her. At least he thought he was—he had the list Anna deciphered, and that's all he knew. "Frau Loeffert?"

"I'm sorry, there is nobody waiting. Perhaps she has not yet arrived."

Stay or leave? The police had his photo, the army had a grudge, and the guy who'd tortured Lorenz was somewhere behind him. He should be keeping his profile low—instead, he ordered a cake and sat on a spindly wooden chair. Was he supposed to wait? Check each location as fast as possible? Wear a yellow fucking rose in his hat?

No idea. No idea except: Anna. That much he knew, running around Switzerland like a besotted schoolboy.

He finished the cake and stepped into the Geneva night, toward the Quai du Mont-Blanc, past buildings with grids of shutters and balconies, and a cobbled plaza with three gnarled trees like the witches in *Macbeth*. At the English Church, a man scolded a sagging horse in an incomprehensible dialect and a cat darted across the street. Grant leaned against the wrought-iron fence, and—

Someone was following him.

A municipal bus wheezed onto Rue de Chantepoulet, a schoolboy slouched against a postbox, men in bowler hats waited at the corner, functionaries of the League of Nations. He turned onto the quay and paused at the Rue des Alpes as if he were enjoying the view of the mountains. Nobody looked out of place. Not the women in furs, not the car sweeping along the quayside toward Les Pâquis, its engine noise blending with the lapping waves in the harbor.

Grant struck a match under a streetlamp that gave no light—none of them did, not since the Nazis demanded the Swiss black out Geneva to keep British pilots from using the city as a directional beacon during night raids. He leaned against the guardrail, listening to the lake, then tossed the dead match into the gutter and drifted toward the Brunswick Monument. He stopped at a city bench, rearranged his shoelace, and checked the street again. Everything was familiar: the two men huddled under an awning, the woman walking briskly past the taxi rank. Somewhere, a door slammed, and he rubbed the back of his neck against a chill.

At the Casino Municipal, he paused below the terrace at the Régence Café. Two boys ran past in dark evening coats, followed by an elegant old woman in a shimmering dress and velvet gloves. No one who could be Magda Loeffert. Five minutes away, a stubborn wind shoved at the bathing machines at the Jetée des Pâquis. Grant boarded the tram, and across the river strolled down the Promenade du Lac, then Rue du Port on the way to George & Cie booksellers. Nothing. He wandered into the narrow ancient streets of Old Town in the shadow of the Saint-Pierre Cathedral, and paused to light a cigarette on the doorstep of the concierge. Nearby, a carved stone lion with flowing curls and a gargoyle face guarded a shuttered window.

Grant paused in the entry of the Maccabee Chapel, watching a woman push a wicker baby carriage. Magda? He tapped ash from his cigarette and a gun barrel dug into his side.

CHAPTER 25

A machine growled in the rail yard outside, and Nadya's hair-brush quivered on the leather chair. She glanced toward the boarded window, then returned to rubbing the ache from her forearms. The floor of the passenger car shuddered several times a day, and the walls shook—and nothing changed, she remained alone in her captivity.

This was no mere prison, though: the isolation and vulnerability tested her faith, and she'd been granted strength. By slow degrees, her prison became her hermitage; the morning prayers, the psalms, the small compline, the three canons, the prayer before sleep. Raised unreligious, Nadya had found faith as a teenager—and discovered it was the beating of her heart.

She said a prayer for her mother, who did not believe, and stepped into the shoe-shine room: she worked for salvation not only in prayer but in the cabinet where the ribbed wooden grate was bolted to the wall. She crawled inside, grabbed the bent fish fork and worked the tines around the bottom right bolt. She'd already dug the top right bolt from the frame, only three more to go. Her arms burned and her shoulders cramped, she closed her eyes and drifted into a haze, scraping and repeating under her breath: *Christ is risen from the dead, trampling on death by death and the stone rolled away and the Angel said, Christ is risen from the dead* . . .

Grant raked his right arm down to knock the gun away and swung at his assailant's face with his left hand. The impact stung the heel of his hand and he followed through, spinning and dragging his assailant to the ground before the details struck: the fan of hair, the scent of face powder, the feminine cry.

And the words: "*Nein! I'm Loeffert!*"

He knelt on her forearm, looking down: dark hair shot with gray, fine wide eyes, and the gun in her hand was a rolled pamphlet.

"Dangerous trick," he said. "Where's your ID?"

"My purse."

He checked her papers, and she was Magdalena Loeffert. He shifted his weight off her arm. "You're a hard woman to find."

"You're working with Anna Fay out of Bern." She got to her feet, raising an eyebrow at his expression. "Maybe I'm not such a fool after all."

"Let's move."

"There is nobody behind you, I've been watching since the tea shop."

"They might be ahead—they got your note."

She made a noise in her throat. "Then quickly, somewhere private." She scanned the street, the towers of the Hotel de Ville. "The university library. Two hundred meters, we'll be safe there."

They started walking and he said, "How do you know me?"

"From watching Frau Fay's house."

"You have the documents?"

She shivered in the moon-cast shadow of chestnut trees on the terrace of La Treille. "I have more than documents."

"What else?"

"News. Disturbing news." She led him across the Rue de la Croix-Rouge, her face white and worried. "Come, quickly."

"Why write the note in Russian code?"

She remained silent until they passed the grim statues of the Reformation Monument. "What note?"

"At the Palace Hotel. We got the second page imprints."

"Second page—? No, that wasn't for anyone but myself." She led him around a row of park benches, onto the university grounds. "I planned to give these documents away, but I was nervous, I wanted to play hide-and-seek before letting anyone close."

"That explains the list of meeting points, but why the code?"

"It's not code, it's my personal shorthand for sensitive documents. I write that way from fear, for security, to keep anyone from following me." She shook her head. "None of that matters. I told one of the Soviets about the tea shop, and you arrived an hour before my—before him. They'll wait, I want to talk to you first."

"Talk? Give me the documents, and I'm gone."

"Who are you?"

"The long arm of Mrs. Fay."

She stopped outside a light brick building. "You said 'they' got my note? The Soviets?"

"Anna only saw one man—probably German. She called him a 'salesman.' "

The woman frowned, then pushed through the library door into a dark foyer.

"My ex-employer often hired Germans, one in particular. A man named Pongratz." She led Grant down a corridor lined with glass display cases, around a corner into a reading room, and stopped at a table beside a long window. "I met him once, he was quiet and polite."

"Like a salesman?"

"Yes." She tapped her fingernails anxiously on a bronze bust of Henri IV on the tabletop. "With nothing human in his eyes."

"Your ex-boss is the one named in the documents?"

She nodded. "He arranged for the Swiss Wood Syndicate to sell hutments—barracks—to the Nazis. Laundering money to fund an SS initiative in Switzerland. Import wood from Germany, construct the barracks, ship them back. That's what started me looking, yes?"

"Sure. You have the documents?"

She lowered her head, hair slanting across her eyes. "I found paperwork, purchase orders and the like, I gave several to Frau Fay already."

"Give me the rest."

"Then today I learned more."

"What's that?"

She turned to the window, staring toward a tree trunk engulfed by spidery bushes. "There's only one thing worse than the Soviets—the Germans."

"Sure," he said.

"And Germany was a democracy, too. The only reason Hitler became chancellor is this: cowards rally to bullies. The Law for the Protection of the People and the State, my foot! More people voted against Hitler than for him, the Reichstag gave him *temporary* powers against an imaginary enemy—"

"Are you gonna tell me what you learned?"

"I don't know yet."

"Decide quick."

After a moment, she nodded. "The Russians sent an emissary to Switzerland, to negotiate a new non-aggression pact with Germany."

"The—what?"

"You heard me. They're working on a second Nazi-Soviet pact."

"They're meeting here?"

"Maybe Hitler's agreed to the talks, maybe von Ribbentrop wants to present a fait accompli—I only heard today, my head's still swimming. The talks start in a few days. If there's peace between Stalin and Hitler, the Nazis will sweep the West away."

He shook his head. "Impossible."

"Do you have children?"

"What? No."

"My daughter won't live under the heel of the Germans, not if I can stop them. Everything hinges on my employer, he has—"

A door opened in the hallway and she froze. They waited, but heard only silence.

"He has leverage on the Germans," she continued, more softly. "Through his firm and his position on a government board, he supports the Reichsbank."

"The credits . . . clearing credits?"

She nodded, her eyes quick with thought. "Anna Fay confirmed that? I suspected, but I'm still putting the pieces together—yet I do know the documents I took provide leverage of our own."

"On your boss?"

"Mm. To learn about his other deals, to force everything he does into the open. But he sent Pongratz after me." Her voiced tightened. "I'm not a woman given to fear, but Herr Pongratz terrifies me. And now this non-aggression pact changes everything."

"Give me the documents, and you're done."

"What can Anna Fay do about the pact? Nothing."

"She might surprise you."

"He said—the Soviets said there's quiet on the front. In Stalingrad, at least. For two days now, no fighting, the precursor to peace."

"Give me the papers, we'll—"

"You think I carry them in my purse? They're not even in this canton, they're with an old friend, I sent my—"

A chair scraped against the floor and shadows climbed the far wall—men burst into the reading room and raced down the aisle, closing fast around the bookshelves.

Grant scooped the bust of Henri IV through the long window.

Glass exploded and he grabbed Loeffert's arm and went sideways into the night, hunched against slicing sheets of glass, and slammed against the tree trunk. Flashes of flame spat from inside the library—Loeffert shrieked and bullets tore through the spidery bushes and a voice called in German, "Not the woman!"

Grant dragged Loeffert down the gap between the hedge and the library wall, until she dug in her heels, coughing into her hand. "Herr Doktor Hostettler," she breathed. "Johannes Hostettler. Has the documents."

Grant yanked her arm—a dead weight. "Are you hit?"

"It doesn't hurt." She sagged against him, her eyes glazing over. "Nothing . . . hurts. I need to—"

"Come. Lean on me. Don't talk."

She smiled weakly, teeth tinged red. "Tell my daughter. I love her."

The Germans crunched over the broken glass behind them, and Grant lifted her into his arms. "Tell her yourself."

"I can't . . . Tell her. Tell Nadya."

He shoved through a trip-wire thicket, carrying Loeffert like a bride, stumbling blind across a dark path. "Hold on. Listen to me. Stay with me."

"Tell my daughter. That every day . . . for nineteen years, I thanked a God . . . I don't believe in. For giving me her."

"Tell her yourself."

"Herr Johannes Hostettler. Has the papers." She coughed and gasped. "Herr Doktor Hostettler, Johannes Hostettler . . ."

Her head lolled back, her white neck porcelain in the moonlight. Dead.

. . .

At the sound of boots, Grant lay the body on a park bench and stepped into the trees. Magda Loeffert, fighting for her daughter, fighting for the West, dead in his arms.

A pigeon exploded at Grant from a spiny bush, and he reeled backward, through a clearing, and burst onto a street. Down the block, a man standing beside a taxi called into a nearby building and two girls, eight or nine years old, skipped toward him, braids spinning like crazy propellers. A taxi. Grant ran forward and a hard metal chime rang, a silenced bullet pinging the base of a streetlamp. Another bullet gouged chunks from the curb, the shooter firing fast and sloppy—not aiming at Grant, aiming at the taxi with the two little girls, to stop his escape.

He snapped into a side street, sprinted across an intersection and into an alley. Car doors slammed and he darted through an archway into a courtyard beneath a stubby tower, with a stack of pallets in the corner and two bicycles leaning next to a drainpipe. He grabbed one of the bikes and saw Magda Loeffert's dying expression, a soft smile of disbelief.

What next? He couldn't think. Another non-aggression pact? Impossible, but . . . but they'd killed her. They'd tortured Lorenz. This was bigger than money laundering, bigger than a prototype aircraft. If the Nazis made peace with the Soviets, they'd win the war.

Through the archway, he pedaled past the roundabout at the Plaine de Plainpalais, jostling up the stone steps into the grassy park fringed by high trees.

Gears ground behind him, a low-slung BMW Roadster prowling into the rotary, then a polished black limousine snarling and shooting south. Grant went north through the park, thumped off the curb onto the sidewalk at the Apollo Theatre, and the Roadster crept from the darkness a hundred meters away. He swerved into a side street and crossed the Place du Cirque, turning onto a diagonal street—and the polished black limousine loomed fifteen feet behind him, engine gunning, windshield reflecting the moon.

He threw himself aside, found his feet and sprinted. The limo ground the bicycle into wreckage, giving him five seconds, and he heaved himself over a wall with a plaque reading CIMETIÈRE DE PLAINPALAIS.

The limousine's engine purred on the other side of the wall, doors opening and closing. A cemetery spread before him in the moonlight, a walled garden, a maze of scattered headstones and marble platforms, drooping trees and meandering paths.

Grant stepped behind a tombstone, watching dark shapes drop over the wall, crouch, and fade to shadow.

A man's polite voice cut the stillness: "Can you hear me? I very much hope so. When you see her again, tell Frau Loeffert we don't wish her harm. My men—trigger-happy fools, these aren't *my* men."

Grant prowled through the trees into a crescent-shaped grotto, looking for a shovel or a thick branch, anything he could use.

"She's in no danger," the man smoothly continued. "Tell Frau Loeffert that she has something dear to us, and we have something dear to her, that is all."

Across a bed of plantings, Grant found the chapel wall—but no weapon, and no safe path back to the wall.

"No answer?" The man's voice slunk through the darkness. "As shy as that? Tell her we'll make an even exchange. What she wants for what we want."

Grant followed a line of trees toward the cemetery wall and two Germans stepped into a moonlit clearing ahead, scanning the darkness, hands bulky with pistols. He sidestepped into the embrace of a slope-shouldered pine and stopped breathing.

"She knows who to call," the man said. "We'll wait . . . but not for long."

A few silent seconds passed, then a minute, and the two Germans faded into the muffled night.

Grant put his palm against the rough tree trunk, thinking of Anna, her quick clear eyes and her blue dress tight around her hips. He'd lost Racket and he'd lost Loeffert: he wasn't gonna lose another fight. Hunted like a dog in a strange city, but his time would come. Take the stick and fly into the attack. He waited, perfectly still, the chill seeping into his bones.

CHAPTER 26

kimov stepped from the Au Mirador doorway, struggling with the top button of his overcoat. Two hours of weak tea and poppy-seed cakes, and after the tea shop closed he'd wasted another hour lurking in the doorway. No sign of Magdalena. He eyed the dark empty street, listening for echoes of Stalingrad—maybe praying for a waft of her lavender perfume. Another dead end.

He started toward the hotel, and a voice spoke beside him. "What went wrong?"

Akimov stopped short. "The hell are you doing here?"

A grip on his elbow propelled him forward and Little Vlad repeated, "What went wrong, Comrade Major?"

"You're here, that's what went wrong." He shook the man off. "She saw you and disappeared."

"She didn't see me, she never came. Why not?"

"You think she left a message in the teapot?"

"She told you she'd be here."

"You scared her off. We're losing Stalingrad and you idiots are playing games—you have no idea. You have no idea what war is."

"Not that way," Little Vlad said, stopping him at the corner. "We're not going to the hotel. We wait for Big Vlad and the others."

"They're here too? Who're *they* scaring?"

"They're checking the city."

"Idiots. Magda's not a fool—she told me to come alone. Are you so completely in my father's thrall that honesty doesn't even occur to you?"

"Your father is a good man. Everything he does, he does for Russia."

"And how convenient for him that Russia always requires his own promotion."

Little Vlad grunted. "So. No message from your ex-wife?"

"No."

They returned to the black sedan and waited in silence, watching the empty street. Akimov rubbed his eyes. Were the streets of Stalingrad as quiet as this? In the de facto cease-fire, were the machine guns silent, did the river not erupt with gouts of water and the streets with gouts of flame? Driven back into the heart of Russia, his countrymen fought with a grim determination that allowed no hope: but he would give them hope, he would buy them time. He'd find Magda and—

"What's it like, then?" the big man asked.

"Hm? What's what like?"

"Stalingrad."

Akimov eyed him. "Do you know the poet Akhmatova?"

"No."

"She wrote a poem, called 'Lot's Wife.' An old *zek* taught me."

"In the gulag?"

"You know the Bible story, Lot and his wife follow an angel out of Sodom, and they're forbidden to look back. But Lot's wife's heart whispers, 'Look back at your native soil, at the square where you sang and the shed where you spun, at the windows of your home, where you bore children for your beloved husband.' "

"And she looked."

"Her native soil, Vladimir, could she *not* look? She looked and was bound, her feet rooted in the ground. And Akhmatova says: 'Deep in my heart, I will always remember the woman who chose to die for the sake of a single glance.' "

Little Vlad was silent, taking a cigarette from his pack. "And that's what Stalingrad is like?"

"Nah, that's just a poem."

Little Vlad chuckled and gave Akimov the cigarette.

He bent over Little Vlad's match, and realized: he knew where to find Magda.

Outside the cemetery wall, Grant dropped behind a row of warehouses. Silence. He slunk past a loading dock—he needed to keep his head down and wait for dawn.

When the city stayed quiet, he jogged into a strange neighborhood with rows of low windowless buildings, and saw the street name in peeling paint: Avenue des Abattoirs. From the cemetery to the abattoirs. Making progress. Get to the consulate, and tell them . . . what? That men in Switzerland were arranging another Nazi-Soviet pact, and for proof he had a dead woman's body on a park bench? And who was he? An escaped prisoner with an assault rap hanging over him, and a wild story about an impossible Nazi prototype.

He turned a corner, and a man stepped from a recessed doorway, wiry in a gray suit. "Some night," the man said, and Grant recognized his voice from the cemetery.

"And not over yet," Grant told him.

"Won't be long now." He reached into his jacket—for a gun?—but no, he just stuck a cigarette in his mouth. "I've been wanting a smoke."

"I'll pass on your message," Grant said. "From the cemetery."

"Then you have hidden talents." The man removed his fedora and ambled closer, moving like a fighter, with eyes crueler than that prison-camp dog. "We found Magda Loeffert where you left her for dead. A pity, I wanted her alive. But you? I don't know you."

Grant backed away. "You don't know what I know."

The black snout of the limousine crept around the corner behind him, and the man smiled. "I'll find out."

"You'll try."

"You're out of your weight class."

"Maybe I'll get lucky," Grant said, and stepped in quick and low.

The man hammered Grant with the heel of his hand. A light flashed and the world reeled and cobblestones slapped his face, cold and gritty.

"I saw what you did," the man said, far above him. "At the taxi, outside the university. The two little girls you chose not to endanger."

Grant rolled onto his hands and knees, and shakily stood. "Yeah?"

The man stepped closer. "Everyone makes mistakes."

"Wait," Grant said, backpedaling. "Wait."

"You're not ready to talk. Not yet."

"Would you wait?"

The man paused. "Why?"

"Just trying to put off the inevitable."

"What's your name?" the man asked, his dark eyes gleaming.

"Ty Cobb."

"You're not Swiss."

"You're Pongratz," Grant said.

"The woman told you?"

"She said—"

He sprang at Pongratz, trying to bring him to the ground where he had a single chance in hell of beating him and keeping the men in the limo from getting a clean shot. But the man was a ghost—Grant caught thin air, felt his arm wrench, and smacked into a brick wall. His vision blurred and his shoulder burned. He felt Pongratz behind him, dropped to one knee and took the punch on his shoulder—twisted and lunged backward and got lucky, his hands closing around a leg.

He heaved, and Pongratz kicked him in the ribs. He gritted his teeth and threw his weight backward into the man's legs, trying to snap a knee, but only found the cobblestones again, the man slipping away like a wisp of smoke.

"You're the best I've seen in sixteen months," the man said.

Grant wiped blood from his lip. "You oughta get out more."

"Ah, you're American—the juvenile humor reveals you. What's an American doing with Magda Loeffert?"

"Watching her die."

Pongratz faked left and Grant took the bait and got a fist in his gut. He bent over and the street echoed with car doors slamming—Pongratz glanced away and Grant took him around the middle and drove him backward. His back caught fire, an elbow to the kidney, and he dropped to his knees, stunned and pain-blind, but no more blows came.

He blinked away tears and turned his head. Around the limo, five men stood in a motionless tableau. Pongratz faced a big man with a flat Slavic face, guns drawn but nobody willing to fire and bring down the police.

Grant rose into a crouch and ran.

CHAPTER 27

Villancourt rested his left elbow on the table and addressed his empty dining room, the scroll-back chairs and Madeira table-cloth. "But you see, gentlemen, we break the spirit of the law if we do *not* increase the clearing credits to Germany. Sacrificing profits for politics is a true violation of neutrality . . ."

He stopped, aware of a faint perturbation in the air. What was wrong? Ah! He switched elbows. Much better. "Now, are clearing credits the firm's best path forward? Yes indeed. Our economy is en-twined with that of Germany, we have ongoing investment and in-frastructural interests—"

The phone rang, and despite the importance of his rehearsal he stood from the table—these were momentous days. He stepped into the hall and answered. "This is Villancourt."

"Herr Villancourt," Kübler said. "I have news."

"I gathered as much, given that you called."

"I have the list you requested, of Bern-based reporters with anti-German prejudices who—"

"You're in Basel?"

"Yes, I—"

"Come to my house, then. This isn't for the telephone."

He returned to the dining room and continued his practice. During the second run-through, the front bell sounded—Kübler, no doubt, Teutonically prompt—and his nephew Hugo stepped into the hall to answer.

Villancourt called: "Hugo, you ingrown toenail! Are you a housemaid, now? Let the man wait, he should learn patience."

Hugo's footsteps paused. "Yes, Uncle."

Poor unfortunate boy, trapped forever in stooped subservience. Villancourt finished his presentation, then wrapped himself in a kimono, silk with excessive embroidery. The bell had only rung once more, but he knew Kübler waited outside, too dutiful to abandon his post yet too proud to continue ringing. He opened the door and was proved correct: Kübler stood at attention, a petite blond man with a square jaw and matching shoulders, like a toy soldier.

"I'm a busy man, Ernst," Kübler said, eyeing his kimono with distaste. "I can't heed your beck and call at all hours of the night. You're overstepping your bounds. That's all I've to say on the matter."

"Care for a drink?" Villancourt asked, ushering him into the drawing room.

"What? Did you hear me?"

"Yes, you said, 'That's all I have to say.' Is there *more*?"

"I—no." Kübler sat on the silk sofa. "I have the list of the Bern-based reporters you requested, the Bolsheviks who print anti-Hitler propaganda."

Villancourt had told him to compile the list before Pongratz tore Pierre-Luc Soyer's name from the hotel clerk, Herr Lorenz. Probably irrelevant now, but he never underestimated the value of information. "Have you? Well, I'm pleased you're keeping out of trouble."

Kübler unfolded a sheet of paper from his breast pocket. "I was forced to call in many favors to assemble this on such short notice."

Villancourt cast his eye over the list. "Only five names?"

"The most biased of them."

"Well, where is Monsieur Soyer?"

"Pierre-Luc Soyer? He's an editor, not a reporter, and a perfectly unexceptional man."

Villancourt tsked. "I've heard differently."

"Did you? From whom?"

"Well, leave him aside for now. Who else have we?"

"The woman is the one to watch."

Villancourt scanned the names. "Anna Fay?"

"A virulently anti-Hitler propagandist."

"Yes, I know the name. Frau Fay came to my attention weeks ago."

"Then she is the one!"

"Came to my attention for investigating the credit relationship between our countries—the clearing credits. She's a complete nonentity, casting about for a story she'll never write."

"She may be casting about for Magda Loeffert, as well. You said Loeffert approached some journalist—this Anna Fay, she's at the top of the list."

"The list has shrunk. Pongratz tracked this down already." Villancourt smiled at Kübler's surprise. "Loeffert was being investigated by a man at the Palace Hotel, and that man was employed by Pierre-Luc Soyer."

"By Soyer?"

"Yes, the 'perfectly unexceptional' fellow. Pongratz will soon be speaking with him."

"Oh. Oh, I'd no idea."

"Chin up, Kübler. Perhaps Loeffert contacted more than one reporter—I'll send the police to question Frau Fay, to be sure. Oh, and well done, arranging those soldiers for Pongratz."

"Took a good deal of asking."

"Worth the effort. The board will extend the clearing credits by an additional 250 million francs, mark my words, bringing the total to near a billion." Villancourt rearranged the folds of his kimono. "I expect a phone call at any moment. Pongratz's in Geneva, speaking with Loeffert—he'll tell her we're holding the girl, and I'll have those documents in my hands by morning. A drink to celebrate?"

"We haven't won yet," Kübler said, waving off the offer.

Villancourt moved to the sideboard. "Do you know who I admire? Your arms manufacturers, the Krupps, selling artillery to both sides during the Great War. Now *that* is taking the long view."

"Krupp is a loyal supporter. For ten years, he pushed rearmament—"

A shadow slipped across the Persian rug, and Pongratz stood in the doorway. No telling how long he'd been there. He stepped into the room, his gaze sweeping the corners before settling on Villancourt.

"What news?" Villancourt asked.

"Loeffert is dead. She was meeting a—"

"Dead?" Kübler said. "Dead?"

"She met an American operative at one of the rendezvous points, we missed the initial meet but found them later—"

"You retrieved the documents?" Villancourt asked.

"Not on her person."

Villancourt's stomach soured. "She gave them to the American?"

"No, the American fled before any business was concluded. We pursued, and were interrupted by men I presume are Red Orchestra."

"Soviets?"

A soft smile flickered on Pongratz's face. "A tense moment."

"Those idiots, we're on the same side of this. We all want these talks to proceed."

"Not entirely the same side," Kübler said. "Whoever controls this blackmail, Herr Villancourt, shapes the negotiation."

"Thank you for that wholly pedestrain observation, Kübler." He looked to Pongratz. "Any police notice?"

"None. The crisis passed, we went our separate ways, but the American got away."

Villancourt ran his fingertip along the rim of his glass. "Where are the documents, then?"

"Hidden, most likely," Kübler said.

"Magda Loeffert's dead," Villancourt said, "so we have no use for her daughter. Dispose of her as you wish, Pongratz, but speak with her first—explain the situation, perhaps she'll remember where the documents are." He considered Pongratz's cold eyes. "We have only two ways forward. The girl and Pierre-Luc Soyer, and you say the girl knows nothing. So you'll sit down with the editor and—what's that on your face? A smile?"

"There is another way forward, Herr Villancourt."

"Don't be coy, Pongratz. You have good news?"

"Before she died, Loeffert repeated these words: 'Herr Doktor Johannes Hostettler.' The American must've left her for dead, but she lived long enough. When we found her she kept saying, again and again, until her last breath, 'The papers are safe with Hostettler.' "

Villancourt bowed his head, awash in relief. "Have you the address?"

"Not yet," Pongratz said.

"Hugo!" he called toward the door. "Come! I have a task for you!"

His unfortunate nephew worked the phone for an hour, tracking Hostettler to an address in Grindelwald, a "hunting box" in the mountains. Nobody answered a direct call—neither staff nor family nor the man himself—which upon reflection might be a blessing.

"Herr Kübler," he said, "take the men to Hostettler's hunting box and find that document. I can't imagine the old gentleman—"

"Take the men?" Kübler had asked. "Me?"

"You and no other."

"Shouldn't we speak with Hostettler first?"

"All in good time. Our first concern is that document—searching his empty house will take longer than bracing the man, but it's best to avoid witnesses."

"You're sure it'll be hidden in his house?"

"He won't be carrying it on his person, not at his age, and if he knows I'm involved he won't trust a bank vault. His hunting box is the first place to search. Always exclude the obvious first, Kübler."

"Very good." A glint of eagerness appeared in Kübler's eyes. "I look forward to commanding such a . . . mission."

"Yes, well I'd send Pongratz but he'll be visiting Pierre-Luc Soyer. And surely you and five soldiers can handle an old man who isn't even at home. And Hugo—don't slouch—you'll head to Grindelwald. Not all the way to the hunting box, you wait at the hotel for a call if—"

"The hotel, Uncle?"

"Don't interrupt, either. The Regina-Alpenruhe, at the station, you'll wait by the telephone. Bring the panel truck, in case it's needed, and watch for these Russians. I don't like the sound of them."

"A fluke," Pongratz said.

"Nevertheless, to set my mind at ease."

Hugo chewed his lower lip. "And you, Uncle?"

"I'm going to bed, I need my beauty sleep for the board meeting tomorrow."

Grant stepped into the hospital lobby and approached the nurse at the desk. "Late business, I'm afraid." He handed her the identification papers he'd stolen from Dubois's house. "I'm looking for Herr Lorenz."

She checked her book. "Fourth floor, Commandant."

He thanked her, and crossed to the elevator. Pressed the call button and the elevator doors slid open, and a policeman stepped into the lobby. Better and better. Grant brushed past him and waited for the doors to close.

The policeman paused. "Late for visiting."

"I'm not visiting," Grant said, coldly. "I'm working."

The policeman shrugged and turned away: nothing was less suspicious than rudeness.

In the room on the fourth floor, Lorenz lay bandaged and dozing, with a tear-streaked Rosine holding his intact hand. Anna sat in a chair near the door, sewing, and Grant stepped inside and asked her, "Did the doctors look at your head?"

"Grant? What are you—what happened in Geneva?"

"Nothing good."

"What does that mean?"

"We should go, a cop got a look at me."

"Go? Where?"

"How's he doing?" he asked Rosine, taking Anna's coat from the hook.

"How do you imagine he's doing?" Rosine said.

"Won't be playing piano anytime soon."

Lorenz stirred. "Trouble with the low notes," he muttered, trying to smile.

Rosine snapped French at Grant, and Anna put her sewing in her bag and stood. "Sleep, Lorenz," she said. "I'll see you tomorrow."

Grant told Lorenz, "Anyone who visits you paints a target on her back, do you understand? You think they won't watch a hospital room?"

Lorenz's unbandaged eye grew grave, and Grant stepped into the hallway. Heard Rosine's voice raised angrily inside, and a moment later Anna joined him. Before she could speak, he said, "Did the doctor look at your head?"

"That was cruel, Grant."

"Not as cruel as Pongratz, if he gets his hands on you or Rosine."

She turned toward the elevator. "Who's Pongratz?"

"The salesman. Let's take the stairs. What'd you tell the police about Lorenz?"

"That a strange man attacked him. Now start talking, Grant."

He opened the stairwell door and started talking. On the first-floor landing, she put her hand on his arm. "Another non-aggression pact? We can't even handle a barracks deal, this is impossible, the talks begin in a few days? This is too big. This is—maybe you're right, Grant, someone is playing games."

"A German squad chased me all over Geneva. They killed Loeffert, they hurt Lorenz. I don't know what this is, but it's not a game."

"There's no way to verify this. Except perhaps with her friend, Doktor Hostettler."

"She said Stalingrad's been quiet for a couple days."

"You mean both armies are ordered to hold their fire?"

"While they hammer out this truce, I guess."

"So if they're not fighting, that proves they're talking?" She opened the door to the street. "Come, we'll ask the colonel, he'll know."

Grant put his back to the door of the colonel's elegant town house and watched the street; bare trees outlined in the moonlight and a scattering of late-model sedans at the curb. Magda Loeffert had to have been the real McCoy—reminded him of Anna, in her quiet fearlessness—but she must have been wrong, too. No way a second Nazi-Soviet pact was in the works. Like Anna'd said, that was just too big.

"Is this guy any good?" he asked.

She pressed the bell. "The colonel knows everyone and every-thing—or so he claims."

The door opened and a maid stood inside, wrapped in a shawl. "Yes, please?"

Anna told her she needed to speak with the colonel, and they were ushered into a dim paneled drawing room. Twenty minutes later, a fat man in a silk dressing gown entered. "My dear Mrs. Fay," he said. "A trifle late in the day."

"I need help—information."

"And who is this fine gentleman?" He engulfed Grant's hand in his own. "I don't believe we've met, sir."

"A friend," Anna said. "I trust him."

"How nice that one of us does."

"He's American, a reconnaissance pilot. An escaped internee."

"You're a fugitive, sir?"

Grant looked at the colonel's throat, the Adam's apple wobbling under smooth-shaven skin.

"None of that!" The colonel raised his hands. "I am discretion itself, I assure you."

"Colonel," Anna said, "I need details about the siege of Stalin-grad."

"Stalingrad? This isn't regarding that other matter?"

"The cryptographer? No."

"But this is equally urgent, I imagine."

"Possibly more so. I need the latest information on the fighting at Stalingrad."

The colonel lifted his hands from his belly, and a little Colt Woodsman glinted between his fingers. "Now, then, Mrs. Fay. This is truly a friend?"

"Of course—put that away."

"I worry that you seem unable to focus on a single request—" The gun swiveled toward Grant. "Please, sir, do not move."

Grant showed the man his hands. "A .22 won't kill me fast enough."

The colonel backed another step. "You're the man she sent to Schürch."

"Put the gun away." Anna stepped between them. "Look at me, Colonel."

"I've seen you appear to better advantage," he said.

"Stop this nonsense—Grant, sit."

The scales hung in the air a moment, then Grant sat on a yellow-and-blue striped love seat. The colonel looked from him to Anna, and Grant hoped she knew what she was doing.

"Stalingrad," the colonel said. "You need to know immediately?"

"As always," she said.

He drifted toward the door like a merchant ship laden with goods. "Make yourselves comfortable."

"That was juvenile," Anna said, when the fat man left. "Were you trying to impress me?"

"Any luck?" he asked.

"I'm impressed that you sat."

In English he said, "You oughta see me roll over."

"I don't understand."

He smiled and lit a cigarette, and was on his second when the fat man returned.

"The Germans' primary objectives in Stalingrad are the Dzerzhinsky tractor factory and the Barrikady gun factory." The colonel settled his bulk into a leather armchair. "The roads are paved with bodies. Flamethrowers, Katyusha rockets, fighting room to room in shelled buildings. On October 7, after fifty-four days of continuous battle, no German tank or infantry assault occurred."

"Nothing?"

"And nothing on the eighth or ninth—as far as I know, this unlikely peace continues as we speak." The colonel took a briar pipe from the table. "The Russians ferry across the river every night, bringing supplies to—"

"I heard the Soviets and Germans are engaged in armistice talks," Anna said. "Here in Bern."

The colonel sucked his empty pipe. "I'll pass that along."

"You don't believe it?"

"Every schoolboy knows the Soviets hate the Reich, and vice versa."

"They signed a non-aggression treaty once."

"Which ended with an invasion. I'll pass this along, Anna. The committee meets Friday."

Anna's face darkened. "If this is true, Friday is too late."

"One day you want a cryptographer, the next you warn of this outrageous scenario. I'll do as you ask . . . on the existing schedule."

"And if I'm right?"

"Then what do you recommend? What would you have us do?"

"I don't know." Her voice was suddenly desperate. "I don't know. Take this off my hands, that's all I ask. Speak to them today."

She pleaded with the colonel but he wouldn't budge. "Then tell me this," she finally said. "Do you know a Herr Doktor Johannes Hostettler?"

"Hostettler? Rings a distant bell."

"Find him for me?"

"At this hour?"

She caught him with a hard gaze. "A man walked into Lorenz's office today and put him in the hospital, missing a finger. You can stay awake."

The colonel inclined his head, and stepped from the room.

"He's a childhood friend of Martin's?" Grant asked.

"You expected someone more like Martin?"

He checked the street through the curtain. "Yeah."

"You were his friend, Grant, and look at you."

Nothing moved on the street. "If your colonel calls the police, there's gonna be trouble."

"He won't."

He heard her stand from the sofa, heard the hush of her dress as she approached. She stood beside him, close enough to feel her warmth and smell her perfume. She put her hand on his arm. They stood that way for a long minute, then he turned to take her in his arms and the colonel entered and said, "Hostettler. Retired professor, has a country home outside Grindelwald he calls his 'hunting box.' " He gave them the address. "What has this to do with the other matter?"

"He's an expert on Stalingrad," Anna said, lying with perfect smoothness. "Thank you, Colonel."

She left, and when Grant followed the colonel murmured, "I wonder if my little .22 would've stopped you."

"Better to live with uncertainty," Grant said. Outside, he caught Anna on the sidewalk. "We could go to Leeger."

"Your brigadier general. Will he act?"

"I was thinking he might confirm."

"Confirm what?" she asked. "This cease-fire? The colonel is not wrong about such things. Or confirm that if the Nazis aren't bogged down in Russia, they'll win this war?"

"I hadn't thought past breaking into Leeger's house and knocking him around."

She didn't smile. "Nothing's changed. We need to get the document from Hostettler's house, that's all."

"This is bigger than a barracks deal, Anna. Bigger than money laundering."

"They're related. Magda's investigation led her to the cease-fire pact, somehow." She considered, then nodded. "We'll ask Hostettler about this pact, and see what names the document gives us. Then we'll know if we can stop the negotiations."

"You didn't tell that to the colonel."

"I trust him, but he's not the only man in Aktion. I need to speak with the embassies about all of this, and—"

"The embassies? What'll they do?"

"Without proof? Nothing." She turned to him, her face flushed from cold. "We cannot allow a cease-fire, Grant. We'll go to this hunting box tonight."

"I'll go. You see what else you can dig up."

"He's more likely to talk to me."

"You stay."

"Why?"

Because he'd already lost two people in Switzerland. "Doctor's orders. That's a nasty bump on your head."

She looked at him. "Thank you. I . . . Christoph is too often alone. You'll need a car."

"Drop me downtown, I'll pick one up."

"You'll steal a car? Off the street?"

"You know my mother's German? Well, my old man's bent."

"What is 'bent'?"

"Crooked."

"Your father was a criminal?"

"Still is."

"Then you're your mother's son."

He smiled. "She says I'm the spitting image. Now how do I get to this hunting box?"

CHAPTER 28

Waves brushed the shore of the cold dark lake. Boats creaked and bobbed in the wind, dying swells simmered around the moss-damp jetty, and the mountains crowded overhead like enemy watchtowers. Akimov stood at the edge of the steamer-office parking lot and watched the night.

Magdalena was dead.

Twenty years ago, he'd loved her like breathing—yet he'd left her to fight for the dream of a future without injustice. Why had she stayed behind? For the affluence of Switzerland, the stability? No, Magda didn't suffer that sort of fear: she simply hadn't reason enough—love enough—to follow. Yet he'd never loved another woman. He'd imagined he'd forgotten her, but now that she was dead he was left empty. A hollow man, he'd never hear her voice or see her face again, he'd never—

Big Vlad clapped a paw on his shoulder. "I'm sorry, Comrade Major."

"The car is here?"

"Yes, back to Bern."

Akimov followed him across the lot toward the steamer office, closed for the day.

"You don't get used to it?" Big Vlad asked. "From the army?"

"To death?" Akimov said. "There's only one way to get used to death, Vladislav. The poetess wrote about that, you know."

"No poems for me, Comrade Major—you might as well dance for the blind."

"I'll spare you, then." He looked at the big man. "Who killed her?"

"Who killed her? We covered the tea shop from a distance, a long ways, and nobody came, not Loefferta, not anyone—at seven o'clock." Big Vlad stopped at the car, but made no move to open the door. "Twenty minutes later, a BMW drives past, four men inside, all of a certain type, you take my meaning?"

Akimov told him that he did.

"They slow at the tea shop, then drive on. We think '*Oh ho*' and follow."

From inside the car, Little Vlad said, "Are you coming?"

"A moment," Big Vlad told him, then continued. "They lead us through the city, slowing now and again, looking I think for your ex-wife. They must recognize her, yes?"

"Yes."

"Because they are quick, looking and driving past. Finally, across the river, they see something, they chase across the city. We lose them, we find them, we lose them . . . and suddenly stumble on them. Guns are drawn, nobody breathes—nobody wants to fire first . . . but that's better than firing second, no?"

"Yes," Akimov said.

Big Vlad nodded. "Yes, firing first is better than firing second. Nobody fires. Then one man, a German, he says, 'We all walk away, this isn't worth the mess.' So we do."

"How did you know he's German?"

"From the cold. He gave me a shiver, all the way across the road."

"Then you found her?"

"We retrace the steps, to the university. She is there alone, on a park bench, very peaceful."

"On a park bench."

Big Vlad nodded and, when Akimov didn't say anything else, opened the car door. Magdalena, dead on a park bench. Akimov refused to allow himself to picture her, abandoned and alone. Instead, he slid into the backseat, and found himself with company.

His father bowed his head gravely. "I would like to say—"

"No," Akimov said.

"I only—"

"Nothing from you."

They drove along the lake, a reflection of the moon fluttering like a tattered flag in the water, through hillside vineyards and orchards pricked by starlight, past castles and churches, and into the amphitheater of the mountains. *Magdalena*. Even in her absence, she'd been the solid ground underfoot.

At length, his father spoke. "And it came to pass that God commanded Abraham to take his only son, Isaac, whom he loved, and sacrifice him on a mountaintop as a burnt offering." His voice was a prophet's deep rumble. "And Abraham rose early the next morning and took his son to the place God commanded. And Abraham bade his son to carry the wood for the burnt offering, and they went together into the mountains." His white head toward the ghostly peaks outside, his face craggy and tragic in the gloom. "And Isaac said, 'My father.' And Abraham said, 'Here I am.' And—"

"I can quote scripture, too," Akimov said. " 'Religion is the sigh of the oppressed creature, the heart of a heartless world, and the soul of soulless conditions.' Do you ache, Deputy Commissar? You're treating the symptom instead of the disease."

"What is my symptom, then?"

"Guilt. And you think I can wash it away."

His father's eyes were black in the darkness. "And my disease? Betrayal?"

"Betrayal is another symptom. Your disease is the man you chose to become."

"A man who raises his country above his son?"

"Without a second thought," Akimov said. "You threw me away without a second thought. You have no idea what I survived."

"But I knew you'd survive it. I know your strength. I know your heart."

The car's headlights, low and hooded, touched the crooked branches of roadside trees, set them glowing against the midnight sky. The engine strained around a steep curve, cold air swept through Akimov's half-open window and mixed with Little Vlad's sweet cologne.

"I remember Magdalena's parents," his father said. "They were rooted in faith—as was she, until you. In the face of a god, Edik, we all fall to our knees. Still, there comes a time when a man is nothing more than a man. You're the last of a line, a long line. I don't ask for your forgiveness, only your recognition."

Akimov met his father's gaze, keeping his own eyes empty. "Does Magda's murder mean we have no hope of influencing the cease-fire?"

A long pause. "There's always hope—if Magdalena wasn't carrying the documents, they can still be found . . . if only we knew where to look."

Akimov nodded, scratching the stump of his arm. He knew exactly where to look, from his conversation with Magdalena:

Remember your eighteenth birthday? he'd asked.

At that fleabag café in—I don't even recall the town.

Of course she recalled the town—Burgdorf—and there was only one reason to lie: she'd been staying there.

They finished the drive in silence, and took the elevator to the suites. Akimov unlocked his door, and his father touched his shoulder. "There comes a time, Edik, when a man raises his eyes to the future. When he realizes the question isn't what he leaves behind, but who."

"Nobody," Akimov said, and shoved him against the wall.

Little Vlad grabbed him and they scuffled in the hallway, until Akimov was pinned, his arm behind him, his shoulder burning.

"Please," Little Vlad said.

Akimov shook him off and pushed into his suite. He locked the door and opened his hand. The car keys, from Little Vlad's jacket pocket. He couldn't drive well with one hand, but he'd make do. He owed Magdalena her privacy, even in death. He'd go alone.

Villancourt woke with a gasp, blinded by his nightcap slipping over his eyes and bathed in sweat. He reached across the bed for the warm indulgence of his wife before remembering: she'd stopped soothing his night terrors years before he'd had her committed. Instead of consolation she'd offered disdain. She'd traded his soft bed for a hard bunk in an asylum dormitory, and he hoped she was shivering in the cold comfort of her self-righteousness.

He threw off his counterpane, burrowed his feet into slippers, and groped for the tincture of passiflorine. The bottle was empty: he'd taken the last spoonful last night, and now instead of the flavor of passionflower, his mouth was coated with bitterness. What was the time? His reflection in the glass of the bedside clock was fractured by the bevels and—

"Good Lord!"

He turned from the clock, shaking his head at his foolishness— he'd missed the most obvious thing in Pongratz's report, and bless his slumbering mind for waking him. Still early enough to fix matters: he need only warn Kübler to expect company at the hunting box. That American wouldn't be long behind.

Nadya stood from the cabinet and said a prayer of thanksgiving in the darkness: the second bolt had fallen, she was half done, almost free. She kissed her baptismal cross and walked the length of her prison, rubbing the ache from her arms. The electric lights were off but she no longer needed them to negotiate; she'd learned a great deal since she'd allowed her captors to divide day from night with the flick of a switch.

Still, the cold-eyed man didn't know she'd delivered Mama's papers to the old gentleman in his mountain home. What would he do when he discovered her lie? She wouldn't think of that. This would soon be over. For weeks now, she'd lived with fear, watching her mother, afraid of nothing, suddenly pale with anxiety. But fierce with determination, too—

The doorknob of the passenger car rattled, and voices raised outside. She rushed to the washroom to erase the evidence of her labor, tugged gloves onto her reddened hands, and offered a jumbled prayer: *Holy Mother of God, glory to the Father, Lord Jesus*—

Nobody entered, the voices were just two men talking in the rail yard near her door. Drunk. Not the cold-eyed man, then—impossible to imagine him drunk. She flattened herself against the wall and listened.

". . . said they have a girl in there?"

"That's what I heard. Pretty little thing."

"They all look the same where it counts." The man raised his slurred voice: "Can you hear me? Say something, *schatzi*, sing to us."

"We've been too long in the barracks—"

"Come out, little rabbit . . ."

She closed her eyes. Only two more bolts to remove, and this is what awaited her on the other side? For a moment, dread and hopelessness washed over her, then she shook her head: *Most Holy Mother of God, cover me with Your protecting mantle*. She refused to despair—with faith, nothing was impossible.

CHAPTER 29

Kübler smiled faintly in the darkness as the car shifted on the mountain road. The Foreign Office was well and good—on his worst day, he was still worth more than any ordinary soldier—yet he couldn't deny he enjoyed commanding a squad of men on a midnight mission.

They drove through Grindelwald, Hostettler's hunting box, closer to the Wetterhorn than town, along the one good road skirting the slope at the Schwarze Lütschine. The turnoff nestled at the edge of a mountain wood, opening into the sweeping drive of a stately two-story château, and they parked under a spreading, bare-limbed tree. He left the car and surveyed the darkness, hand to his holster.

Silence, as expected. Still, he sent the acne-faced soldier to reconnoiter, then nodded crisply at the report: No signs of life.

One of the men forced the door, and Kübler led the squad through the country house: a formal parlor with a narrow door leading to the servants' stairs; a large dining room with a table and sideboard draped in dust cloths; a library and two parlors and a morning room. At the rear of the house, a patio room opening to a flagstone deck, and on the upper floor, white cloths covered the chairs lining the wide corridor and the furniture in the bedrooms.

Well, what better place to hide a document than a closed house?

After the initial reconnoiter, he searched the dining room himself, the sideboard and twin hutches, checked the walls and floor then prepared the table as a work space. A moment later, the first soldier entered with an armload of loose papers. "From the kitchen, sir."

"Put them here, I'll sort through and—" There was a crash, and Kübler reached for his pistol. "What's that?"

"Schmidt with the ax, sir. Searching a locked trunk upstairs."

"Ah, very well. Carry on, and—wait." He sniffed the air. "Do I smell smoke?"

"We laid a fire in the back-parlor hearth, sir."

"Idiots. Extinguish that immediately."

"We thought, seeing as there isn't another house within ten kilometers—"

"Smoke travels. Now stop thinking, and start searching."

Kübler stifled his annoyance, and over the next hour his men came and went from the dining room and the pile of paperwork grew. He finished inspecting a box of correspondence with university letterhead and the phone rang in the front hall.

He stood, weighing his options. Could be Hostettler, or someone calling for him—but at this time of night? He hesitated, his hand hovering over the phone, then answered: "Hello?"

"An American man met Frau Loeffert in Geneva," Villancourt said.

"Herr Villancourt!"

"You expected someone else?"

"Well, no, I—"

"Pay attention, Kübler. An American met Loeffert before she died, yes? She likely told him about Hostettler, so presume he has the address."

"Here? At the hunting box?"

"Almost certainly."

"Well, we're almost finished, we'll load the paperwork into the car and sift through later—"

"Turn out the lights," Villancourt said. "Hide the car. Make no sound—and when he arrives, don't let him leave."

"Ah." Kübler's pulse quickened in anticipation. Searching for the paperwork was vital, of course, but confronting an enemy combatant was infinitely more satisfying. "As you say."

"Take him alive if possible. I'll be there soon."

Kübler relayed the orders to his troops, then settled into the wingback chair in the patio room, feeling the comforting heft of his Walther. Ten minutes passed, then twenty. The silence was complete, but for the song of some night bird, the brush of wind through trees. And, finally, a low whistle from the sentry in the front of the house: someone was approaching.

Grant crouched behind the mossy stone fence. The place wasn't a hunting box but a country house, an English manor, a rectangle of dull yellow brick with two stories and three chimneys. Ivy crept around the windows and the front door opened onto a close-cropped lawn interrupted by low boulders. No car in the drive, no light behind the curtains, and no scent in the air but rain and wood smoke.

The place looked empty, but a vague caution pricked the back of Grant's neck. That's why he'd parked off the main road, why he crept forward instead of . . .

No. No excuses. Knock on the front door, ask Hostettler what Magda had told him, get the document, and be gone. An owl hooted and he stood, knees cracking, headed for the front then stopped: there were two other entrances, the side door and the French doors around back.

What did that matter? Like a frightened little boy, he was play-

242

ing hide-and-seek alone in the dark. Still, he threaded through the ironwork chairs on the deck to the edge of the French doors and glanced inside. A coal glow from the fireplace outlined the room, chairs on fringed rugs, a carved mantel with statuettes, portraits of skinny men in armor and fat women in nothing at all. How old a fire? Hostettler was probably upstairs asleep. Grant blew steam into the cold pine air and slipped inside, surrounded by silence, the scent of port and wood smoke.

He took the flashlight from his pocket and a pistol cocked, and a man said, "Don't move. Raise your hands."

"What's this?" Grant blurted in English, gaping at the short man with the square jaw and blond hair. "Where's Johannes? You speak English? *Sprechen Sie* English?"

"Raise your hands," the man said, in English.

"You have—that's a gun! What do you—"

"Or I will shoot."

Grant raised his hands, flashlight pointed to the ceiling. "I don't know what you want, but—"

"This way." The short man gestured toward a doorway. "Turn around, hands high—thank you. Into the corridor."

Oil paintings crowded the hallway, and Grant didn't know how to play this, didn't know why he'd spoken English. To confuse the man, keep him guessing, keep him asking questions instead of pulling the trigger.

The short man guided him into another parlor and aimed at his chest. "Now we wait."

"What've you done with Johannes?" Grant anxiously asked, trying to maintain the pretense.

The man hitched his hip against a silk striped chair. "You were seen in Geneva, speaking with the woman."

"Frau Hostettler?"

"There is no Frau Hostettler. You met Magdalena Loeffert." The short man called toward the doorway: "He is secure, gentlemen."

Footsteps sounded, and two young soldiers entered, and Grant heard more in the hallway. Too many. Even if he talked the guy into getting close, there was no beating those odds.

"We know everything, I'm afraid." The short man circled behind Grant, spoke to the back of his head. "Except the details. What is your name?"

"Cy Young."

"You're not British."

He watched the man's reflection shimmer along the edge of a cut-glass vase on the sideboard. "South African."

"You're American, don't lie. Lying won't serve you—" The short man stopped at the sound of a car door slamming, and addressed the soldiers: "Ah, he made good time. Well, this fellow's taken alive as reques—"

Kübler's throat tightened—at the words, "taken alive," the American changed from a caged animal to a cornered one: visible in the set of his shoulders and the clench of his hands. Kübler's finger tensed on the trigger and he knew he should fire—aim for the leg, the shoulder—but he wasn't Pongratz, couldn't shoot an unarmed man without a moment's inward preparation. Pongratz, that's who the American reminded him of, loose-limbed as an animal—

The man's flashlight whipped toward Kübler's face and he flinched and the man dove over the sofa and scrambled behind the pianoforte. The soldier shouted warnings, and Kübler's vision narrowed to a tunnel and he fired. The glass-front cabinet shattered and the man sprinted through the open door to the servants' stairs.

Kübler's palm stung from the Walther and glass crunched underfoot as he ran to the stairwell and crowded the doorway with two soldiers. They pushed through, and the stairway was empty, the American already upstairs. The youngest soldier took the stairs three at a time, pistol raised, and was almost to the top when a chair swung into the stairwell from the hallway. Carved dark beech wood with a broad seat and wide back, spinning in the air, slamming the wall and chopping toward the soldier, who raised his arms to protect his face.

The chair crashed to the soldier's feet, and Villancourt spoke from behind Kübler: "He's upstairs? Is he armed?"

"Yes. No."

"Then go after him—go, go!"

The soldiers shoved the chair aside, and the jug-eared one crept upstairs, wary of another chair. Silence and stillness, almost to the top stair—then a flash of movement and the soldier shrieked, twisting and clutching his stomach, falling sideways down the stairs.

"Fuck!" The soldier crumpled in a heap, blood seeping through his fingers. "Jesus! An ax, he hit me with an ax."

"Press down hard with your hand," Kübler said. "You two— take the other stairs, at the front door. There's no rush, he's unarmed."

"Except for a fucking ax," the jug-eared soldier said through gritted teeth. "Oh, God . . ."

Kübler turned to the youngest soldier. "Slowly now, climb. Don't let him close, you have the gun. I'll cover you."

He braced against the wall, his Walther steady, and listened as the wounded soldier started weeping. Glass smashed somewhere and time slowed. They had all night. The American was trapped. The youngest soldier paused at the top, peeked around the corner, and through the front parlor an engine howled and pebbles kicked against stone, a car roaring down the drive.

"That's my Mercedes." Villancourt ran to the window, shoved aside the curtains, and the car was a blur of moonlight at the end of the drive. "Good God, is nothing sacred? At least tell me you found the document."

"The papers are collected," Kübler said, "but I haven't yet sorted through—"

Villancourt turned to the soldiers, who'd gathered in the parlor. "Find the American, the only road out of Grindelwald leads west toward Interlaken, take—"

"There's a mountain road, sir," the acne-pocked soldier said. "East to the motor-post route."

"Passable this time of year?"

"He could drive to the end, hike for Meiringen."

"Which of you is best overland? You? Take the Opel in the garage. How many other cars have we? Two in the garage, plus the American's. Search toward Grindelwald, it's a Mercedes 230, two-tone, and the man—you all saw him?"

"Yes, sir. What are our orders?"

"Alive is better than dead, and dead is better than nothing. Now go. Herr Kübler, you and I will load the car with the papers."

The injured soldier staggered into the doorway, blood soaking his shirt and staining his fingers. "And me, sir?"

"You keep still. Where's the telephone? The American is headed toward Hugo at the Regina-Alpenruhe."

"Your nephew?" Kübler asked. "What can he do?"

"Use the truck to slow the American down."

Hooded headlights glimmered eighty feet ahead of Grant and the side panel of a small truck gleamed in the moonlight: a makeshift roadblock.

Driving too fast on strange unlighted roads, the mountain road snaking under his car—he smiled into the blackness and tasted blood. He'd flown naked against Japanese fighters, this was his ele-

246

ment. His grip relaxed on the wheel and he punched into the curve. The falling moon filtered through a cloud and showed a tall skinny man standing beside the truck. Something like a photo-recon shot flashed in Grant's mind, freezing the tableau, and he hit the accelerator.

The steering wheel jerked on impact with the man's legs, the windshield splintered as a white face loomed and vanished. Grant fought the bucking car, stomped the brakes and squealed to a halt. The windshield was ruined and broken glass covered the seat, but he wasn't cut.

He threw the car into reverse, backed until he hit something then worked the gearshift and heard another engine, a drone echoing from the hillside. He stomped the accelerator, drove fast and blind into the night, blinking at the deafening air. The pain in his forehead sunk to his neck, and he banked into turn after turn and chased the road from the hills to the lake.

The wind lashed his face. Without warning an old sedan loomed, and he yanked the wheel and swerved too hard—ran the tires onto gravel, jerked the wheel, and found tarmac again. The road was a dark whir, his tears blurred what his dim headlights touched. Past the junction for Langnau and Lucerne, the road vanished and he slammed off an embankment, jolted twenty feet over grass and rocks, and rammed into a gully.

The silence was absolute. There was something he needed to do, but he couldn't remember what. He killed the ignition and fell across the seat.

CHAPTER 30

A pretty town on a pretty hill, crowned by a pretty church: Burgdorf. The station of the electric railway, the Emmental line, was still closed for the night, so Akimov scanned the post board at the shuttered ticket kiosk. Railway timetables, church schedules, brochures for an Austrian cobbler and an iron-water spring. He'd check the hotels first. He'd find Magda's room and the document, and dictate the terms of this cease-fire. In memory of her.

He spoke with the night clerk at the Guggisberg. Only forty beds, yet the man had never heard of Magda, didn't recognize her from the photograph. Akimov stuck a cigarette in his mouth and went outside to watch a truck rumble through the center of a cobbled plaza. In Stalingrad, a surgeon was cutting through a homesick boy's thigh, and a junior nurse's dying emotion was shame that she'd loosed her bladder. He needed this cease-fire for his men, for all the soldiers and civilians, for the country whose pain he felt like the ache of his phantom arm.

He asked at the Stadthaus, with no luck, and knocked on the doors of three pensions. He cornered the night manager of the *Bahn-*

hof hotel and spoke to one of the maids, then the railway office finally opened for the morning. He waited until there was no queue, then showed the ticket agent Magda's picture.

"You say she's your wife?" the man asked.

"That's right." Akimov took his wedding photo from his breast pocket. "That's me without wrinkles, you have to squint. Have you seen her?"

The ticket agent nodded. "She's in and out of Burgdorf like a swallow. I tell her to buy a pass, but does she listen?"

A wave of relief hit Akimov. "She comes in a taxi? On the motor coach?"

"Perhaps you should ask her."

"Well, I . . . I'd rather you told me."

"I'm not sure I understand, sir."

"She left me," Akimov blurted. "There. She left me. I only want to talk to her, but no. She refuses."

After two minutes of commiseration, the man said, "A boardinghouse by the river, she mentioned that once."

"The river?"

"Yes, she said she should've stayed closer to the station."

The man knew nothing more, so Akimov thanked him and went outside, and fifteen minutes later was on a long curving riverside street. Both directions were equally uninviting so he turned left—a good Communist—and asked at a shop that sold gravestones where he might find a boardinghouse.

The man told him that wasn't the business he was in.

He knocked on doors until his knuckles ached, crossed the river and followed a sidewalk into a neighborhood of exhausted mansions with wide porches and flower gardens trampled for clotheslines. He passed a dozen private homes, a club for a Spiritualist Society, finally found a house offering lodging by the week or month. It took him twenty minutes and ten francs before he believed the manager's words: none of the lodgers were Magda.

Back on the street, the early-morning wind tossed the trees around. Nobody answered on the first half of the next block, no lodging on the second. Across the railway tracks, he knocked at a funeral parlor then found another boardinghouse, with a porch covered with dainty houseplants and small twisting trees.

The front door opened into a foyer smelling of wood polish and cooking oil. He called hello, and a man stepped around a stairway with a chipped banister, holding a violin by the neck. "Ah—yes?"

"You're the landlord?"

"All full, I'm afraid." The man smiled in apology. "We only let five rooms. You might try Frau Rees, down the road."

"I'm looking for Magda Loeffert."

"As am I," the man said. "Her rent is due."

Akimov offered a silent prayer of thanks. "I can help with that."

"You're a friend of hers?"

He half smiled. "A friend of the family, from back home."

"*Tovarich!*" the landlord said, with an awkward accent. "*Pozdravlyayu!*"

Pozdravlyayu meant "congratulations," so Akimov said, in Russian, "Congratulations for what?"

"*K sozhaleniyu, ya poka ne govoryu po russki,*" the man recited carefully. Sadly, I don't yet speak Russian. Then, in German: "I'm still learning."

"No matter, my German needs practice. You expect Frau Loeffert back soon?"

"From Russia!" He glanced at Akimov's empty sleeve. "You are not here on vacation, I think."

"Trade commission."

"League of Nations?"

"Yes, industrial commission, import duties. Frau Loeffert's room is upstairs?"

The man tightened a string on his violin. "I'm not a Party member myself, you know. Interested only in the—the cultural heritage, the language and so forth."

"An academic interest?" Akimov said.

"Exactly so."

"And Frau Loeffert—" No reason to admit she was dead. "She's not in?"

"She travels on business a good deal." The landlord plucked at the violin and a string quivered and hummed and fell silent. "Why are you here? You needn't be coy, I've nothing to hide."

Nothing to hide? Akimov shifted closer to the man. "Haven't you?"

"She's a good tenant."

"Which room is hers?"

"Quiet and tidy, and kind to Mother, too."

He hardened his voice. "Comrade, please—which room is hers?"

"You shouldn't have come," the landlord said, suddenly defensive. "I haven't attended a meeting in years, I canceled my subscriptions, I don't even listen to the radio."

The landlord thought Akimov had come to inspect his Party bona fides? "All I want is answers. Tell me about Magda Loeffert."

"I've nothing to do with that anymore. As I told Frau Loeffert, at any sign of political activity I'll contact the authorities."

"That's fine," Akimov said. And he understood why she boarded here—for the security, the landlord a nervous yapping dog. "When did you last see her?"

"She hasn't been home in days." The man pinched his nostrils. "Perhaps I should call the police . . ."

"Perhaps your mother knows where she is."

"My mother is ailing, bedridden."

"I'll need to see her room."

The man paled. "Mother's?"

"Frau Loeffert's," Akimov said. "I'll pay you."

"No. You leave. I'll shout for my lodgers, I'll call them right now if you don't leave, they'll—"

"Let me see her room, that's all."

"I have rights, too," the man said, voice quavering. "I have rights. You get out."

"If that's what you want, *tovarich*." Akimov turned toward the stairs.

"By the time you return downstairs," the landlord said, "I'll have my rifle."

If he had two arms, he'd force the matter—and if he had wings, he'd fly. He adjusted the strap of his satchel, then stepped outside. Across the street, a mottled mutt sniffed his shoes, hoping for a bite of the roll in his satchel. He threatened a kick, but the dog just cocked his head so Akimov gave him a crust.

"In Stalingrad," he told the dog, "you'd be roasted with onions."

He rubbed the stump of his arm, then went down a rickety wooden stairway toward the riverside, to wait.

Villancourt watched the red stain eclipse the pupil of Hugo's right eye. He cradled the boy's head in the backseat of the car and the world outside was far away, the dawn-lit treetops and the sweeping road. The engine sounded a gruff lullaby, the seat stank of blood and leather. Kübler drove slowly, his shoulders erect as a shudder ran through Hugo.

Villancourt crooned a few words. They'd found the boy crushed and keening by the side of the road, and he'd worried about moving him. But no further harm was possible: half his face was sheared away, his mouth an open stew of blood.

The boy's ruined lips twitched. "I tried to stop him, Uncle . . ."

"You did a good job, lad."

"I'm . . . sorry."

"You slowed him. Well done, Hugo, well done."

Hugo's right eye closed. "Please . . . tell Mother . . ."

"I will," Villancourt promised. "I will."

And he'd find the man who killed his nephew. Find the American, and punish him.

Anna sat by Christoph's bed, watching the rise and fall of his chest under the duvet, his eyes closed and fluttering. Nothing was sweeter than his face, even chased by uneasy dreams. The hour was so early and she was so alone—she wanted to lock her doors to the world, to reject every responsibility but one.

Christoph's breathing changed, and she stayed beside him until he yawned himself awake, then went downstairs to fix breakfast. Set out bread and butter, marmalade and cheese, and decided to make a pot of *Kabissuppe*. She ground nutmeg, chopped onion and cabbage, and was suddenly exhausted. She'd slept uneasily and woken anxious: Where was Grant? Dawn was long gone, and still no news. She needed that document, needed one clear-cut victory, needed to salvage her pride in her country and herself—needed to prove Martin wrong about her.

She splashed water on her face and was coring apples for a tart when the back door opened and shoes scuffed into the corridor. She grabbed the paring knife—Christoph was asleep upstairs, *hit first, hit hard, keep hitting*—and a shape darkened the kitchen door: Grant, his hair mussed and his eyes flat.

She exhaled. "You almost killed me."

"You're not the only one."

"What? What happened?"

"They were waiting at Hostettler's. Waiting inside."

"Did they follow you? They know you're here?"

"I ditched the car. I—slept in the front seat."

"And the document? They have the document?"

"I don't know. No, they were still looking." He slumped against the wall. "You made your calls?"

"Was Hostettler there?"

"Nobody but the Germans. You called the embassies?"

"Nobody believes me—I hardly believe myself, based on nothing but a dead woman's words. We must stop this thing ourselves."

"I can't see straight, and you're making soup. 'We' who?"

She brushed stray hair from her face. "There's nobody else."

"What about the camera?"

"Rosine will ask about the crash site. We'll know tomorrow."

"Yeah, well—" Grant swayed suddenly and grabbed the hall table to stay upright, knocking the pen set to the floor. "Sorry."

She took his elbow. "Come upstairs."

In the guest room, he took off his shoes and lay back on the bed. "They're military. The men at the hunting box."

"German?"

"Yeah. Could be Swiss, but . . ."

"The SS is funding the barracks deal," she said. "They're the ones laundering money to establish a Nazi intelligence network in Switzerland. German soldiers make sense. If only we knew who Magda's boss was—and how the money laundering relates to the cease-fire negotiations. Simply because the same men are involved, or is there another connection?"

She considered the possibilities, and when she looked back to Grant he was asleep. She pulled the quilt over him and watched his face. What next? Find Hostettler? And then what?

She returned to the kitchen, finished the tart, and started coffee. She was going in circles. She'd been researching the clearing credits, trying to find the Clodius memorandum, until Magda Loeffert told her about the barracks deal: the Nazis laundering money through the Swiss Wood Syndicate. Thirteen million francs was an easy trail to follow . . . or so she'd thought. But were the clearing credits and the barracks deal backed by the same men? Could she use Magda's proof of the money laundering to influence the clearing credits somehow? Could she even *find* Magda's proof, now that Grant had failed at Hostettler's hunting box? How was the Nazi-Soviet non-aggression pact connected to the barracks deal? Through Magda, who'd planned to blackmail the Swiss business-men into telling everything they knew—including about the nego-tiations. And the clearing credits provided leverage, allowing these Swiss men to effect the cease-fire negotiations. Because of the clearing-credit loans, the Swiss had leverage over Germany. Except Anna didn't even know who was involved, or when or where—

The front bell rang, and she bit her lip: surely the hospital would have called with news of Lorenz. She smoothed her house-dress and opened the door to find two police officers on the stoop.

"Frau Fay?" one asked.

"What's wrong? Is it my mother-in-law?"

"Nothing like that, ma'am. We've had reports you're harboring an undocumented alien."

"I'm harboring a—? This is nonsense."

"Still, we're obliged to check."

"This is not a convenient time," she said. "My son is due at school and I—"

"I'm afraid we're not asking, ma'am."

"This is my home," she said. "You cannot—"

He shoved past, begging her pardon, and entered the parlor as his partner moved toward the kitchen. She said something about waking Christoph and ran upstairs to Grant's room. The bed was empty. Heavy footsteps sounded on the stairs, and she was fluffing the pillows when the policemen entered.

They eyed Grant's wallet and cigarettes, the jacket on the hook and shoes on the floor. "Whose room is this, ma'am?"

"Do you think those shoes are mine?"

"Your husband's?"

"I can't imagine my domestic arrangements are any concern of yours."

"And where is your husband at the moment, ma'am?"

"As a matter of fact—"

A knob rattled in the corridor, and the bathroom door opened. Grant stepped out, a towel around his neck and his hair brushed forward. Shirtless, with the left side of his face lathered with shaving cream and a straight razor held down by his hip.

"What's this?" he said, frowning.

"Police, darling," she said. "They have reports of an undocumented worker in the area. They insisted on coming upstairs."

"Insisted?"

"They barged in, I couldn't stop them."

The policeman said, "May we see your identification, sir?"

"You can wait in the parlor," Grant said, "like guests in my home."

"I'm afraid we—"

Grant gestured with the straight razor. "Who's your commanding officer?"

The policemen looked at each other. "Chief Signer. Why do—"

"Of Bern canton?"

"Yes, of course."

"Well, you tell Signer—"

Christoph padded into the hall from his bedroom, his hair mussed. "Maman, I can't find my—" He stopped when he saw the policemen, and stepped beside Grant. "Papa—what's this?"

"Back to your room, Christoph," Grant said.

"But Papa—"

"What did I tell you?"

Christoph eyed the policemen. "Did somebody rob the bank?"

"Nobody robbed the bank," Anna said.

"I bet someone did!"

"Christoph," Grant said warningly, "don't make me tell you again."

Christoph returned to his room and didn't quite slam the door.

Grant made an exasperated noise, the harried father. "He's a handful."

"I have a nephew that age," one of the policemen said.

"He gets nightmares," Anna confided. "He's usually better behaved. Can I make you gentlemen some tea?"

They looked at each other. "No, thank you. This is—I'm sure we were misinformed, but we ought to finish searching."

She turned to Grant with what she hoped was wifely submission, and he shrugged and told the police, "Knock before you enter my son's room."

He returned to the bathroom and the policemen clumped downstairs and she straightened the guest room. She was folding the bedspread over the pillows when Grant entered. He went to her and she thought he was going to kiss her. He bent close and she saw a smudge of shaving cream behind his jaw. She wiped the cream away and told him there were fresh shirts in the drawer.

He dressed and they went downstairs, where she poured coffee and fed him bread and a bowl of Birchermüesli. The police checked the cellar, refused another offer of tea, and left via the back door, searching the vineyard. •

Grant sipped coffee, watching the guards. "Birchermüesli?"

"For Dr. Bircher's slimming diet, which I forever plan to start next week. You don't like it?"

"I wouldn't mind sausages."

"I haven't any, unless Joris brought them." She opened the refrigerator. "How's your head?"

"Not bad."

No sausage. She closed the fridge, and Christoph stood in the doorway, his hair combed and tie straight. There was a light in his face she hadn't seen in too long. As she and Grant turned to watch him, he tugged his tie self-consciously.

"Come here," Grant said.

Christoph went to stand in front of him.

Grant's face was hard and empty, a stranger's face. He measured her son with his eyes, and she realized there was something between them from which she was excluded. Finally, he said, "Not bad, soldier."

Not bad? A young boy steps between him and the police, and he says "Not bad"?

Christoph lowered his head and beamed at the floor.

CHAPTER 31

The kid left for school and Grant watched Anna peer out the kitchen window. He tore a chunk of bread from the loaf to keep from staring at her legs, the fullness of her hips, the curve of her ass. He'd wanted to toss her onto the bed upstairs, take her wrists in his hands and taste the hollow of her throat—only having cops in the house had stopped him.

"The policemen are still there," she said.

"In the vineyard?"

"Sitting in their car." She turned from the window. "We should leave before they ask the neighbors about my husband."

"Then let's go. Is this hat okay?"

"What happened last night?"

"I'll tell you while you pack."

"Am I packing?"

"You're leaving—you and Christoph. They know where you live, sending the police, they know you're involved."

She bit her lower lip. "I'll have my mother-in-law take Christoph until—"

"Too easy. Does Joris have family?"

"He's related to half of Ticino. Do you really think—?" She saw his face, and nodded. "I'll have him take Christoph to the country, after school. Let me put together a bag for him."

"Joris can pack his bags—we've gotta go."

She went into the hallway and handed him two empty suitcases from the closet. "The small one's for you. Now tell me about last night."

"I got lucky. I got away."

"The unabridged version."

"They were waiting inside the hunting box—"

"From the beginning." She led toward the stairs. "I dropped you at Münsingen. You got a car?"

"At the asylum."

"You stole a car from the lunatic asylum?"

"Crazy, huh?"

She shot him a look. "Keep talking."

"I drove to Grindelwald and ditched the car down the road—"

"Why didn't you drive to the front door?"

"I don't know." He shrugged. "Because of Racket and Magda. And Lorenz."

"And then?"

He told her: slipping through the unlocked doors, springing the trap, being on the wrong side of the gun—then hearing they wanted him alive and making his move. He paused at the top of the stairs, remembering. Told her about swinging the ax, smashing a window onto the second-floor balcony, driving away and hitting the man on the road. When he finished, she peppered him with questions: What exactly did the man say? Then what? And you said? In those words?

"You're certain they're German?" she asked.

"Yeah. He spoke English better than me but—"

"Than I," she said.

"No, you speak pretty good."

She laughed, her eyes suddenly bright. "You do me good, Grant."

Nothing warmed him like her laugh. He would've said something, but the words didn't come.

"I'm sorry," she said. "What else?"

"Nothing. I went out the second-floor balcony, the keys were in the car in the drive—I told you the rest. Go pack."

She went into her bedroom, and he watched the doorway, feeling the pull of her bed. Martin's wife. With Racket dead and a man tortured, running from Swiss police and freelance Germans, trying to stop a non-aggression pact and get the pictures of that prototype aircraft—all he wanted was Martin's wife moving beneath him on that wide warm bed, a flush on her skin and damp in her hair, eyes dilated, crying out for—

He shook himself. Acting like a schoolboy. He washed his face at the bathroom sink, then went into his room, and tossed what little he had into a case. In less time than he expected, she came to the door and said, "We'll stay at the Palace for a day or two."

"That's pretty high profile."

"Not if we get the right rooms, and use the back door."

"Speaking of which, those cops are still outside."

She crossed to the window. "Perhaps just eating breakfast in their car."

"And trying to remember why I look familiar."

"They have your photograph?"

"My service photo, yeah. I have a bad feeling about this, Anna, we should— What are you doing?"

"Tidying. Nervous habit."

He laughed and grabbed their suitcases. "Let's go."

"We need to find Hostettler and ask what Magda told him about—" She stopped, lifting a curled pamphlet from the bedside table. "What's this?"

"No idea." He looked closer. "Oh—Loeffert pretended that was a gun barrel."

"You got this from Magda?" She scanned the front, then the back. "A vocational school policy pamphlet? With the Palace Hotel phone number written in her handwriting."

"Scratch paper."

"This isn't some tourist brochure, available everywhere, this tells us where she'd been."

"A vocational school?"

"In Burgdorf. This was near the phone when she got the Palace number. We should—"

"We should talk on the way."

She nodded and they went downstairs and slipped out the side door, where she jabbered in Italian to Joris, telling him to take Christoph to Ticino after school.

"I will see he is packed," Joris said in rusty German when Anna finished. "All the things. And Christoph safe and warm."

"I'll call you."

"There is no *telefono*," he said. "I will call you."

She kissed him on the cheek and they followed a faint vineyard path to the maintenance steps of a hillside railcar. They went down to the street below, where the scent of river was strong but the traffic was light. Walked a quarter mile, then climbed back up a long flight of stone stairs, Grant's shoulders aching from the weight of the cases.

Anna led him through the windy terraces of the Bundeshaus, her hair rising in tendrils—and stopped. "Wait. The keys were in the car?"

"What?"

"At Hostettler's hunting box. You went out the second-floor balcony and found a car with keys inside?"

"Yeah."

"I thought you stole the car."

"No, this is a different one, after they—"

"Whose car was it, Grant? Did you check the registration?"

He shook his head, struck by the sudden realization of failure: if they knew who owned that car, they could pin a name on one of the men involved. "*Scheisse.* No, I didn't even get the license plates."

"Where did you leave it?"

"In a ditch. Must've been towed away by now. I was shook up, Anna. No excuse."

She bit her lip, eyes distant. "The police will have a crash report on the car, they'll know who the owner is. Whoever he is, he's deep into this."

"Will the police give you the name?"

"Me? No. But they'll tell the newspaper—maybe. Come along."

She led him through a dingy paved tunnel, flat calm after the terraces, to a hotel service door. Inside, they skirted a steamy laundry to a stairwell, where they climbed to the third floor. Grant said, "What about guests?"

"This corridor is empty." She unlocked a door into a room the color of sunflowers and mahogany, with a four-poster bed and a nook with three leather chairs. "They retire sections when occupancy is low."

"And you have a key?"

"That's one benefit of working with Lorenz."

He lay the suitcases on the rack, eyeing the room. "Not bad."

"Don't make yourself at home," she said.

"We're heading out?"

"I'm off to ask Pierre-Luc—at the newspaper—to help find the car owner. You're going to Burgdorf."

"Why? Because Magda once stopped there for lunch?"

"Because that's the only lead we have."

"We have Hostettler."

"Who's missing, and whose house is closed."

"You think he's in hiding?"

"I don't know. I'll look into him, you backtrack Magda. Ask for her at the vocational school, find her hotel room." She touched his arm. "Pick up her trail somehow, Grant—maybe that'll lead to us Hostettler, or the documents."

The Select Committee convened in Bern, and Villancourt spent the journey from the funeral home in preparation. Commerce halted for no man, for no grief . . . yet still he heard the echoes of his sister's indrawn breath, her broken sobs: *My baby, my Hugo, oh my boy.* He'd been oddly moved by her anguish, and had wasted valuable time extricating himself. But that was over now. He closed his eyes, steeling himself for the task at hand—increase the clearing credits, expand the industrial base, and Swiss economic dominance would inevitably follow, war or no. Vengeance could wait.

Stepping off the elevator at the top floor, he took a cigarette from his case and entered the boardroom, a shrine to serious purpose, with lead-glass windows overlooking the world so deservedly below them. He arranged his portfolio, his left elbow, his right eyebrow, and focused on the first task, safeguarding the productivity of the daughter corporations.

"Gentlemen," he said, after the introductory business was concluded, "we face a moral dilemma. We must deplore the German use of unfree labor, let the minutes show we are resolved on this matter: the exploitation of workers within the Reich is indefensible." A susurrus of agitation rose around the table, and he continued. "Sadly, however, we cannot openly challenge this behavior. While the war rages, we are obliged to retain a firm association with the Reich. We act as a moderating, a civilizing influence on the Germans. The question is simple, gentlemen, do we condemn the German use of unfree—"

"Condemn?" the deputy chairman interrupted.

"Internally, discreetly. Condemn the Germans *and* consolidate our commercial ties with them. Thus we build the foundation of future growth while—"

Herr Gohr, the idealistic young nitwit, rapped his knuckles on the table. "You speak of moderation, but you *mean* collaboration. The use of slave labor—"

"You recommend we refuse to trade with our principal account?" Villancourt politely inquired. "If we do so, we violate neutrality . . . and risk angering the Nazis."

"Then let us anger them!"

"For what purpose? To salve our pride? Our pride—*your* pride, sir—would enslave us. We must anticipate Germany's needs, we must make ourselves indispensable and exert our calming influence." He bowed toward the head of the table. "Mr. Chairman?"

Chairman Ochsner said, "We can curb German excesses best—and profit most—as a trusted partner. My vote is with Herr Villancourt."

There was pro forma discussion, then the voice vote. Ten stood with him, four against: the first hurdle easily overcome. Villancourt bided his time as the meeting continued, enjoying the action of his favorite pen, golden pearl celluloid with a two-tone nib, truly mightier than the sword—a few strokes could bury a thousand battalions and erect factories for their headstones.

For morning tea, the board members were given scones with tart cherry jam, assorted finger sandwiches, and cookies with mascarpone. After the plates were cleared, Chairman Ochsner intoned a few words and nodded gravely.

"As you know, gentlemen," Villancourt said, "more than eighty percent of German payments to Switzerland are currently handled via the clearing-credit system. This novel approach forges an intimate bond between our private and public sectors, allowing us to—"

"If you please," young Herr Gohr interrupted, virtually on cue. "The true results of this approach are economic bodies exempt from democratic controls. Impervious to scrutiny and beholden only to personal cronies and—"

"Personal cronies?" Villancourt's voice swelled with outrage. "Do you consider those at this table anything but Swiss patriots?"

"Don't be ridicu—"

"Your implications are not to be borne. These gentlemen represent the finest of our ancient democratic tradition. We're at war and—"

"We are at war, sir! We must follow the lead of General Guisan—'armed neutrality' is *not* for the military alone. The financial sector should give the Nazis nothing beyond the bare minimum required by law."

"You would see the country occupied, then?" Villancourt asked, mild as tomorrow's milk.

"Would they squander troops to occupy us, and risk foreign trade?" Gohr asked, red blotches rising on his cheeks. "We must pacify them with the minimum, not support them with the maximum."

Villancourt flared with righteous indignation, secure in the knowledge that he'd won. "Are you implying that the members of this body blindly support the Germans?"

"Of course not, I—" Gohr exhaled slowly. "This is about policy, not personalities. Your clearing-credit treaties haven't been officially published, Herr Villancourt, in violation of all legal precedent."

Villancourt appealed to his fellows with open hands. "An idealistic young gentleman, but perhaps we wiser and"—he permitted himself a small smile—"regrettably, older, heads must take cold stock of the situation."

A ripple of laughter and relief swept the table.

"Consider the proposal I've submitted—" Villancourt stopped when a footman slipped him a note, and scanned the message. "Ah. My apologies, gentlemen, my wife is unwell, and . . . yes. If you'll read the paperwork, I'll return in two shakes. With your permission, Chairman?"

"Family comes first," Chairman Ochsner said. "I applaud your priorities, Herr Villancourt."

What the chairman applauded, in fact, was the profit potential of the clearing credits—positioning Swiss firms to expand with the unstoppable Wehrmacht. And in the unthinkable case of a Nazi defeat? Well, they would expand on the ruins of the Wehrmacht, then. Who better to entrust with the industrial infrastructure of a defeated foe than a neutral country?

Down the corridor, the footman ushered him into a private office. Villancourt crossed toward the telephone, and a shadow drifted from the corner.

"Herr Kübler is on the line," Pongratz said.

"Good God!" Villancourt said. "You'll kill me one day, appearing like that."

"I spoke with the editor, Pierre-Luc Soyer. He isn't involved."

"Ah. Then the hotel clerk lied to you?"

"Lorenz. Yes, I'll pay him another visit. The editor gave me a name, though. Anna Fay."

"Frau Fay? So Kübler was right to send the police, bless his plodding heart. And he rang to crow? For this he interrupted the board meeting?" He lifted the telephone. "Herr Kübler, the meeting has reached the crucial moment, a billion francs hang on my words and you call with a complaint about shoeblack?"

"What? No, I have urgent news, Herr Villancourt. I've gone through the paperwork we took from the hunting box and—"

"You found the document?"

"No."

"Then what? Speak up already."

"It seems Hostettler has another house, a second home in Bad Ragaz. This is why the hunting box was closed."

"And you think we'll find the document there?"

"We'll find Hostettler himself. I tracked down his domestics and they confirmed he's there's now, as we speak."

"You have the Bad Ragaz address? Tell me, I'll send Pongratz to inquire." Villancourt ripped the flyleaf from a book, scribbled the address, and handed the page to Pongratz. "Well done, Herr Kübler. And I understand you were correct regarding Anna Fay, as well."

"Did Pongratz tell you? The officers who searched her house weren't informed of any, er, extrajudicial reasons for the investigation. They were told only of a suspicion of an illegal alien."

"A wise precaution."

"After I heard Frau Fay was involved, I called them personally. They found nothing, they said. All in order—the woman, Anna Fay, her son, and her husband."

"A lovely domestic picture. Your point?"

"Her husband is long dead."

"So she has a lover?"

"The officers interrupted him shaving, his face was obscured with lather, but after hearing my questions they checked the posters again and—"

"They recognized him," Villancourt said.

"He's an escaped prisoner. An American pilot wanted by the police for assault."

"God loves me, Kübler. What else?"

"They showed me his photograph—he's the man at the hunting box. The man who killed Hugo. Lieutenant Grant, of the United States Air Force."

Villancourt felt his lip curl. "And he's staying with Anna Fay."

"Indeed."

"He murdered my nephew." The words came unbidden from Villancourt's throat. "Ran him down like a dog in the street."

Silence on the line.

"I want him dead, Kübler."

Villancourt cut the connection and went into the hallway, trembling with anger, hearing echoes of his sister's sobs. Knowing the killer's name changed everything. Lieutenant Grant. This was no longer merely business, this was the blood that pulsed in his veins. He stopped and breathed outside the conference room doors, then stepped within. From a distance, he approved of the resolve with which he concluded his presentation: "For the future of Switzerland, the future of a Europe unfettered by Bolshevism, the clearing credits must be extended in the amount of 300 million francs."

From a distance, he answered questions and overruled objections. From a distance, he watched the final vote: *All in favor say aye. The motion passes.* From a distance, he saw the future unfold, in blood and gold and glory.

CHAPTER 32

Grant missed the turn to Burgdorf and drove twenty minutes before the distant peaks raised a chill of memory. He checked the map and yeah, he was closing fast on the punishment camp. Racket would've laughed at him, lost in the clouds without his navigator. He turned at a hill town with a patchwork of fields, back the way he'd come, checked the map again and found the vocational school without trouble.

At the front desk, he showed the woman the policy pamphlet. "My son is a handful," he told her. "He left home and this isn't the first time, but— Well, he left a number, on this pamphlet from your school. You see? I'm wondering where he might've come across it."

She said, "Pardon?"

"I want to know where he found this pamphlet."

"That's for enrolled students. About school policy."

"Yes. Right. Do you give them away? Where?"

Her brow furrowed. "We give them to all students. What is this concerning?"

"My son. So there's no way to figure where this came from?"

"That particular copy?"

"Yes."

"No."

He took two more runs at her, then returned to the car and watched the street. What else could he do? Nothing. Except take a page from Anna's book and play reporter, try to find the crash site himself. Call the police, the military, the newspapers. Worth a shot, anyway. He drove across the railroad tracks, past a few industrial buildings, and into a ramshackle neighborhood where a one-armed man waited at a bus stop.

Drab suit, drab hat, battered satchel. The officer from the Palace Hotel, in Burgdorf. And Russian, like Magda.

The mottled mutt dozed under a nearby bush, and Akimov finished the roll and watched the street until the front door of the boarding-house finally opened.

An elderly woman stepped onto the porch and savaged the plants with pinking shears, then swept the cuttings into a wicker scoop and returned inside. Ten minutes later, the landlord appeared and followed a trampled path around the rear of the house. Four cars puttered past, a cluster of schoolchildren chattered along the sidewalk. The front door opened again and two middle-aged men headed for the street. The landlord hailed them from behind the house, and all three left together.

On the porch, an earthy sugared smell hung over the plants. Akimov pushed inside and followed the stairway to the second floor, where he found an open sitting room and two varnished doors, both locked. In the bathroom, a shaving kit with a still-damp brush sat on the blue tile counter—a men's bathroom. He climbed to the third floor. Another sitting room, with heavy blankets in a pile by a painted fire screen, this one more feminine. A cough sounded down the hall, and a floorboard creaked—the land-lord's mother?

That left one door. Akimov forced the lock and found a suite with a sitting room and two bedrooms. Stepping inside, he was struck an almost physical blow: Magda's perfume. The quirk of her smile, the flare of her nostrils, the sweep of her hair on his chest. And there, in the first bedroom, the pillow where she slept, the closet filled with her clothes. He said her name into the empty room.

In the next bedroom, embroidered cloth draped a large icon on one wall, with a Bible, an incense burner, and three smaller icons on a table below. There was a stopper of holy water, a leather prayer ladder, and an oil-burning vigil lamp. Akimov sniffed the lamp: olive oil. Had Magda returned to the fold? The table and dresser were empty, except for the photograph: Magda and a girl, the daughter from her second husband. *Madame et Mademoiselle Loeffert.*

The daughter reminded him of Magda as a child, coltish and quick and—

The room tilted. Akimov reached for the wall with his missing arm and stumbled, then caught his footing and sat heavily on the bed.

He stared at the photo. The girl was his. His daughter—she was his daughter, the same mole under her mouth, which was his mouth, and her eyes were his eyes and . . . she was his. He'd re-turned to the Soviet Union, and Magda hadn't betrayed him—no, she'd stayed behind for their unborn child. She'd let him return, and raised her daughter, *his* daughter, in the sanctuary of Switzer-land. Had she dreamed of joining him in the worker's paradise, once achieved?

Her new husband had adopted the child, gave her his name—What *was* her name? He found a crumpled note in the bureau, a shopping list. *Nadya*. Milk, bread, cheese. Nadya Eduardovna Akimova. No, her name was still Nadya Loeffert—but *his* daughter, his flesh, look at her.

A sudden fear cut him, like the sound of a falling shell: Where was she? Magda was dead, the landlord said nothing of a daughter. Her room was empty, where was she now? Was she safe? He slipped the photograph into his pocket, went into the sitting room—and the door opened.

He expected the landlord's mother, but the man from the bar in the Palace Hotel—the Australian—stepped toward him, face hard. Akimov's first instinct was to run, but you never show a predator your back.

Instead, he raised his hand. "The door slams."

The man stopped, caught the door.

"You're following me," Akimov said. "What do you want?"

The Australian closed the door with a gentle click. "This is Loeffert's room? She's Russian. You're Russian."

"I'm family."

"Yeah?" He looked at the shelves, the open drawers of the bureau visible inside the bedroom: "Is that why you frisked the place?"

"She's never been tidy."

"Why are you here?"

"If you don't know—"

"No," the Australian interrupted softly. "Tell me."

A short silence. "I should call the police."

"You can try."

Akimov played a hunch. "For me, the police are an embarrassment, but you'd rather not speak with them at all."

"There's plenty I'd rather not do."

The room was suddenly charged with threat—Akimov knew men like this, raised rough and raised wrong, good animals if you held the leash. "You're better than that."

"You sure?"

"I hope." A handful of seconds slunk past, and the tension eased from Akimov's shoulders—if the man hadn't gone for his throat yet, he wouldn't. "What are you doing here?"

The Australian shook his head ruefully. "Wish I knew. Did you find anything?"

"If I had, would I still be looking?"

"Probably," the man said, and the door opened again.

A rifle barrel twitched into the room, followed by a floral sleeve and the landlord's mother, clutching the weapon unsteadily in spotted hands, finger on the trigger. "You there!" she gasped, aiming the rifle everywhere at once.

"Lower that weapon," Akimov roared. "This instant!"

"You—you're in my house—"

"Sergeant!" Akimov barked at the Australian. "If she doesn't lower that—"

"Oh!" She aimed at the floorboards. "I'm sorry, I didn't know— the army? My son is away on business, I'm so sorry."

Akimov took the rifle, and the Australian stepped close beside him so he couldn't use it.

"We're looking for Frau—Fräulein Loeffert," Akimov said. "Nadya Loeffert. Where is she?"

"She's not here." The woman's voice quavered. "She only stayed with her mother two or three times. She's not here."

"Where is she?"

"Has—has something dreadful happened?" she said, still not answering the question.

"You know where she is."

The woman paled. "Oh, I haven't any idea . . ."

Wind scraped from the river and whistled toothlessly past the house, and the Australian disappeared into stillness, despite his suffocating presence moments before. Akimov checked the rifle. He couldn't unload one-handed so he gave the weapon to the Australian—made no difference—and waited.

"I was worried," the woman finally said. "Frau Loeffert is in some sort of trouble, but her daughter is a good religious girl, she doesn't wear lipstick or nail varnish, she wouldn't do anything wrong."

"We watched your son this morning," Akimov said. "Leaving the house."

"What? He—he's at work—"

"We know of his youthful indiscretion, ma'am, a member of the Communist Party."

Tears welled in her eyes. "He's a hard worker, a good boy. Only his firm wouldn't understand . . . What will you do with him?"

"Nothing, if you tell us where the girl is."

The woman wilted. "She didn't—she asked me to tell nobody. She needed advice on travel, her mother left early that morning and . . ."

"Would you rather we asked your son?"

"No—please. She took the train east, to Graubunden canton, to Bad Ragaz." She swallowed, and tears ran down her grooved cheeks. "She was visiting a friend of her mother, an important man. In Bad Ragaz."

"His name?" Akimov demanded.

"Herr Hostettler," the woman whispered. "Professor. Herr Professor Hostettler."

Anna cut across the street at the tram stop of the Gurten railway, toward the newspaper offices. Despite the solid Bernese street, the ground shifted underfoot, the investigation spinning beyond her control. Too many strands to follow—the barracks deal, the clearing credits, the threat of another non-aggression pact. She paused in the foyer to straighten her hat and strengthen her resolve. One thing at a time: first, convince Pierre-Luc to produce the police report on the car Grant crashed, to find the owner's name. Perhaps then they'd know who was behind this.

But on the fourth floor, the receptionist shook her head. "I'm sorry, Madame Fay, Monsieur Soyer won't be in the office today. He's home with an illness."

"That's not like Pierre-Luc."

The receptionist smiled. "No, but if you'd heard him on the telephone this morning . . . the poor man sounded like death warmed over."

Anna thanked her, and stepped back into the corridor. Would anyone else give her access to the police report? Not without Pierre-Luc's blessing.

Twenty minutes later, in a leafy neighborhood across Bern, she rang the bell of his house and waited. No answer, so she grabbed the lion's-head knocker and the door swung open into an empty foyer.

"Pierre-Luc?" she called from the bottom of a sweeping staircase. "Hello?"

Silence . . . except for a faint high piano note: *plink, plink*.

"Hello?" Coming from the corridor. She followed the sound into a gloomy drawing room, curtains drawn and lamps dark. *Plink, plink, plink*. "Pierre-Luc?"

She reached for the light switch, and a man slumped at the piano in the corner said, "Don't."

"Pierre-Luc?" she said. "What happened? Should I—"

"You've done enough." He tapped the high note: *plink-plink*. "Go away, Anna."

"Are you ill? What happened? Pierre-Luc, tell me what's happened." No answer, so she forged on. "I need your help. The balance of the war is—"

"He threatened my children."

"He what? Who?"

"You tell me, Anna. You led him to my family." Pierre-Luc's voice remained flat. "My children—he knows their names."

"I'm so sorry, I—"

"Don't apologize, Anna. Just get out of my house."

"No." She stepped closer. "If you want to be rid of him, Pierre-

Luc, I need your help." *Plink plink plink plink.* "I need a police report. Once I get that, he'll never return."

"He never will. I saw to that."

Something in his tone chilled her. "What did you tell him?"

"Whatever he wanted. Mind your own child, Anna—mind your own."

"What did you tell him? Pierre-Luc, what did you tell him?"

His fists crashed on the piano keys. "Get out! If you don't leave now, God help me—I won't be responsible for what I do."

CHAPTER 33

The professor's house was on the shore of a small mountain lake, five miles outside Bad Ragaz as the crow flies—but they weren't flying the crow. Grant was driving and the Russian navigating, each afraid to let the other out of sight. An uneasy unspoken partnership, born the moment they stepped from the boardinghouse and headed the same direction.

Grant accelerated into a curve. No other choice: keep your friends close and your enemies closer, and he wasn't sure which Akimov was. He was Russian, though, and knew about Loeffert's daughter—best to tag along, see where this was heading. Closer to Hostettler, at least.

A wary silence stretched through the drive east, broken only by directions until they reached Bad Ragaz. The mountains, the clouds, the winding roads with buses and a convoy of trucks: Grant was tired of Switzerland. Give him gray drizzling England, the familiarity of the pub and the village and the air base—hell, give him Burma, with landing strips carved from tea plantations and birdcage cities, the foreignness comfortably absolute. Akimov was both foreign and familiar, sitting in his rumpled suit with his missing arm, the model of every bearish commander Grant ever saw . . . but Russian.

Still, Grant had logged ten thousand hours in cockpits with bored men, and his gut told him this one was okay. Of course, his gut told him all kinds of things—that's why he was here instead of the hotel, instead of chasing down the crash site and camera. Because his gut told him: Anna Fay.

They stopped for directions to the professor's house at the post office: past the cable railway and woods, through a little village with a big church. They returned to the car, and Akimov unfolded a photograph of Magda Loeffert and a girl with a high forehead and dark demure eyes.

"That's her daughter?"

"My daughter," the Russian said, like he was surprised. "She's my daughter."

Grant looked at him. "You're the first husband. You really *are* family."

"Yes."

"I thought the daughter was from her second marriage."

"She never told me." Akimov stared at the picture. "Look at her."

"She looks like—" he stopped, not wanting to say too much.

"Her mother. You know Magda?"

"We met."

"You're after the document she found," the Russian said. "Yes, I know about that. You think Nadya gave it to Hostettler for safekeeping."

"And what're you after?"

Akimov looked at the photograph, and didn't answer.

The countryside was rough but the road wasn't as bad as the postmaster warned. A dozen houses dotted the valley, with Hostettler's house a quarter mile down a turnoff, a two-story châlet with

279

an Alfa Romeo in the tree-lined drive. Four or five houses perched at the edge of the lake, but none were too close—when Grant stepped from the car, the buzz of insects around a late-flowering bush was the loudest sound.

"Not Australian, are you?" Akimov said.

" 'Course I am, mate."

"American?"

Grant gave up. "Yeah."

The Russian grabbed the iron hoop on the door and knocked. "The accent is a little different."

"You've met Australians?"

"This isn't my first war—and in the '20s, I did some traveling."

"They let you travel?"

"In the '20s, 'they' were me." He rapped with his knuckles on the glass pane beside the door. "A car in the drive, but nobody answers."

Grant checked the knob: unlocked.

"Trust is a wonderful thing," the Russian said.

Above the sharp frozen peaks, the wind shoved the clouds around, and twenty yards away a wooden pier jutted from a sudden mossy bank. Nobody in sight. Grant opened the door and was greeted by the homey scent of roasting pork.

"Herr Professor?" Akimov called, stepping inside.

Hats and boots cluttered an alcove to the left of the door, and beyond that a timber-beamed room sprawled the width of the house, with book-lined walls and a reading chair by the fireplace.

"Herr Professor?"

Grant headed past the stairs to a modest kitchen. Near a door opening onto a little garden, a white mug lolled sideways on the table in the breakfast nook, like a defeated king in a chess game, and fresh-spilled coffee stained the tablecloth and dripped to the floor. The top of the cookstove glowed dull red, and under the scent of roasting meat Grant smelled something damp and animal: fear.

The hair rose on the back of his neck. He heard footsteps behind him and said, "What the hell happened here?"

The Russian brushed past. "Nothing good."

A metal box gaped open on the countertop, with copper handles and a keyhole: a safe box. Charred paper and ash wafted inside, where documents meant for safekeeping had been burned to powder.

Grant touched the handle. "Still hot."

"Whoever started the fire," Akimov said, "he isn't long gone."

"If he's gone at all," Grant said, taking a knife from a block on the counter. He pointed to his chest, then pointed upstairs. "Watch the doors."

Akimov nodded and crossed to the sink as Grant went into the hall. He prowled through every room, opened every closet, kept himself loose and ready. Nothing on the first floor. The staircase was a choke point, though. He cracked his neck, his palm dry on the knife handle—and saw motion through the dining-room window: in the woods, a man with a backpack and a walking stick.

Not a walking stick—a rifle.

Down the hall, through the open door, he tackled Akimov at the kitchen sink, sending them crashing to the floor.

The Russian groaned and cradled his stump to his stomach. "*Blyad!* My arm!"

Grant rolled away, staying low, and the quiet wasn't shattered by a gunshot. "Rifle," he said. "Outside."

"The mountain or the road?"

"The hill, there. One man, with a—a heavy pack, parallel to the house."

"That's not a pack—" Akimov squeezed his stump, trying to ease the pain. "It's a body."

"Hostettler?"

"Safe bet. The killer got Magda's document—you saw the empty safe box. Opened with a combination he tortured from Hostettler. Did you find a rifle rack?"

"I'll look."

"*I'll* look, you get to a window and watch. How many ways into the house?"

"Three or four, plus maybe a bulkhead or coal chute."

Akimov stood, his face ashen. "You couldn't have hit me on the other side?"

"Next time."

Grant went upstairs, holding the knife ready. Nobody was waiting, not in any of the four bedrooms, the closets, or the bathroom. He twitched back the master bedroom curtain and scanned the hillside. A granite outcropping, scattered pines, the blue-gray sky above dirty white clouds. Nothing.

A few quiet minutes passed, then Akimov came upstairs and stood in the doorway. "No rifle rack. Not a violent man, the professor. A bad way to die."

"You sure he's dead? I didn't see any blood."

"The rifleman cauterized what he cut." Akimov gazed at the hillside. "The other side of that ledge—he can circle around, approach from the back."

"Do you think—"

Akimov stepped into the hallway, out of sight. "There are four entrances to watch," he called. "If he gets inside we're in trouble."

"His rifle's no good inside."

"You willing to bet your life he doesn't have a sidearm?" Akimov asked, voice muffled.

Good point. "So what's the plan?"

"We watch, three of the windows overlook the four entrances."

"Three windows, two of us."

"We'll patrol, guest room to the bath to the master bedroom."

"Duck duck goose," Grant said in English, going toward the bathroom.

"Dancing 'round the Maypole," the Russian said, also in English, passing him in the hall. "Or is it the 'mulberry bush'? There's a children's rhyme, no?"

Grant stepped into the bathroom, watched the lake and lawn from the cloudy window over the tub. "Why'd he take Hostettler with him?" he said, loud enough to carry.

"To hide the evidence."

"Maybe he's not dead."

"He talked, why keep him alive? The killer saw us coming, dragged the body away." Akimov tapped the bathroom door as he passed. "Toss him in a ravine, maybe—an old man twists his ankle on a path, let animals finish the job."

Grant went back to the master bedroom and watched nothing happen on the circular drive and the hill beyond. "You've got all the answers."

"Not all."

"And the safe box?"

"Whoever wanted that document found it."

And only one person wanted it burned—the man it implicated. "We could make a break," Grant called. "One of us out each door."

"And if he has the car in his sights?"

"How about the lake?"

"I don't swim, but don't let that stop you. Perhaps he's gone— or a bad shot."

"On the other hand," Grant said. They were safe in the house, and the rifleman was saddled with a body he wanted to dispose of. While the daylight remained, they could see outside better than he could see in. "But how long're we gonna play ring around the rosy?"

"Is that like the mulberry bush?" They passed in the corridor again and Akimov shot him a sidelong look. "Ah! A pilot."

"Yeah?" Grant stepped into the children's room. "What do you fly?"

Akimov laughed. "Are you familiar with Anna Akhmatova?"

"No."

"A poetess who spent a great deal of time looking out windows." His voice changed, reciting: " 'Look back at the rose turrets of your native town, the square where you sang, the pool where you swam, the windows peeking from your cozy home. Lot's wife looked and was bound, her feet rooted in the stony ground.' "

Grant went to the bathroom door. Inside, standing at an angle to the window, Akimov rubbed the stump of his arm. He turned and met Grant's eyes, and they stood like that, then Grant moved to the master bedroom.

Time slunk past. He smoked one of Akimov's makhorka cigarettes and listened to the empty house. In the bathroom again, he knocked cigarette ash into the sink.

"How'd you lose the arm?" he called.

"A wall fell on me."

"Which war?"

"This one."

"And the scars around your eye?"

A slight hesitation. "That was a boot—I was in prison."

"In Russia?"

"Kolyma."

"Never heard of it."

"In Siberia, a labor camp five times the size of France, broken into a hundred camps. Two million prisoners."

"What were you in for?"

"The birth pangs of the future. It was a *zek*—an old prisoner— who taught me the poem, he knew all her poems."

"Is he still there?"

"He's dead." Akimov paused, maybe remembering. "Sometimes the last man to fall in would be shot as a *dokhodyaga*, an idler. To teach the rest of us a lesson."

"Is that what you were arrested for? Idling?"

"No, I was accused of anti-Party propaganda—I wasn't sufficiently guarded in my speech, I complained about the arrests."

"Talked to the wrong person, huh?"

Another pause. "My father denounced me."

"Your father? Shit, and I thought mine was bad."

"A political necessity. As a tsar's man, he needed to prove his loyalty, so he gave them me. His only son, whom he loved."

"Some kind of love. Then you're a—what's your rank?"

"Major."

"A major and an ex-con."

"They needed officers, they paroled us from the gulag—those still alive."

"And after prison, you still fought for them?"

"Not for *them*. For my countrymen and my country, for the sort of Communism the world has not yet seen—and against the Fascists."

"Is that straight? Your own father ratted you into prison?"

"At least there was a reason. I knew men fingered by debtors who didn't want to repay a loan, a woman who spent eight months in Lubyanka for a clerical error."

"Some country." They passed in the hall and Grant said, "You got another cigarette?"

Akimov gave him the tobacco pouch. "Roll one for me."

In the guest room, he opened the pouch and straightened the rolling papers.

"All countries are built on bloodshed," Akimov said, his voice distant. "Look at yours, you slaughtered Indians for land and enslaved Negroes for money."

"That's history."

"We're a young country, our history happens now."

"That doesn't mean—"

"You live in a stolen house and say crime is history. Our troubles will pass and our children will deplore them—and they'll profit, as you do, from the blood their fathers shed." The Russian fell silent a moment. "We all live on graveyards."

Anna would know how to answer that, but Grant didn't. Next time they stepped into the hall, he gave Akimov a lighted cigarette and said, "You can't change the past. The present's all we have."

"And the future."

"You're talking about your daughter?"

"My daughter." A smile cracked the man's hard face. "I want to shout the words from the rooftops."

Grant watched him disappear into the bedroom, then went to stand at the bathroom window. Finished his cigarette, tossed the butt in the sink, changed rooms five more times. He needed to move. He met the Russian in the hall and said, "Let's go."

"Not yet."

"When?"

"The hill with the pines is the best sniper nest, then the outcropping." The Russian glanced at the window, where the sky was washed with gray. "When the sun's in his eyes, we go."

"If he's still there."

"Even better if he's not."

Grant looked at the sun. "You've commanded snipers."

"And faced them. Go back to your window."

He went back to his window. Fifty minutes passed, same as all the other minutes, then Akimov's voice came: "You were infantry before air force?"

"No."

"You were born for the infantry."

"Not anymore. I was in Nanking, the tail end of 1937." The shadows lengthened in the woods, across the lake. "Yeah, everything's built on a graveyard."

"You got out alive."

"Mostly."

He heard footsteps behind him, and Akimov was standing in the doorway.

Grant shrugged. "Before Nanking, I was fearless, I was . . . a bear trap. Trip the wire and the jaws close, no hesitation."

"The killer instinct." Akimov said something in Russian, then back in German: "Instinct is for animals. Men have souls."

"Fat lot of good they do."

Akimov smiled, maybe sadly. "Time to go."

They went downstairs, eyed the sun and the woods. A dusting of snow fell from a clear sky and disappeared. They ran for the car and Grant gunned the engine, sped away from the lake. There weren't any gunshots, there weren't any roadblocks, there was nothing but the empty mountains and the long empty day.

CHAPTER 34

The radio played a Wagner song cycle in the dark dining room, the glossy telephone out of place at the head of the table. Villancourt sat motionless, like a snake conserving energy. In board meetings and conferences, with investors and bankers, he'd never hesitated—yet cradling a dead boy's head in his lap had been new. Watching the life fade from his nephew's eyes had been new.

The German soldiers encircled Anna Fay's house; once Lieutenant Grant returned, the phone would ring. Pongratz had tracked Hostettler to Bad Ragaz; once he had secured the documents, the phone would ring. Then Villancourt would strike.

On the radio, "Im Treibhaus" ended and "Schmerzen" began—from "In the Greenhouse" to "Sorrow"—and Villancourt heard his sister's sobbing woven through the song. Almost comic, yet for some reason he found himself moved.

The phone rang and he snatched it up. "This is Villancourt."

"It's done," Pongratz said.

"You have the document?"

"Destroyed."

"Thank heavens! You're certain?"

"Of course."

"No additional copies? That's what the man told you?"

"Yes—and in the end he convinced me."

"Then this is over?" Villancourt asked. "No more complications?"

"This is finished, yes, but there are complications. Two men interrupted my . . . discussion."

"After you succeeded?"

"Yes. They're just a hanging thread, connected to nothing and no one."

"Except, possibly, the girl."

Pongratz grunted. "You might ask her what else she knows. Although without the paperwork you cannot be touched."

"Indeed," he said. "I'll speak with the girl before you finish her."

He rang off, wondering about the two men. Well, so long as Pongratz had destroyed that document, success was inevitable. All that remained were the negotiations, the nitty-gritty of finance and industry . . . and the soldiers waiting for the American murderer.

The *Wesendonck Lieder* ended, and the phone rang again. One of the soldiers from Anna Fay's house. "Herr Villancourt," he said. "We searched the woman's house and—"

"You entered her house?"

"Yes, sir."

"Were you instructed to enter the house?"

"Not . . . entirely, sir. But they've left. The man's clothing and toiletries are gone—not a trace of him."

"He's gone?"

"The woman, too, we think. Possibly. And the boy, the son, his dresser is completely bare."

"You're telling me—you're telling me this murderer is gone?"

"I'm sorry, sir."

A cold certainty rose from Villancourt's chest. He'd find this Lieutenant Grant and punish him, whatever obstacles rose in his path, however long it took. Every time he blinked he saw Hugo's blood-clouded eyes urging him onward; he would do as they commanded.

"We went through the woman's papers," the soldier continued. "Her correspondence. There are a dozen friends and family they may—"

Villancourt glanced at the clock. "In the paperwork, did you find the son's school?"

"Pardon? The son?"

"Yes, the son. Christopher? Christoph."

"But it's the man you want, no?"

"The man is gone. The boy is Anna Fay's family, as Hugo is mine, and if she cares more for this American than her son, perhaps she won't miss him when he's gone, perhaps she won't do as she's told, but I will see her suffer for her—" He heard the anger in his voice, and calmed himself. "What is the son's school?"

"His school?"

"The name of the school the boy attends. I don't know how to express myself more clearly. Where is his school?"

"One moment, sir, I'll ask." The soldier's voice muffled as he relayed the question, then returned. "Yes, we found a grade card. He attends a local school, not far away."

"Go to the school. Right now. Take the boy."

"Well, sir, he's most likely with his mother."

"You said his dresser is empty?"

"Almost entirely."

"But his mother took so little you can hardly tell if she's even gone? She didn't pack for him, they left separately—and she'll expect he's safe at school."

"What shall we do?"

"See that he's not."

· · ·

A billow of steam rolled across the railway platform and enveloped a porter slouched under a brass placard. The American angled forward and Akimov touched his elbow, to keep him from knocking the porter around: they couldn't afford a scene. The landlord's mother had told them Nadya took the train to Hostettler, chances were she took one back, too—problem was, Grant had realized the same thing. For now, at least, they were a team.

The American slowed, and Akimov asked the porter, "What's your name?"

"Stosser, sir."

"Stand up straight."

The porter shoved himself off the wall with his shoulders.

"Herr Stosser." Akimov took the photograph from his breast pocket. "You recognize the younger woman."

The porter picked at his cheek. "Can't say I do."

"Look closer."

"She was on the train today?"

"Four days ago."

"A thousand passengers since then . . ." The boy sighed. "Shall I fetch the head porter?"

"Do that," Akimov said, and watched him slouch across the tracks.

"He doesn't like you," Grant said.

"A boy that age—if he were Russian, he'd be at Stalingrad. At least I didn't kick him."

"I'm getting impatient."

"What's your urgency?"

"I'm wasting time, I want this in my rearview and shrinking." The American offered him a cigarette. "You?"

"She's my daughter."

"And this is your duty. You're not working for the army." Grant struck a match and lit their cigarettes. "Security service?"

"The army—always and forever."

"You never told me what you're after."

Akimov inhaled a lungful of smoke. No reason to mention the cease-fire talks. "Magda's dead, and her daughter is missing. My daughter. My daughter. What do you think I'm after?" The truth of his words rang inside him like a bell. "And you? What do you want, now that document is burned?"

"Whatever she knows about it."

"Why do you think she knows anything?"

"Can't hurt to ask."

A man in a porter's uniform with extra gold braid crossed the tracks, and Akimov thanked him for his help and showed him Nadya's photograph.

"But excuse me," the man said, "who exactly are you?"

"She's my fiancée," Grant said. "She ran away with this bastard's brother."

"Watch your language," Akimov said.

The head porter's eyes sharpened. "Please, gentlemen."

"You recognize her?" Grant asked.

"There are so many faces . . ."

They tossed the story around for a few minutes, then a ten-franc note appeared between Grant's thumb and forefinger. Five minutes of negotiation, another ten francs, and the head porter went to his office for the ledger.

"You think he bought any of that?" the American asked.

"Maybe the francs bought him."

"Or he's calling the cops."

"*My* papers are in order," Akimov said.

"Sure," Grant said. "Mine, too."

Akimov blew a cloud of smoke, wondering if he'd imagined that hitch in the American's voice, then the head porter returned with a ledger and showed them the entries. "She may have been third class, we don't record those. First and second, yes, but no Fräulein Nadya Loeffert. She is Russian?"

Grant twisted the book away from the man. "Maybe you missed the name."

"Please! This is not allowed. Return that at once!"

Akimov glanced at the page: lines of entries, with tickets and compartments and prices, luggage receipts, columns of obscure marks.

"You cannot," the head porter sputtered. "That is the property of the railway!"

"He's right," Akimov said, scanning the rows of names. "Give him back his book."

Grant didn't look up from the page. "Twenty francs."

"Here!" The man produced the bills from his vest pocket. "That is not your property. You must return it at once, or—"

Grant handed the book over and Akimov took the bills from the man's fingers. They left the station, passed the diner to the street. They'd both seen the name: Hostettler, one second-class ticket to Zurich. The professor had driven her to the station, bought the ticket, and waved goodbye.

Christoph toyed with the inkwell on his school desk as the other students filed from the classroom—biding his time, heart fluttering like a hummingbird. The bully Horst usually caught him in the hallway after this class, and most days he scurried immediately to the dubious sanctuary of chapel services. But not today. Today he waited for Horst, today he was a soldier. *Not bad, soldier.* He wasn't tough like his father, but tough like Mr. Grant, like *Lieutenant* Grant—an American, a fighter pilot, an officer. The second kind of tough.

293

He took a deep breath and blew the specks of eraser rubber from his desktop, then gathered his books and left the classroom. The hallway was empty save for a chauffeur waiting near the courtyard door and four students rushing past on the tile floor. Christoph followed them at a distance, nervous but also eager.

What would Lieutenant Grant say when he heard Christoph faced the bully? Well, he'd probably just—

Horst stepped from a doorway niche, smiling his rosy fat-cheeked smile. "Late for chapel, Chrissy? Maybe your *father* can call the headmaster." His smile drooped as Christoph headed straight for him, but he continued: "Oh, you *haven't* a father."

"And you haven't a—"

A man's voice echoed in the corridor: "You're Christoph Fay?"

He stopped, heart pounding, a foot from Horst. Slowly turned to the man, the chauffeur, and said, "Um, yes sir."

"The car is waiting."

"For me? So early?"

"I'm afraid so, Mr. Fay. I was told to pick you up." The chauffeur checked his watch. "Five minutes ago."

Christoph turned to the other boy. "Sorry, Borscht. The car is waiting."

Red spots rose on Horst's cheeks; he hated the nickname. "You're lucky."

He laughed, and followed the chauffeur outside. What a fine day, the best he could remember—he hoped it never ended.

A checkpoint blocked the entry of the Zurich rail station, half a dozen bored Swiss reservists inspecting papers. Grant drove past and parked beside the Metzgerbräu, wondering if they had his picture, wondering if Martin's papers would pass. Wondering what he'd do if they didn't.

"You coming?" Akimov asked.

Grant grunted and stepped from the car. They crossed the plaza, and an Italian businessman outside the Commerico Hotel asked for a light. Grant struck a match and said, "Trouble at the station?"

"You mean the checkpoint?" the Italian said. "No, they're just looking for German saboteurs again."

"How long've they been there?"

The man shrugged. "A week? They're afraid of frogmen at Lake Constance, so they check papers in Zurich."

"The Swiss," another Italian said. "Always thorough."

The Italians laughed, and they crossed the street toward the Bahnhofplatz. The Russian scratched the stump of his arm, eyed the checkpoint, and said, "They may be logging names."

"You think they took your daughter's name?" Grant asked.

"Could be."

"If she left the station instead of boarding another train."

They merged with a knot of businessmen, flashed their papers at the Swiss reservists, and walked past, easy as that. Inside the station, the offices were tucked behind a glass case containing a model Swiss town, down to the trees and snow and cows. Grant asked for the station manager and they landed in a room with a view of the switching yards, where a secretary stood at a chrome desk, putting a dustcover on a typewriter. She was blond with cheerful blue eyes and belonged on a Swiss Tourist Board pamphlet.

"Is the station manager available?" Grant asked.

"The office closes early today," she said, tugging at the dustcover. "I should be gone myself."

"If you could spare a minute," Grant said. "We have a—an awkward problem."

Her cheerful eyes grew wary. "Yes?"

"My friend—he's Russian—show her your papers."

Akimov obliged. "I'm a member of the trade delegation in Bern."

"His daughter lives in Switzerland," Grant said. "We're afraid she's gone missing."

The secretary put her hand to her mouth. "I'm so sorry."

"She's been gone three days."

"Four." Akimov showed the picture of the girl and her mother. "This is her, with my wife."

"We think she came through Zurich. She—" Grant shook his head. "There was a gentleman, er, flattering her."

"Not a *gentleman*," Akimov said. "Hostettler."

"They came from Bad Ragaz. We're sorry to keep you late, but Nadya . . ."

"She's a good girl," Akimov said. "Only she imagined herself in love, and this man . . "

Grant murmured, "He's married."

The woman snapped into action—asked a few questions then lifted the phone to speak with someone named Hartmut. "I have a passenger, a Miss Nadya Loeffert, she arrived from Bad Ragaz on a second-class ticket under the name Hostettler. Check the logs and—yes, now, please. Yes? Yes—thank you." She rung off and turned to Akimov. "Your daughter's ticket was through to Bern but she missed the connection in Zurich. No outbound ticket was purchased under her name or Herr Hostettler's."

"So she stayed in Zurich?"

The secretary nodded. "At least on that day."

"What about her luggage?"

"She had no voucher, and hadn't booked anything into the heavy compartment." She cocked her head. "You must know she didn't pack a trunk."

"We're thinking of *his* luggage," Grant said. "What if she bought a new ticket, with another name?"

"A false name? Not in the past week, with the heightened attention, but she may have gone unreserved third class . . ." She lifted the phone and spoke with Hartmut again, then said, "There were two trains after the Bad Ragaz line, and third class was full on both. She didn't leave by train. Perhaps they took a motor coach, or hired a car?"

"And now could be anywhere," Akimov said.

Grant thanked the secretary and she turned off the lamp, and the three of them walked outside together. Dirty clouds slid across the sky, streetcars grumbled around the corner, and the secretary looked toward the checkpoint. "Four days ago," she said, "they were recording all traffic. They may have taken note."

Grant wasn't sure he wanted to give them another look at him. "They don't seem too thorough."

"Only today. Their duty officially ended this morning, yet they were told to report here just the same." She smiled at a red-haired reservist, approaching. "Are you still here?"

"Keeping you safe, my dear," he said.

"A girl came through, four days ago, Nadya Loeffert. Check for her, won't you?"

The reservist glanced at them, and Grant tried to look harmless while he figured how he'd get ahold of the man's sidearm.

"I promise they're not frogmen," the secretary said, and told the story.

The reservist clucked his tongue at the folly of young women and ran his finger down a page in the logbook. "Four days . . . Loeffert? No."

"She didn't come through the checkpoint?" Grant asked.

"Not that day, she didn't. Nor any other."

Grant glanced at the bored man. "You're certain?"

"We were keener, before today."

"But she disembarked here?" Akimov asked.

The secretary nodded. "That's right."

"So she left her train," Grant said, "and didn't board another . . . but didn't leave the station?"

"It's impossible," Akimov said.

"She didn't pass this checkpoint," the reservist said. "That's all I can tell you."

There was no answer, an hour later, when Akimov knocked on the final door in the administrative wing of the Landesmuseum. He backtracked, spoke with the guards at the Hallwil Collection, learned nothing, and headed outside, through the park to the river promenade. He'd try again at the buildings on Bahnhofplatz: some trace of his daughter must remain, some witness must remember.

On the street, he passed the bar at which he'd left the American, claiming he had business in St. Gallen. If Grant knew he'd planned to remain in Zurich to search, he'd given no sign—probably hadn't cared. Was he Allied intelligence? Was he truly American? In any case, he was gone, and Akimov needed to find Nadya, to discover what she knew. And, more urgently, to look into her eyes and see: his daughter. The one thing that remained of Magda, the one thing that remained of his own youth and dreams. The one thing of beauty he'd brought into the world.

He spoke with clerks, with janitors and bus drivers. None had seen Nadya. She'd arrived in Zurich and vanished, either avoiding the checkpoint or secretly boarding a train. Neither seemed likely, but there was no other option, there was nothing—

Akimov stopped on the street corner. There was one final possibility: she was still in the station.

Grant drove over the bridge toward Schanzenstrasse, found the Women's Hospital and parked in a cluster of cars, unfolding a newspaper for cover. Derailing these talks oughta be easy, with the Commies and Nazis killing each other—but where could they start, now that Magda's document was ashes? Unless Anna found the police report, they were done.

He lighted a cigarette. So what next? Find the crash site and expose this German prototype. Of course, with a cease-fire on the eastern front, it didn't matter what the Luftwaffe was flying—the Battle of Britain would look like a training flight. But these talks started today or tomorrow, and the embassies wouldn't listen to a fugitive American and a Swiss housewife. Well, maybe Anna got the police report. If they had one name—the owner of the car at the hunting box—maybe they could unravel this whole thing.

He flicked cigarette ash out the window, and Anna slid into the passenger seat and said, "You got my note."

Under the door of his hotel room, asking to meet here. "Why a woman's hospital?"

"I've been all around town, trying to call in favors. The consulates, the newspapers. I know a nurse here with family in the Nazi Party; I thought perhaps she'd heard something."

"Did she?"

"Nothing helpful. Tell me you have a lead, Grant, please."

"No luck with your editor?"

"The opposite of luck. Pierre-Luc refused to help find the owner of the car. And he told me . . ." Anna lifted a hand to her throat. "He said . . ."

"Said what?"

"Something about Christoph. He'd been threatened, Pierre-Luc had. His family, his children, threatened. He said I should mind my own child." Her eyes clouded. "If I hadn't already sent Christoph away, I'd worry."

"You're still worried."

"I'm a mother." A smile rose and faltered on her face. "These men, what they did to Lorenz . . . I'm just glad Christoph is safe and gone. Now tell me what happened."

He looked at her for a moment, then adjusted the rearview and pulled from the curb. "The vocational school was a dead end, but I recognized a guy in Burgdorf, from the hotel, a Russian named Akimov. Turns out he's Magda's husband—her first husband, her ex-husband."

"Did he see you?"

"See me? We spent the day together. The daughter is his, from the first marriage, only he didn't know until recently. The landlady told us the girl went to meet Hostettler at his other house."

"He has another house?"

"In Bad Ragaz."

"I've been asking about Herr Hostettler," she said, rubbing her eyes. "Didn't hear about this other house, just that he's an anti-Fascist, a good man."

"He was."

She lowered her hand. "You didn't—what happened?"

"I didn't anything. We got—"

"You and Akimov."

"Don't look at me like that, he's a straight shooter."

"What's he doing in Switzerland?"

"I don't know."

The car hit a bump, and she steadied herself on the dashboard. "You don't know."

"He's a major in the Red Army, he heard about his daughter, I guess, got himself to Switzerland—"

"He's Magda's ex-husband, Grant, they sent him to find her. Only the Germans found her first, so he went after the daughter, and you saw him."

He turned that over. "Makes sense."

"And the professor? He's dead?"

"Yeah, he— He'd been asked some hard questions."

"I haven't any idea what you mean."

"Someone hurt him first."

"Like Lorenz?"

"Yeah, probably Pongratz. Hostettler gave up the combination of his safe box, and the killer set fire to whatever was inside. Nothing left but ashes."

She closed her eyes. "He burned the document. We can't find the men behind the barracks-deal money laundering. We can't use Magda's proof to pressure them—blackmail them—into influencing these talks. It's over."

"There's still the police report, find the owner of the car."

"That's no use without the documents for leverage, Grant. You found Hostettler dead and the papers burned. What happened next?"

"The guy was still there when we showed—"

"Pongratz?"

"If it was him, yeah." He told her about playing 'round the mulberry bush. "We waited for the sun to move, and left. No sign of the rifleman. I figured, stay close to the Russian, find the daughter, maybe she'll know something. We went to the local station—Nadya caught a train, landed in Zurich, and disappeared." He parked on a dead-end street and finished the story. "Akimov stayed in Zurich, I came back to Bern, hoping you'd found something."

"Magda's dead, her daughter's vanished, the document's burned." Anna spoke flatly. "Yes, Grant, I found something."

The pressure in the car changed, and he knew better than to say anything.

"Failure," she said. "That's what I found."

"The talks don't start until—"

"No. Martin was right. He never respected me, not really, not from the heart." She twisted her wedding ring. "He never trusted me to make him proud. He knew I wasn't the woman he deserved. And all I wanted—all I wanted was to prove him wrong."

"We're not done yet."

"What else is there?"

"You'll think of something."

Anna turned away. "He regretted marrying me. His mother told him he'd married beneath himself. She was right. She blamed me when he didn't come home." She lowered her head. "She was right about that, too."

Grant wanted to recite a poem like Akimov, but he didn't know any. He wanted to take her in his arms and hold her. Instead, he said, "Somewhere in Switzerland, the Nazis and Soviets are negotiating a cease-fire. You want to cry over something, cry over that—the Thousand-Year Reich. Forget Martin's mother, his son's gonna be living in Greater Germany if we don't stop this truce. You wanna cry over something, cry over that."

She said, "Take me home."

He pulled the car around, turned right past a Catholic church, toward the hotel.

"Not the hotel," Anna told him. "Home."

"Your house isn't safe."

"Stop here, Grant."

He looked at her, then pulled to the curb. "Martin would've been proud of you—any man would."

"Don't be a fool," she said, and walked away.

Twenty minutes in the night air cleared Anna's head, and cooled her temper. She stopped at a postbox and for a moment didn't recognize the neighborhood, then saw the Alhambra Theatre across the street. Maulbeerstrasse, closer to home than the Palace Hotel—and how dangerous could her own house be? She'd failed to achieve anything, to accomplish anything . . . surely such mediocrity didn't inspire opposition.

At least at home she'd have her own bed, the memory of Martin, and the scent of her son. Joris and Christoph must've arrived in

302

Ticino already—thank God she'd sent them away—but she'd still be surrounded by evidence of her family and of herself: Anna Fay, more than a failure. What was at the Palace for her? Not Lorenz, still in the hospital, tortured for helping her. Rosine? Yes, Rosine was there, and Anna had a new job for her, a new man to seduce— but how much longer could she use the girl without destroying her? And what else waited for her at the hotel? Grant?

She paused at the crossroads, deciding.

CHAPTER 35

kimov sat on a stone bench outside the Zurich station, shoulders bowed under the weight of despair. Nadya wasn't in the station, not the public halls or restrooms, the railyard or offices or mechanic's shed. He'd sorted through three bins of found luggage, and discovered nothing with her name. None of the signalmen or stevedores recognized her picture, nor did the shunters or porters or ticket agents. They'd killed his wife, and his daughter had faded like an echo into silence.

The sunset dimmed and icy drizzle filled a puddle, raindrops splashing like shell splinters in the Stalingrad mud, where good men died on stretchers, in dugouts, in sewage tunnels crossed by charred beams. Rain collected in the trenches, and soldiers drowned in two inches of muck. Soon the Volga would freeze.

He opened his tobacco pouch, but had nothing left.

Why is our century worse than all the others?
Because we touched the foulest wounds—and left them
*   unhealed.*

Dawn glows in the West but here Death already chalks a
* door,*
And summons the crows, and the crows fly.

Akimov hired a taxi and returned in bleak silence to Bern. Inside the Palace Hotel, the elevator rose swift and smooth as an executioner's ax, and upstairs he knocked at his father's suite. Little Vlad opened the door and said, "Where's the damn car?"

"Burgdorf. The *bahnhof* parking lot."

Little Vlad swore. "The deputy commissar wants to see you, two hours ago."

"Then let me past."

"Not here, he's in conference with the Nazis, an introductory meeting for the unofficial negotiation of the preliminary talks." He snorted. "Only the fucking Germans. They're in the second-floor conference room."

When Akimov stepped into the private meeting room, his father was shaking his head at the German negotiator, demurring in his resonant voice: "That's a generous offer, but the Soviet delegation will remain at the hotel."

"Nonsense, you'll come stay at our embassy."

"We shouldn't like to impose upon your hospitality, Herr Kübler."

"It's no imposition, Deputy Commissar," the German said, a short man with a smart suit and square jaw. "It's our pleasure. The embassy is more secure than the hotel. More comfortable, as well."

"Herr Kübler, if we might discuss more productive—ah!" His father brightened at the sight of Akimov, or pretended to. "Here is my wayward son. Might we adjourn for ten minutes?"

"Of course, Deputy Commissar."

When they were alone, his father turned to Akimov. "Tell me you found Magda's document. Tell me we can prove the money laundering, tell me we have leverage against the Germans and

305

you didn't run away only to sulk. This smug bastard wants to move the talks to his embassy, as a token of our complete capitulation."

"The document is gone. Destroyed."

His father grew still. "Are you sure?"

"I found Magda's boardinghouse—found the man to whom she entrusted the papers that prove the barracks deal. He'd been tortured and killed. A pile of ashes in his safe box."

"Then we have no evidence of Swiss complicity in a Nazi intelligence ring? No names, no leverage? Nothing?"

"No."

"If we can't use the illegitimate Swiss support of the Reichsbank to sway these talks, capitulation is our only choice. We'll take whatever crumbs the Nazis offer."

Akimov shrugged. "So long as the siege of Stalingrad ends."

"You'd give them all of the Ukraine?"

"They want the Ukraine?"

"What won't they ask for? This war won't end until they're all dead, or we are."

"You need to buy time, that's all."

"I need a drink." His father rubbed his eyes. "I need—I need a man to stand beside me, shoulder to shoulder. Someone I know from the bone, do you understand?"

"Someone who won't betray you?"

"Will you never forgive me?"

"Perhaps I would—if you gave me a reason."

"You're my son, look at you. You have my eyes, my nose—my blood beats in your heart. You think your mulishness came from nowhere? Your bloody-mindedness, your anger, your idealism? I have nobody else, Edik, I have no one. I'm a deputy commissar, a confidant of Beria, sent to Switzerland to negotiate the pact which will save our country, and I have nothing but you."

Akimov looked at him—his thick white hair and heavy brows,

his strong arms and wide shoulders—and saw, for the first time, an old man. He opened his mouth, but before he could speak the Germans filed back inside.

Returning to his seat at the table, the German negotiator smiled at his father. "I've had news from a wayward wanderer, myself."

"Have you, Herr Kübler?"

"Yes, I learned of a little fire, at an old friend's house. Oh, but don't worry, nothing of value was lost." Kübler sipped water from the glass at his elbow. "Only some paperwork."

"Is that so?"

"A few documents, some old purchase orders. Now, where were we? Ah, yes—have you given more thought to reconvening at the embassy?"

"I have. We'd be honored."

"And you'll stay in our guest suites?"

His father bowed his head, defeated. "Our pleasure. Tomorrow morning?"

"Excellent. Now, if we wish our superiors to profitably continue this discussion we must address issues of industry and commerce . . ."

Akimov listened to the slash and thrust of the discussion, remembering another negotiation, another world, when he'd turned a Stalingrad corner and found four of his men dragging a machine gun into the shadow of a wall:

We lost the building, he'd told them. *We're falling back, you're going the wrong direction.*

See there, Comrade Major, across the street, past the shell craters? The staircase leading to nowhere?

That's a chimney, a toppled chimney.

Toppled onto a staircase. The four of us will crawl over, climb the stairs, and fire from above.

You won't get halfway before they start shooting.

We're not going halfway, Comrade Major. We're going all the way.

The four of you? You too, Filya?

For a change of scenery. I've packed a picnic.

Akimov had looked across the still-smoking rubble to the staircase, a suicide mission. *Hold Fritz long enough*, he'd told them, *and we'll retake the courtyard.*

We'll hold them forever.

If you crawled as fast as you talked, he'd said, knowing they'd be dead by noon, *you'd already be there.*

The cost of peace was high, yes, but his men weren't sitting warm in a luxury hotel. Perhaps the Nazis would demand concessions that cut too deep—still, tomorrow would care for itself, or his men wouldn't live past today. And *his* future? He wouldn't leave Switzerland without seeing Nadya, without hearing her voice. She was the only path open to him, the only path that didn't lead across a shelled square to a toppled staircase. Everything was a dead end, everything but her.

At length the meeting ended, and his father took him aside. "Come, Edik. There's a club at Viktoriaplatz with a fine reputation. I need to forget."

Akimov looked at the old man. "That bad?"

"Not another word until I have a drink."

At the club, a maître d' whisked them into a long dining room with white-jacketed waiters and the scent of parsley and roast fish. A glossy black bar stretched the length of the room and ended near a cluster of booths. Akimov and his father were shown to one of the booths, and the Vlads were given a table nearby.

Akimov watched the Vlads cast suspicious gazes over the room, and said, "How much security will you have inside the German embassy?"

"I'm in no danger, not anymore. They've neutered me." His father raised a finger and a sommelier materialized. They spoke about the Bernese lake wines, the Gordola Nostrano, the Lavaux wines of

Vaud. Then Akimov asked for a bottle of vodka, and his father laughed and said, "Two bottles."

They ordered duck breasts with peppercorn, onion soup, and chicken roulade with Gruyère. When the vodka came they each downed a glass, then his father raised his second in a toast. "To words."

Akimov sipped. "Will words matter, without leverage?"

"Words always matter . . . and often fail me. I haven't asked about your arm."

"A wall fell on me. At Rostov."

"I know what happened, Edik, I read the report." He poured another glass. "But I haven't asked how you . . . What does one ask? If you miss the arm?"

"Every time I button a coat."

"You cope well."

"There's nothing to which a man can't grow accustomed," Akimov said. "How do the negotiations stand? Can you recover from the loss of the document?"

"I can mitigate the damage. Slightly."

"That bad?"

"Yes. We'll be forced into painful and dangerous concessions, like an amputa—"

He stopped short, and Akimov laughed. "That's not like you, a faux pas."

"As I said, words fail me." His father's eyes were grave. "At least with you."

"So. Dangerous concessions?"

"Most cease-fires are built from suspicion, but this one is built of certainty. We *will* fight again—Fascists and Communists cannot co-exist long. We both wish to buy time, that's all, the Germans to defeat one enemy before engaging the next, and we—well, you know the situation at Stalingrad, the impossible possibility of losing the city. We're haggling not over peace but over strategic gains."

The soup came, and they ate in silence. Setting the bowl aside, Akimov noticed the Vlads gazing hungrily across the room.

At the bar, a young woman bent over a candle to light her cigarette, the flame glowing across her cheekbones and mouth and all the fine bones of her high-strung face. Her eyes were an exotic slant, her shimmering dress cupped her breasts and caressed her long smooth flanks. She crossed her legs and laughed at the bartender, and all her elegance vanished into unconcealed pleasure—and promise.

"Nothing reveals a woman like her laughter," his father said.

"Not even her conversation?"

"More words. And nothing, Edik, reveals a man like his son."

Akimov took the photograph from his breast pocket. "Or daughter?" He laid the photo in the halo of candlelight on the table.

"Magda's child?" his father asked, bowing his head to look.

"Yes."

His father's brow creased, then smoothed. His breath caught, and he lifted a trembling finger to touch Nadya's face—this from a man who'd condemned his son without a tremor, who'd sacrificed love on the altar of duty. He turned the photograph to the light and his astonished smile spread into awe. "She's yours. She's ours." Tears stained his cheeks. "She looks like your mother."

"Her name is Nadya."

"Nadya. My granddaughter. My—" His breath caught. "Tell me everything."

Akimov did: the boardinghouse bedroom with the prayer ladder and vigil lamp, the journey to Bad Ragaz, following Nadya's trail to the Zurich *bahnhof*, where she vanished like a soft scent in a hard wind.

"Find her," his father said. "She's a . . . a new way forward, Edik. My granddaughter, your daughter. Already I feel her, close as my own pulse. Close as my own son—who I love, who I wronged. You must find her."

"How? In the morning we move to the German embassy."

"Not you. No—you find her, find Nadya. Return to her board-inghouse, go through her papers."

"There's nothing there, that was a hotel room not a home."

"Look at her eyes, so like your mother's, in which nothing is hidden. She has the— Do you think she has the same cast of mind? Icons in her room . . ." A wondering smile rose on his face. "She's our only hope. For the talks and for . . . What if Magda entrusted her with more than the documents, what if she also told her what they said? This is our final chance, this is—*she* is my final chance, do you see? I've spun everything else into dross, I was given a mountain of gold and melted it for slag—"

"Will you ever stop crying?"

"Am I crying?" His father touched his face in surprise. "This doesn't call for tears, but celebration."

"Another bottle?"

"Not for you. Take Little Vlad and force this landlord to talk."

"He knows nothing."

"Are you certain? Are you willing to bet the lives of all the men at Stalingrad?" His father reached across the table and grabbed his wrist. "You must find her. She's all either of us has left."

Nadya dried her face in the beveled mirror over the sink. Her cheekbones were sharper and her lips fuller, her eyes deeper and darker, as if without the anxieties of freedom she was reduced to es-sentials: soon all that would remain was faith.

Faith, and the grate in the shoe-shine room. Only one bolt re-mained. She went into the narrow corridor, and stopped as if struck. She hadn't felt a breeze in days, but now fresh air brushed her cheeks and her calm almost fled. *Be merciful to us sinners, You created us, have mercy on us, though we have sinned, forgive us.* She exhaled and entered the lounge and found a man there, with a face like the assistant manager of a village bank, his overcoat draped over his arm.

"Fräulein Loeffert," he said. "I am the bearer of glad tidings. May I sit?"

She gestured to a chair.

"After you," he said.

"I prefer to stand."

"Of course." He cocked his head. "Do you know, I'd imagined you'd find my company distressing, but I see I was wrong."

"I'm not so easily distressed," she said, and was surprised to realize she spoke the truth.

"No? Well, we shall see. I know you delivered a document to Professor Hostettler at his house in Bad Ragaz. Even that doesn't upset you?" He set his overcoat on the love seat. "Will you please sit?"

She sat, empty of curiosity and fear and hope—a comfortable absence.

"Thank you." He settled into a chair and lifted a cigarette case from his pocket. "Now, my man retrieved the—"

"I'd rather you didn't smoke," she said, because in her small way she'd consecrated the room with her prayers.

"Of course." He returned the case to his pocket. "You are sufficiently comfortable?"

"Yes."

"You aren't—you must wonder why you're being held."

"I know why." A test of faith, a lesson of faith.

"Do you?" he said. "I'm afraid I don't understand."

She inclined her head at his perplexity. "You have a question?"

"You don't—" He inspected her face. "Well. You're still being held, you see, to answer questions about the documents your mother stole from me."

"You're Herr Villancourt."

He inclined his head and laid a sheet of paper on the table. "My man secured the documents from Hostettler's safe box and destroyed them, leaving only the cover letter for me. To satisfy this juvenile desire . . ." He folded the page into a square, set fire to the edge, and dropped the blazing paper into the ashtray. Smoke rose to the ribbed wooden ceiling and diffused into a fine haze. "And so all evidence vanishes. That is the first of my glad tidings. There is a second."

She said nothing.

"You won't ask? Stubborn girl. The gentleman who escorted you here is peeved with you, as you didn't mention Hostettler to him, or the house in Bad Ragaz, and he takes such things to heart. He's a sensitive soul. He hopes to visit you again, to press you for— ah, now *that* gives you a start." His preening smile contained no warmth. "It should. This is my proposition to you, Fräulein. You tell me everything you know, and I'll not allow him to question you. At length. Alone."

She slid the fire-smudged ashtray across the table. "Then you'll release me?"

"I will," he said, too easily.

"You'll unlock that door and send me home?"

"Don't be naïve, Fräulein Loeffert. However, I will release you."

Understanding spread, yet her calm remained. "You'll kill me if I tell you?"

"Painlessly. Your only alternative to Herr Pongratz."

"No."

"That quickly? No hesitation?"

"Suicide is a mortal sin."

"Allow me to explain. Tomorrow morning, the Germans sit down with the Communists to negotiate the ground rules of an armistice treaty. If formulated correctly, great benefit accrues to my firm and myself. If, on the other hand, I'm constrained by blackmail . . . tragedy. Now, the papers your mother stole are destroyed, but I'm a careful man, and must see that all loose ends are snipped.

Kübler is an adequate negotiator, but this Deputy Commissar Akimov is not a man to—" He stopped, peering into her eyes. "What?"

"Nothing."

"There is a barracks of soldiers just outside—shall I invite them in?"

"No. No, it's truly nothing. Only 'Akimov' is my father's name, my mother's first husband—he returned to Russia before I was born."

"Your father? Curious." He flicked his cigarette case opened and closed. "And *his* father? Who is your grandfather?"

"A diplomat at the Russian embassy before the Revolution, I never met him."

"Ah. Then I may have a use for you yet."

"But—this deputy commissar is my grandfather?"

A chill smile flickered on Villancourt's face. "The bonds of family, Fräulein Loeffert, are impossible to escape. Speaking of which, you'll soon have company. But don't worry—he won't be here long."

When the crash sounded, Grant rolled from the bed, slammed to the floor, and kept moving until he hit the wall. He rose into a crouch and remembered where he was—Switzerland, the hotel room. Nothing moved in the hallway or the street. Nothing moved at all, except the suspicion of a memory: a pale face looming at him on a deserted road, then shattering into splinters of glass.

He sat on the edge of the bed, head pounding. Was there anything in the dream he needed to know? He took himself back to the mountainside roadblock, made himself face the memory. Nothing there for him.

Then why was he awake?

Only one reason.

CHAPTER 36

A voice woke Anna in the dark. "It's me."

"No!" Anna sat up in bed, duvet clutched to her throat. "What? Grant?"

"I thought you never slept."

She turned on the lamp. "Apparently I don't. What's wrong?"

"Nothing."

"What time is it?"

"Late. Early."

"Close the door before you wake Christoph."

"We're in the hotel."

"Mm? Oh." Memory returned—Christoph was safe in Ticino, and she was at the Palace with Grant next door. Except he was here. "Turn around."

She stepped from the bed, drew her robe around her, and saw he'd been watching in the mirror. He crossed the room, took her shoulders in his hands, and leaned close, lean and hard as a schoolgirl fantasy—but she was no schoolgirl. She was a mother and wife, past the age of melting into a man's demanding arms.

"Martin," she whispered.

Grant stopped, his mouth an inch from hers, and dropped her shoulders. "You loved him," he said.

"That's my terrible secret," she said. "He never cared for me, never trusted me. But I loved him. I'm sorry, Grant—you're a good man."

"I've got a beautiful soul."

"And nice hands."

That surprised a laugh from him. "Go on, make this harder."

"I can't help thinking I'm at fault here."

"Don't be a fool," he said. "Of course you are."

"Me? I didn't burst into your hotel room in the middle of the night."

"Let me just—"

He touched her face and kissed her, and she closed her eyes and sunk into dizzying darkness. His hands were hot on her neck, her hips, the small of her back, and she felt herself waver and unfurl.

Anna's hair felt like silk, fanned over his chest as she traced soft lines on his stomach. He cradled her close, her skin warming him. After a time, she lifted her head from his shoulder and said, "Tell me how he died."

"What good does knowing do?"

"Perhaps he'll be easier to bury."

He said, "It started in December '37," then stopped.

"Grant?"

He couldn't do this with her in his arms. He disentangled himself, tugged on his pants, and sat in the bedside chair, then took a minute to find the words. "After the shelling . . . There were craters in the road, this is the first week, the Japanese wanted to level the ground, open the city for traffic. They lined up Chinese, whole families, and used machetes."

"They killed them?"

"For road fill, easier than moving rocks. Patching potholes with bodies."

Anna stood and pulled a robe tight around herself.

"There were men—fathers—they made them . . . with their own daughters, sons with mothers." He looked at his hands. "Martin was a rock, but there came a time, even he couldn't watch anymore."

"What happened?"

"Dusk. Dusk happened. Like every other hour after Nanking fell."

The clock ticked off a minute, and she said, "He died at dusk?"

"A squad of soldiers stopped a wedding procession. They took the bride from the sedan chair—scrawny cross-eyed girl, maybe fifteen—to keep in the barracks for a week or two. Martin told them to let her go, they said his choice: either the barracks for a few weeks or a 'social club' for months."

"What did he do?"

"He chose. He wasn't a man afraid of hard decisions. Then a couple of days later, the same squad comes into the courtyard—behind one of our houses, where a hundred refugees were living. Looking for enemy combatants, they said." He shrugged. "The bride didn't keep 'em busy for long, I guess."

"And Martin?"

"He put himself in the middle."

"They killed him."

"Yeah."

"This isn't your burden, Grant. He was my husband, this belongs to me."

"You want to know? They cut off his head. They cut off his head, tossed it on the pile."

"And you?" she asked, after a blank pause.

"Me what?"

"Did there come a time when you couldn't watch?"

"I'm not Martin. When I couldn't watch anymore, I stopped watching."

"You started caring."

"I lost my edge, that's all."

"I don't know what you were before Nanking, Grant, but I know what you are now. When that girl died in your arms you didn't lose something, you learned something, you—" There was a scratching at the door, and Anna's voice tightened. "The police—they found us."

"Cops don't knock," Grant said.

Rosine's voice came from the hall. "Anna?"

Grant opened the door and saw the girl standing there, her dress ripped off her shoulder, a bloody handkerchief at her nose. He pulled her inside and said, "Did they follow you?"

"No. Th-there is nobody." She looked at his bare chest, then to Anna in her robe. "Oh! Anna, finally!"

"Rosie, what happened? Let me see your shoulder." Anna touched a purple bruise on the girl's collarbone. "Can you lift your arm? Wiggle your fingers." She unfastened Rosine's collar. "Step outside, Grant."

"No," Rosine said. "Stay, I have news. I meet the Russians last night and—" She saw Grant's confusion. "The Russians, the men Anna tells me to approach."

"After you spent the day with the Russian," Anna explained, "I asked Rosine to learn more about the others at the hotel. They claim to be a trade deputation, but . . ."

"They are not," Rosine said. "Last night, they ring for a taxi to a theater club—I arrive early and skulk at the bar. Four men, speaking Russian. Two leave after dinner, but the white-haired man, the deputy commissar, stays for dessert."

"He did this?"

"*Non*. His bodyguard. He is afraid I spy on the commissar, he wants me to confess I speak Russian. I refuse, and so . . ." Her teeth chattered and she hugged herself tight. "But the commissar is gentle, he wants comfort more than pleasure and never stops talking, words flow like a river. The Soviets are losing Stalingrad, the Germans fight on too many fronts. This is a meeting *exploratoire*, more tenuous than tenuous. Only if the first step succeeds will . . ."

She faded, and Anna said, "Rosine?"

"Run her a bath," Grant said. "Is there any liquor in the room?"

"She needs a doctor."

"I've seen men hurt before."

"She's not a man."

"She's as tough as you are, Anna."

Anna stepped into the bathroom, started the water then stood in the doorway. "Then everything is true. There is a Nazi-Soviet pact."

"We already knew that, *non*?" the girl said. "But the deputy commissar, have you seen him? A head of white hair like a prophet, and a voice to match. He meets the Germans at the embassy tomorrow—today, this morning, right now—he's the *émissaire*. And he has a granddaughter he never knew. Nadya Loeffert."

"He's staying here at the hotel?" Grant asked. "What's his name?"

"Yes, at the hotel—he's Deputy Commissar Akimov."

"Akimov?" He shook his head. "Nadya's his granddaughter?"

"He must be your Russian's father," Anna said.

"He only learned of his granddaughter today," Rosine said. "That she lived, that she's Swiss. He's struck by thunder over her, he says—he weeps with fear for her, and hope."

"Why did he tell you?"

"He talks Russian, he thinks I didn't understand, but I do. I understand enough. He says there's no victory without sacrifice—his wife, his son. He says, five times over he says, 'I *will* have my granddaughter.' "

"He's the linchpin," Anna said. "Without him the negotiation fails."

"Him and the German emissary," Grant said.

"The German is replaceable—but they can't easily replace the commissar, not so far from Moscow. And he's in the hotel, Grant. Sent to negotiate a cease-fire—we cannot allow that. You must stop him." She caught him with her eyes. "Do you understand?"

"Yeah."

"Will you need a pistol?" she asked.

"You don't have one."

"Give me an hour."

Rosine shook her head. "He's leaving this morning, for the German embassy. Early this morning. Once there, he's safe behind walls."

"Can you do this without a pistol?" Anna asked.

Grant said, "I can try."

CHAPTER 37

übler unlocked the door of his embassy suite and mixed a
martini at the sideboard. He wasn't a man to drink his breakfast in the normal course of affairs, but today was extraordi-
nary—everything in place, and success completely assured.

Yesterday, the Russian negotiator had clutched at straws, yet
Kübler had *still* felt a shiver of unease: a scheming and untrustwor-
thy man, Deputy Commissar Akimov, possibly a Jew. One mustn't
be complacent when facing such cunning. However, after being
woken by Villancourt's telephone call in the wee hours of the morning, Kübler's last twinges of concern vanished. The pound of flesh
would be cut from the Communists, not the Reich.

He opened the safe to savor Foreign Minister von Ribbentrop's
communiqué. Hitler hadn't yet given his personal imprimatur to
formal talks, but once Kübler secured favorable terms, von Ribbentrop's initiative would move forward. The ice tinkled in his glass as
he reread the memorandum commanding him to achieve "sufficiently favorable terms" at whatever cost . . . and Nadya Loeffert
was that cost. Another order faithfully executed. He sipped his

drink and smiled, remembering the phone call that had startled him from sleep:

"Kübler, you lazy dog," Villancourt had said. "Sleeping again?"

"Villancourt. What time is it?"

"Time for happy news. We have the old man's heart in a cage. At the meeting this morning, you'll tell him—"

"What? Who? Slow down, Villancourt."

A heavy sigh. "Deputy Commissar Akimov. We have his granddaughter. I spent—"

"His granddaughter?"

"His son's daughter—surely you're familiar with the term? We have her in custody. I spent the night confirming this matter, and first thing in the morning you'll take a sounding of the deputy commissar, do you hear?"

"A sounding?"

"What concessions will he make to guarantee the release of his granddaughter? What concessions is he allowed? He will tell you everything, every instruction he received." A brief pause. "Can I trust you to present the matter forcefully?"

"I should hope so!"

"With hope and two centime, Kübler, I can buy a bag of nuts. In the morning, convene a special session—I'll send Pongratz. And don't fuck this up, or you're finished."

The curtains were drawn and the walls bruised with darkness. Akimov sat at the hotel writing desk, eyes half closed, watching the cigarette in the ashtray send gray threads toward the ceiling. He held a pen over a sheet of hotel stationery and had nothing to write.

Last night, he and Little Vlad had hired a taxi to the Burgdorf station, retrieved the car, and driven to the boardinghouse on the Emme. They'd braced the landlord in his bed and Little Vlad beat him bloody before asking a single question. Well, what were a few bumps to the wounds at Stalingrad, the infections and gangrene? Akimov had seen worse there, every day—and yet. And yet he'd never sickened himself before.

The landlord babbled hysterically, everything he knew of Magda and Nadya, which amounted to nothing, and they'd searched the rooms and two hours later admitted defeat. Nadya was gone. Did she even know her mother was dead? She was completely alone now—except for him. He wrote her name on the notepad, her true name—*Nadya Eduardovna Akimova*—then stood at a noise from the adjoining room.

The door swung open and the American shouldered him aside. "Where is he?"

"Who?"

"Your father, the commissar."

"Deputy commissar."

"He's not in his room, his luggage is gone—where is he?"

"He left twenty minutes ago. What do you want with him?"

"Front desk says he hasn't checked out."

"He'll keep the room until—" Akimov shrugged. "If he needs to return."

"Where is he?"

"Why?"

"Answer the question, Akimov."

"An answer for an answer."

A woman stepped from behind Grant, with clear eyes and rose-wood hair. "Please, Major," she said, "tell us where he is."

"He won't return today."

She locked the connecting door and turned to Grant. "Can you make him talk?"

The air in the room thickened and Grant asked Akimov, "Could I?"

"Given enough time."

Grant told the woman, "Never."

"He's at the embassy," the woman said. "The German embassy."

"Find out," Grant told her. "Call them."

She lifted the phone. "The concierge will know if they hired a car or—"

"Don't bother," Akimov said, because the fewer people involved, the better. "You're right. He's at the embassy, a guest of the Nazis."

Anna replaced the phone, and exhaled. She looked at Grant, not for his response but for his solidity. If the Russian was telling the truth, if his father was already safe in the German embassy, she was left with nothing.

No matter how tenuous the talks, she couldn't upset them now—the embassy was too well guarded, the blackmail document was destroyed, the negotiations already begun. She considered the angles of Grant's face, his easy subdued strength, and nodded once: they needed to find the girl, Nadya.

Not for influence, not to scuttle the talks. It was too late for that, with the Soviet delegation already behind locked doors. No, they'd find the girl to *help* the Russians. Between Stalin and Hitler, the choice was obvious—one was an ally, however unpleasant, and one a mortal enemy. The talks were beyond Anna's reach, but not beyond Akimov's: if they learned anything from the girl, Major Akimov would inform his father and the Soviets could demand terms. Yes, she'd failed to stop the non-aggression treaty—she'd failed herself and her country, she'd failed Martin. Yet if she could sway the pact against the Nazis by aiding the Soviets . . .

She nodded again.

· · ·

324

Akimov watched the woman's eyes cloud with thought, then sharpen into clarity. "You're Swiss intelligence?" he asked her. "What do you want with my father?"

"I want what you want," she said. "Your daughter."

Sudden hope quickened his heart. "You know where she is?"

"I know Switzerland. Tell me everything, I'll help you find her."

"Why?"

"We're allies."

He laughed. "That's not what you thought a moment ago, locking that door."

"Your daughter's missing, your wife is dead. Have you a better plan?"

"We know about the cease-fire talks," Grant said.

"We know your wife stole the papers," the woman said, "trying to blackmail a Swiss industrialist. She intended to give them to me. Not you, not your father: me. Do you know the industrialist's name?"

He shook his head slowly, sitting at the table. "They took me from Stalingrad to find her, and I never even saw her face. Maybe I flushed her like a quail, for the Germans to kill. No, I don't know the man. I know nothing but my daughter's name."

"Without us, how will you find her?"

He looked at his hand, curled into a loose fist on the tabletop. Without help, he wouldn't find her. Without help, he'd never hear her voice. He told the woman everything: the dead ends in Zurich, the boardinghouse in Burgdorf.

"You missed something," she said when he finished.

"The apartment in Geneva? That was searched by professionals."

"Not the apartment." She went to the phone, spoke at length in Swiss-German, and hung up. "Now we wait for a return call."

"Or your reinforcements," Akimov said.

"I have Grant," she said. "Why would I need reinforcements?"

He nodded again, rubbing his face with his palm. He needed his daughter—needed to stop the fighting at Stalingrad before the Soviet Union lay in ruins beneath the tread of German tanks. Yet here he sat, lost in a hotel room.

"Did we interrupt your breakfast?" the woman asked. "I recommend the lamb kidney with smoked bacon."

"What am I waiting for?"

"Indulge me." She paced the room, absently tidying until the phone rang, then asked a few questions and listened to the answers. "I have confirmation," she told Grant, upon breaking the connection. "The deputy commissar is at the German embassy."

"That's all you were doing?" Akimov asked. "Confirming my father's location?"

"No. I also found your daughter."

CHAPTER 38

Villancourt turned from his office window and frowned at the acne-pocked soldier standing beside his desk. "Your men are still watching Anna Fay's house?" he asked.

"Yes, sir."

"No sign of her or the American?"

"Not yet, sir. Just the gardener, yesterday."

"That was poorly done."

"He attacked Schmidt with a pitchfork, screaming in Italian and—" the soldier shrugged. "We needed to quiet him."

"You succeeded."

"A blow to the head is tricky, sir. We didn't intend to kill him."

"Enough excuses. When Fay or the American appear, you know what to do?"

"Tell them the boy is safe, and alert you and Herr Pongratz."

"Tell them the boy is safe 'for now.' You had no trouble convincing him to join you?"

"None at all," the soldier said. "He saw the chauffeur's uniform and didn't say a word. If I may say so, sir . . . that's an odd sort of a prison."

"Sadly, I haven't access to the municipal jail, so must use what is already at hand. Now return to your men—and be sure you don't disappoint me." The white-and-gold telephone rang, and Villancourt shooed the soldier outside, then answered. "This is Villancourt."

An officious woman's voice: "Hold for Chairman Ochsner, please." In a moment, the chairman came on the line. "Herr Villancourt, you are happily settled in Basel, I believe?"

"Quite at home, thank you."

"Then you would be reluctant to relocate."

"For the firm, I wouldn't hesitate. There is a branch in need of assistance?"

"Not quite yet, but let me say that we are aware of your contributions. The clearing credits, the question of foreign labor, the marriage of probity and profitability . . . You threaded the needle with a steady hand. I offer my congratulations—and my condolences. I understand there's been a death in the family?"

"My nephew, yes. An accident on the road."

"My thoughts are with you, a very sad affair." Ochsner grew silent for a moment, then continued briskly. "In other business . . . Apparently one Herr Rothenbuehler, of the Basel customs office, has been to see you—or, rather, he hasn't."

"Herr Rothenbuehler? A customs officer?"

"Yes, the poor fellow's been trying all week, and can't get past your anteroom."

"Is that so? I've been sadly busy with other matters."

"Indeed. However, one mustn't neglect the humdrum routine, don't you agree?"

"Of course. I'll contact Rothenbuehler in the morning and—"

"This is regarding freight forwarding, I believe? There's an expiry of liability, you know, if the firm doesn't take receipt by the agreed-upon date . . ."

"I assure you, Chairman Ochsner, I am perfectly conversant with—"

"The deadline is today. Herr Rothenbuehler is at this moment outside your office door. Accompany him to the customs offices at the Reichs depot and complete this transaction. That is all."

After the chairman broke the connection, Villancourt caressed the phone with the pad of his thumb, almost purring in satisfaction. The conversation revealed Ochsner's rising panic over the consolidation of Villancourt's position, not sure if he should praise Villancourt or slight him. Well, he was right to panic; today, Villancourt would run along to the Reichs depot on an errand boy's task, but tomorrow his campaign for the chairmanship would begin.

Glassware chimed in the dining car of the morning express train to Basel. Anna pushed scrambled eggs around her plate and looked beyond Grant to the river valley sweeping past. *Mind your own child*, Pierre-Luc had said. She'd found Akimov's daughter's trail, yet didn't know where her own son was—somewhere in Ticino. Why hadn't Joris left a message at the hotel? Wasn't like him to forget. He probably couldn't find a telephone.

She hated herself for ignoring Christoph, at school and at home, and now she'd even sent him away. And for what? A vague fear, the rush to find Nadya Loeffert. And she didn't know if helping the Soviet Union was her best option.

She dabbed at her mouth with the napkin. She'd failed to stop the cease-fire talks—with the negotiators safe in the Germany embassy this wasn't merely her best option but her only option.

The Russian poured coffee, watching her. "And now, will you tell me where we're going?"

She set her fork down. "How did Nadya leave the Zurich station?"

"That's the question. She didn't pass the checkpoint, she didn't buy a ticket or travel third class."

"There's only one other possibility: she boarded a German train."

"There weren't any," Akimov said.

"I'm not speaking of passenger trains. German boxcars travel through Switzerland on rail lines untouchable by treaty—night and day, the workhorses of industry. One such train passed through Zurich the day Nadya disappeared, and a car was added, a Blue Star club-lounge car."

"A passenger car?"

She nodded. "Heading north."

"You think she boarded this Blue Star?"

"I know she did."

"And these cargo trains, the German boxcars are based in Basel?" Akimov asked.

"In an extraterritorial German railway yard, the Reichs depot—that's where Nadya went." She looked back to the window. "Pray we pick up her trail."

Kübler stood when the Russian entered, and murmured a greeting in French, in the spirit of internationality. The deputy commissar answered more fluently, with an accent of unmistakable refinement, and Kübler felt his smile turn cold. But no matter, in moments the man would be pleading for mercy.

He invited the Russian to sit and said, "May I begin with a question?"

"By all means, Herr Kübler."

"What are the best terms you're empowered to offer?"

"An admirable directness! We should be finished by lunch, if only—"

"Where is the line you cannot cross? What is the greatest sacrifice you can make?"

"Yes, I quite take your point, Herr Kübler. You wish to ensure the greatest benefit for your Reich, while I—"

"We have your granddaughter."

"—wish to . . . Pardon?"

"Your granddaughter, Nadya Loeffert, Nadya Akimov. We have her."

"She's not—" The Russian cocked an eyebrow. "Is she here at the embassy?"

Kübler shook his head. "She's safe."

"Well, I'm pleased to hear that. Of course, you do understand I've never met the girl. And besides, I'm not what you might call a 'family man.' Didn't I consign my only son to the gulag?" He chuckled, clearly amused at Kübler's attempt to control him. "Now, unless you have some observations about my third cousin or my great-aunt, may we continue?"

Kübler's face heated in shame. Damn Villancourt, making him appear the fool. Still, he was a man who did his duty to the last breath. "No more about the girl, then. If she means nothing to you, we have no use for her. She'll be dealt with. Now, to our first order of business—"

"Nevertheless," the deputy commissar said, no longer so amused. "I wouldn't like to see her hurt."

Cold triumph rose in Kübler, and he told the man, "You won't see a thing."

For the first time, the Russian's gaze wavered. "What do you want of me?"

"Your granddaughter will remain unharmed until, on your return to Moscow, you recommend that our agreement be ratified."

"I need proof—proof you have her."

"Listen to your heart, you know I have her. Now begin, Deputy Commissar. What are the best terms you can offer?"

The Russian pinched the bridge of his nose. "*Nyet*."

"No?"

"I agree to nothing. You need me as much as I need you."

"All I stand to lose is a promotion."

"And a war," the Russian said. "I want Nadya and you want terms—we have a standoff. Kill her, and you lose. Not as much as I, perhaps, but still a loss. No. Release the girl and we'll negotiate in earnest."

Kübler sipped water from his glass. The Russian was NKVD, of course he wouldn't break as quickly as a civilian—still, his position was untenable, and easily altered. He touched the button and said, "Let me introduce a man you ought to meet, Deputy Commissar."

Pongratz entered and swept the room with his uncaring gaze, even his quiet politeness somehow menacing.

"There are acts from which most of us would recoil," Kübler explained. "But not him. He's the one I'll send to Nadya."

"If he kills her, the talks die too."

"Did I say 'kill'? No, your leverage is a onetime affair, while mine extends into endless degrees. We'll keep your granddaughter alive for weeks. If you don't cooperate now, at this moment, then we'll go our separate ways—and in three hours I'll ask you again. She'll still be alive . . . though not quite the same."

"You can't—"

"And three hours after that, and after that. You work for Beria, you've seen young women in eager hands."

"This cannot—"

"Imagine your granddaughter, in their place."

Something died in the Russian's eyes. "I need to see her. Before I tell you anything, I will speak with her."

Kübler let him suffer for a minute, then nodded. "We'll go to Basel, show you she's alive—then we'll talk terms."

In the Basel rail station, Grant watched Anna slip through a herd of businessmen, past the air service inquiry desk to the ticket booth.

The longer they chased these cease-fire negotiations, the farther they got from the finish line. Killing the deputy commissar he could understand, no better way to scuttle the talks, but now . . . what? Find Akimov's daughter and hope she knew something about the barracks deal that the Russians could use against the Germans? So now Grant was working for Stalin, for "Uncle Joe"? He shrugged inwardly. Well, as long as he was working against Hitler— he trusted Anna to guide him right.

He absently watched her in the ticket queue, then glanced at a city map on the wall and whistled. "Germany's right here. Look at that, not even a mile away."

"Yes," Akimov said. "We're in Basel."

"Didn't know the city was smack on the border."

"Too close for your taste?"

"Unless I'm flying a bomber."

Anna returned with the tickets and said, "It's a ten-minute trip by streetcar to the Reichs *bahnhof*, the German station."

"That's the cargo terminal?" Grant asked.

"There are two sections, the Reichs *bahnhof* is for German passenger lines, and the Reichs depot is cargo warehousing and inspections." She led them outside to the streetcar. "That's where we'll find what we're looking for."

"If any trace remains," Akimov said, taking a seat. "How extraterritorial is this depot?"

"Officially, I don't know. It's not an embassy."

"And unofficially?"

"The passenger terminal is comfortably Swiss, but the cargo terminal?" She set her purse on the seat beside her. "Welcome to Germany."

The streetcar pulled from the station, rattled past Kirschgarten and Handelsbank, and Anna said, "Have we a plan?"

"Do you know the layout?" Grant asked.

"Of the depot? No."

"Okay. Nadya left Hostettler's house heading for Basel, but at the Zurich station she boarded this German line, right? We need to figure where she arrived at the depot, and how she left."

Two soldiers boarded, and they fell silent. The streetcar passed the St. Elisabethen Church, crossed the river, and finally jerked to a halt outside the Reichs *bahnhof*, where they stepped into a busy passenger terminal with wide corridors and hanging clocks.

"We need a map of the depot," Grant said. "Or a good vantage point."

"I'll get a map," Anna said. "You wait at the newsstand."

She walked briskly away and Akimov said, "How do you know her?"

"I watched her husband die. Should've been me."

"To die, or to be her husband?"

"Yeah," Grant said.

He bought cigarettes and gave one to Akimov. They smoked in silence until Anna reappeared and led them to the privacy of the lowest platform, with concrete floors and dingy walls. Dim daylight crept from the level above and brushed the postage and baggage cars on sidelined tracks. She spread the map on a bench with peeling paint. "This blank space, here, this is the Reichs depot."

"The blank space is blank," Grant said.

"No public access, so no public map. This building is customs, these are switching stations, I suppose. Warehousing over here. A great deal of storage. These, I don't know."

"Any Swiss army presence?"

"Not within the Reichs depot. No army, no police, nobody un-invited except customs agents."

"It's fenced?"

"Very much so. Million of francs pass through the depot, Oer-likon ammunition, fuses and components, machine tools."

"Nadya's train came on these tracks?" Akimov traced a line on the map. "And she left though customs?"

"As I understand, yes."

"So we talk to the customs agents, show her picture."

"We can't approach them openly," Grant said. "Not in de facto German territory."

"Then what?" Akimov asked him.

"We need to figure who might've seen her. Maybe find a customs officer, follow him outside the station, convince him to call in a question. I see two ways—"

A door opened in the wall, and a mail clerk rolled a cart onto the platform—and beyond the door there was unexpected daylight. A direct route into the rail yard. The clerk pushed the cart down the platform, the door clicked shut, and the three of them looked at one another.

After the cart clamored around the corner, Grant tried the knob: locked tight.

"I have a hairpin," Anna said, opening her purse.

"My skills stop at cars," Grant said. "I can't pick a lock."

"Move aside." Akimov took a knife from his satchel and worked the blade into the jamb, muttering in rhythmic Russian.

"More poetry?" Grant asked.

"Poetry and forced entry, they're mother and child." A train groaned in the distance, and Akimov said, "Ah!" and opened the door.

They went through, into a paved courtyard with half a dozen loading docks and brick walls on three sides. "Stay here," Grant told Anna.

"How solicitous," she said.

"Look around, how many dresses do you see?"

"But a one-armed man and a hoodlum—you're inconspicuous." Anna took a stenography pad from her purse. "There, I'm your secretary."

Not a bad idea, taking dictation to make them look legitimate. They headed into the yard, where the air was warm with exhaust, full of the rumble of truck engines and the call of workers. Down a short flight of stairs, they crossed two sets of tracks on a walkway bordered by a picket fence, past a structure like a covered bridge with three men inside smoking, listening to the radio. Grant said hello and the men nodded and eyed Anna as she passed.

"There's a view from the roof," Grant said, checking the sky-line.

"And from the ground." Akimov nodded across the yard. "At the gravity sorting yard, see the tower? Behind that."

The tower was a three-story metal frame in front of a hill of dirt. They went through the sorting yard, and when nobody shouted Grant took Anna's arm, her heels unsteady in the scrub, and helped her uphill. Good view. The Reichs *bahnhof* yard teemed with passenger trains and cargo, carts and trucks and men yelling directions. At the northeast corner, a third of the yard was sliced from the activity by a high spiked fence into a long rectangle, with towers and turntables, switch tracks and machine sheds and freight scales: the cargo depot, an outpost of the Reich. The traffic con-verged at two points, one at each end of the Reichs depot yard: at the farther side, German soldiers lounged on a platform, smoking and playing cards; at the nearer, rail guards in green-and-gray uni-forms inspected a train that'd just rolled into the yard.

"A search like that," Grant said, "Nadya didn't slip away unno-ticed."

Anna tapped her stenography pad. "What if she tried, and was arrested?"

"Arrested?" Akimov nodded. "Yes. Yes, what if she's been in jail for days now?"

"Nothing we can do about that," Grant said, eyeing the Reichs depot.

Only six breaks in the fence: two for the trains, one at customs for movement between the depot and the terminal, and two flank-ing a gate over a paved roadway for truck traffic. The gate itself made six. Oh, and a seventh: street access at the other side of the depot, locked and guarded like the Germans thought Swiss pedestrians might suddenly attack.

"A waste of time." Akimov rubbed his eyes. "We should talk to the police."

"We'll wait for a customs official to leave," Grant said, "and follow him."

Anna grabbed his arm. "No, over there. Look." She pointed across the depot to where a royal blue passenger car sat apart from the cargo cars, the words BLUE STAR painted in silver script over windows covered with planking. "The Blue Star club lounge from Zurich. Boarded for privacy."

"A hideout?" Grant asked.

"Or a love nest. She could still be inside."

Akimov massaged his stump. "We need to get closer."

Villancourt rested his attaché case on the table in the lobby of his firm, enjoying Rothenbuehler's impatience. A petty satisfaction, but gratifying. The customs officer glanced at the front doors, shifted his weight, and finally said, "The tram, Herr Villancourt, is two steps away—"

"We'll take the company car."

"But surely—the Reichs *bahnhof* is only a forty centime fare."

"Do you imagine I ride the tram, Herr Rothenbuehler?"

Villancourt stood before the customs officer could answer, followed the driver outside, and slipped into the backseat. Even today, with triumph at hand and the negotiations under way, he was forced to suffer idiots.

A few moments later, Rothenbuehler joined him, shifting uneasily. "A tiresome excursion," the man said, as they pulled from the curb. "I apologize for dragging a man of your station to the, er, station."

Was that an attempted witticism? Villancourt didn't bother responding.

"Customs clearance and warehousing," Rothenbuehler continued. "Ten years ago this wouldn't have been necessary. Still, the current requirements have noble antecedents, so to speak. In 1933, the—"

"Noble antecedents? There's a subject about which you must know very little."

They rode in silence until the driver pulled beyond the fountains at the Reichs *bahnhof*, and stopped at the customs house. Villancourt stepped from the car and finally addressed the customs man. "Now, let us waste no more—"

He froze. Beyond the warehouse fence, a man crossed the yard. Villancourt recognized him from the photograph: the American, the murderer. Lieutenant Grant.

CHAPTER 39

At the bottom of the dirt hill, Grant released Anna's arm and paused, summoning a bird's-eye view of the rail yard. Took a second to figure, then he headed past a fenced pen of barrels and pallets.

"The train car is that way," Akimov said, pointing the other direction.

"This is close as we'll get," Grant told him, "without breaking into the depot."

They went behind a round building, where the sun was high and the cold wind thick with the machine stink of grit and oil. Heavy couplings rattled as they climbed a flight of exterior metal stairs. At the terminal, a passenger train arrived and another departed. They paused on a landing where Grant made a show of pointing to various buildings and Anna pretended to take notes.

"The water's connected," she said, eyeing the Blue Star car. "For the plumbing. Isn't that a water pipe?"

"You think she's still inside?" Akimov said.

"I hope not." Grant looked to a watchtower. "That side is the Reich—check the uniforms. We're not getting any closer."

"I don't know." Akimov's craggy face sagged. "Maybe she came, maybe she's still here."

"The talks start today?" Anna asked.

"Informally, they started this morning."

"Officially?"

"This afternoon. Preliminary talks, nonbinding. We'll draw a line west of the Volga. If we lose Stalin's city, the damage will—"

"If there's a cease-fire in the east," Anna said, "the Nazis will attack west."

Akimov gestured with the stump of his arm. "Three million dead Russians isn't enough for the West? For you, the fighting kills two birds with one stone." He looked across the yard, past the terminal and warehouses, past the city and mountains. "There's a boy in Stalingrad, a stretcher bearer, he crawls through the ruins into no-man's-land and follows the whimpers, you understand? He has sharp ears so we call him Fox—"

Footsteps rang on the metal staircase below them—a man said something about rail migration and expansion gaps, and another man answered. Grant gestured Anna and Akimov upstairs to the domed top of the building, and eyed the windblown trash at the base of a metal door: crumpled newspaper, wet leaves, a rusted alligator wrench.

The footsteps stopped and one of the men yelled, "Hey! *Schafseckel!* Up here!" Grant moved for the wrench, but the man continued. "Next time bring a spare shirt, you won't go home naked!" Calling to a friend about a poker game. The answering shout was lost in the wind, back and forth and ending with a volley of friendly insults. Then the man said, quieter, to his buddy on the stairs, "Poor Thorsten still thinks a straight beats a flush."

They kept talking, twenty feet below and Anna murmured, "This is turning into a goose chase."

"We know she was here," Grant said. "We just need to find someone who—"

"Look." Akimov's attention sharpened on the train car. "There."

Inside the Reichs depot fence, a man in custodial coveralls climbed to the end platform of the Blue Star car, stopped at the turnbuckle coupler. He hoisted a cumbersome case onto a shadowed sill, opened a panel into the railcar, and transferred the contents: a serving tray with dishes and silver.

"She's still there," Anna said. "She's inside."

Akimov looked at Grant. "Help me free her."

"Free her?"

"You don't screen a love nest with wooden planks. That's a prison, they feed her through a hole in the wall. They kidnapped her to pressure my father."

"How do they know she's his granddaughter?" Anna asked. "You didn't know yourself until yesterday."

"You knew."

"No," Anna said, tapping her notepad in thought. "They kidnapped her, you're right, but not because of your father."

"Then why?"

"To pressure Magda. You remember, Grant—when Pongratz chased you into that cemetery in Geneva, he gave you a message for Magda."

"He said he had something dear to her."

"Yes, her daughter. They kidnapped Nadya to make Magda return the blackmail document, not to influence the talks. They don't know she's the commissar's granddaughter."

"Would your father even care?" Grant asked Akimov.

A slow sad smile. "Yes. We must free her."

"Look at that fence, look at those soldiers. You'd need an army."

"All I have is you."

"You don't have him," Anna said. "If we call attention to her, they'll realize she's important. They'll use her to steamroll your father in these talks."

"Don't underestimate my father."

Grant looked at Anna and stepped toward the stairs. "Time to go."

"Wait," Akimov said. "They'll kill her."

The official car of the German embassy, a seven-seater Horch Pullman limousine, growled to a halt at the gates of the Reichs depot. One sentry demanded identification as another moved to inspect the trunk, and the deputy commissar leaned close to Kübler, his face a mask of polite indifference.

"If she's hurt," he said, "I'll kill you."

"If she's *dead*, you'll kill me," Kübler corrected. "If she's merely hurt, you'll do as I say."

"She's unhurt," Pongratz told the Russian. "For now."

A soldier tapped at Kübler's window. "A communication for you, sir, cabled from the embassy."

Kübler took the note, marked URGENT. "Received when?"

"Just now—we were told you were *en route*."

"Forwarded from Villancourt," he told Pongratz, reading as they rolled into the depot. "He's apparently alarmed that— My God! That man is here at the Reichs *bahnhof*, the man from the hunting box."

Pongratz opened his door. "Where?"

"On the other side, near customs. I'll raise a general alert."

"Don't. That'll warn him."

"Well, how will you catch the man? You can't—"

New sounds broke over the commotion of the cargo terminal: a gong repeatedly struck, an alarmed outcry, hoarse shouts.

Pongratz loped toward the noise.

• • •

Grant stopped at the top stair.

"They'll kill her," the Russian repeated. "If they don't know she's leverage, they'll kill her."

"If they do know," Anna said, "they'll use her."

"She's my daughter," Akimov said, and hammered the metal door with the rusted alligator wrench. The sound boomed over the yard and he yelled, "Here! Guards! Here!"

Anna flew at him, twisting the wrench from his grip, but men at the livestock pens were already pointing and shouting. Grant dragged her away from Akimov and down the stairs to the two rail-men smoking on the landing—put his hand on the closer man's face and shoved. The railman fell backward into his buddy and they tumbled in a tailspin, ended in the middle of the stairs in an ugly heap. Grant trotted down, lifted Anna over them, and was at the base of the stairs when four burly guys came around the corner.

Four guys, shit, maybe firemen or shunters, with Akimov still shouting above them, and nothing in Grant's mind but silence.

"He's up there!" Anna pointed wide-eyed to the stairs. "Go, go! Stop him!"

CHAPTER 40

When the car door slammed behind Pongratz, Kübler told the driver, "A change of plans. Take us to the central guard station."

The limousine turned, and the deputy commissar murmured, "Who's the man from the hunting box?"

"A dangerous animal—but he'll be put down shortly. We'll spend the next few minutes out of harm's way."

"I must see my granddaughter."

"And you will." The car pulled to the base of the central guard tower. "From a safe distance."

"I must speak with her."

"Perhaps." Kübler opened the door into the industrial clangor of the depot. "If you behave."

The deputy commissar's shoulders slumped in defeat as they climbed to the lookout above the rail yard. The soldiers inside straightened at Kübler's arrival and he scanned the yard past the waist-high barrier enclosing the concrete box. Pongratz was nowhere to be seen, but the yard was busy and the Blue Star passenger car secure.

Anna's feet throbbed from trotting through the yard, half dragged by a silent purposeful Grant. Men shouted behind them, harsh directionless voices echoing between concrete and steel, but he didn't look back, didn't slow, guiding her through the maze of boxcars, over weedy tracks toward the station building.

Into a dead end.

The station loomed in front of them, they were caught in a U edged with halfhearted shrubs and brick walls stained by the imprint of ivy. Grant swore and led her back between the boxcars. "You have the map?"

She showed him her hand—instead of the map, she was holding the corroded railway tool. "Just this."

"We need a platform, mix with the passengers."

"What if they stop the trains?"

"For some trespassers and a wild-eyed Russian?"

"And the workmen you knocked downstairs."

"No, you handled that—they oughta blame Akimov."

He grabbed her arm as three men came around a corner thirty feet away, two in work clothes and the third in a green-and-gray rail-guard uniform.

"That's them," one of the workmen said.

The guard scrambled for his pistol and Grant told him, "You don't want to do that."

The rail guard hesitated. "You'd better come with us."

"Our pleasure," Grant said. "Do you—"

Another man stepped forward, wearing a dark suit and a high-crowned felt fedora. The salesman, Pongratz. Anna's breath caught from fright, and Grant yelled, like he was warning Pongratz, "Helmut, run!"

The rail guard spun toward Pongratz, his hand at his holster, and Grant shoved Anna around the nearest boxcar. A surprised shout sounded behind them and Grant dragged her across an aisle and beneath a metal coupling, pulling her forward as she tripped and skinned her knee on the gravel. She gasped down an aisle and he lifted her into an open boxcar that stank of rawhide, climbed in after her and prowled the length of the gloomy dark interior.

There was shouting outside, footsteps. Grant tensed, and she made herself exhale—she was a journalist, she was a Swiss woman in Switzerland, the worst she'd done was trespassing . . . and aiding a fugitive. Maybe assault. The scuffing outside grew louder, gravel crunched. Grant stepped between her and the open boxcar door, and she put her hand on his shoulder to steady herself—or him—or both of them. The crunching stopped, started again, faded to nothing.

She dropped her hand and they waited, listening to the sounds of the rail yard.

"You were a kid when you met Martin," Grant murmured.

"I was seventeen."

"You'd never left Switzerland?"

"I'd hardly left my hometown."

He rubbed the back of his neck. "Fifteen years ago."

"Yes."

"Three days and two dozen letters," he said.

"Mm?"

"That's all I needed."

She didn't know what to say. Three days and two dozen letters, and she felt something entirely unlike the admiring devotion she had for Martin. Her feet ached and her knees burned and she was cold and frightened—but not alone. Grant stood beside her, with his strong hands and quick smile and—

She put her hand to her mouth.

"What?" He eyed the boxcar door, tense. "Anna?"

She loved him. The man he thought he was and the man he wanted to be—the warmth he showed nobody else. She loved him and said, "No—nothing."

He flashed a grin at her. "You little liar."

"I've no notion what you're talking about."

The grin turned to a boyish smile. "Wait 'til later, I'll explain."

In the dark of the boxcar, she felt herself blush. She started to speak but he lifted a finger, silencing her. Footsteps crunched on gravel outside, a train wheezed to a stop. She waited, not quite watching Grant, not quite thinking about him.

"Let's go," he said, and vaulted from the open door.

But instead of lifting her down, he turned suddenly, watchful and still. She peeked through a seam in the boxcar slats—and at the end of the aisle, Pongratz was as intent on Grant as a cat on a mouse hole.

"Why call yourself Cy Young?" The German removed his fedora and stalked forward. "Nobody lost more games than him."

"Or won more, either."

A cold smile flickered on Pongratz's face as Grant backed away. "Don't run. If you run, I make do with the hausfrau."

She was afraid to move in the darkness, her breath ragged and thin. Pongratz was going to pass the open door of her boxcar, terrifyingly close; she pressed herself against the wall and put her hand in her purse and felt the cold corroded metal tool. *She* could run, race panicked from the boxcar and keep running.

"Best pitcher in the world." Pongratz hung his hat on a boxcar hitch. "But you—you're out of your league."

She drew the tool from her purse, heavy and rough and long as her forearm. The man was only feet away, the air too thick to breathe. *Hit first, hit hard, keep hitting.* If she missed, Martin's mother would have the raising of Christoph. *Hit hard, hit first.* The boxcar darkened as Pongratz passed the door and she bit her lip to keep her teeth from chattering.

• • •

Grant sidled backward, drawing the guy away from Anna and doing what he'd told Akimov never worked: putting off the inevitable. Out of his league, sure, but he'd like to see Pongratz in a cockpit. What he needed was a baseball bat—or his service revolver. He wasn't gonna walk away from this, he just needed to hurt the guy hard enough to keep Anna safe.

Pongratz stalked closer, and Anna loomed in the boxcar door behind him, and Grant couldn't help himself, he glanced at her. A half smile twitched on the German's face—he thought Grant was giving him an eye-fake—and she dropped, swinging the alligator wrench, and caught Pongratz off center, a glancing blow down his temple, clipping his ear, smashing his collarbone.

Grant sprang forward and Pongratz pivoted—his ear torn, one arm dangling—and Anna swung again, eyes squeezed shut. She split open his cheek, snapped his head back, and a sweep of blood splashed her face. Pongratz swayed and dropped to his knees and, eyes still closed, Anna swung and missed and stumbled off her heels and Grant kicked Pongratz in the stomach.

The German grunted and Anna opened her eyes and with a wild sobbing one-arm swing caught him hard on the back of his head.

CHAPTER 41

In the room behind the security office, the gray-haired guard handcuffed Akimov to the railing. "Herr Kübler, you say?"

"At the German embassy in Bern," Akimov told him.

"He'll vouch for you?"

"Yes—please, call him."

"And your accomplices?" The guard glanced toward the square window overlooking the rail yard. "They're also Russian?"

"They're not my accomplices."

A rubber stop held the door open to the security office, and Akimov slid the handcuff along the rail to look through, hoping to catch another guard's attention. File cabinets crowded the other room, a coatrack and a radio in a tombstone cabinet, and three guards sat at heavy wooden desks—all ignoring him.

"Call Kübler," he said. "Tell him I must speak with him. He's at a meeting at—"

"Yes, yes—I heard the first time."

"Please." The only way to keep Nadya alive was to be sure the Germans knew who she was. "Just call him."

"You think I'll call the Foreign Office on the word of a trespasser?"

Akimov shifted, rattling the handcuff. "You saw my papers," he told the guard. "I'm trade commission, why am I trespassing?"

"Bolsheviks. Why do you do anything? You're certain this Herr Kübler is at the embassy?"

"Yes, and all I ask is—"

The guard snorted. "That shows what you know. He's not there, he's here." He gestured toward the window. "On the other side."

"Kübler's in the depot?"

"At this very moment," the guard said. "Now, then—are there any other lies you'd like to tell me?"

Following the shadow of a rolling coal car, waiting for the guards to shout an alarm, Grant dragged Anna to a windowless building with codes stenciled on the side. He pulled her into a deep niche along one wall and wiped blood from her cheek. She tried to speak then covered her mouth with her hand.

He stroked her hair. "You did good, Anna. You did good."

"How did he find us? Pongratz, he—" She breathed hard, almost hiccupping. "Akimov will tell them the girl's a hostage and—the talks. We must stop the talks, we must."

"First, we get out of here."

"We need a plan. What do we know? We have to think." Using words to steady herself, to calm the shock. "We need to know what's happening. We need to stop this. How do we stop this?"

"We don't, Anna. We wait for a passenger train, and we leave. Get the camera, do what we can."

"So we've lost?"

"That happens, when you fight."

She turned to watch a passenger train rumble toward the terminal, and even pale and trembling, she was beautiful. He took her hand and stepped from the niche, walking straight and slow behind the arriving train until they could climb the platform and merge with a cluster of passengers. Back in the safety of the *bahnhof* crowds.

"Thank God," she said, and started shaking.

He led her into the passenger terminal and up a flight of stairs, stopping on the landing in front of a wall of windows. The sunlight set fire to her hair and when she started to speak he took her and held her. She stilled, cheek against his chest, face to the sun. She smelled of sage or rosemary, some plain herb at the border of a wildflower garden, worth a thousand long-stemmed roses.

Then she pushed away. "That's an official Nazi car, a diplomat's car."

He followed her gaze to a limousine parked below a guard tower deep inside the depot. "Yeah?"

"There, in the tower. Look."

"Can't see anything from—" He caught a glimpse of windswept white hair. "Akimov's father?"

"Who else? But why is he here? Why in a guard tower?"

"No idea."

"An official car, the Russian emissary . . ." Her voice trailed off. "I was wrong. They *do* know Nadya is the deputy commissar's granddaughter. They brought him here to prove they have her. She's a hostage to these talks."

"You don't know that."

"They're here, Nadya's here, the talks start today."

"Yeah, but—"

"If they sign another non-aggression pact, nothing can stop the Nazis. We must end this now." She put her hand on his arm. "We have one shot."

"Take out the Russian?" Grant eyed the guard tower. "Too far for me, I'm no good with a rifle."

"Can you get close enough to use a pistol?"

"The man's in a guard tower, Anna."

She fell silent, then nodded. "Nadya's not. She's alone in that train car."

"Break her out? Can't be done, the place is a prison."

"Can you get to her?"

"Even if I could, I'd never get her away."

"I know," she said, her voice thick.

For a moment he didn't understand, then his stomach twisted. "What are you asking me to do?"

"Stop this truce."

"By killing the girl?"

She pressed an unsteady hand to her chest. "If that doesn't scuttle these talks, nothing will."

In the guard tower, a blond soldier turned from the telephone and told Kübler, "They found a body, sir, on the Reichs *bahnhof* side of the fence."

Kübler blew a cloud of cigarette smoke: so much for Lieutenant Grant. "Did they find identification?"

"They have a name, sir. 'Pongratz.' "

"No," Kübler said. "I mean the dead man."

"Yes, sir. Pongratz."

Kübler steadied himself on the railing, the concrete cool and rough on his palm, the noise of the depot fading to a sudden hush. The American killed Pongratz? Impossible. He felt himself turn to the soldier, heard himself say, "Close the gates. Stop the trains. Sweep the yard."

. . .

"It's the only way." Anna watched a light die in Grant's face. "There's nothing more important to the commissar than his granddaughter, and— You need to do this."

"There was a girl in China," he said. "In the wrong place at the wrong time."

She touched his cheek. "Like Nadya."

"You said I've seen too much innocent blood."

"And now I'm telling you to shed more. I'm sorry, Grant—I'm so sorry."

He stared out the window. "That's not the man I want to be."

"You'll do this because somebody must, and nobody else can. That's the man you are."

After a long moment, he nodded, the decision deepening the lines on his face.

"Can you get inside the depot?" she asked, her breath shallow and quick.

"Maybe through customs."

"They'll see you, the guards are twenty feet away."

"I need cover, someone the guards recognize. I'll grab the next businessman who steps outside." His gaze flicked over the space between customs and the passenger terminal. "It's a long shot."

"And once you get in?"

"Easy enough."

"Grant, I—"

He tucked a strand of hair behind her ear. "I know."

"I wish . . . everything was different."

" 'Kill your sled dogs.' For us, there's no other choice."

She looked into his warm wounded eyes.

"I'm just going outside," he said, like the arctic explorer who'd disappeared into a blizzard. "I may be some time."

CHAPTER 42

Villancourt rapped his knuckles on the desk in customs agent Rothenbuehler's empty office, coming to a sudden decision. He'd telephoned a warning to the German embassy and now should simply wait for the American to be apprehended—but this was more than business as usual. This was family. Only he knew what the American was wearing, only he knew exactly where he'd been spotted. Villancourt left the customs house and walked into the parking lot, his eyes peeled for—

An arm wrapped his throat and dragged him behind a goods van.

He flailed, his elbow smacking the van: "Please—no!"

"You're gonna walk me into customs," a man said into his ear.

"I don't—"

The arm tightened. "Past the guards, into the Reichs depot."

Villancourt's panic subsided into sudden realization: this was Lieutenant Grant, delivered into his hands.

"If you tip them off," Grant said, "I'm the *second* to die, you understand?"

"Please," he gasped. "Please."

"Through customs into the depot. Yes or no?"

"Yes."

His knees buckled, and only the man's arm kept him upright. Genuinely frightened, yes—but still calculating the costs and benefits. He would reveal nothing except fear until the final moment, then he'd seize his chance.

Grant punched his shoulder. "Move."

"But the guards!"

"Start talking, we're old friends. One wrong word, and I break your neck."

Villancourt pasted a smile on his face as they approached the guard hut, and he heard a soldier inside asking, "Close the gates?"

"All of them," another answered. "Stop the traffic—"

"Close the gates?" Villancourt interrupted, stepping into view. "Impossible. At this hour? Mark my words, I will issue an official complaint."

"Save your breath," the guard said.

"Your superiors will hear a thing or two!"

"Go on," the guard said. "We cleared you twenty minutes ago."

Muttering darkly, Villancourt escorted Grant past the hut and into the building. The door shut behind them and the corridor was airless and claustrophobic. The American held himself too close: even if Villancourt warned the guards, he'd be in the line of fire. No, he needed to lull the man, wait for the right moment . . .

Ten feet away, the second set of sentries were alert, watching. Villancourt smacked the guard counter and demanded, "Where's Herr Rothenbuehler? He's kept me waiting outrageously."

"Pardon?" a guard asked. "Oh, Herr Rothenbuehler, he—"

"We'll wait in his office for ten minutes. Tell him that, do you hear? Ten minutes and not one second more!"

Two hurdles down, one remained: the primary security office adjoining the depot doors. *Those* guards wouldn't be so easily deceived, they hadn't already waved Villancourt through once that day—he needed to focus, to remember Hugo's ruined face and his sister's grief.

Around the next corner, a few guards chatted over a murmur of radio in the security office. One stood in the doorway, a buck-toothed man in green-and-gray who said, "I'm sorry, the Reichs depot is closed."

"Impossible," Grant said, half a pace behind Villancourt. "At this hour?"

The bucktoothed guard eyed him suspiciously. "Perhaps you'd like to wait inside?"

Grant said, "That's fine," and herded Villancourt into an office with desks and file cabinets, two guards in chairs and a third in the doorway of a back room.

"Your papers, please," the bucktoothed guard said.

"I don't have any," Grant said.

The seated guards exchanged glances and stood. "No sudden moves," a gray-haired guard said. "Raise your hands."

"He fits the description?" another asked.

"What's this?" Grant moved aside, spreading his hands against a file cabinet. "I don't want trouble."

Finally, his chance! Villancourt opened his mouth to warn them, and from the back room a man yelled, "That's him! Stop him!"

Akimov stood at the window, ignoring the murmur of the guards in the outer office until he heard a familiar voice. He wasted seconds in disbelief—why was Grant still here? why break into the depot?— then he realized, and his heart turned to ice.

The American wanted to kill his daughter. The only way to stop the pact.

Akimov slid the handcuff down the railing and saw Grant in the

356

other room, surrounded by guards, his hands spread on a file cabinet. He shouted a warning, and Grant thumbed the lock of the drawer under his hand, yanked the heavy cube free and spun it into the nearest guard, crushing his scalp with a sharp metal corner. Before the guard fell, Grant took the drawer in both hands and rammed a second guard's face, breaking his nose and maybe teeth, and the third guard swung wildly at him. The American heaved the drawer upward, catching the guard's jaw and snapping his head back, then dropped the drawer and punched the guard in the throat, and turned to the last guard, standing in the center of the room pawing at his buckled holster. Grant took a handful of his gray hair and flung him across the room into the radio cabinet, beating his head until blood speckled the glossy wood.

He crossed the room when he saw the pale businessman crawling toward one of the guard's guns—grabbed a telephone from a desk and hammered the man's head, the chime sounding like a child's toy. When the businessman stopped moving, he straightened and kicked the second guard, who was keening on the floor with his ruined face in his hands, until there was silence in the room.

For a moment, all was still. Then Grant straightened and took a guard's cap and overcoat from the hook, collected three sidearms, Walther P38s, checked the magazines and worked the slides. He glanced at a holster but instead stuck two guns in his belt like a buccaneer and draped another coat over the third P38 in his right hand. He turned to face Akimov and they looked at each other.

"Don't," Akimov said. "Please."

"You said it. 'Everything's built on a graveyard.'"

"I'm begging you."

One of the guards moaned, and Grant headed outside.

Akimov scraped the handcuff along the railing to the window. The concrete towers were dark against a cloudless sky, guards ranged over rail tracks in the Reichs *Bahnhof*, past sheds and storehouses, but the depot was quiet—they didn't expect trouble inside the gates. Grant stepped into view with an easy rolling saunter, and covered twenty yards before three guards turned a corner fifteen feet ahead of him. One started to speak and the overcoat on Grant's arm jumped and gunshots sounded. The guard fell and the other two froze, and Grant steadied the gun with his left hand and fired until he was alone.

Through the window Akimov heard a siren wail at the sound of gunfire, and a speaker crackle with commands. A Kubelwagen engine gunned and the soldiers in guard towers signaled: the attacker was inside the Reichs depot, not beyond the fence.

Grant dropped the overcoat and sidestepped a crane and disappeared. No movement for thirty seconds. Behind Akimov, a guard moaned—the one with the ruined face, crawling blindly in the security office, a key ring jingling at his hip.

Akimov looked at the key ring, and decided. He sat on the bench murmuring encouragement, pitching his voice like his father's: "Come, come—this way. I'll help you. Follow my voice. Everything will be fine, just come along this way . . ."

The guard crawled sobbing into the back room and crossed to the bench, but Akimov couldn't reach the key ring, not with his hand cuffed to the railing. He crooned gentle commands—*stand, I'll see to everything, just stand and I'll help you, you'll be fine*—and when the man shakily rose he lunged forward and took the key ring in his teeth.

An awkward minute later, he unlocked the handcuff and heard a crackle of gunfire through the window. A train rumbled over tracks, men shouted, a machine gun chattered. Watching the yard, Akimov told himself this was over, Grant was dead. The machine gun must've—

There. Near the Blue Star club lounge, a lone guard trotted across a turntable, unhurried and intent: Grant.

And if he got inside, more than the truce was dead.

Give me bitter years of pain,
Steal my children and lovers and my mysterious gift—
This I beg, after exhausted days.
And in exchange, let the stormcloud over dark Russia,
Become a crown of sunlight.

He shook his head. "No."

No more bitter years of pain, and nobody would steal Akimov's child. He checked the key ring—found a key marked FORD EIFEL—then in the other room tugged at one of the unconscious guards.

At first Nadya thought the gunshots were wine corks popping, then she realized and stood from her meal, saying a quick prayer. Perhaps in the chaos they could flee. In any case, there was nothing but patience and prayer, there was *never* anything but patience and prayer. The lessons of—

A gunshot cracked directly outside, and she spun to the door. Would the cold-eyed man enter? Another shot, and the door flung inward, and a man vaulted the steps into the aisle. A stranger, with gentle eyes and a gun. "Miss Loeffert?"

"Yes."

"Your mother sent me to bring you home."

She almost laughed. "I'm surprised she didn't come herself."

"She sends her love," he said, softly. "Are you ready to go?"

"Of course."

A motorcar engine roared outside, and the man nodded toward the door. "I'm right behind you, there's nothing to be afraid of."

"I'm not afraid," she said. "I have faith."

"Then you'll be fine."

She looked toward the bathroom. "Let me just tell—"

The girl turned away, not toward the door but the narrow hallway. One shot, then Grant would step outside into the gunfire, quick and clean. He raised the pistol, hearing the roar of blood in his ears— this would stop the Nazi-Soviet truce, this would save the West. His finger tightened on the trigger, his heart beating impossibly slow and—

"Sir?" Christoph's voice. "It's you! I knew you'd come!"

Christoph? Here? Everything shifted, like dropping from a cloud to find yourself flying into a mountain—no time for panic or confusion, just the light touch of your hand on the stick.

Christoph stepped into the lounge and wrapped himself around Grant. "I told you he'd come," he said to the girl. "Didn't I tell you?"

"This is Lieutenant Grant?" she asked.

"I told you!"

"Christoph, what are you—" Grant stopped, no time for questions. The Germans couldn't fire through the walls for fear of hitting the girl, but they could rush the door. "We need another way out."

"We can't use the front?" the girl asked.

"Not anymore," he told her.

"The grate in the shoe-shine room is loose. I've been digging at the bolts with—"

He pushed past her, found the shoe-shine room—on the wall opposite the front door—and said, "Where's the grate?"

From the doorway, the girl pointed at a bottom cabinet. "There."

Inside, a wooden grate hung on a single bolt. "Stay back," he said, and fired at the bolt, the shot deafening in the small room.

Fired twice more, and something snapped.

. . .

The man Grant slipped through patrols like a wraith—dressed as a rail guard, daring the machine guns to fire. Too late, Kübler ripped field glasses from a soldier's hands and surveyed the yard. Too late, he realized he should've ordered the men to defend instead of attack. Too late, he knew the American's target.

"The girl," he said. "He's after the girl."

The Russian elbowed him aside. "My granddaughter? If she—"

"Tell them to hold their fire!" Kübler shouted at the soldier with the phone. "Do not shoot into the passenger car!"

He shoved to the stairwell and raced down, the Russian thundering behind him, into the asphalt heat of the yard, following the soldiers converging on the Blue Star car, where men massed at the train car with rifles raised.

Too late: from inside the Blue Star car, a shot cracked. Then two more, and silence.

Kübler eyed the train door. Was the girl dead? Could he still salvage this?

He needed the girl alive, or her grandfather would render "sufficiently favorable terms" impossible. Send his men into the train, with orders to kill the American and pretend the girl still lived? Yes, and refuse to let her grandfather see her. The deputy commissar wouldn't ordinarily believe such a crude ruse, but desperate men could believe anything to keep hope alive.

He turned, and the Russian wasn't watching the train car—instead, he was staring at a rail-guard van shuddering to a halt nearby. The man driving returned his stare, then flicked his gaze toward a row of oil drums . . . where three forms crept toward the van, then paused—unable to get closer without revealing themselves.

The American, and the girl. Sudden relief almost buckled Kübler's knees and he drew breath to shout the order.

• • •

The engine grumbled at Akimov's crude handling, and he looked away from Grant and his daughter—his *daughter*—to see his father, white hair shining like a beacon. The old man met Akimov's gaze, then followed his nod to the row of barrels . . . and Nadya. Young and strong and beautiful, and radiating calm, even now.

His father's eyes grew bright and fierce as he nodded his understanding, his intention—his redemption. He'd make whatever sacrifice was necessary to save his granddaughter. Fifteen yards away, and they'd never been closer.

Akimov mouthed: "*Otets.*" Father.

Grant watched Akimov, tensed to move. The Russian had come to save his daughter, they were all in this together now, but no way to cross to the van without a dozen soldiers seeing them. He lifted his hand, telling Christoph and the girl to stay behind him. Not yet . . . not yet. At least they hadn't been seen, and—

And the German from the hunting lodge looked directly at Grant.

Before he could move, Akimov's father lifted his arm, a Walther suddenly in his fist, and shot the German in the face. The man's head snapped back into a red mist, and Grant straightened, murmuring, "Come, now—slowly."

Chaos in front of the train car: scattered shouts, panicked gunfire, a scream of enraged fear, the soldiers under attack by an unseen enemy.

A volley of gunfire crashed into the Blue Star car and Grant opened the rear doors of the van and shoved the girl and Christoph inside. Through the windshield, he saw Akimov's father take aim and step close to a white tank on a low-bedded rail truck—a propane tank. The perfect diversion, yet the commissar was so close he'd be caught in the blast. He fired anyway, and his third bullet caught a spark, and the propane tank exploded into a column of flame, blinding and hot.

A white glare washed the world, then dimmed when Akimov eased the van around a corner, toward the gates.

The locked gates.

"Pull over," Grant told him. "Maybe they'll open the gates before they realize what happened."

Akimov nosed the van behind a stack of pallets. "Won't be long, one way or another." He glanced once toward the fire that was his daughter's salvation and his father's funeral pyre.

Grant turned to Nadya and Christoph, huddled in the rear of the van. "Stay there," he told the girl. "If I give the word, take the boy out the back door. Get to Bern, to his mother. You understand?"

"I'll see that he's safe," she said.

"And you," he told Christoph. "Take care of her, soldier."

"Yes, sir."

In the front of the van, Akimov moved to the passenger seat, looking away from Nadya with a clear effort of will. "So the cease-fire dies with my father," he murmured. "And the bloodshed continues."

Grant slid behind the wheel. "You'll return to the front?"

"If we get out of here alive? Yes—back to Stalingrad." The Russian raised his head at the sound of sirens from the road. "A pity you can't join me, I could use a man like you."

"Would be an honor, serving under you."

"And you?" Akimov asked. "Back to England?"

The gates opened for a fire truck, and Grant eased the van forward. "After I do one last thing."

Find the crash site and get the camera to the embassy. And ask Anna to marry him. Easy enough.

CHAPTER 43

Chairman Ochsner caressed the glossy desktop, burr walnut with a hand-carved gadroon edge. Quality and elegance. He hummed a happy little tune and signed the document. Flipped the page, signed again, and twice more. With four strokes of his pen, the firm's future was assured—the firm, the country, the splendid heritage of neutrality.

He spun in his chair to the windows overlooking the lake, the bright choppy water winking praise and congratulations. Effort was rewarded, simple as that, risk was rewarded. So long as one was nimble. Poor Herr Villancourt. The chairman grieved for him, of course—beaten quite literally senseless by that fugitive American pilot—but at least he'd been found a bed in the same sanitarium as his wife. Something romantic there, twin souls bound forever and all that rot.

And his legacy would endure: the clearing credits that the chairman's signatures had just enacted would lay the groundwork for the expansion of Swiss industry, regardless of which side won this most profitable war. One must be nimble, that was all.

EPILOGUE

Despite the late-March sun shining warm and bright, a light snow dusted the mountainside, drifting in eddies and clinging to pine needles. Anna tugged off one glove with her teeth and checked the map again.

"Maman," Christoph called, trotting toward her along the path. "Over here!"

His face was flushed and his eyes bright. She smiled. "Slow down, Christoph, you'll fall off the mountain."

"I found it! Come, come!"

She shifted the hamper into her other hand and followed him around the bend to the edge of an alpine meadow. Twenty yards away, the crashed airplane splayed in a broken hump under a rind of snow, like a long-dead bird decomposing into a skeleton.

"How did he *survive*?" Christoph asked.

"With a steady hand," she said, "and the grace of God."

But of course his navigator hadn't survived—not for long. And Joris, poor dear Joris, killed in his beloved garden. She gazed somberly at the wreckage, and Christoph caught her mood and fell silent beside her. They stood together for a time, then she picked her way carefully to the cockpit, and looked at the pilot's seat.

"He's a fighter pilot now," Christoph said. "Can you imagine?"

"All too well."

"He'll come back, don't worry Maman."

"He promised?"

"No. He said, 'Don't hold your breath, kid.' "

"And that convinced you?"

Christoph nodded. "May I go inside?"

"In *there*?"

"You know what Lieutenant Grant would say?"

"What?"

He grinned. "He'd say 'yeah.' "

"He'd also say he doesn't know much about kids," she told him, trying not to smile.

"Horst doesn't bother me anymore."

"Christoph! That's nothing to be proud of."

He ducked his head in faux remorse, and she turned in a circle, looking for the biggest fir tree at the edge of the meadow.

"That's where he hid the camera?" Christoph asked.

She nodded, and he raced off to rummage among the roots.

The camera itself was long gone; Grant had come last October, after she'd located the site, unearthed the camera, and brought it to his embassy. The Americans refused even to acknowledge they'd developed the film, but still, a small victory.

She set the hamper down. Victory. The cease-fire talks died at the rail yard with Akimov's father—any budding goodwill between the Soviets and the Nazis destroyed in the explosion. Poor Major Akimov, his heart overflowed for his daughter but his duty required he return to the front. Perhaps one day he'd come back; in the meanwhile, Anna stood as a surrogate mother to Nadya. She'd even been a bridesmaid at Rosine and Lorenz's wedding.

Victory. Anna had discovered the name of the Swiss financier—

Villancourt—too late to change anything. Hospitalized by Grant, the man was no longer complicit in the Swiss support of the Third Reich. Yet she knew other Swiss took his place. And while she still hadn't found proof—not of the clearing-credit loans to Germany, not of the barracks deal that laundered money to fund a Nazi intelligence network—she'd never stop looking.

She nodded, her resolve as strong as ever. In Stalingrad, a month after the explosion at the Basel rail yard, the Nazi onslaught had split the Russian defenses at the Volga. For days, the Reich teetered on the edge of victory, but thickening ice crept over the river. The Red Army had massed to the east, and after losing half a million soldiers at Stalingrad, the Soviets crushed the Nazi war machine. That was victory—not something achieved but something averted. A pact unsigned, a siege unbroken. Half a million men killed . . . but the Nazis defeated.

The wind rose and Anna lifted her head to the scent of spring sweeping down from the east. Snowmelt and mountain pine, like a promise. One day, her country would stand firm against evil. One day, Grant would return. One day, this war would end.

AUTHOR'S NOTE

The aircraft Grant and Racket saw on the German border was the V3 prototype airframe, which initially flew in July 1942—built for the world's first operational jet fighter. Although the Me 262 was 150 miles per hour faster than anything on the Allied side, production was slowed by Hitler's personal requirement that it function as both a fighter and a bomber . . . and possibly by the Allied response to getting Racket's photographs.

As a neutral nation, Switzerland was legally required to prevent Allied internees from escaping. However, punishment camps like Straflager Wauwilermoos violated Swiss and international law: internees weren't allowed military tribunals, were sentenced for longer than allowed by law, were quartered with violent criminals, and were beaten and placed in solitary confinement. The commandant of Wauwilermoos, Captain Andre Beguin, a Nazi frontist known to sign his correspondence "Heil Hitler," was court-martialed after the war and sentenced to several years in prison.

During the war, eighty percent of German payments to Switzerland were handled through the "clearing credit" system, which permitted commercial traffic without any exchange of currency. This was critically important to Germany not only because the Reich lacked foreign currency but because it required Swiss goods. Such as—per the "Clodius memorandum" which Anna sought (which was drafted, in fact, on June 3, 1943, after the events of this book)—"special, technical equipment whose shortfall, especially in the next few months, would seriously affect, inter alia, the German tank and remote-control programs . . ."

The Swiss government granted Germany 150 million Swiss francs in clearing-credit advances in 1940. These interest-free credits were increased a year later to 850 million francs, and again in 1943 to more than a billion francs. As the German military used the credits to buy Swiss machines, farming products, and—primarily— war materiel, the loans almost certainly contravened the law of neutrality.

Finally, newly declassified testimony revealed that a "barracks deal" in 1941—in which Swiss-built barracks were sold to Germany for use at the Dachau concentration camp—was designed to give Nazi intelligence access to Swiss contacts and funds. An agent of the Reich Economics Ministry was ordered by the Waffen-SS and the SS Economic-Administrative Main Office to initiate the deal, soon signing a thirteen million franc contract and establishing a Swiss corporation to serve as a front for German Intelligence.

ACKNOWLEDGMENTS

Special thanks to Yan Mann and Ray Wells. Many thanks also to Kurt Bamert, Danny Baror, Phyllis Grann, Jennifer Lultschik, Henry Morrison, and Anatol Schenker.